FRACTURED DARKNESS

Fractured Darkness

Published by Red Cabin Publishing

Spokane, WA

10 Years Anniversary Edition: April 2024

4 6 8 10 9 7 5 3

Fractured Darkness edited by Amber Beuschel

Cover Art and Typography by Evelyne Paniez at www.secretdartiste.be(Resources listed on Acknowledgement Page)

LCCN: 2015931718

CIP data for this book is available from the Library of Congress

Paperback: ISBN: 0692374132, ISBN-13: 978-0-692-37413-9

Hardback: ISBN: 979-8-9877165-2-6

Also by Morgan Wylie

Thank You...

It has been almost 15 years since I began envisioning and sharing the journey of Kaeleigh, Daegan, and the crew's adventures in Alandria. This special edition is to celebrate 10 years of being published!!

Writing can be a very solitary experience, and yet there are so many people I want to thank who have been a part of my journey, bringing this story to life from beginning to present. From author friends offering support, advice, encouragement, etc. along the way to the technical support of editors and graphic designers to beta, ARC, and proof readers... my book wouldn't be what it is today without you. You know who you all are, I love and appreciate you! This edition is what I have always imagined this story could be and it finally is!!

To my husband, Steven, you inspire me, challenge me, and encourage me to be the best version of me I can be even when I wasn't sure who that was, thank you. And to my beautiful daughters, I continue pursuing my dreams so that you know you can pursue yours. I love you. Also to the rest of my family, you have been an incredible support and encouragement. Thank you for believing in me and cheering for me. Especially my momma: I can't tell you how much it has meant over the years that you liked my story, believed in it, and invested in it...me.

As in life, we grow, evolve, and take on new iterations of ourselves to become the best version of ourselves, so has this project...

From the foundations of this book, I want to thank the creative team: Claudia at for her creative genius with the cover art and Ashley at The Bookish Brunette for her beautiful fonts and layout. Thank you both! Your art has been a part of this journey for over 10 years.

In this edition, I want to give credit and thank Evelyne Paniez at www.secretdartiste.be for her amazing cover design, all created by her human layering process (no AI used)!

All good fantasy stories need a map! (At least I think so). And Alandria has gone through several versions when it's come to the map. From my scratchy drawing to Donna Dull with Sharp Covers who brought it visually to life to then Bill Morgan's edition, giving it that extra push to Gerralt at Dimension Door's (https://www.dimensiondoor.nl) current spectacular version... I thank all of you!!

Thank you to Amber Beuschel—the wordsmith!—who took my story and my characters and helped me discover their greater potential all whilst getting crazy with ALL "there was" to highlight ;) the 2nd time around. You have made me better and for that I will always be grateful. Christine LePorte, you took a novice writer and helped shape my story in the very beginning, thank you.

Also a special Thank You to Steven James Wylie and Blair Masters for your beautiful original soundtrack *Silent Orchids* inspired by this book.

I would most especially like to acknowledge you, the reader. For it is with you that my story has wings. Thank YOU for 10 enchanting years and here's to many more!!

Cover Art Resources Used By Secretdartiste:
FONTS: Lucy Rose (title) and Athelas (other text)
RESOURCES:
Foliage back: depositphotos 310708970
Texture snakes: depositphotos 230230888
Branches and additional leaves: www.hwwostock.com
Snake 1: depositphotos 200497132
Snake 2: depositphotos 491023036
Snake 3: depositphotos 505198294
Snake 4: depositphotos 505198302
Glass and crown particles: www.fantasybackgroundstore.com
Fireflies: www.neo-stock.com

Mortal Realm
Caves of Vuldün
Ary'th
Forest of Dul-Isteach
Bridge of Revealment
Hunters Cottage
The Stone Forest
River of Rancier
La
Mandü Tré Lan
Shadow Ridges

THE AGE OF

ALANDRIA

NALRINIA

ELNYE

GUARDIAN GROVE

GARALDRATH
MOUNTAINS

FERAÁNMAR

OSSING AT LUMEI

FOREST OF LUMEI

EXHILE

ANISE
(LORTUNA)

LUMARI

ADETTLYN

TYLÍNYTH

EHSMIA

KLAVAÍ

KÁNDRI

KANDRIAN MOUNTAINS

LENORIA

PROLOGUE

EXHILE. THE LAND OF THE
UNFORGIVEN DEAD.

"**M**aleina has failed me."

The woman residing inside the mountain—the one known to those who know of her only as *She*—turned from her scrying pool nestled in a cradle of rock. Hundreds of lit torches floating all around the cave reflected dancing flames in her eyes. It was striking against the creamy, smooth complexion of her face, both pure beauty and pure evil. Her jet black hair, long and flowy and half pulled back draped down her backside, swished as she slowly turned and gazed fondly at something up in the corner of her craggy residence. Red eyes appeared out of the dark, where there was not more than a crevice in the rock.

"Not yet, my pet. Our timing must be precise," she crooned, responding to a silent plea. Drumming her long, graceful fingers tipped with the colors of fire and blood on her nails against her chin, *She* was deep in thought. "The warrior being freed will only be a minor diversion from the plan. The girl gaining access to the core of her power—that could pose a problem. The girl is all that matters. We must get her here, out of Alandria." A devious smirk began to cool the fires of her eyes, returning them to the solid black of their unnatural state. An altered plan was taking shape in her mind.

"Perhaps your time will come sooner than I had planned, my pet. All I ask is a little more patience from your kind." The creature that was of the Droch-Shúil slithered like a ghostly snake from one corner of the cave to another, slowly making its way closer to its master. *She* patiently waited until her "pet" was close enough that she could almost touch it. Extending her hand, palm out, *She* allowed it to come to her, displaying its loyalty.

The Droch-Shúil approached her like a shy puppy, then nuzzled her hand while wrapping the rest of its darkness seductively around her. The woman closed her eyes, allowing the cool shadows of darkness to rub against her, to seep into her very being, and fuel the fire already burning deep within her. *She* took as it gave, leeching the power of its darkness to feed her magic. Taking a deep breath, inhaling through her nose, *She* absorbed all she could. Her eyelids fluttered with euphoria before opening once again revealing eyes now two glowing orbs of power. Eerily, she looked to the creature made of shadow and darkness. Bending toward it, *She* coaxed it closer to her face.

"It is time to visit our guests. The *Orchids* have been busy in my absence. They need a reminder of who is Queen in this land." The Droch-Shúil untangled itself from around the woman, floating to one of the walls of the cavernous room used for her rituals, then dissipated into it, becoming one with it.

She sashayed toward the opening in the cave. The walls of the interior were smooth, but the edges in the doorway were rough, sharp, and jagged. Placing her hand on one wall, *She* infused a measure of her most recent accrual of power into the rock itself. Her magic allowed her to mix the dark energies of the Droch-Shúil with the essence of not only the mountain, but the land in Exhile as well, strengthening her bond with it.

Satisfied that it had been done, the mistress of darkness stood straight, basking in the heady remainder of the magical energies swirling about her. *She* smoothed her hands down the front of her stomach to her thighs, habitually removing nonexistent wrinkles. It was a memory lost to time, but the actions remained. Her long black dress clung tightly against the shape of her body. *She* was an attractive woman, appearing in her forties by mortal years, but the obsidian depths of her eyes spoke of agelessness... and darkness; the two seemed at odds on her. There was a part of her that clung to a memory of blue skies, wheat fields as far as the eye could see, and the warm smell of baked apple pie. *She* did not always know if it was a real memory or something she had seen through a soul that had slipped through with the transference of dark magic between her and the Droch-Shúil. Something warmed her chest when *She* thought on it, but quickly squelched the feeling... because those kinds of feelings only brought pain, pain she didn't have time for. The intense darkness of the cave enveloped her as she disappeared through the tunnel in the mountain. *She* had *Orchids* to deal with.

CHAPTER ONE

THE WAY OF ADBERTOS. SOMEWHERE NEAR THE GÁRALDRATH MOUNTAINS.

"It's open!" Finn shouted as the shimmering veil in front of the cave wall stretched and pulled into a shape large enough for a person to step through.

Chel sighed with frustration. "Let's get going. Who knows how long it will be open and I, for one, do not want to have to live in here until I die, which let's face it might not be that long because I might shift and take one of you poor souls out and then you'd have to kill me."

"Chel, stop rambling and help Kaeleigh get up," Finn instructed as he examined the opening.

"I'm fine," Kaeleigh said breathlessly as she sat up, attempting to get up on her own. She swatted Chel's hand away trying to prove a point, which earned her a glare from her best friend. Softening her countenance, she was about to allow Chel to help when a strong hand reached under one of her elbows and pulled her swiftly to her feet without giving her the chance. As he held her arm steady, she gained her balance and turned to see Daegan's impassive face. It was as if he was not even truly seeing her, but instead he—once again—wore a mask of undeterred guardianship. Kaeleigh's heart sunk. She thought they were past that.

Looking unfazed into his eyes, she said the thing that weighed on her most heavily. "He's dead." A tear built up in the corner of her eye. Spilling over, it trailed down her cheek. "Hunter... he's dead. I saw it. In there, in the light, I saw it." Her voice wavered as a sob threatened to choke her. Daegan's face fell and his eyes softened. Regret passed over his gaze.

"I am sorry, Kaeleighnna," Daegan whispered, wiping away her tear before it fell from her jaw. Kaeleigh's lower lip quivered, threatening to break her. But not here. They needed to get to somewhere safe.

"We must go now," Finn demanded roughly, not sure what to do with the emotion of the situation.

Chel flipped Finn off, lovingly of course, then wrapped Kaeleigh in a tight embrace, whispering words of love and strength. Kaeleigh took a deep breath and hugged Chel tightly in response. "We have each other," Chel uttered into Kaeleigh's hair.

They moved to follow Daegan as he stood at the veil they hoped to be their exit out of the dark and damp cave that had not only been their prison, but their shelter.

"Have we been granted permission to freely leave, Kaeleigh?" Aidón spoke from the shadow of the far cave wall. He had been so quiet, simply watching.

Kaeleigh turned to him and looked into his eyes, really looking unabashedly like she was searching for something. "Yes, I will explain, but we are free to leave. Sacrifices have been made and more will be required, whatever that means, but for now we are free."

He reached out to gently place his hand on her forearm. "It is regrettable about your grandfather. I am sorry for your loss." His voice caught with emotion as he turned and walked straight through the veil without hesitance.

Watching the entire interaction, the others looked at each other and then back to Kaeleigh.

"Well, let's get out of here." Kaeleigh pulled herself together and gestured for someone to lead the way. Daegan went first.

Finn turned to her. "You all right, Kae?"

She looked to him thoughtfully and nodded. "I will be. You knew him as well, probably more than anyone here, right? I'm sorry, Finn." She reached for his hand and gave it a squeeze.

"Maybe." Finn frowned. "Will you tell us how it happened?"

"Let's get out of here first. We can talk later."

They walked in silence for quite a ways, stepping lightly and moving like shadows between the side of the mountain and the shelter of the trees. Constantly aware of any and every movement around them, they were almost afraid to breathe lest they draw the attention of those who sought them.

Daegan, in the lead, paused with his hand held behind him, halting everyone following. Chel grabbed Kaeleigh's hand. Kaeleigh took in everyone around her: Daegan at the front, Aidón in front of her, Chel by her side, and Finn trailing behind them, constantly turning to ensure no one followed.

Taking a step forward to whisper something, Kaeleigh stepped on a twig that she didn't see and *snap*. Daegan shot fierce, reprimanding eyes on her carelessness. Kaeleigh flinched. No one moved for several seconds, waiting for anything to move that should not be there. When there was nothing, Daegan signaled to move forward.

The silence was maddening. Kaeleigh looked to Chel with crazed eyes like she might explode, then signaled toward Daegan and made choking gestures with her hands. Chel couldn't help but to stifle a giggle. Kaeleigh smiled at her friend's momentary relief. No one else could hear it, but when Kaeleigh heard Finn silently snort she turned back towards him with a smirk. He simply lifted the side of his mouth in a hint of amusement before he turned back around to survey the forest behind them. There was nothing in sight but trees and more trees: big ones, thin ones, young ones, old ones.

Kaeleigh took deep breaths to calm her anxious energy. Thinking on everything that had occurred, she got lost in her mind. So much had happened. She didn't even know how much time had passed since they had been in that cave but it didn't seem like it could have been more than a day. The light of day was now fading into twilight and it was easier to blend into the surroundings of the forest, but it also meant more shadows, natural or otherwise, and they still gave Kaeleigh chills. She reflected on how Daegan had risked everything to free them from their prison within the rock. She knew he could never go home and it was because of her. Seeing him tortured internally, struggling on the ground after they were freed, tore something deep inside her. Feeling his pain as her magic infiltrated him had broken her heart. She had been given a glimpse into his soul. She felt closer and more tied to him somehow. Too bad he didn't seem to feel it as well.

For a brief moment, Daegan looked back, his deep brown eyes finding hers. They were not questioning, but openly aware as if he sensed where her thoughts had been. Perhaps he had. Or perhaps he could sense the pain and anger, along with sympathy and discouragement, surging within her, stirring her energy both magical and emotional. Unable to talk, he turned back around, leaving her to her own thoughts.

Kaeleigh watched from behind as he took in everything around him in a very precise and cautious manner. The tense lines of his shoulders, the rounded curves of the strong muscles in his shoulders and biceps, the flex of his fist as one hand gripped his knife, the defined lines in his back that couldn't help but be followed lower—every move and decision he made was that of a practiced warrior. It was natural. She envied his strength and confidence. Her fingers itched to run up the back of his neck strained with tension and into the blue-black waves that were now starting to grow out from his head longer than when she first met him.

Whoa, Kaeleigh, rein it in! Kind of have a focused situation going on here. Yes, he is a dream, but why can't I think about this at a more appropriate time? She talked mentally to herself often at the most inappropriate times. *If only we could talk, my mind wouldn't wander so much. I want to believe that what I see in his eyes is because he cares.*

Her mind brought her back around to being in the cave—the Way of Adbertos, literally meaning the way of sacrifice. She didn't know what had happened from the time she tried to free Daegan from his bond to Maleina to waking up in the cave. Walking into that light and speaking with the guardian of Adbertos, whom Kaeleigh nervously and inappropriately named "Abi" and watching Hunter be killed right in front of her by Maleina, stirred not only deep sadness and utter loss but an anger and a rage that she didn't know what to do with. Her breathing became labored and her energy levels began to rise higher and higher.

Chel gripped her hand tighter, trying to get her to calm down, but it wasn't working. The next thing she knew he was there at her side, turning her toward him, gripping her shoulders gently.

"Kaeleigh, look at me," he spoke with soft authority. His words and his touch infused within her a calm energy as his magic wrapped around her. "Focus your magic. Contain it... only for now. I will find you a place and a time to grieve, but it is not safe here for us."

At that, Kaeleigh suddenly sensed she was not alone. She could feel Finn at her back with his hand against her. Chel held her hand, gripping so tightly she thought her hand might break. Daegan in front of her, the gentle tone of his voice talking her down while his magic soothed her own, and their new companion, Aidón, watched her with eyes of compassion. She felt love and reached for it desperately, pulling her out of the despair she quickly had spiraled into. Taking deep breaths, she felt a peace come over her. She could feel Hunter with her—she didn't know how, but she could actually *feel* him near her so strongly she even looked around and up into the trees for him or the white bird his spirit had taken on. Kaeleigh saw nothing, but held onto the hope that perhaps he had not really left her.

With a barely audible whisper for fear of making noise, she said, "Thank you." Looking into each of their eyes she gave a grateful nod, lingering a bit longer on the chocolate orbs directly in front of her that held her gaze intensely as he searched her strength, finding it solid. Turning abruptly, he took the lead once again as they slowly made their way deeper into the shelter of the ancient forest.

Trying a new tactic, Kaeleigh decided to see if she could make contact with her inner magic. She wanted to understand her magic and become more in tune with it. The best way she understood to do that was to become familiar with it—how it felt and moved within her, how it responded and reacted to her emotions. She took deep breaths of the clean, oxygen-rich air of the forest into her lungs. Holding it for a second, she then slowly released it, focusing on the way it felt. The way the air moved from her tightly expanded lungs, bringing a feeling of peace and relief as she exhaled it. It was heady and even made her a little light-headed, but there was power in the control she was exercising. Feeling her magic respond to her gentle coaxing as she mentally stirred it deep within her core exhilarated her and pushed her to stir it even more. She kept control for the first time. Kaeleigh willed it back into submission, then stirred it up again. Unsure of what she was doing, Kaeleigh felt like it was working—she felt right—so she kept at it as they walked.

Wanting to experiment, Kaeleigh looked out at the forest around her to see what perhaps she wasn't truly seeing with only her eyes, if anything. At the same time she internally guided her magic from its source in the core of who she was up her chest, through her neck, and up the back of her neck into her head, culminating at her point of sight. She could feel the buzzing electricity of her magic as it seeped through her eyes. Not knowing what to expect as she looked out with eyes of magic, she remained open to anything. Nothing unusual until... there! Off in the distance there was a large old tree with a canopy of branches that extended over a large expanse. This tree had a vibration of energy that was stronger than any of the other trees around it. It reminded her of Holly—the tree she had met by the stream before they had gone to Feraánmar—except the energy in this tree was even stronger than hers. She could see the green threads of energy that flowed swiftly throughout the trunk, into each branch, then cycle back. There was no beginning and no end to the magic.

At her intake of breath, Finn was right at her back. "Kaeleigh? What is it?" He was poised for a fight, his hands gripping sheathed daggers in anticipation.

She shook her head back and forth, having a hard time putting words to what she was seeing, afraid that if she spoke she might break her shaky grasp of control over her magic. Hoping he would understand there was no threat, she signaled an "okay" sign with her hand—cheesy, but effective.

"You're all right?"

Kaeleigh simply nodded. She could hear them just fine, even though Chel spoke like she couldn't hear them. "Why isn't she talking?"

Both Daegan and Aidón had also stopped looking for a sign of a threat. Aidón looked at her and followed her gaze out to the trees. "I think she is looking into a glamour or possibly just seeing what is beyond your sight, but I am not seeing it either."

"The trees. I think she is seeing the energy of the trees. She is not in danger. I can feel her awe." Daegan shifted a little, sounding uncomfortable revealing that.

"Do you see the trees as well, Daegan?" Aidón asked curiously.

Daegan turned out towards the trees, giving a slight and awkward nod. Aidón patted Daegan on the shoulder. "There are not many who can so easily see into natural glamours. It is a gift. Your secret is safe with me."

"How is she doing that?" asked Chel.

"She must be trying to learn about her magic," Aidón mused.

"She is doing quite well. Kaeleigh has been practicing for the last few hours. She learns quickly," Daegan said quietly as he turned, surveying other areas of the forest. "We have remained here too long as it is. We must continue if we are to make it somewhere safe to camp."

Finn spoke after a long time of silence. "Where are you leading us, Daegan?"

"There is a place I know that will be well guarded and safe for a short period of time to rest. It is where the base of the Gáraldrath Mountain ridges gets swallowed by the heart of the Forest of Lumei."

Finn nodded thoughtfully. "Taking the back way into the lands of Kandri?"

Daegan nodded slowly in return, watching Finn's response.

"That seems wise. There are ruins to hide throughout that area as well. That should help traversing towards the Kandrian Mountains. Thoughts, Aidón? Do you know that land well?"

Finn seemed to direct his question pointedly at the newcomer to gauge his reaction. There was something Finn didn't trust about their tagalong. Daegan, too, seemed to watch the man carefully. The more he noticed of him, the more he realized the man's appearance had actually changed quite significantly since they had first entered the forest upon fleeing Elnye. He had begun an old and weak man only to gain in strength and stature, growing younger again as if reversing time itself upon his physical being. Leading to one solution: he was himself glamoured. But why? He obviously appeared to be an Elf with his pointy ears, fair and opalescent skin, sharp features, and silver hair. His build was thin but strong, similar to Finn's structure. He was shorter than the average Elf.

Suddenly feeling Chel's receptive hand squeezes, Kaeleigh made a note to be more aware of her surroundings when she was activating her magic. Feeling the uncertain tension building between the three men of their entourage, Kaeleigh whipped around to see Finn and Daegan glaring warily at Aidón. Daegan spotted her eyes on them first, breaking contact with the newest member. Then Aidón turned his eyes toward Kaeleigh. Eyes of sharp emerald green pierced her own. *Wait! They were blue. Weren't they blue?* Kaeleigh cocked her head to the side, confusion clearly written on her face. Both Daegan and Finn reacted to her expression, stepping back from Aidón and drawing their weapons in case something dangerous was about to be revealed.

Aidón's eyes grew large with surprise and shock. "You can see through it?"

"Your eyes... they were blue, weren't they?" Kaeleigh stammered as she continued to stare at him. She refocused her eyes several times and squinted to try and see what else was revealed.

"They still look blue to me, Kaeleigh," Chel interjected.

"This glamour is one of the strongest created. I had no idea your gifts would be able to decipher it." He spoke as if in awe and not concerned with what she was about to see. "I... Kaeleighnna, I was hoping to share this with you at a better time, but I do not know when and if there will be one. I know you will be able to see through it given some time, but I am not sure how you will react to my presence."

Still confused, Kaeleigh took a deep breath. "You're not going to make this easy for me, are you?"

"I'm curious how far you can push your magic while still bound," he plainly asked.

Furrowing her brow, Kaeleigh looked to her friends. "Wait. I'm still bound? What happened while I was unconscious?"

"Kae, there's still a lot we don't know and we don't have time for it here. We have to find shelter," Finn reminded them all.

"Right. Just one more second. I feel like I'm so close to seeing what is behind Aidón's glamour. I'm assuming"—she addressed Aidón—"that since you are letting me break your cover, you are not going to turn into a dark monster and eat us as soon as I de-cloak you or whatever."

Chel whispered with a sparkle of excitement, "De-cloak him. I don't know what that means, but do it, Kae!" She giggled. But then she thought and added, "You aren't a monster, are you, Aidón?"

He chuckled under his breath. "No. I am not a dark monster, but I guess you will have to take my word for it until your magic is strong enough to puzzle it out." Aidón winked at them then gestured for Daegan to lead the way. "We should keep going."

"I will figure it out. But you're right. We need to keep moving." Kaeleigh looped her arm through Chel's as much for her own comfort as for that of her friend.

CHAPTER TWO

"**A**re you hiding something, Aidón?" Chel asked innocently.

"I told you we shouldn't trust him to come with us," spat Finn from the back of the line.

Kaeleigh knew by his tone that Finn was clenching his knives at his side not only for what might come from the outside, but also from within. She took a deep breath. Kaeleigh felt an urgency to help Aidón get in touch with his magic and to unveil himself once again. She had a good feeling about him. There was a sense of familiarity in his magic. She could almost put her finger on it when she tried to strip the glamour back from him, but it would then slip from her grip.

"Patience, Finn...please," Kaeleigh whispered to him, looking back at him with pleading eyes. His gaze found hers, then consented with a short nod, but still he moved up behind her right into her personal space. His eyes were concerned and warm; he took a deep breath when he whispered in response, "Be careful, Kae."

Tiny butterflies swirled in her stomach at his close proximity as she remembered how Finn had kissed her. It had seemed ages ago and yet still not long enough to make the awkwardness she felt a mere memory. She didn't want Finn to be hurt; he was her family but she still resented that he took that step. At some point they were going to have to discuss it. She couldn't lose him. Her love for him as a friend was sincere, but she couldn't give him more than that.

Kaeleigh focused again, pushing her magic to swirl around Aidón as they continued to walk. She could see his shoulders flinch when her magic touched him, and then they relaxed again, allowing her attempt to chisel away at his glamour. She could almost *see* the glamour dissolving as she focused on it doing that very thing. Aidón's hair began changing from silver to dark, wavy, shoulder-length hair. Just when she thought she was making progress, the image would falter and so would Kaeleigh's steps. Chel was there gripping her arm to keep her from falling.

Aidón's shoulders sagged momentarily, then he turned to her with a sad smile. "It is hard to focus out here on the road under the threat of possible capture. When we are safe, please feel free to attempt another try." He turned and continued to follow Daegan down a slight decline in the landscape.

At the front, Daegan's steps staggered and he rubbed his forehead with one hand while leaning briefly against a thin tree that was suddenly quite close to him. "No, no, no..." he muttered. Then shook his head and stood straight and in control once more.

"Daegan?" Kaeleigh whispered as she moved closer to him.

"I... I am all right. I had a dull pain that was similar to the ones..." His voice quieted then he looked her in the eyes. "But it was not the same, it could not be."

"We can rest for a moment." Kaeleigh reached out and gently grabbed his arm, igniting the tiniest of blue sparks. He pulled away from her abruptly, causing Kaeleigh to jump back at first, and then she raised both hands in mock surrender. She shook her head with annoyance as she returned to her place by Chel.

"We must get as far as we can. I feel their pursuit is not as far away as we would like. Or perhaps it is not even Maleina's men." Daegan looked slowly about the forest all around them, seeing with more than his eyes. "Hurry. We do not have much time."

The five of them began to move quickly across the thick forest floor, skirting around trees and shrubbery, rocks, fallen branches, and roots that rose up from the ground to slow their movements. The trees seemed to grow thicker the further they went. Kaeleigh was surprised to find how large the forest in this part of Alandria truly was. She thought by this time the forest should be thinning, as they had to be getting closer to a town or village. They had been walking for so long. Her feet hurt and she was tired.

Suddenly, the hairs on the back of her neck began to rise and a dangerous feeling began to creep around them. Looking behind him, Finn saw the look in her eyes. Fear. He grabbed her arm and yanked both her and Chel so they ran even faster until they arrived side by side with Daegan at the front.

Daegan, unfazed by what they were doing, pulled out his large sword from its holster attached to his back. "Stay close!"

"I do not have a weapon." Aidón looked to each of the warriors. "I can fight. I will help." He held out his hand expectantly to Finn, but it was Daegan who gave him one of his knives that he pulled from a holster at his waist.

"I know you were in that prison for a reason. Do not make me regret this," he growled out.

No longer was there time for debate, nor was there time to run. The only time they had was to prepare to fight whatever was rumbling through the forest behind them. Kaeleigh and Chel were once again pushed into a tight triangle of fierce protection. They had been backed up to a large tree, their strong male defenders on every other side. Eyes searching everywhere, looking for the enemy, but Kaeleigh's eyes found Chel. She had gone white with fear. Mumbling something incoherently, she closed her eyes, trying to breathe. Kaeleigh's senses picked up no sound other than a strong wind picking up not far from where they were. A flash of images flew through Kaeleigh's mind. Images of darkness surrounding them and flying like the wind throughout the dense trees, and images of red eyes that were locked on hers. She gasped deeply.

"What is it?" Finn shouted now that the rumbling had grown louder. It sounded like the roar of an earthquake.

"Not warriors. Darkness with red eyes. Almost here." Choppy and broken, she tried to get the warning out as fast as she could.

Daegan uttered something that sounded like a curse in another language.

Finn grew pale as well. "The Droch-Shúil?" he questioned hoarsely to Daegan, who only nodded.

"We have to find a way out of here," shouted Aidón nervously. "We cannot fight and win like this."

"Daegan?" Kaeleigh whispered for his ears only. As his eyes found hers, they were filled with fear... for her. "I do not have my sword, like last time. It's gone."

He looked from her to Chel and then to the other men. "We do not need it. When I give you the order, you run. No questions. Do you understand?"

With understanding, her eyes got wide. "No!"

"Kaeleigh, this is not negotiable. Do you understand?" His fierce gaze bored into her soul. Another might assume that he resented her, but she could see the truth in his eyes; they were full of a life of loss and he could not afford one more on his count. She nodded.

Braced for battle, they waited what seemed like forever as anxiety reached heightened levels. The sky darkened. The few sounds made from creatures of the forest silenced. Low moans and creaks arose from all around them and behind them.

Chel looked about with a little more color in her cheeks and her eyes hopeful. "The trees are helping us again!" The trees were not actually moving, but something was happening, she was sure of it.

Kaeleigh looked to her, confused. "Again? Did I miss something... again?"

Chel was about to explain what she meant when Finn interjected. "Later!" he shouted at them, confounded they could have conversations at the most inopportune times.

Slowly, the darkness circled about them, weaving in and around the trees not too far out from where they stood. The wind roared so loudly, Daegan flinched and Kaeleigh couldn't help but cover her ears. Swords were extended at the ready, but there was nothing solid to even pierce the darkness in front of them. Kaeleigh's sword was special, the metal enchanted with magic and infused with light, but they did not have it this time. Not for the first time, she wondered where it went when it left her. The black, inky wind moved faster and faster, creating a funnel cloud that threw loose and broken parts of the forest all around, branches coming close enough to strike them.

"KAELEIGH!" screamed Chel.

They all turned just in time to see multiple small twisters come out of the larger one, morphing into long, sinewy tentacles made from the darkness. Each snakelike appendage reached out from the center of their funnel, wrapping around Kaeleigh's waist from different directions. Those tentacles of smoke and darkness seized her and lifted her off the ground and out of reach, a nightmare come to reality. It did not take her away, but held her right in front of her friends trapped in its octopus-like clutches, suspended in air and surrounded by other moving shadows of darkness. The only clear things visible were eyes of red.

Kaeleigh felt weightless as she was lifted into the sky, but it was not a peaceful feeling. She was caught in evil's grasp. This was not just a malicious wind, this was the Droch-Shúil and it had found her. It felt as if the wind was holding her up by pressing in around her from all sides, while the darkness pulled. It was tight. She could not move. Her skin crawled under the touch of the dark and evil residue of the wind as it moved around her. It was dark, and she could no longer see her friends. She had no idea where she was.

Eyes, a blood-thirsty red, opened right in front of her. Her hair whipped wildly about her, but her arms were restricted to her sides unable to pull it out of her face. Panic threatened to explode from her, but she kept breathing. There was no one with her to help her. She had to find a way out of this herself. Kaeleigh felt for her magic, gently stirring it up, hoping for some kind of miracle.

"*She* wants you," the voice hissed darkly all around her.

"*She* can't have me!" Kaeleigh declared boldly.

"*She* always gets what *She* wants. I will take you with me," the darkness hissed out again. It was creepy how the eyes never blinked or moved, even as swirls of darkness moved around and around like smoke in the darkness.

Kaeleigh's magic stirred within her, spinning at a comparable speed to the darkness echoed outside of her. It grew in intensity similar to what it felt like when she tried to free Daegan, like it would explode. Kaeleigh could feel real sparks at the edges of her fingertips ready to ignite the darkness—that had never happened before. Pressure bubbled up in her stomach, moving upward through her chest, pushing outward, looking for release. Throwing her head back, she strained against her own magic, afraid of what might happen if she did let loose, but also afraid of what would happen not only to her but to her friends if she didn't. It was painful holding back such a tidal wave of energy.

There was a gentle, peaceful push into her mind and a whisper: "*Release it, Kaeleighnna.*"

That was all she needed. Kaeleigh looked fiercely one last time into those eyes full of bloodlust and unspeakable darkness and shouted, "*She* cannot have me!"

There was a simultaneous thunderclap and explosion of light, the brightest white Kaeleigh had ever seen. The darkness around her screeched a bloodcurdling scream and the tentacles released her from its grip, shriveling into the sky and disappearing. Then she was falling.

Chel screamed as she was hit and slammed to the ground by something large. "Kaeleigh!" she grunted out breathlessly from under her fallen friend.

Breathing heavily, Kaeleigh rolled off Chel, looking around frantically to see the result of what had just happened. "Sorry, Chel, did I hurt you?"

"Of course you did! You fell out of the sky on me!" she shouted as she threw herself onto Kaeleigh, squeezing whatever life she still had out of her. "Couldn't you have fallen into the arms of one of these hunky warrior guys we have around here? Now that would have been amazingly romantic, just like in the movies." Chel sighed with a wink, then sobered quickly. "We didn't know what to do, we couldn't reach you. I thought I was going to lose you again." Chel's eyes filled with emotion.

"I thought I was lost too." She looked up, confused. "I thought it had taken me somewhere."

Kneeling on the ground close to her was Finn. Aidón stood close by with his knife out, standing guard. She felt Daegan at her back. Looking up and back, she watched him as he stood fierce and protective, intensely scanning the forest. But in the back of her mind, she heard his voice sighing with relief, "*You are safe now.*" She nodded and when he looked down at her, puzzled, she realized that he had not meant for her to hear that. Strange, but she was beginning to like his voice in her mind.

Hearing the sound of a twig snapping off to their side, they all reacted. Jumping to their feet, they held their swords at the ready. However, what they saw coming through the tree line was the most welcome sight.

"Ella," both Daegan and Finn said with relief then looked at the other in confusion unaware of the other's knowledge of the Ehsmian.

"Hello, boys," Ella smirked. "Always one for an entrance, aren't you, Finnlan?" Ella sauntered her way through the brush and moss of the forest floor like she could slide right through them. She was not alone. Five Faerie men were with her. They were definitely warriors, but looked very different from the Ferrishyn that Daegan was. These Faeries had only a slight tint to their skin whereas, Ferrishyn were more of a tan complexion. They were also thin and tall, but athletic looking. All of them, including Ella, wore a cream-colored material that definitely did not allow them to blend in with their surroundings. Ella's hair was a pixie cut—short and jagged—and frost white; the others' hair seemed normal—by mortal realm standards of color—but they each had a variety of styles of braids with knots and ties in them. Some had shaved the sides of their heads. They carried spears, shields, and multiple ornately carved knives on their belts. Ella seemed to be the only one with personality as those with her remained expressionless and surveyed Kaeleigh and company.

"Unless you want to wait for the Droch-Shúil to come back or the dark forces that are tracking you to catch up, I suggest we move now and talk later," Ella directed at Daegan.

"Wait. Who are you? How do I know we can trust you?" Kaeleigh stepped forward in front of Daegan, putting everyone with her behind her.

Ella raised an eyebrow at Kaeleigh. "Good, you have a backbone. You are going to need it. I know you have gone through a lot, and will continue to go through even more." At Kaeleigh's befuddled expression, she continued, "I know more about you than anyone here does... him included." She pointed to Finn, who rolled his eyes.

Finn rolled his eyes. What is going on?! Kaeleigh looked to Chel to see if she saw what just happened. Apparently she did since her mouth was agape and she was staring straight at him.

Ella continued, "You are about to find what you have been seeking, but only if we get to the mountain and my grandfather. So I'm asking you to blindly trust me at least for a little while... Princess."

The last word she spoke very quietly so Kaeleigh knew she was aware of her sensitive hearing. Kaeleigh didn't like not knowing who she was with, but neither Daegan nor Finn would let them walk into something dangerous without knowing it. She nodded and gave Ella a small smile. There was something about Ella's confidence and directness that made Kaeleigh want to like her.

"By the way, good timing releasing your pent-up power surge, Kaeleighnna," Ella spoke softly. Her voice triggered the sound of the voice that spoke to Kaeleigh while she was trapped in the funnel cloud with the darkness.

She gasped. "That was you? You spoke to my mind."

Ella nodded. "And you listened. We made a good team." She smiled.

Chel jumped in. "Did you make that bright light?"

"I did. While Kaeleighnna—"

"Kaeleigh, please call me Kaeleigh. My friends do," Kaeleigh interrupted.

Ella smiled again. "While Kaeleigh was releasing her power, I released the light of the Quarian sun, our sacred star, thus blinding the darkness long enough for her power to break its hold. It was good we got to her when we did. You might not have been able to defeat it on your own today."

"The glorious Ella! Please tell us more about your great deeds," Finn laughed.

Kaeleigh was baffled for a moment, causing her to lose any comebacks. *He laughed and talked like a mortal teenager... what is up with Finn?*

Kaeleigh was deep in thought when Chel elbowed her. "Did you hear how he just talked?"

Kaeleigh nodded, dumbfounded.

"What? It IS what happened," Ella replied with the slightest smile. "Kaeleigh's power is still blocked, and she does not have the sword as it is in the mountain. So no, you were not getting out of that darkness by yourselves. I helped. Simple fact. Deal with it, Finnlan." She winked at him and began walking, followed immediately by a couple of her men. The other three stayed to follow at the tail end of the group.

"Thank you. Thank you for coming, Ella." Kaeleigh, even though shocked by Finn's behavior, felt a slight twinge of jealousy at his familiarity and ease with Ella. She could also clearly see the truth in what Ella said. They would not have survived, or worse, she could have been taken to this mysterious "She" had Ella not intervened. One more puzzle to solve.

Chapter Three

The Way to Sanctuary.

"Where are we?" Chel asked, looking around in awe. They had walked in stressful, contained silence for quite a while until they finally reached a place where the forest began to thin, the mountain began to grow, and the ground cracked open into a canyon just beyond it. They followed a narrow rock path that went down the side of the canyon until the ground fell away from them and turned into a sudden long drop down the face of a cliff. Luckily, they had turned into an opening in the mountain that then led through a maze of tunnels and caves until it brought them to one unimpressive underground cave room. There was nothing in it except large rocks and boulders.

"We call it 'Sanctuary.' It is my home away from home. It can be yours as well, you might find it comforting here. This very spot is an overlay in the realms, which is usually where a gate is put to govern who goes in and out, but this one was protected... or hidden I should say, so no one but us knows about it. It also has its own portal entrance into the mortal realm and also one near the entrance into Ehsmia."

Kaeleigh was relieved to see that not only did she and Chel have confused looks on their faces, but Aidón and Daegan did as well. She couldn't imagine that Ella lived here. There was nothing homey about it.

"What does it overlay, Ella?" Finn asked, suddenly very serious.

She stared at him for a moment. "I was unable to show you until now, Finnlan, I beg your forgiveness. It was foreseen." Ella looked down in an odd show of humility.

"Where?" Finn growled out impatiently.

"Locast Ridge." She looked at him sheepishly but also with a glimmer of hope and excitement in her eyes.

Finn's eyes lit up. "Really?! I can't believe it. Why you couldn't tell me about it, I don't understand. I could've gone back and forth the whole time and no one would have known."

Ella briefly shifted her gaze toward Kaeleigh then back to Finn. He seemed to get the message and slightly changed the subject.

"Can we go there?" Finn asked. "I haven't seen the boys in quite some time."

"Yes, I think that might be best for now anyway. You all can rest, then we will continue on to the mountain." Ella looked to Daegan and his scowl.

"I do not know this place. How far is the mountain entrance from here?" he asked.

"It is almost a day's journey, Daegan. You all need rest, shelter, and food. Kaeleigh needs to rest, her energy is draining. If we got attacked again on the way, none of us would survive at this point."

Daegan took a deep breath. He looked to Kaeleigh, taking a moment to really sense her, then nodded back to Ella.

"So one more time: where are we?" Chel began again.

"I will explain as soon as we get settled, Chel. But for now, know that it is safe and it is a part of your mortal realm." With that little nugget, Ella walked around a very large boulder that was much taller than all of them and into a dark crevice that couldn't be detected by the naked eye.

"What?!" both Kaeleigh and Chel said at the same time. They looked to Finn and then to Daegan.

"We are going back into the mortal realm? Do you know where? Can we go home?" Chel began firing questions in rapid-fire succession.

"I don't know, Chel, calm down." Finn held his hands up trying to hold her back while Kaeleigh just started forward and followed Ella into the dark.

"Kaeleigh, wait!" Chel whisper shouted.

Unprepared for what she saw, Kaeleigh had no frame of reference for where in the mortal realm they might be. They emerged from behind a large boulder similar to the one they had entered around on the other side. Behind them stood nothing but solid, smooth gray rock. The same rock was above them at a spacious distance, curving all the way down to the ground about thirty feet away. It was mostly smooth, but with jagged outcroppings and even small holes placed at various intervals. Several young men and a couple older ones stared at them with menace, pointing spears in their direction. There was no doubt that they would shish kebob Kaeleigh and her friends had Ella not stepped out from behind Kaeleigh with her hands up.

Finn and Daegan were instantly in front of Kaeleigh and Chel, pushing them back behind them, but moving slowly, hoping not to provoke the spears that were mere feet in front of them.

"You may look like Ella, but what is the secret password?" one of the older men asked.

She nodded appreciatively. "Very good. Do not ever take what you see at face value. However, please never use the phrase 'secret password' again. We are not children." Ella smiled. "The word is 'Fantasyland,' as picked by Tina this week." Instantly, the men lowered their spears and took what few steps they could back to create more space.

"It seems all is well?" a different man asked. He was in his late thirties perhaps, with scruffy facial hair and wearing thick pants, hiking boots, and a heavy flannel coat and hat.

"There was a small delay, but nothing I couldn't handle. I have arrived with the guests I was looking for." Ella inclined her head toward Kaeleigh and her friends. The men in front of her did nothing more than nod and then continued speaking to Ella. Some of the younger men shook hands with the warriors that had been with Ella in Alandria. Although the warriors appeared to be trying, they still seemed awkward with the interaction.

"What is happening here, Ella?" Daegan asked, unwilling to take Kaeleigh any further without explanation.

Ella took a deep breath. "Daegan, you will have to trust me once more. This is something you will need to see to understand. I am about to show you something that everyone in Alandria believes to not exist. This is a colony of Twined mortals and Twined beings of Alandria that have fled the realm for safety. There are few that know of this place and even fewer who know the numbers within it."

Daegan looked troubled. Not only was he trying to fathom what Ella had spoken of, but if it was true, he was concerned about his presence there. "I should not come with you," he stated flatly.

Kaeleigh looked up at his face and then bit her bottom lip in concern. "The headaches?" she whispered and he nodded slightly.

Ella stepped forward, looking directly into his soul through his eyes. "Yes, there is still a connection. I can almost *see* it, but this place is heavily warded. It is essentially an extension of Ehsmia. She cannot permeate our wards while you are there. You will not be a danger to us. Let us head to the entrance."

A glimmer of hope stirred in Daegan's eyes. It made Kaeleigh's chest tighten to know there was still a connection between him and Maleina; that she hadn't been able to free him entirely of his bond. She could tell that Daegan wanted to see what Ella was about to show them, but his concern for the safety of the people/beings he didn't even know outweighed what he desired.

Without thinking, Kaeleigh placed her hand around the back of his bicep. At her touch, the spark that had been there before ignited once again. His muscles bunched underneath her hand. Even though she didn't want to let go, she did. Then followed the group that was already trailing Ella down a dirt path cut through a grassy hillside. Above her, the sky was overcast and gray. There was a slight breeze that oddly brought confusion and dizziness when Kaeleigh tried to look around too much.

Looking behind her, Kaeleigh's eyes grew large. Where they had just exited through a crevice of rocks, there was now only a decaying forest of broken branches and lifeless limbs. Through the dying trees, she could see a large decomposing house; something out of a horror movie or a haunted house. Drained of all color and life, boards broken, and shutters barely hanging by their hinges, it gave Kaeleigh chills.

"Wha... What happened to the rocks?" she stammered.

Next to her, Chel snapped her head around in confusion. "Where are we?"

Kaeleigh could see in her friend's eyes the beginning of panic. Kaeleigh could sympathize with her—suddenly feeling trapped, not knowing where she was. Turning back toward the way they were headed, Kaeleigh gasped, seeing the exact mirror image of the decrepit house that was behind them now suddenly also in front of them. Trying to stay calm for her friend was suddenly not working well for her. Swiveling her head back and forth between the two houses, she felt disoriented and lost; she almost began walking off in a random direction.

A large hand with worn callouses gripped her wrist, sending jolts of electricity that both calmed her and cleared her head, but also stirred the butterflies deep in her stomach, sending them soaring all throughout her chest. She took a deep cleansing breath, the dizziness gone.

"It is an illusion. Similar to a glamour, but it is meant to cause confusion to keep anyone out that should not be at the entrance," Daegan explained quietly in her ear as he pulled her back onto the path. "Something not seen with purely Alandrian magic."

She looked over at him, then down at where his large, strong hand encircled her small wrist, and then back up into his eyes.

"We need to stay together," he said, and Kaeleigh nodded. "We need to stay with the group," he amended. She looked over and realized Daegan was guiding Chel as well with his hand on her elbow.

Kaeleigh gave her head a strong shake to clear her mind completely, then stood up tall and tried to focus on all the people in their group. Seeing Finn up closer to the front, talking to Aidón but following closely behind Ella, made Kaeleigh wonder about how they knew each other. Finn normally wasn't that far away from her and she realized she felt a spark of something... *Jealousy? No I shouldn't be jealous. After all, he can talk to whoever he wants to just as I can. He doesn't belong to me... no one does.*

"Something is wrong. What is it?" Daegan asked quietly, leaning in to her ear. She could feel his breath tickle the sensitive skin on her neck, sending friendly chills down her spine.

"It's nothing. You don't need to worry about me, Daegan."

His grip squeezed her wrist so she knew he was there, but that was something she didn't want at the moment. His hot and cold mood swings were irritating. As she pulled her hand out of his grip, she pulled up so she could grip his hand in hers before she let go and pulled away completely. Before she moved out of his reach, she heard him mutter under his breath, "But I do."

They found themselves carefully walking up rotted steps, unsure if it was an illusion. And if it was, could they still be hurt if they fell through the decaying boards? Soon they were all crowded into the entryway of what once could have been a beautiful old mansion. It was three stories tall with floor to ceiling windows on the first level, though most were either boarded up or broken. There was a grand staircase off to the side of the entry. There was no color in this place. It was a void, lifeless and muted, but it was all a deception.

Chapter Four

ELNYE. THE CASTLE IN ELNYE, THE
CAPITAL OF FERAÁNMAR.

"**M**y Lady, Maleina. It is always a pleasure, but I am afraid I have journeyed, personally, to bring you disappointing news." The man before her inclined his head slightly, keeping his eyes downcast awaiting her to acknowledge him.

Maleina stood regally, poised in front of one of the tall windows off to the side from her throne. She appeared to be entranced, watching something far off in the distance. Fully adorned in her finest, knowing she was to have company, she wore silks of red and orange. The skirt was full with layers of bright fabric, while the bodice was sculpted against her outline. It was without sleeves, except for the short dress jacket she wore with it. Her mane of fiery red curls was, unusually, left down this day. She wore pins of exquisite jewels and several pieces of her hair were roped with strips of fabric that matched her dress.

She made the man in her presence wait longer than was hospitable, but then she did not desire to be accommodating. When she heard the fabric of his clothing rub together from his fidgeting, she took a deep breath and turned slowly to grace him with her attention. *He looks nervous. Good,* she thought. There were two other men—Elves—standing some distance behind the man in front of her. They stood as sentries, on guard for their master with their hands holding their spears and shields in front of them as if they were prepared for battle. In front of her stood the Elf who called himself "king" of Adettlyn—for the time being. She had other plans for him, but not just yet. She needed him for now.

"What is the news you bring, Syén?"

"I have eyes in the eastern woods of Lumei. They report to me of a group traveling under the cover of night and the trees. My spies watched them while they waited to hear my instruction, but then lost them when they were under attack from the Droch-Shúil and saved by a blinding light of sacred magic. When their vision was restored, they could neither find them nor track them. It was as if they had vanished."

Maleina's eyes burned with flames of fire. Her fists clenched at her sides. The king in front of her lowered his head, but continued to watch her. He took a step back, which he regretted. He did not like her superiority over him—after all, he too was a king—but he honestly feared her more. He preferred to send messages, but he owed his crown to her.

"I was counting on your resources to regain what is mine, but I shall now have to take matters into my own hands. Unfortunately, I know where they are headed and it is somewhere my reach does not grant me. *She* must have sent the Droch-Shúil on her own. I will have to resort to some unfortunate means to get results." Maleina turned back toward the window, ignoring her company but not yet dismissing them. She mused the situation over to herself until she lighted on a certain outcome.

"You are dismissed for now, Syén. Do not stray from your kingdom, however, for I feel you will be needed there in the future." She smirked condescendingly at him. He inclined his head and quickly left the throne room with his men behind him.

"Guards." Her voice carried across the long room to the men stationed at the throne room entrance. "Bring me my son."

CHAPTER FIVE

TYLÍNYTH. THE POCKET REALM OF THE TWINED.

T he heavy, creaking door of the haunted mansion closed loudly behind them, causing Kaeleigh and Chel to jump and grab onto each other's arms.

"Fan-freaking-tastic. How did we go from a fantasy world to my nightmare?" Chel whispered.

Kaeleigh held tightly to Chel's arm; she hated all things horror. There was a reason she didn't watch those kinds of movies and now she was in one. She tried to take steady breaths. "It's going to be okay, Chel. It has to be, right?" Kaeleigh whispered back. She didn't turn around, but she felt Daegan at her back, his presence bringing a sense of calm and safety with him. It was almost like he was touching her, but he wasn't. As much as she coveted the feeling of calm he gave her, it also drove her emotions and hormones crazy.

Ella muttered something in another language, and then there was a light a short ways down the hall in front of them. She started walking again. Apprehensively, they followed.

"Look," Chel said under her breath and nodded towards the front.

"Oh wow," Kaeleigh responded. "Is that her marking? It glows. That is pretty cool." Kaeleigh and Chel both looked at Kaeleigh's wrists as she pulled back her bracelets and material she used to cover them up to see if her marking glowed like Ella's did. Disappointed to find that neither of them did, Kaeleigh shrugged. Then she felt Daegan nudge her back with what must have been the back of his hand. Distracted by Ella's mark, they had gotten a bit behind and took fast steps to catch up.

Ella led the group through the bright light that created the gateway into the pocket realm. She and her grandfather, along with a hand-selected small group of powerful and trusted members of Alandria, made it a habitable and thriving environment for the Twined. The group was made up of half mortal/half Alandrian beings and halves from two different races within Alandria who had escaped to flee recent persecution. No one knew how many there actually were in existence until they had begun to come from all over the mortal realm, looking for sanctuary. They either did not understand why they were the way they were—similar to Kaeleigh—or they had been taught some of their birthright from their parents, but wanted to be taught more and/or to be a part of what could be the hopeful future of Alandria. Ella had hoped that Kaeleigh would feel at home in this place. If there was anyone the Twined could relate to, it might be Kaeleigh—born of two Alandrian races, raised as mortal.

"We are here," Ella said with her arms wide clearly proud of what was before her. "Welcome to Tylínyth."

They stepped out from behind another cluster of large rocks and boulders. As they looked up behind them, they saw an enormous, white snow-capped mountain through the man-sized crevice they had walked through.

"Wow," Kaeleigh breathed out in awe. Everyone, except for those who came with Ella and had obviously been there before, stood still for a moment in silence taking in the scene.

There were people busying about doing what appeared to be "normal" things in a village nestled at the base of a mountain chain. There were small houses, some more fortified than others that were more log cabin-esque, and there were larger structures that looked to house supplies if the strings of food and weapons hanging in the windows were any indication. Some of the houses that seemed to be more lived in even had gardens and greenery thriving around them. Off in the distance, there was a treed area—not nearly as old or mysterious looking as the forests in Alandria. Next to that were fields of wildflowers that went on for miles leading up toward a range of mountains. They were striking, tall and all capped with snow. They created a beautiful wall, proud and protective. The air was fresh and crisp. Even though the sun—no wait, was that two... three suns?—were high in the sky, and there was a spring chill in the air. There were birds chirping nearby and even a butterfly or two passed in front of them as they remained by the entrance to this familiar feeling place.

"Is this somewhere in Alandria?" Kaeleigh asked. "It looks more like something out of one of my Geography books, except for the three suns."

"What did you do, Ella? I feel like I'm looking at a postcard," Chel fired off. Ella uncharacteristically blushed. Backpedaling to not offend her, Chel added, "I mean it's beautiful, it just seems too perfect."

"It looks like somewhere in Switzerland," Daegan said matter-of-factly. Several pairs of eyes shifted his direction in questioning shock. He shrugged his shoulders. "I know more about your world than you do. Yes, Chel, I think that is exactly what Ella has done, quite masterfully I might add. Except for the three suns, that is not a part of the mortal realm."

"No, but as there are Alandrians living here as well, I tried to combine the realms to make everyone comfortable." Then she huffed in frustration. "And they are not all suns. It is one sun and two moons, but for some reason I can not get the moon cycles to work quite right so they pretty much stay there permanently and just change shades at night." Crossing her arms over her chest, she seemed to still be considering how to alter it.

Kaeleigh jumped in. "Ella, please show us around. This is truly incredible." Ella's eyes lit up and gestured for them to follow her.

They were shown around the different living quarters, the eating and meeting hall which was just a larger building, and the training arena out in one of the fields. Ella had explained that even though it looked as if you could go for miles, for now, it was just for appearances and you could really only climb up one side of the mountains before you had an "urge" to go back down to the bottom. The camp or village itself was not as large as it first appeared. Kaeleigh began yawning as they neared the end. She didn't want to make Ella feel bad, but the events of the last while were suddenly catching up to her quickly. She needed a long rest.

"Ella, is there somewhere that we can rest?" It was Finn. He nodded imperceptibly at Kaeleigh, covering for her. Though it was not always wanted, she did appreciate him and his heart, looking after her.

"Yes, let me show you." Ella walked back towards the larger of the buildings. Right before they reached it, Ella stopped and gestured to a smaller structure next to it. It was larger than most of the "homes" they had seen along the tour. It was also extremely simple in construction, basically four walls and a flat roof, creating a box with a door and two small windows in the front.

"This is one of the bunk buildings. It is usually used for newer guests or those that don't stay long enough to want or need their own residence. There is no one using it that I am aware of, though, so it should be peaceful for you all. I apologize there are not more individual accommodations for you, but with the recent events I assumed you would all prefer to remain close anyway." Ella eyed Finn with a slight question in her eyes, but as soon as he nodded appreciatively she opened the door and entered what essentially was a big open room with only one door in the back—hopefully a bathroom.

Each wall was lined with bunk beds. There were a couple trunks in the room. Ella pointed at one of them. "There are blankets, linens, and towels in these." She then pointed toward the door to the back, "The bathroom is simple, but it is at least modern plumbing." Ella looked to the girls with a small smile.

Both Kaeleigh and Chel sighed with relief. They had been using the eau de toilette de nature quite a bit in Alandria while they trekked all over.

"It's a shame having magic powers doesn't give you the luxury of not needing a bathroom anymore," Chel mused. Kaeleigh giggled at Chel's blunt observation.

Ella interrupted their laughter calmly. "There is a meal in the main hall at sundown. I would like to introduce you to everyone." Oddly she looked only at Kaeleigh, awaiting her reply.

After a second, Kaeleigh looked up from the bed she was about to stake a claim to. "Oh, yes, I would be honored to meet everyone." She blushed at not realizing she was being spoken to.

Ella nodded as she walked out, but before she had gotten far, she gestured for Finn to follow her out. Kaeleigh almost missed it, Ella was so subtle. But then Finn followed her out, and Kaeleigh couldn't help wonder if they had been "together" before Finn had been kicked out of his home to take care of her. A momentary stab of guilt pierced her heart, but then she remembered that he would have been sentenced to Exhile or death anyway; it wasn't her fault he had to leave.

Without realizing it, Kaeleigh started to sway. The exhaustion from their journey and its events was catching up to her all at once, draining away any semblance of energy that she had left. Chel was immediately by her side.

"Daegan, help," Chel said as she tried to hold Kaeleigh up with an arm around her waist and gripping onto one arm. "Okay, let's get you onto a bed before you faint on us." Daegan tried to help Chel by grabbing her other side but his height in contrast to Chel's made it awkward and he didn't want Kaeleigh to fall. His solution shocked Chel as he leaned over and swiped Kaeleigh's legs out from under her and cradled her in his strong arms and simply carried her over to a bed.

"Wait!" Chel practically shouted at him before he laid her down. Daegan looked at her and then around the room, guessing at what her outburst was for. "She will kill me if we lay her on a bed that who knows how many people have laid on without putting a blanket down."

Daegan got a crease in his forehead as he took in what Chel had said and watched as she strewed blankets and linens from the chest onto the bed. "She has slept on the ground and on a prison floor, I do not think she will notice there are no sheets on this bed."

Chel's mouth gaped open. "Even more reason to make her a bed that she might feel a little more comfortable in! Don't you think?" Daegan looked to Chel and then to the bed and then down to Kaeleigh, now sleeping in his arms. He noticed how much she had changed in such a little time. Extreme situations had a way of doing that to a person. "Yeah, that's what I thought," Chel said as she busied herself first making a bed for Kaeleigh and then another on the bunk above her. Then she moved to make the other two bunks next to that one. She watched Daegan out of the corner of her eyes as he gently laid Kaeleigh down and then began to take her shoes off with extreme care. "That's far enough, buddy. Don't be removing anything else." Chel was serious but she snickered at her comment.

Daegan practically growled at her, "Do you think so little of me, shifter? That I would not honor her with respect?"

Chel stared him deep in the eyes. She was not afraid of him; in fact, in that moment, she knew beyond a shadow of a doubt what he probably did not yet even understand himself. "I'm just being the best friend..." She looked at Kaeleigh with soft eyes then continued, "she's been through a lot. But I do trust you with her, maybe more than you trust yourself." She looked back at the shock in Daegan's eyes, seeing that he saw the weight of what she said, but didn't know what to do with it. She decided to help him out. Gesturing around at all the beds she asked, "So, warrior, which bunk do you want? I'll put sheets on it as well."

Daegan nodded toward the bunk across from hers and Kaeleigh's but closer to the door so he could watch the entrance. "Bottom."

Chel cocked her eyebrow at his statement.

He cleared his throat at the feisty little shifter in front of him, "Excuse my manners. I prefer the bottom, if you please... and thank you, Chel."

"Oh, and I do please. I prefer the bottom too, but I think Kaeleigh might prefer the top," Chel said with a suggestive wink then went to work. She giggled to herself and when she turned to spy Daegan out of the corner of her eye, he seemed flustered. Flustered! He even had a slight tint to the tan skin of his cheeks. Could he be blushing? Chel was shocked she was able to rattle him. Oh, this could be fun. But before she could go further with her teasing, he changed the subject.

"Please make a place for Finn here on this bunk at Kaeleigh's head. I want someone on this side able to jump in front of you both if necessary." He cleared his throat again and stalked to the door. "I will be right outside for a moment."

"Need some fresh air there, warrior?" He stormed out the door, pretending not to hear her. Chel giggled again. It felt good to laugh a bit. It felt good to rest and feel safe, even if for a short time.

Chapter Six

Tylínyth.

The door swung open, slamming against the wall. Jumping up from her bed, Chel peered through sleepy eyes at the stranger that had just froze in the doorway. Squinting, she couldn't see much of the tall masculine figure that was shadowed as light filtered in from the outside surrounding him. It wasn't anyone that traveled with them. She was sure she would recognize all their profiles anywhere. Suddenly, she was wide awake as she realized that it was only she and a sleeping Kaeleigh alone in the cabin.

"Oh! I'm sorry. I didn't realize anyone was in here." A rough timbre of a man's voice broke through her surprise.

"Shhh... I swear if you wake her up, I will take you down myself if the big warrior behind you doesn't do it first." Chel smirked as the shadow of a man still in the doorway turned to see Daegan standing with his arms folded behind him with a scowl on his face.

Daegan moved back, inviting the shadowed man back outside with him. She could hear Daegan's low voice interrogating the man. "Who are you?" There was a quick response from the man. "My name is Cyrus." The rumble of their continued talking almost lulled Chel back into dreamland. After looking at the bunk below her to see Kaeleigh still out cold, Chel rolled over and quickly sank back into blissful sleep.

❖❖❖

Restless in her sleep, Kaeleigh tossed and turned as she dreamed in flashes.

A familiar scene of endless trees sped by her as she moved swiftly through the familiar forest, her friends by her side. She could feel eyes on her—as they fled. Darkness was on the outskirts, she could feel it. Why she didn't sense it sooner in reality, she wasn't sure because here it was obvious they were being pursued... tracked... hunted. Brought to a clearing, she and her group were surrounded by the darkness, by the Droch-Shúil. There wasn't hope of escape this time, but then a light brighter than she had ever seen exploded. Ella had helped rescue them.

Her focus slowed as it paused on Aidón as she watched his glamour shift and shimmer and morph around him, but never fully lifting or stopping on an image that seemed to fit him. He looked back at her with an expression that pleaded with her to try again. He was trapped within himself, wanting out of his fleshly prison, being captive to a body that was not his own. Over and over she watched her magic seek entrance into the shell of glamour that seemed impenetrable to her. She wasn't strong enough yet. She could see what needed to happen, but wasn't quite able to reach it. There was an intense magic around him.

Suddenly, the background changed. She was with Aidón at the base of a tall snowy mountain, nearby a flowing stream. Down on a knee, he awaited her as she drew upon her magic, stirring it to epic proportions within herself. She placed her hands on him, one on his chest and the other opposite it on his back. Her magic swirled around them as a funnel of wind. Still it was not enough. Approaching from behind, Daegan along with Finn and Chel surrounded Kaeleigh and a kneeling Aidón. Each placed their hands on Kaeleigh, uniting their magic and energy with her own. Again, a bright light exploded.

Kaeleigh jolted upright in her bed. Forgetting where she was, she smacked her head on the bunk above her. "OW!"

"Oh no... That was not quite the wake-up call I was hoping for," Chel grumbled from the top bunk. "You okay?"

"Forgot where I was," Kaeleigh mumbled as she rubbed her head. Suddenly remembering what her dream was about, she practically shouted, "I know how to release him!"

"What? Who?"

"Aidón. I've been trying to break down his glamour."

"Oh. Are you sure that's a good idea? We don't even know him." Chel swung her head down to look Kaeleigh in the eyes, hanging upside down with all her hair falling in and around her face.

"You look like a bat," Kaeleigh laughed.

"You'll regret that comment when I get my shifting abilities down. I might just turn into a bat and terrorize you." They both laughed then quickly sobered.

"He was making light of it, while we traveled... maybe to test me, I'm not sure. In a dream I saw him, he's trapped in a glamour kind of like I was, except he knows it whereas I didn't. He wants out... And I know how to do it," Kaeleigh said with determined excitement. "But I'm going to need all of you." Kaeleigh sought her friend's expression, expecting uneasiness, but once again Chel bounced back.

"Then let's get this deliverance underway," Chel said snarkily, wiggling her fingers in Kaeleigh's face. Kaeleigh shook her head, smiling, as they both jumped out of their beds and straightened their clothing.

"I feel gross," Chel complained, swiping her hands down her shirt.

"Yeah, a nice hot shower sounds heavenly about now, doesn't it?"

"And some new clothes," Chel grumbled as she took in Kaeleigh's and then her own attire—she refused to call the rags they were given in the prison an outfit; it so wasn't even close.

"Let's get cleaned up first and then go see if we can find everyone," Kaeleigh said as she grabbed a couple towels out of the open chest in the center of the room and threw one at Chel.

"You go first, I'll guard the door from any unsuspecting warriors that might come wandering in." Chel winked.

Several minutes later, Kaeleigh stuck her head out the door wrapped in a towel. "Remember when I said 'nice warm shower'?" Chel nodded. "Yeah, they may have plumbing, but they are missing the 'nice warm' part."

"Great," Chel grumbled sarcastically. "Well, at least Ella brought us some new clothes to wear." Chel threw a wad of cream-colored linens at Kaeleigh, who almost dropped her towel to catch the haphazardly thrown clothes which only made Chel laugh.

A moment later, Kaeleigh walked out wearing clothes that looked like those worn by many of the other residents that she had caught glances of when they took their tour. They were simple, but comfortable. Everything was a cotton-linen blend. For whatever reason, it reminded Kaeleigh of some kind of refugee camp or a new world resistance where everyone looked the same and dressed the same. It kind of gave her the creeps and left her feeling void and colorless. But at least they were clean.

A high-pitched wolf whistle broke her out of her thoughts. "Nice duds," Chel said from the bottom bunk near the bathroom door.

"I am but a mere vision of what you have to look forward to," Kaeleigh said sweetly as she twirled around playfully showing off her linens.

"Lovely." Chel jumped up and took her turn in the bathroom.

Standing under a tree a short distance off to the side of a clearing that was the training area, Daegan watched a group of young people, both men and women, Faeries, Elves, and even some shifters, training and practicing together. It wasn't a sight he was use to seeing. In Elnye, the Ferrishyn all trained together but it consisted mostly of males. Something warmed in his chest as he continued to watch. They were lacking in their training and what he thought they should be able to do as warriors—even half-human ones, but there was something very right about how they functioned together. He continued to evaluate their weaponry, how they held it and how they wielded it, until someone noticed him.

"Would you like to join us?" a young wisp of a girl with curly white-blonde hair asked.

Just as Daegan was about to warn her that her partner was still coming at her with his sword, she turned swiftly and blocked his strike with her own weapon that resembled a staff or a spear without the point. In fact, as he looked closer he saw it was more a stick than anything. She quickly disarmed her partner who was bigger than her and waited for him to acknowledge defeat, then she turned back to Daegan's awaiting smirk of approval.

"Well done," he said and nodded at her.

She beamed up at him. "So would you like to join us?" Daegan approached their group of about twenty or so, all of whom had stopped what they were doing to watch his interaction with the young girl. "You came with that new group that got here earlier, right?"

"I did." He gave the group a quick glance.

The girl's partner, a young man of about seventeen, jumped up from the ground and stepped closer to her protectively, which Daegan found slightly humorous, as did the girl apparently since she rolled her eyes at him. A very human response reminding him of something Kaeleigh might do, and for sure Chel.

"You could join us if you would like. We could use another warrior," a different boy chimed in a little too excitedly.

"All right." Daegan nodded to the young boy. He found it a little hard to tell for certain what race of beings these younger ones belonged to. He had guesses based on certain characteristic markers or the way they fought, but they were not marked like those of Alandria. And their appearances were slightly off from what he would expect them to be since they were, of course, Twined—being part human and part Elf or Faerie or shifter. "I am not sure how I will fit in with your group and your normal routine, but I will do my best." Daegan surveyed the response of the group which as a whole seemed to be accepting. "Where shall I begin?"

"You can partner with me at first." The fiery young girl who had just taken her partner down a notch had a gleam of excitement in her eyes.

Daegan nodded at her and stepped back, pulling his shorter sword from his hip holster. Everyone around them took similar positions nearby. He could see her original partner standing not far off in case he needed to save her from the "big bad warrior" guy. Although lacking some formal training, as a whole, they seemed to be able to hold their own. To his surprise, his young new sparring partner, who looked like a mortal version of a pixie, was steady with her staff and more competent with it than he had originally given her credit for. Apparently, she had been holding back with her original partner when Daegan watched from the sidelines.

"I know you are going easy on me, push me a bit more," the young girl protested.

Daegan's eyes squinted in consideration. "Not yet. You are a skilled young warrioress but I can help you learn a few more strengthening skills and moves that will play to your advantage with your size."

The girl looked as if she were about to argue, but then took a deep breath and looked him square in the eyes and nodded.

"What is your name?"

"Metrí."

"And what is your race, Metrí?"

Suddenly the atmosphere in the field shifted from camaraderie to an animosity that Daegan had not sensed in any of those present thus far. They had, of course, been apprehensive and skeptical of him and the others, but they had attempted to accept him into their circle nonetheless. Daegan did not step back and he did not apologize; however, he did hold a hand up asking them to wait.

Metrí's original partner stepped up next to her, showing he was ready to step up to the plate to interfere if he needed to.

"I ask because in Alandria, where I come from, we are marked with a marking such as this one," he spoke as he turned and presented his inner forearm with the circle crest of the Ferrishyn to those near him. "It distinguishes one tribe from another."

The young man next to Metrí spoke out. "Does it not also separate you? We are distinguished from one another, but are joined in what makes us different from other humans... from others of our kind."

Daegan considered what he had said before responding to him. "In a way, yes it does. There are positives and negatives to knowing your heritage. Why I am asking is so that I may know what particular strengths are attributed to your particular race. For example, within the shifter race, there is great strength and there can be great speed. Whatever strengths that come from the specific animals you are gifted to embody are yours as well. The race of Elves has extra speed, mobility, agility, and a great wisdom that comes from the depths of their magic. Faeries of Feraánmar, where I am from, have magic that cultivates and can be very useful in a fight only if necessary, but their true magic is vital after the battle for re-creating that which was destroyed."

He looked around to see almost all of them intrigued by the words he spoke, as if they had never heard it presented that way—and perhaps they hadn't. "As it stands, there is much separation and division because of the races, but if they can come together as you do here on this field and work together with each strength unique to you as individuals, there would be great strength in Alandria." Daegan's voice grew quiet. "What I see here is the potential to realize a dream many have thought to be impossible... what I thought was impossible."

"Why haven't you already done this in the realm of Alandria? Surely, we are not so unique?" a voice called out from the group.

"It has been tried, but it is not easy. It is my belief that it was not attempted genuinely." Daegan quickly shook off his contemplations and refocused on the group of would-be warriors. "Now, will you allow me to continue to practice with you?"

He saw a few in the crowd shrug their shoulders indifferently and a few who appeared skeptical, but the overall feeling was acceptance and even hope. Metrí was nodding her head emphatically. She whispered, "Yes," as her eyes caught Daegan's while her companion stood protectively close with a scowl on his face. Daegan looked him directly in the eyes, not challenging his spirit but his mind to give the possibility a chance. After not even a few seconds, the young man nodded and relaxed his posture. Daegan noted the brief flicker of what he perceived to be possibilities bubble in the young warrior's soul.

"Let us begin again. But first if you would, could you inform me of your parentage so that I might understand how to assist you if I am able?"

"How is it you think you can train a Shifter or an Elf?" another young female voice asked as she stood in the back of the gathered group.

"I hold a position in the courts of Feraánmar that has ensured I am trained quite sufficiently in all types of combat, but I also have had the opportunity to work with several from various races that I may be able to pass on to you. Is that sufficient?"

The warrior nodded, accepting the answer.

"I only have one request: let's refrain from the use of the word *warrioress*, shall we?" Metrí asked with light attitude.

Daegan smirked playfully. "No? Where I am from, there are very few female warriors. Those there are, that is what they are referred to. I thought it to be a title of honor, but if you do not wish it, then it will be stricken from this field." He awaited her answer.

After a moment, she responded, "Hmmm, well, I will think about it then. I don't want to miss out on any titles of honor." She smiled playfully back.

Then a voice rang out from the group, followed by another and another as one by one, the eager warriors in the field started speaking out their race. Daegan sat down cross-legged on the ground, indicating to the others around him to do the same, as many took turns sharing a brief history of what they knew of their parentage. Some had been left in the dark as their parents had either hoped they would not need to know this side of the heritage for their own safety or they simply never had the chance to tell them. Many of them did not know if their parents were still alive or not. Overall, there seemed to be a large number of Shifters in the group, only a handful of Faeries, and an even smaller amount of Elves; most not knowing much about their non-human side.

As they continued to share their stories, the young warriors watched his every move and his every reaction with eager observation. Daegan remained stoic, listening and absorbing the new information. The last to share her story was Metrí, the fiery little slip of a girl who wielded a staff like one of Alandria. Her short and curly white-blond hair was pulled back from her face with clips, her gray eyes intense like the coming of a storm, and the pinkish tints on her cheeks stood out from her porcelain white skin. There was something akin to shame or unworthiness in her eyes as Daegan watched her closely, waiting for her to announce her parentage. She took a deep breath and looked up at him like not many of the others would dare to do.

"I don't know."

"You do not know who your parents are?" Daegan asked carefully.

"No. I know nothing of my family and I do not know which race I belong to. I have no extra powers that I am aware of."

"How did you know to come here then?"

"They found me. I mean Ella. She found me. She said that her grandfather sent her and that I was to be a part of this world. She told me that it would be 'revealed in the right time.'" Metrí used air quotes as her youthful eyes betrayed weariness and sadness. She continued, "I don't know what that means though. Anyway, I had nowhere else to be and no ties so I figured it couldn't hurt. Plus something about her felt right, so I went with her."

Metrí looked around at everyone else, realizing that they had never asked nor had she ever explained herself to them. "She never told me what my race was or any gifts I might have, just that I would have some and to learn whatever skills I could while I was here." She shrugged it off. "So, now that I've gone all emo on everyone, can

I get back to kicking everyone's asses? I think we've all shared our sob stories. It's time to start training." She paused, "Teach us, sir. Please?"

Daegan smiled at Metrí's spunky attitude. "Yes. Pair off again and begin your routines like you were doing before I stepped in. I will walk around and give comments and adjust as needed. Begin." Daegan turned to Metrí. "Practice with your original partner once more, and I will observe."

"His name is Peter," she informed him.

Daegan nodded at Peter. He then turned to watch the others get into their formations, expecting them all to do as he asked. They did. The sounds of swords clashing together was like a soothing balm to his ears. There was something that ministered to his being within the sounds of metal scraping against metal. He did not enjoy the acts nor the results of war, but there was something that sang a song into his very soul when he was being who he was created to be. It was refreshing.

He watched carefully as the men and women of this camp moved and flowed with their strikes and parries. Walking around each group, he would make a comment here and there critiquing, but also praising, their skills. Overall, Daegan was impressed with what he saw for a group that had no true warrior training or that barely knew what skills they should have being part magical. His eye kept being drawn toward Metrí and her partner, Peter. She was a little thing, but she had fire in her eyes and a determination to prove she could be good at what she was doing; clinging to it as if it was all she had, the only thing she had ever wanted to hold onto—and maybe it was. Just by watching for a mere moments, Daegan could see that she was already better than Peter, but she held herself back for his sake. She needed to be pushed, to be challenged to see what she was really capable of. There was something inside him that was drawn to the potential he saw there. He knew he could make her great. Daegan felt something stir within him. Something he hadn't felt in quite some time... a reason... a purpose—one that felt true and genuine.

Continuing to walk amongst the group, he would raise an arm holding a sword and tip it at slightly various angles, or adjust someone else's stance or grip on their weapon. He could feel their initial hesitation but then their response and acceptance. More than once, he would even feel their anticipation as he approached, their hunger to learn and excel. Pride began to rise in his chest just as a tickle of awareness slid up the back of his neck; he was being watched.

Adjusting his position in the slightest to the side allowed him to peer beyond his current student into the tree line where he first stood. Even though he didn't need to; he knew who was there—Kaeleigh. He could feel her. He could always feel her presence when she was near. He didn't know why, but it gave him comfort knowing she was near and safe. But it also drove him mad like an itch he could not scratch, mostly because he did not understand their connection and because he was beginning to grow accustomed to it. Knowing she felt it too did nothing to help his discomfort. Daegan knew he was keeping her at an arm's length, but it was too much right now. He didn't know what she expected of it or of him.

He looked up more directly only to find her smirking at him. She knew he had seen her. For not being an empath as he was, she could read him pretty easily, and perhaps that was the true reason for his discomfort. Her friends would not let her out of their sight long, so where she went he had to assume that Chel or Finn would be close by. Although, since they had gotten there, Finn had seemed quite preoccupied with something else. After Daegan had cornered the young man who had barged into their cabin while the girls were sleeping, he heard Finn and Ella arguing in hushed tones about something related to the Twined camp; something about how in Finn's previous position she was not able to trust him with it; something about a letter she had intercepted addressed to the Paladin.

There was more but he could not pay attention as he had been dealing with Cyrus. He was determined to find out what Finn was up to. Daegan could feel that he was hiding something, but Finn was able to mask his emotions well, except when Kaeleigh was around. She had him tied in knots. Finn watched her when she didn't know he did. From what Daegan could feel from Kaeleigh—even though he tried not to pry into the privacy of others—she did not return the same feelings Finn had. Daegan did not trust everything about the Elf, but he knew Finn's motive to protect Kaeleigh to be genuine. After all, he had done just that for the last many years. That story was still yet to be understood. So much had happened in the short time that Kaeleigh and her friends had come into Alandria. So much had happened to her personally, he did not know how she was coping with it all. Something in his chest tightened, thinking of Hunter and her feelings of loss as well as his own. Shaking off his brief sadness, he looked at her with a question in his eyes.

Kaeleigh took a step forward from the tree line with Chel right on her heels. When the two saw the group training, their eyes lit up. There was a bounce in Chel's steps as she moved closer. He knew they both wanted to learn to fight with weapons. They had only had one opportunity to have a training session right before they left Hunter's and they both still needed to train in order for him to feel comfortable that they could even attempt to protect anyone, let alone themselves. Kaeleigh had not done too badly for herself, but he feared it was mostly adrenaline and the magic of her sword. He decided to remedy that and soon. Perhaps they could join this group for training while they were here.

Walking toward the group of people training in the field, Kaeleigh was struck by how many were young like they were. Then there was Daegan, who stood out among the group—but then he stood out everywhere he was. There was such an air of authority and an ease with commanding, but not only that, there was a genuine passion that flowed out of him as he worked with the others. Her breath caught as something gripped her heart as their eyes met even across the distance of the field. He had changed into clothes from the mortal realm: snug blue jeans and a tight white shirt similar to everyone's that stretched across his broad, muscular chest. *Why*

didn't Chel and I get blue jeans too? Kaeleigh wondered briefly. Daegan really was a sight to behold. His dark brown eyes and his blue-black hair that was longer in this realm than it was when he had been in her world... well, her mortal world. She liked it longer, she had distracting desires to run her fingers through it. Blushing, she pulled her focus back onto the group in front of her that had now all stopped what they were doing and watched her and Chel approach, some with open curiosity and others with blatant skepticism.

Daegan turned to face her and nodded in her direction. Kaeleigh gave a slight smile at the recognition, even though that was pretty much how he acknowledged most people, unless he chose not to acknowledge them at all. So there was that. Suddenly feeling slightly deflated, she took a breath and remembered why she was looking for him. He had that effect on her often—distracting her from her present focus. She heard a subtle clearing of a throat next to her as Chel popped up beside her. Kaeleigh relaxed as her best friend stood with her.

"Kaeleigh. Chel. This is the Twined training ground." Daegan spoke as if welcoming them without the actual feeling of a welcome, but more questioning their presence.

"Thanks, Captain Obvious," Chel retorted. There was a snort from behind Daegan and then the young white-haired girl shot out around him.

Metrí looked up at Daegan then back at Chel then back to Daegan. "I like her."

Daegan looked down at the girl with a frown. Then Metrí glared back at Daegan. "We don't like to be referred to as Twined. We understand that is what we are and that society feels to label us because we are different and it makes sense if we need to be referred to as a group, but as a whole, we don't like it. We just want to be who we are and be a part." Her stance was strong with one hand fisted at her waist and the other gripping her staff at her side.

Chel grinned and nodded toward Metrí. "And I like her."

Kaeleigh pushed her way forward to be acknowledged, impatient to get on with why they were here. Aidón. She was suddenly feeling impatient and irritated because the little imp of a girl made her feel... made her feel... what? Not jealous. Couldn't be jealous. "I apologize to everyone, but I really need to speak with your new instructor in private." Kaeleigh looked at Daegan with eyes pleading and continued politely. "We need to speak with you if you could spare a moment to come with us, please?"

"We have been training, could it wait? I would like to try a few more drills with them. Actually, I was going to see if you and Chel wanted to join and practice the skills you have learned."

"No, I mean yes, we would like to, but perhaps a bit later? And no, it really can't wait. I think I know how to release Aidón from his glamour, but I am going to need your assistance... I think," Kaeleigh stumbled, suddenly unsure of what she had, moments ago, been sure about. Taking a breath, she looked back up into his eyes so he could hopefully get a clear read on what she was feeling. Apparently understanding she needed to do this soon, he nodded.

Turning to the others behind him, "I will hopefully return soon. Keep practicing the adjustments I showed you. Thank you for allowing me to train with you."

Metrí jumped forward with a sparkle of anticipation in her eyes. "Can I help you? Is there anything I can do?"

Kaeleigh was about to turn the girl down when something nudged the back of her mind. It was just a feeling and she couldn't even decipher what it meant but there was a rightness at having the girl there even without knowing if she had any magic of her own, but she knew that wasn't really what was important. "Yes, thank you, I would appreciate your help. I'm Kaeleigh, by the way, and this my friend Chel."

"I'm Metrí. And before you ask, no, I don't know what it means or where my name came from." She stuck out her delicate hand in Kaeleigh's direction.

Kaeleigh and Chel both shook her hand and smiled. Kaeleigh then turned to head back toward the main camp area, but saw Chel's quirked eyebrow in question. Kaeleigh shrugged and kept going, feeling Daegan behind her... always feeling him when he was near.

Almost back to the village where the cabins were, Kaeleigh felt a pull just past the main area. She looked around as they slowly passed, looking for Finn.

"Chel, do you see Finn? I am going to need him too."

"Is he the one all in black with a surly-looking expression?" Metrí spoke up from quite close behind Kaeleigh.

Kaeleigh startled slightly; she hadn't realized the girl was so close to her. Chel responded instead, "Yep, that's him, sunshine and daisies, that one." Chel winked at the girl as she let out a short laugh. "I'll get him, Kae." Chel jogged toward where Finn was leaning against one of the cabins intently focused on something. He did not see Chel coming up on him until she was quite close. She animatedly waved her hands around, explaining something to him. He looked up and beyond her to stare directly at Kaeleigh. There was a flash of guilt or regret in his eyes that quickly vanished. He nodded and gave a just-a-minute signal with his finger. Chel jogged back toward them, as Finn seemed to finish whatever conversation he was having with a shadow of a man.

"Who is he talking to?" Kaeleigh asked Chel.

"I'm not sure. He was pissed that I totally interrupted him but I thought this was more important." Chel paused, thinking about what she had interrupted. "He was saying something about how it was almost 'time.'" Chel shrugged, unconcerned. "You ask him, here he comes."

"Did you use your nose, Chel?" Daegan asked quietly. When she looked at him with part confusion and part insult, he explained. "You have incredible senses being a shifter, Chel. You need to learn to use them to your advantage. You never know who may depend on it." He spoke like he was educating her, but he also inclined his head in Kaeleigh's direction.

Kaeleigh put her hand protectively on Chel's arm to comfort her. "Don't put that pressure on her, Daegan, she will learn when she is ready."

"No, Kaeleigh, he is right. I want to. I just need to focus more." Chel looked into her friend's eyes, trying to convince her she was fine. "Let me try and see if I can remember."

"The scents are much harder to recall after the encounter for any shifter, let alone an untrained one. Do not feel bad if you do not," Daegan added.

Chel closed her eyes and tried to focus on her brief encounter with Finn and the stranger. Her eyes squinted together in deep concentration. Suddenly, she opened her eyes to find both Kaeleigh and Daegan staring at her in expectation. "Well, I remember he smelled kind of like you do, Daegan, but not quite as strong." Kaeleigh leaned closer to Daegan, attempting to sniff him, which only earned her a scowl as he moved away slightly. The girls giggled.

"You do kind of smell strong," Kaeleigh admitted with humor, then she winked at him.

"So he is probably Faerie. That is most likely the similar underlying scent you are picking up," Daegan stated, trying to ignore Kaeleigh's comment.

"But there was more," Chel began again, suddenly serious. "I was picking up more from the birds in the trees. At first I thought it was odd because in this place, there are not many animals and creatures other than the people. But there were some birds that apparently had been following him since no one else should be able to find it other than those invited. I picked up suspicion and caution and..."

"What's so important, Kae?" Finn interrupted what Chel had been about to say as he walked up to the group. "Why are so many people following you?" Finn eyed the group that had gathered, apparently unbeknownst to Kaeleigh if her shocked expression was any indication.

"Oh, I didn't realize so many of you had come." She paused, looking at the several new additions that had joined them from the training ground. "Thank you. I would appreciate any assistance you are able to lend. I will explain when we get there what I need you to do." She looked back to Finn. "I know how to break the glamour over Aidón and I want you all to be there to help, but also... to see if you know who he really is."

She was hesitant and Daegan reached toward her then dropped his hand before it came close to her as he spoke. "There is no reason to be concerned. We will be there to determine the situation. I do not, however, feel him to be a danger. His motives have appeared to be genuine thus far; however, this glamour is almost as strong as yours was and I am unsure if what I feel from him is authentic."

Finn, slightly distracted, refocused on what they were saying. "Lead the way then. I'm with you." He gestured with his arm for her to continue.

Kaeleigh frowned at her friend of many years, suddenly concerned for him. She couldn't feel him as Daegan could, except that hadn't he said that he couldn't really read Finn? But she could tell by looking at him that something was not quite right with her friend. She would find time to ask him about it later.

"We need music," Chel said randomly as she began to hum. At Kaeleigh and everyone else's confused expressions, she gestured with her hand at everyone following them. "We look like a parade... minus the floats." She shrugged. "I always wanted to be in a parade."

Chapter Seven

Aidón was exactly where Kaeleigh saw in her dream: down by the lazy river, sitting serenely on the bank. He tilted his head toward the sky, enjoying the warmth of the sun upon his face. She could feel the pull of his energy as soon as she had left the training field, zoning in on his destination. It was as focused as an electric current, pulling and guiding her toward him. It was like one of the threads that she had seen before—the ones that connected her to those around her when their energies had connected; like an aura but more whiplike than a glow around them. Aidón's energy was a green similar to Finn's, marking him as an Elf, but with a trace of something different making it his own. Those of stronger magic could contain a mix of their own color, Hunter had explained to her, whereas the mass of the races had the same subdued color marking them to the race they belonged with. Kaeleigh reminded herself to examine the energy colors of those from the Twined camp when she was finished. Her curiosity had her wondering what colors theirs would be. She didn't see the thread at all times, but only when she focused her inner magic or when an energy was loud enough that it practically slapped her in the face.

As they approached, Aidón turned toward them with a pinched expression on his face. Taking in everyone tagging along with Kaeleigh, he rose and slowly began to approach her. "I know you are here to attempt to remove the glamour, or the magic encasing this glamour, but I am not sure it is a good idea for you." Disappointment flashed across his features before he steeled his resolve.

"Aidón, I'm not sure why you wouldn't want me to keep trying, but I think I know how to do it now... no, I'm sure of it—I can *feel* it. I want to try once more," she pleaded.

"It is not that I do not want you to try, it is just that it might not be"—he sighed in his pause as he took in Finn and Daegan on either side of her—"safe. It might not be safe for you." As she expected, the warriors at her sides stiffened with bristling agitation and began to move in front of her as if Aidón was attempting to harm her. Kaeleigh waved them back with barely a frowning glance and stepped further in front.

"I saw it in a dream...or a vision...or whatever. I *know* I can do this. I saw that I would need help and that is why they have all come with me." Her hands gestured toward those behind her. "I can help direct their energy into dissolving the glamour. I know I can't do it on my own—I could feel that much from my earlier attempts. I'm not strong enough yet," she declared with an edge of frustration. "Please let me try."

"I don't know, Kae, if he doesn't think it's a good idea maybe he knows more about it than we do. We don't even know him, and I won't let you put yourself at risk for him. There is too much at stake," Finn tried to reason with her.

Kaeleigh looked at him with pure aggravation, "You won't *let* me? Finn, really? You do know me, right?" Chel came up along Finn's side, seeking something in her friend's eyes. Kaeleigh patiently allowed her inspection, hoping to find support. Chel took a slow breath and nodded to Kaeleigh. "Okay, if you need to do this, I am with you."

Kaeleigh turned back to Finn, barely pausing at Daegan's eyes as she did, afraid for the fight she would see there as well. *One at a time*, she thought. She gave Finn a questioning glance as if to say, "Would it be too much to ask for that kind of support?" Finn practically growled at her. He folded his arms in protest but nodded, relenting. "You have my support. You know you always do."

She had started to move toward Aidón when a strong masculine grip held onto her arm just inside the elbow. Somehow, that simple touch and placement of Daegan's hand sent shivers racing through Kaeleigh's body. She looked up into his eyes to see cauldrons of boiling dark chocolate. She saw his concern, but also saw the struggle he seemed to be having within himself. Kaeleigh could feel his protest for her protection, of course, but also he seemed to be decided in letting her follow her path.

Daegan bent toward her, and for her ears he spoke softly. "My energy, my magic, belongs to you. Take what you need." He paused for a moment, then added, "If you are in danger at all, you back away or I will pull you out myself. Understood?" As he took a step back, she looked up into his face again and saw fear and something else. Something that made her heart feel warm. Instead of putting up a further fight, she gave a quick nod.

With all of that out of the way, Kaeleigh took a deep breath and walked with confidence and anticipation toward Aidón. Not only did she feel the rightness of what she was to do, but she had the support and help of her friends. Now to find out who this man, who had become a mystery to their little group, really was.

Kaeleigh took a moment to stare at Aidón. She let the magic in her energy assess him. In her mind's eye, she visualized the thread of her own energy as it approached him. It moved freely around him, poking and prodding with fingers of static electricity. The glamour around him was extensively created, but her energy sought any weakness it could find in order for her to know how to go about disbanding the magical entrapment that he was living within. On the path there, Kaeleigh had seen a sneak peek at what she assumed was his true self when she had attempted to break down the magic. She was slowly learning and at a time like this, when she was confident in her actions, she felt free—as if her magic had endless possibilities. Aidón patiently let her assess him, opening himself to her magic as he could. When she looked back into his eyes with a resolve of steel, she asked, "Ready?"

He looked back at her friends, specifically to her warriors behind her, and spoke. It wasn't a request. "Her life and presence here is more important than mine. If something should go wrong, let me go or remain as I am, but get her out." He knew they would do just that. Looking back at Kaeleigh, he nodded. "Ready."

"I am going to place my hands on Aidón's shoulders as he kneels. When you feel your own energy guiding you, place your hands on me or the ground surrounding us," Kaeleigh instructed the others as she moved back to Aidón, already kneeling on the ground. "Life is energy. Energy is power. We are energy. Release your energy focused on freedom, focused on dissolving and consuming the excess energy surrounding Aidón, and push it toward me as I guide it around his glamour."

Kaeleigh took a deep breath, closed her eyes, and did exactly as she told the others. She could feel the power of their energy one by one as they drew close to her. She could feel it in the ground at her feet. It was uniting with her own energy, growing within her before she released it. It was more power than she had ever felt before, but it still seemed like it wasn't quite enough. The power was turbulent, like the rim of a volcano, roiling unstable at the edge, enough to remain active not yet enough to force a blast. Until she felt him. When Daegan's familiar energy collided with hers, it was explosive with raw power. She unleashed the energy in a controlled burst unlike the flailing power surge she had with Daegan back in Elnye. Kaeleigh could feel all the individual threads of energy uniting into a chord of power. She applied mental pressure, guiding it gently around Aidón's glamour. She could hear gasps from various people as all those with her could visibly see the energy in this concentrated magnitude.

"Stay focused," she whispered with effort.

Kaeleigh couldn't help her own gasp as she watched the power swirling around Aidón begin to erode the magical barriers. She could sense the glamour was not ill intended, but quite the opposite. It was forged for protection with one of the greatest magical energies: LOVE. Having had her own glamour of a similar nature, she felt emotion bubble through her chest resulting in her own tears. Selfishly, she relished the familiar feel of the magical traces entombed within Aidón's shell. Hunter. Her chest pinched; she missed him.

"*Let him go.*" Daegan's whisper floated through her mind.

On a shaky breath, Kaeleigh poured out all the energy she had available to her and pulled a little more from those surrounding her just to be sure. With a final swirl of the thread of energy, the last of Aidón's glamour crumbled away from him, leaving him panting in a fetal position on the ground near the river bank.

Everyone pulled away also panting, but recovered quickly. Kaeleigh took a step back and practically sagged right into the arms of a very strong Ferrishyn ready to catch her.

"I have you. Breathe. Well done," a gravelly and somewhat hoarse voice spoke near her ear. Daegan settled her gently on the ground. With a simple smile of gratitude, Kaeleigh nodded her head. Her hands trembled almost as fiercely as her insides from having that extreme amount of power within her one moment, then feeling dry as an emptied river bed.

"All good?" she asked as a general question to everyone as she inspected her friends. At all their nods, she relaxed back onto the grass. Kaeleigh was impressed with herself that she didn't pass out this time at the use of so much power. Hopefully, she was getting a better grasp of her own magic and its abilities. Still, she felt practically paralyzed with exhaustion and was glad she and her friends were in a safe spot to rest.

Just then a low, mournful cry tore through the camp. Startled, Kaeleigh crawled toward Aidón—or at least tried—just as Finn stopped her.

"No. Stay back. Let us handle it," he commanded her.

Finn and Daegan—knives out—warily approached the older Elf curled on the ground, crying out as if in agony. Daegan stopped with his head cocked to the side, staring intently at Aidón. He dropped his knife and relaxed his shoulders then knelt closer to Aidón on the ground.

"What are you doing?" Finn spat out.

"There is no threat here," Daegan said. "Lower your weapon, Finn."

"What? How do you know that?" He looked confused, but kept his weapon extended.

"Trust him, Finn, he knows," Kaeleigh interjected as she began to move closer once again, knowing Daegan wouldn't stop her since he had basically given her the go-ahead.

At first, Finn reacted as if she slapped him, and then something dawned on him as his expression lit with understanding, and he stared at Daegan. "You have the gift of empathy?"

Completely ignoring Finn's question, Daegan looked to Kaeleigh. "There is great pain in his past. He is mourning it all over again, but he will recover."

Kaeleigh nodded as she placed her hand on Aidón's head for comfort.

"That gift is rare, Daegan. Why have you not told us of it? I'm sure that comes in handy with what you do for the Paladin." A greater revelation hit Finn, one he wasn't sure how to process. "Wait. They don't know of this gift. Do they?"

"No. And they must not find out either. Please, Finn, they would abuse it," Kaeleigh demanded. Daegan shot her a slight glare. Kaeleigh met his glare with her own and shrugged a shoulder. "What?"

"I would appreciate it if you did not reveal this. But if you must, then that is your choice." Daegan stared at Finn for a brief moment, then looked back at the man on the ground. His appearance had altered but in the state and position he was in, he had not been seen yet. Kaeleigh had moved close behind Aidón on the ground and she kept placing a hand either on his forehead or on his shoulder for comfort, but something dark and agitated rose within him at the sight of it. He shook it off, disconnected once more.

"There is nothing more we can do here. Perhaps we should return to the training field and continue practicing while we await to meet the real Aidón," Daegan strongly suggested.

Kaeleigh gave him a questioning brow, but didn't say anything.

"I'll stay with them," Finn gestured toward those on the ground.

Daegan gave a nod then began to walk back the way they had come, but then stopped at the sound of the small voice he quickly recognized as Metrí's.

"Kaeleigh, may I try something?" Metrí asked boldly as she approached. Kaeleigh watched the girl doing something strange that looked like drawing on her arm with her opposite hand. Oddly, she didn't feel anything apprehensive about what the girl was doing. She nodded and gestured the girl forward.

"What is it you are doing?"

"I... I'm not really sure. I've never really done this before, but I just feel like I should. That doesn't make sense, I know, but I..." Metrí started to back up, suddenly unsure.

"No, I think you should try. Follow your instincts. That's all I'm doing. Sometimes it doesn't work but sometimes something amazing happens. Please, try," Kaeleigh encouraged.

The girl smiled a small smile, then knelt down next to Aidón but did not touch him. Instead, tall on her knees, she began to draw strange shapes and patterns in the air above him. She looked at the air as if she could see what it was she was drawing. No one else could see it, but it was there nonetheless. There was an intricacy to the movements she made with her fingers, but it was also simple. There was an energy that permeated the air around her. Daegan had come back to Kaeleigh's side as he watched. The others as well moved closer so they could watch one of their own do things no one knew she could do. In a moment, Aidón had gone from stiff agony to a more peaceful relaxed state.

"He is at peace now. Did you heal him?" Daegan asked.

"You can heal people?" Chel asked as she knelt near Kaeleigh.

"No. At least I don't think so. I've never done that before... but I think I was offering him a healing of the mind, or a peace to allow himself to deal with whatever it is he is going through." Metrí paused in her explanation, thinking about it. "Yes, that's what I was thinking about and my fingers just started moving. What does this mean?"

Everyone was quiet for a moment. Metrí looked around at confused and blank faces.

"I've never heard of that type of gift in Alandria," Finn offered. "But maybe it is something new, given your heritage that we are not familiar with."

Metrí scrunched her face up in contemplation. There was a rustling from the side as Ella approached them.

"I felt the energy you all had released all the way over at the meeting hall. That was quite powerful, we will be fortunate if it was not felt outside of this realm." She paused then looked to Metrí. "I agree with Finnlan. Your gifts will begin to emerge the more they are exposed to other magic and energy. You will need to be trained in how to use them as they continue to come forth, but Kaeleigh's advice to follow your heart and your instincts is good. That is one of the best ways to grow and learn within ourselves." Ella smiled toward Kaeleigh.

The moment was interrupted as Aidón stirred and tried to sit up. All those gathered around him quickly scooted back to give him some room. He sat up and smiled a sad smile. His voice scratchy and somber, he choked out, "Thank you."

Kaeleigh gasped when he looked her in the eyes. Green eyes. Those eyes were familiar—she had seen them before.

"I know you," she whispered.

CHAPTER EIGHT

ELNYE. THE CASTLE IN ELNYE, THE CAPITAL OF FERAÁNMAR.

"The Sol-lumieth is growing in power," Maleina spoke to the window, her back facing the extravagant room of her private chambers. Awaiting the arrival of her son, Halister, she took some time to conspire alone. The room was not small, but it was not large. It had several tall windows encased with long, thick draperies made from a cranberry dye that overlooked the gardens a story below. The small couch and settee were plush and sophisticated in dark colors that still looked feminine. An ornately carved desk took up one end of the room, a vanity at the opposite end. Even with the windows, though rarely exposed from their coverings, there was a sinister oppression in the heart of the space. Through her thin, barely there tie to her lost Ferrishyn, she felt the aftershocks from that surge of power released not long before. Even though most of the threads of energy connecting her to Daegan had been severed, there were still a few remaining and they were mending. She could still feel him. Though she may not be able to get into his head the way she could before and see through his eyes, she could still *feel* him. It was not enough to track him directly, but she would not need to rely on it solely. She had another source. He would be found, he and that *girl* who had no right to possess the power that appeared to be hers.

A simple knock sounded at her door.

"What is it?"

"Master Halister is in the throne room when you are ready, my Lady," the messenger replied through the thick wood of the door.

"I will be there momentarily." Maleina approached the vanity and took one look into the mirror at the sneer upon her face and schooled her features into those of a concerned mother. She took a deep breath and pulled a random curl or two from the perfected up-do that confined her fiery chaos. Maleina stepped out her door into the short breezeway that returned her into the throne room.

"Halister, my son, something terrible has happened." She approached him with haste and concerned eyes.

Halister stiffened as she came closer. Looking her over, he noticed she seemed uncharacteristically out of sorts. "What is it, Mother? What has happened? Is Father all right?" He appeared confused and apprehensive.

"Your father is fine. But I fear that Daegan, the brother of your heart and duty, is not." She looked out the window and then down to the floor as if afraid she would not be able to speak her next words.

"What do you mean, Mother?"

"The king in Adettlyn was just here. His guards saw a battle within the forest: a battle with the darkness." Her eyes were large and fearful. "They said there were various surges of power and then everything in the vicinity was destroyed by a blinding light." She inhaled sharply. "It is my hope that he survived, but I do not know for certain."

"I felt a surge of power not long ago," Halister said with a deadpan expression. Even though the surge he felt was from Kaeleigh's blast of power, he could feel the familiarity of Daegan's combined with hers. Not everyone could decipher each other's power, but they had fought and trained alongside each other for so long that he could determine without doubt Daegan's energy.

"You must go find him, Halister. I know he betrayed us, but he is still family and I will always welcome him home. I fear for him." His mother had moved to stand in front of him, her hands on either side of his shoulders.

Halister took a step back from her. Her eyes widened in surprise. "I am not this easily manipulated, Mother. You want him back, but not as a part of this family. You would use and destroy him if you could, of this I have no doubt."

Maleina's eyes grew dark. "Perceptive, son," she sneered at her only son and heir to her throne. "You are right, I do want to punish him. He betrayed us... his family! He would be nothing without us! That little wretch of a human girl has bewitched him somehow and turned him from us!" She began pacing agitatedly in front of him. "We have to find a way to break her spell over him, then perhaps he will come back to us willingly." She looked at her son with maddened false hope glistening in her eyes.

Unmoved, Halister pierced her with his stare. "I will not be a part of your schemes for power. I do not know what you are trying to accomplish, Mother, but I want no part of this at all!" Hal was fuming, his fists clenched. He turned to leave then turned back to his mother. "Daegan is no enemy. And Kaeleigh is not either. Not of Alandria or ours!" He knew he crossed a line when he saw a spark of fire and a twitch in his mother's eyes. He turned and stole from the throne room. He did not run, but his steps were wide with great purpose.

Once the doors closed on Halister's retreat, Maleina turned to the window nearest her that looked out upon most of the grounds around the castle entry. Halister stormed out of the castle carrying a small bag and headed straight for the stables.

Maleina smirked as she watched him ride out. "Good boy."

Seeing one of her guards step out from the shadows of the stables and look up at her window, she nodded at him. He mounted his own horse and took off in the same direction as her son, keeping his distance. Maleina would find them; *She* was waiting.

Chapter Nine

Tylínyth. The Pocket Realm of the Twined.

"**H**ow do I know you? Are you... Are you my father?" Kaeleigh knelt down in front of Aidón hesitantly. She could feel the eyes of everyone around her, watching and waiting. Her heart fluttered and her throat was tight.

Aidón looked at her with compassion as he lifted his hand to her cheek. "No, child, I am not. I... I am truly sorry." He grabbed her wrist as she began to pull away from him, putting space between them. "I am, however, your uncle." Kaeleigh gasped, her face flushed with hope. "Well, to clarify, I am your father's uncle, your grandfather's brother."

"What!?" "No way!" Her warriors drew their weapons while Chel gripped Kaeleigh's elbow right next to her. Kaeleigh stared at them with piercing eyes, in shock.

"Why do you have your swords drawn? He's my uncle!"

"Your 'uncle' was killed by his son during the last battle, Kaeleigh. This cannot be him, I'm sorry." Finn looked at her with genuine hurt in his eyes. He hated to dash her hopes again.

"True," Aidón began when all their eyes whipped back to meet his. "My son, Syén, killed me to strip me from the throne I had been given in your grandfather's absence. Only, he did not complete it." With sad eyes, he looked down to the ground and took a steadying breath. He looked up to Metrí. "Thank you for what you did to alleviate the grief and pain. It helps. I do not understand your magic but it is a gift, indeed." Metrí gave a small smile. "He meant to kill me. My own son. It was Ryek, your grandfather, who found me and brought me into hiding with him. I was not able to deal with the grief and betrayal of what my son had done to me and to his mother. What he did not accomplish with me, he did to my wife. She was lost. He encased me in a glamour so tight that the details of what had happened would be fuzzy until I was strong enough to handle them. It was meant to protect me and to save me."

"How did you end up in Maleina's dungeon?" Daegan asked him.

"Ah, yes, I had been out gathering intel and passing along messages with a contact we had near Adettlyn, and I was captured. Apparently, someone believed me to be a thief and reported me. I think Syén recognized my energy in the area. I was careless and had used additional magic. For a simple thievery, they should have placed me within the barracks of Adettlyn, but instead had me sent to Elnye. There I have been until now."

"Aidón, do you know about my grandfather?" Kaeleigh asked with a small, broken voice.

"I do, child. We had a bond. I felt it change not long ago." He looked out at the mountains towering in the distance, his eyes full of grief and memory.

"I'm so sorry for your loss," Kaeleigh said as she placed her hand on top of his in comfort.

"And I am sorry for yours as well," he said with a small smile, patting the top of her hand.

Both Daegan and Finn had lowered their weapons and stepped back to give Kaeleigh and her uncle some room. Chel, however, remained close to Kaeleigh.

"Thank you for freeing me from Maleina and that dungeon. There was darkness there that drove me to madness at times." He looked to Finn, then Daegan and Chel. "I am in all of your debt."

"We couldn't leave you there," Chel huffed out. "And now you are one of us." She smiled proudly as she squeezed Kaeleigh's arm. Kaeleigh looked to her friend with a beaming smile.

"That's right," she nodded.

"Is your name really Aidón?" Chel asked, suddenly looking at him strangely. She looked taken aback by a look Kaeleigh gave her. "What? Hunter wasn't really your grandfather's name and they were HIDING so it would make sense," Chel stated with attitude.

"I know that, I just didn't think of it," Kaeleigh defended apologetically.

"Yes, it is. We decided it was unnecessary as Aidón is a common name among the Elves and I was already pronounced to be dead." He shrugged as if no big deal.

"Now what, oh mighty warriors?" Chel asked, looking up from Daegan to Finn.

"If I may?" Aidón looked to Daegan to interject. Daegan nodded. "I have seen the way you fight," he said, looking at Kaeleigh specifically. "While you fight with heart and powerful energy, your skills need some attention. I think it would be wise to spend some time here in training."

"Agreed," Daegan stated.

After silent observation Ella spoke. "You may use the training field and join with those here." She gestured to the group of Twined beings that had joined Kaeleigh. "They would also benefit from your instruction. Then I feel that you must not tarry here longer than that. Arileas is awaiting our presence in Ehsmia."

Finn reached down and pulled Aidón to his feet then gave him a handshake in welcome. "I did not recognize you or your energy. Forgive me if I insulted you in any way," he said humbly with his head inclined.

Aidón placed his other hand on Finn's shoulder. "No apologies necessary. You are a guardian and you performed your job well. I remember you in service to Ryek." Then suddenly a strange expression quickly passed over his face before he turned a strained look back to Daegan.

With a frown, Finn's glance found Ella watching him. Quickly, Daegan's eyes were blazing with suspicion and shot to Finn. Finn now realized Daegan was sensing Aidón's reaction to him.

"Come on, guys," Kaeleigh yelled back as she and Chel were walking back the way they had come. Daegan frowned at her, suddenly distracted from the brief encounter of guilt he watched wash over Finn's features. He still had a hard time reading Finn's emotions even when he tried. Something strong blocked him.

On their way back to the training field, Kaeleigh and those with her passed by the large main cabin in the center of camp. A slight breeze ruffled her hair, bringing within it the sweet smoky smell of campfires and a crispness in the air that reminded her of her home in Montana. It had just been the beginning of fall when they left. She didn't know how many days they had actually been gone since Finn had tried to explain that time moved a little differently in Alandria. The smells wafting from within the meeting hall were so deliciously strong that Kaeleigh and Chel's stomachs both grumbled at the same time, resulting in giggles from the girls.

"We need to stop to eat," Finn spoke to those around them, but especially to Daegan as he nodded at the girls.

Nodding, Daegan turned toward the food. "I am sure Aidón could use some food as well to recover."

Kaeleigh and Chel followed Metrí in and grabbed their food. Some of the others from the camp were sitting at a table that looked like it had been carved straight out of a huge tree. It was rough with bark on all the edges, but the top had been smoothed to near perfection and it was clean. They chatted about things of no consequence for the most part and got to know those they sat with. Peter had come from the Midwest. Silas had come from sunny Florida. Loraina was from California and there were even a few from across the great pond sporting beautiful English and Scottish accents, along with a couple from Australia. They were all from various ethnicities and backgrounds. Hearing them talk like nor-mal—mortal—teenagers made Kaeleigh homesick. Chel was getting a rise out of several of them with something funny she had said, but Kaeleigh couldn't help but observe them. She tried to focus on their threads of energies without being too obvious about it. It wasn't that she wouldn't tell them or that she was trying to be sneaky, but people were usually more relaxed and allowed their true selves to shine a little more when they don't realize they are being examined.

"I don't understand," Kaeleigh mumbled out loud.

All conversation fell as everyone near her stared with confusion.

"What don't you understand, Kae?" Chel asked nonchalantly.

Kaeleigh looked around at each of them, suddenly realizing she had spoken out loud. A slight blush creeped up her neck. "Oh, sorry." She cleared her throat at the awkwardness. "I was trying to get a read on each of your energy threads." She wrung her hands and looked down at the table then took a deep breath. "I'm sorry, I should've asked but you were all relaxed which makes it easier for me to try. It's just something I am starting to get a grasp on. I don't even know how to do it right because it didn't really work."

One of the boys was scrunching his eyebrows at her—Silas, she thought. "So, we don't have energy threads? Because we are different?" He sounded a bit offended.

"No! No, that's not it. I mean I can see your general energy signature that says, you know, that you're alive. It's the specific energy marking you as one of those with magic from Alandria." She took a deep breath, suddenly feeling the need to back-pedal. "I can't sense it all the time anyway, but I just thought I'd try. I'm still trying to get the hang of it, obviously."

"Obviously," the same boy—Silas—responded dryly. Which earned him an elbow in his side from Metrí. She might be petite, but she was not afraid of the much bigger warriors.

"Okay, try me." Metrí bounced with anticipation, her short white-blonde curls mimicking her enthusiasm.

"Are you sure?" At the girl's nod, Kaeleigh readjusted her po-sition so she could fully focus on Metrí. "Please don't feel bad if I don't get anything. Like I said, I don't have a handle on it. It comes and goes, usually when I am not looking for it." Kaeleigh knew she had gotten much better at using her magic, but for some reason it wasn't working well with this group and she didn't want Metrí to feel bad.

"It's okay."

"All right. Just relax and be yourself... I guess." Kaeleigh took a deep breath and watched as the girl of about fifteen or sixteen did the same and closed her eyes. She then focused her inner magic, stirring up her energy. Kaeleigh was growing to love the feeling of her magic moving inside her. In her mind's eye, she watched as it swirled then moved from her to Metrí. It gently and quietly swirled about her then returned to its owner. Kaeleigh cocked her head as she examined the thread that she saw now linking Metrí to herself. It was similar to what she saw with Chel and the others, but it also had its own uniqueness. Its texture was thicker, coarser. Possibly because of her mixed blood? The color of it was different from what she knew represented either the Elves or the Faeries or even the Shifters. Kaeleigh knew there were other races in Alandria that she had yet to discover, and Metrí's thread definitely felt different.

Suddenly she picked up on a strong male presence coming close behind her. She was sure Daegan must have felt what she was feeling and had come to discover it himself, but she didn't react to him. Kaeleigh wanted to re-examine the thread before she said anything to Metrí—maybe even ask Arileas about it when they went to meet him.

Kaeleigh sat back and relaxed. "You can open your eyes now, Metrí."

Metrí slowly squinted her eyes open one at a time as if she was about to see something different. "So? Did you see it?"

Kaeleigh paused, unsure if she should tell the girl or wait until she knew something. Was it better for her to think she couldn't see it or to be honest and know that she didn't understand it? That she would be different... once more. Kaeleigh thought if the roles were reversed how she would handle it.

"It's not there, is it? You can tell me."

"No, it is there." Kaeleigh paused as the girl's eyes grew wider. "But I'm going to be honest with you because you are strong and I would want to be told. I went my whole life with secrets that should have been told to me. I don't know what it means. I could see your thread, but it is different from any of the other ones I have seen before." Metrí lowered her eyes, downcast, but then suddenly shot them up so not to show her disappointment. "Don't be discouraged. Like I said, I don't know what it means. And I am obviously new at this. It didn't feel negative by any means." Kaeleigh took on a wistful expression. "In fact, I'd say it felt peaceful and full of balance. Don't ask me what that feels like, but those are the images I get when I think of it."

"I, too, felt what Kaeleigh has described," Daegan spoke with a deep thoughtful timbre. "It is unlike what I know, but it felt strong. I think we should take you with us to Ehsmia and ask Ella's grandfather, Arileas. He is an Elder in Alandria. Since Ella was the one who brought you here, I'm sure she won't object."

As if on cue, Ella stepped up beside Daegan. "She is not ready to go into Alandria, but I am afraid that might be the only option at this point to help get her in touch with who she is inside. It will be significant in the coming days."

Peter, the young man she sparred with, shot up from the other side of the table. "Oh, no! She is not going anywhere with you all. Ella said it: she's not ready!" It was obvious that he had affection for the girl, but there was also a spark of jealousy that he was not the one being invited to go.

Just as Daegan was about to say something to the boy, Metrí stood up and looked right into Peter's eyes. "I go where I want to, with who I want to, when I want to. Is that clear?" Her expression softened then she looked into his eyes with big full eyes, pleading for him to understand. "I need to know, Peter." She stared at him a moment longer, then he sighed and gave her a short nod. Metrí turned back to Ella and Daegan, who were standing behind where she and Kaeleigh sat at the picnic-style log table.

"When do we go?"

Daegan and Ella shared a brief look, and Ella nodded back at him. Kaeleigh's eyebrows pinched at their silent communication.

"We leave at first light." That was all Ella spoke before she turned and left the meeting hall.

Daegan turned back to Kaeleigh and Metrí. "We had better get some more training in for the both of you. Metrí, will you work with Kaeleigh when we return to the field?"

Metrí bobbed her head up and down with a smile on her face. Kaeleigh couldn't help but smile in return. Just beyond the table, she watched as Finn walked out of the meeting hall following in Ella's wake, wondering not for the first time what was going on with the two of them. She brought herself back to Metrí animatedly waving her hands while she demonstrated to Chel across the table a new technique she was working on. Apparently, she had talked Chel into joining their duo, now making it quite the training triangle. Kaeleigh smiled as she watched them discuss the mechanics of how it would work.

On the training field, everyone was matched up with a single partner, except in the girls' case. Aidón looked like he had miraculously regained all of his strength and even looked younger than he had originally when the glamour was broken. He was still quite old if he was Hunter's brother, but his appearance wore youth a little better than Hunter had. Aidón was grabbing one of the practice weapons on a rack where one of the locals had shown them. They were told to take their pick. He walked toward one of the warriors already waiting on the field and bowed to him like a warrior with honor. Aidón then stretched his arms and swung his weapon around, gripping it and admiring it as if reuniting with an old friend. A moment later, he took his stance as his partner looked on with an expression of slight confusion before nodding his head and taking his own stance.

As all the partners were ready, Daegan began to call out beginning instructions, then as each was perfected he called out harder combinations of steps and swings, choreographing a dance. The girls tried several times to get some kind of syncopated movements together in their coordination. Finally, Metrí stopped them and called out her own instructions, directing it by name. She kept the order of their names the same until they had a rhythm. It worked. She would thrust to Kaeleigh, who blocked then spun to throw her arm toward Chel, who blocked, then did the same motion at Metrí. They kept it slow until they were comfortable with the motions.

Kaeleigh had practiced more than Chel, so Metrí would call out her own steps to Kaeleigh then Chel would know what was coming in order to prepare. Eventually, Metrí stopped calling them and Chel got the hang of it. Without the added energy Kaeleigh's sword provided, the girls were almost evenly matched. Metrí had been practicing longer and had more skill, but Kaeleigh and Chel both caught on quickly. Unaware of what was going on around them and how long they had been at it, Kaeleigh finally noticed—actually felt— Daegan standing at the edge of their little group.

"You are doing well. Keep going, I am going to take over your instructions. Get ready. I am going to add in another," Daegan said, watching them.

"What?!" Chel exclaimed.

"Just keep your focus. Loraina, step in."

Without questioning what he was asking, Loraina, a Twined girl that sat at the table with them during lunch, fluidly inserted herself into the controlled chaos, the result causing the girls to pair off.

"No. Do not pair off, keep on guard of all those around you. You will not always have the luxury of pairing off with an enemy. Fight what comes near you. If you see an opening, switch to another opponent. Keep them guessing. Remain alert, but be the offense, be in control. Discipline your instincts."

It took the girls a few tries before they understood what it was he was asking. And once they did, he destroyed their balance.

"James, in," Daegan commanded without averting his eyes from the fight before him. Most of the other fighters had joined him in watching the new technique.

"Daegan, are you trying to kill us?" Chel shouted out, to which he actually chuckled.

"If I had wanted to do that, I had many opportunities while you slept."

Chel's face paled, but she didn't lose her focus as a sword came close to her face. "That is not funny!" she shot back.

"Good focus, Chel," he replied.

James had just slid in with a block to a shot Kaeleigh had intended for Loraina. Loraina had circled backward and began her own dance with another partner.

"Very fluid, James. Metrí, keep on your toes. Good. Chel, do not be afraid of Loraina. You are a fighter, it is in your blood. You are a shifter, do not fight it... accept it." Daegan continued to admonish the different fighters and added in a couple more.

"Aidón, fight Kaeleigh." He was complete business.

Aidón was skilled beyond any in this realm, possibly even including Daegan himself. He had fought through battles and it showed. Daegan watched him carefully. Watched how he tempered his moves with each of the fighters but especially as he fought with Kaeleigh. He had a way of moving with his sword that was full of skill, but there was definitely more yet to be understood about Aidón.

"Give her more, Aidón. She will not break."

So he did. Daegan could feel Kaeleigh's frustration that she purposely sent his way. Daegan almost laughed out loud. Then as Aidón began pushing her more with each swing and each thrust, she began to fight back. He could feel her energy change as it united with her sword—even though it was not the ancient sword that had attached itself to her. The sword began to give off the slightest bit of a glow, and being that it was daylight, no one really noticed unless they were paying extra attention, which he was. Aidón noticed it too as his eyes widened slightly, but he continued to fight her. Her confidence grew. Daegan could see it in her countenance and stature. She was not just training, she was fighting back and she was fierce. It was hypnotizing to watch; she was almost holding her own against Aidón.

Kaeleigh felt stronger than she had ever known was possible, and fighting Aidón had been exhilarating. She was afraid at first, but then she could feel her energy rising up to meet his and counter it. But, she also felt herself quickly tiring. Her stamina was not ready for long physical fighting along with using her magic.

"Enough." Daegan's voice carried across the training area. Everyone stopped where they were and lowered their weapons, the new additions panting heavily and the practiced warriors just barely winded. Daegan was rubbing the spot high on his arm that made Kaeleigh's eyes narrow in on him.

"Well done, all of you. Be prepared. Something is coming. I must find Ella," he said as he turned and left the field.

"Daegan, wait!" Kaeleigh yelled as she ran to catch up with him.

"Stay with the others, Kaeleigh. I will return as soon as I know what it is."

"No. It's your arm again. I thought she was gone." Referring to Maleina sent chills down her spine. Kaeleigh reached out to touch his arm, but he pulled away and moved even faster.

Kaeleigh spotted Ella and Finn moving just as quickly toward them with concern written on their faces. She wondered where they had been.

"There is a unit of Ónarach not far from the entrance to our realm. They are close, but not close enough. Not yet at least." Ella spoke calmly, but looked Daegan straight in the eyes. For the first time, Kaeleigh saw something that looked like shame or guilt in his eyes. Ella paused, but then nodded and looked to Finn. "We must get all the Twined into the caves in that mountain for their protection should the wards and the walls not hold. The warriors can stand guard on this side where the portal opens."

"Wait. What's going to happen? They can't get in here, can they? It was hard enough for us to get into the realm," Kaeleigh interjected.

"There are ways of blasting one's way through the barriers we've created if they are able to find them," Ella calmly explained.

"Let's get a group and go out and fight them," Kaeleigh replied with passion.

"You cannot fight them, Kaeleigh. You and this group are not ready." Finn spoke with authority, but because Kaeleigh knew him so well, she could see the fear in his eyes.

"It is already settled," Daegan said.

"What is settled?"

"This is not your concern, Kaeleigh. Stay with the others. Help keep them safe. Stand with Aidón, he will instruct you." Daegan was staring straight ahead, looking at no one.

"Someone has to go out there! To distract them at the very least …" Kaeleigh started rambling, trying to come up with some way to help.

"Someone is."

"What? Who?"

"I am," Daegan replied flatly.

"You think this is your fault?" She was lost. "Daegan—"

At her obvious attempt to change what he said, he put his hand out to stop her. "This is my fault. The connection I have to Maleina is regenerating. I thought it was severed before… but it has slowly been reconnecting. I do not understand why. They found this place because of me. I will lead them away."

Kaeleigh looked to both Finn and Ella, hoping they would say something to stop him, but they didn't. "Seriously? You both would just let him go out there alone to possibly die protecting this place and you would do nothing?" Kaeleigh was aghast.

"We do not do nothing, Kaeleighnna. This is the order of things. He offered protection. We have accepted it. There is much more at work here and this place is worth the sacrifice. Though I do not think it will come to that. Daegan has a greater purpose in all of this," Ella explained.

"I was not saying this place, nor its people, were not worthy of a sacrifice. That wasn't what I meant—"

"We know that's not what you meant, Kae, but we have to protect those here," Finn interrupted her.

"What I meant was that..." She took a deep breath. "I am going with him."

"No," they all said together.

Kaeleigh looked up at Daegan. "If you get to choose the sacrifices you make, then I do too. I want to help. It is as much my fault that it didn't sever and that I didn't make sure it was." Daegan looked at her like she was nuts and as though she might have been reaching a bit with the explanation—and she knew she was, but she wasn't going to let him go out there alone. At least with another he might have a chance.

"No."

"Yes, Daegan, I am going with you."

"Kaeleigh, please don't do this." Finn tried to order her, but his eyes pleaded with her.

"It's my choice, Finn."

Daegan stared at her, reading her soul with the intensity of his eyes.

Finn sighed. "Fine, then I am going too. We need to tell the others." He and Ella kept moving toward the field.

Kaeleigh turned to follow them, but Daegan was rooted in his spot. She stopped, afraid he would try to leave without her. There was a sudden flare of panic in her chest.

"I will not leave without you, Kaeleigh." He sighed with frustration and ran his fingers through his bluish-black hair. "You should not be doing this. I... I cannot..." He looked to the sky, his words stuck in his throat. *I cannot lose you* was the thought running through his heart, but his head was arguing the logic of that.

Kaeleigh looked into his eyes, letting her heart speak through her own eyes before she spoke with words, as if she had heard his heart's cry. "Then don't." She stood tall and walked slowly back to the field with confidence that he would follow. He did.

"You do not leave my side out there, understood?" he whispered behind her.

"I will follow your lead," she replied with her heart racing.

They walked up, hearing Ella instruct the gathered group, Kaeleigh's old and now new friends, along with many Kaeleigh had not yet had the chance to meet. Kaeleigh's heart hurt; this beautiful place they had called home might soon be under attack.

Ella spoke with authority. "There is an enemy close. There will be a battle. Those who fight, take your positions. Those who do not, get to safety. Elder Tillin will take you into the caves in the mountain. They will lead you to the mortal realm like you have practiced. James, you will get the warriors positioned at the entrance to that cave. You know the signal if you are to evacuate as well." She stared at him a moment to ensure he understood. He nodded. Ella continued instructing as her people watched and listened intently, nodding at their given positions.

"Where will you be?" Finn questioned her.

Ella paused, then looked back to Kaeleigh and Daegan before she answered his question. "I am going with you," she said saucily with a wink. "Someone needs to distract the enemy."

Kaeleigh could hear Finn growl under his breath. She had to remember to find time to ask him about who Ella was to him.

"Well, I am going wherever Kaeleigh goes," Chel blurted out irreverently.

"No, Chel, stay here and help protect this place," Kaeleigh asked.

"Hell, no. I go where you go. We are in this together, remember?"

Kaeleigh's eyes filled, but didn't spill over as she gave her friend a grateful nod.

"Well, I already had decided I was going with you, so I guess this is as good of a time as any," shot Metrí. She linked arms with Chel, who was right beside her.

Kaeleigh could hear Daegan sigh quietly behind her. He was not happy.

Chapter Ten

Alandria. Ehsmia.

The way out of Tylínyth was not nearly as elaborate as the way they had entered. It was actually quite simple. As the small group slid behind the large rock covering the entrance, they walked back through what seemed like a cave that went on for a while. At one point Ella stopped and spoke words in a language that none of them understood and waved her hand. There was nothing to be seen, but as they walked through, Kaeleigh could feel a tingle of the residue of magic as it washed over her skin. It must have been the portal. She wanted to ask but no one spoke, afraid to alert the enemy with any sounds. There was the soft, smooth sound of liquid—probably water—sliding down the wall of rock just before it dripped onto the floor of the tunnel. The noise echoed as it hit the ground with a splash. It was dark but there was just enough light from the marking—shaped like a vertical eight-pointed star—on the back of Ella's neck. The tunnel smelled of must and the air was thick with dampness. As they walked, there was only the slightest sound of shoes connecting with water. As they approached the entrance to the tunnel—or their exit—a breeze flowed toward them, carrying with it the freshness of the outside air.

Kaeleigh inhaled deeply, relishing the cleanliness of that air. She hadn't realized how stifling the air in the tunnel had been until it couldn't compare. She could hear both Chel and Metrí taking deep breaths as well. They were just behind her in the narrow cave.

Suddenly, the broad, muscled back that she had been following stopped abruptly causing her to hold her hand out to brace herself from falling completely into him. Daegan. Kaeleigh still couldn't believe he was going to go out to face who knows what alone... well, she could but she still didn't think he should have thought that way. Although, situation reversed... yeah, she probably would have too. She left her hand on his back for what was probably an inappropriate length of time needed to gain her balance, but she couldn't help it. Even though it was warm in the cave, the warmth that came from touching him soothed something deep inside her. Feeling the ridges of his muscles bunch under her hand simply made her feel like a teenage girl giddy with hormones instead of a lost princess trying to fight for the lives of her friends and of her own as they attempted to regain freedom for an entire realm. No pressure. So, yeah, she took a second or two longer for a self-indulgent moment before she removed her hand. He didn't flinch this time when she touched him; maybe she was making progress. Although the brief head turn toward his shoulder without actually looking back at her suggested maybe not.

Ella's whispered voice floated on a breeze to the back of the line. "This is the gateway to Alandria. If they are not right outside this entrance, how do you want to proceed, Daegan?"

"Quietly and quickly make our way in the opposite direction. Lead them away from this entrance. If they are there, then fight like nothing else exists but getting through alive because you must."

"Great pep talk, D," Chel snorted.

A giggle from Metrí earned her another point in Chel's book as they bumped fists in the dark.

"Together or split up?" Kaeleigh asked.

"Together, until the situation is assessed."

Daegan then looked back at Kaeleigh, caught her eye, and spoke into her mind. "*Always together... out there.*" She nodded. It had been some time since he last spoke into her mind, and she realized she had missed it. It made her feel special and safe.

"Okay, weapons and magic at the ready," Finn instructed as he led Ella out of the cave entrance, sliding behind another huge boulder mirroring the one in the other realm. They moved with grace and stealth. First Finn, then Ella, followed by Chel and Metrí, then Kaeleigh and Daegan bringing up the rear along with Aidón, who had quietly joined them. Kaeleigh gave a confused look at him as he came up beside them and then focused. All eyes roaming, seeking, searching for any movement behind rocks or in the trees or even in the sky above. Nothing. It was silent and eerie. They moved further away from the entrance and even faced opposite directions to look like they came from another direction.

After several minutes of finding nothing and hearing nothing, Chel held her hand up to stop everyone. She gave a finger asking for a moment and cocked her head to the side, listening intently with her eyes focused on the ground.

"What do you hear?" Finn came up and whispered close to her head.

"Nothing."

With a look of frustration, Finn started to move back to his position.

"No. I mean I literally hear nothing." Chel was shaking her head in frustration. On guard even more than he first was, if possible, Daegan began to move forward and circle them together with his short sword in one hand while he pulled out his long sword from the holster at his back. "I always hear *something*. It's almost like everything has been silenced," she continued to whisper as she looked around. "Every living thing has a vibration of energy. Kaeleigh, you can see it sometimes, but I can hear it. I hear nothing."

"It's been silenced by magic, dampened by darkness." Ella looked around in frightening wonder. "They are here somewhere. Be ready."

From behind one tree, not even a whole clearing away, stepped a lone figure clothed in black and shrouded in darkness. It had the form of a physical being with an appearance similar to the Elves. Where an Elf's skin radiated light in its very skin, this creature, sickly pale and sullen, was void of any light at all. Its hair was stripped of vibrancy, now greasy and the color of ash. It walked slowly and limped with one leg as if it dragged something. Golden eyes pierced through the shadows of its hood; its arms were raised at its sides as if in welcome. It emanated evil.

"Is it the Droch-Shúil... or their servants?" Chel stammered out, remembering those who had imprisoned her.

Kaeleigh gripped Chel's hand, but it was Ella who answered.

"No. It is one of the Ónarach. Do not misunderstand, they are just as dark, and if they get you, they will strip your magical essence from you simply to make them stronger."

"They once used to be from the race of Elves," Finn said with disgust and anger. "They turned from their true nature and went against all they were created to be, choosing instead to be... this," he spat out, pointing at the creature before them. It moved no closer, but stared into them with hatred and hunger.

"Well, he is just one, can we take him?" Metrí asked, speaking up for the first time in a while.

"Am I?" the creature spoke with a deep but smooth and sensuous voice. It made them all cringe, even the warriors among them.

"That is just wrong on so many levels," Chel stated. Kaeleigh and Metrí nodded their agreement with scrunched-up faces.

"I have never fought one before so I'm not sure their tactics." Finn looked to Daegan.

"Nor have I, I have only heard they are ruthless to encounter so do not underestimate it in any way."

"This one is cunning, I can feel it. It has a massive volume to its darkness, I can't read much more than that from it." Ella spoke as if she had studied it thoroughly. Perhaps she had.

Just when they all held up their weapons to advance together, the strangeness increased. The creature took one more step toward them, but stopped. Another creature—a duplicate—stepped out from behind it. Then another and another until the one at the front created the triangle tip of a small army.

Gasps came from the girls as both Finn and Daegan's eyes had widened in surprise. But what was almost more surprising was that the army of Ónarach simply stood there as if they awaited a command.

Daegan looked past the creatures, and all around, but did not see anyone else around. "Steady, there is something...someone else here. I can feel it, but cannot see it."

"Is it... her?" Kaeleigh whispered.

"Maleina! Show yourself," Daegan commanded.

With a sultry, evil cackle Maleina appeared off to the side of her little evil army. "Very good, Daegan, my boy. Are you surprised to see me?" She must not have intended to get her hands dirty this day. She was dressed in one of her finest gowns for court. Maleina wore blue tinted with purple—the color of the Alandrian night sky. Her thick red hair was braided down to her back but slung forward over one shoulder. She sneered in Kaeleigh's direction, but Kaeleigh only stood taller and more confident. Maleina took in the others among their group with barely a care.

"This is quite the band of misfits you have with you, Daegan. Train them yourself?" Daegan didn't give her an answer, nor did she wait for one. "Are you not the least bit curious how I came to find you here"—she waved her arm around in the air—"in this place? Where are we anyway? There is a strong concentration of magic in that general direction." She pointed toward the hill covered in rocks that was beyond the tree line just behind where they stood. Exactly where they had come from.

They had circled away from the entrance, hoping to detract from the portal entrance, but someone trained to look and feel out magic would be able to decipher it if they were looking specifically for something hidden. Metrí, being young and unfamiliar with an actual encounter with Maleina, stiffened at the mention of her home. Unfortunately, it didn't go unnoticed by Maleina. She raised an eyebrow in Metrí's direction.

"I do not believe I have seen you before. Who are you?"

"She is of no concern to you," Ella spoke out.

"Foolish girl, just by saying that, she has suddenly become a 'concern to me.'" Maleina walked a few steps closer to Metrí then returned her focus to Daegan. "Did Halister not find you? He was so worried for your well-being that he set off to find you in this very direction." Maleina blanched innocently as if she had just revealed something top secret... then she leered at them.

"You used your son to find us?" Daegan's hatred for Maleina rose to a new level. He knew there was great potential within her for selfish gain, but had been blinded to the depths she would go to.

She feigned innocence. "We all are concerned for you, Daegan, traipsing around Alandria with these"—she waved her hand in the air as she searched for the right word—"lower-class citizens." Gesturing toward Finn and Ella then to Kaeleigh, Chel, and Metrí, she said, "And these that do not even belong here!" Her voice raised, adopting a hint of anger.

"You used your own son as bait! To find us! For what... to gain power? To take out potential threats to your power?" Daegan's voice was now raised in anger.

"No, dear boy," she began with a slippery smoothness to her words. Then she spoke words laced with her own brand of dark power. "The ultimate power." A flame flickered in her eyes as said power began to surge underneath her skin.

"Of course I used him! I am no fool and I use whatever tools are available to me. Obviously, he did not find you as he is not here, is he?"

"Am I not, Mother?" Halister spoke as he walked out from around a large tree with a quiet casualness off to the other side of where Daegan faced off with Maleina.

If Daegan was surprised to find his friend there, his expression gave nothing away. However, Maleina's did. Her eyes, wide with surprise, quickly narrowed, taking in the situation.

"Son." She raised her chin to him in challenge. "It is time for you both to come back to Elnye with me." Daegan stayed in his place as Halister moved closer to him. "I see." The same flames flickered in her eyes, brighter than the first time Daegan had seen it.

"Whoa, did you see her eyes?" Hal pretended to whisper.

Daegan knew Hal was afraid, he could feel it coming off him in waves, but they all were. "Enough of this, Maleina. Leave it and go back to your throne."

"I do not think you understand what my little friends here"—she waved over to the small army of Ónarach still waiting her command—"are actually capable of. You are no match for them."

"Do not do this here, Maleina. You will only call further retribution down upon yourself," Ella spoke out without a trace of fear in her voice.

"We are not alone," Halister said, straightforward, as the bushes behind him rustled and a numerous amount of beings stepped out of the shadows armed with bows and arrows notched at the ready. Ella gasped with a twinkle in her eye. The Faeries of Ehsmia had come to assist in their escape. There were not enough of them to fully take on the battle and win completely, but it would be enough to stir things up and get them out of there, most likely alive.

"Yes!" Chel hissed between her teeth as she bounced on the balls of her feet.

"We are not so unevenly matched as you had planned, are we, Mother? No, you see, I had learned of your plan—albeit a little too late—but rerouted myself in search of assistance against whatever you might have planned. Now I understand." Hal paused and when he looked back into his mother's fierce eyes, he was resolved. "I am no son of yours."

Out from behind the same tree that Hal had come stepped Arileas, Elder of the Ehsmia, clothed in leathers and armed with a sword and spear. He stared Maleina down. "We meet again, Paladin of Feraánmar."

If Maleina could turn into a dragon, she would have spit fire. She glared at Arileas, then back to Daegan and her son. "So be it." She turned, her dress swirling out from her as she vanished. Her leaving, however, set off the Ónarach as they began to move as a unit toward them.

They moved in sync, a freaky entourage of clones. Draped in black cloaks, they each hobbled with the same lame leg. As they got closer, their faces were revealed, their eyes golden glowing orbs in deep-set sockets. Their faces ashen and expressionless.

"Are they zombies?" Chel asked in disgust.

"No, but they are something similar in that they aren't completely alive, but neither are they dead. Actually, I guess they are kind of like zombies, Chel," Finn responded thoughtfully.

"I don't really care what they are, but what they can do! And what do *we* do?" Kaeleigh replied, revealing her growing fear as they kept getting closer.

"They seem to move kind of slow, can we just out run them?" Metrí asked.

"No. And who are you?" Hal asked with a large grin that was entirely out of place for the situation at hand.

"Metrí. And Halister, was it?"

"Hal will work just fine. You are kind of a little thing to be hanging around with this crazy crew, aren't you?"

"I can manage."

"You better watch your mouth, Hal, she could probably take you down," Chel replied with a playful hand on her hip.

"Nice to see you too, love," Hal returned with a wink.

Chel's expression cooled. "Watch your mouth, palace boy."

"Focus!" Finn jumped in, shouting.

Daegan had not taken his eyes off the creatures as they watched the immature interaction with interest.

"What do you see, Daegan?" Hal asked, suddenly focused again.

"I can still *feel* them. It is so chaotic and sticky in their heads. Confusion. Hunger. Bound to obey. Longing... longing for their essence, who they were before." Daegan's face held an ounce of sympathy and pain, until it suddenly went pale and then a sickly green. He looked as if he might lose what meal he had last eaten. He shook his head and closed his features off as everyone looked on in horror at his reaction.

"Whoa, that bad, huh?" Chel asked.

Daegan took out the shorter knife he had sheathed at his hip and threw it straight into the heart of the creature leading the pack. He went down immediately.

"I guess so," Chel commented as the others looked on in pure fascination.

"Holy..." "Oh my..." Metrí and Kaeleigh said at the same time. The lead Ónarach that Daegan so quickly dispatched rose up in a slow-motion reversal of how it just had gone down, unfolding itself.

"That can't be good," Hal said flatly. "No, not good at all."

"You think?"

"Chel, not the time," Kaeleigh whispered. Chel nodded at her friend. Kaeleigh squeezed her arm; she knew Chel was scared. They both were.

"Archers at the ready," Arileas commanded. "Take your mark. The rest of you get ready for diversions and chaos." He looked them each briefly in the eyes. "This fight is not meant to be your last. You will live for tomorrow." He signaled to his people and everything after that went extremely swiftly.

Arrows soared through the clearing, fired straight and true one after another. The Ónarach were each hit and responded accordingly. They began to move slightly more independently of each other as if being struck over and over severed their ties to each other. Each held a small black dagger that had been unseen beneath their cloaks. Moving freely, they did not swing their daggers but instead waved them at the arrows haphazardly, attempting to block them. Individual winds began to swirl around each creature, causing their cloaks to flap around them. It was an eerie effect, if nothing else. The winds picked up and assisted in blocking the arrows fired at them by changing their directions.

"Remember, at my side," Daegan whispered fiercely into Kaeleigh's ear as he prepared to fight off whatever might come at them. She had no intention of going anywhere else at that moment. They all stayed pretty close.

"I have an idea. Kaeleigh, use your magic to light the tips of the arrows as they are released. Everyone else focus your magic on blocking the wind," Finn said hastily, voice trembling a bit with excitement.

"I don't know if I can, Finn."

"I know you can, Kae. Try... Now!" Finn almost shouted at her.

Thinking desperately of fire and picturing their tips igniting as she saw the first of the arrows fly, she was disappointed not to see them burst.

"Try again."

She took a deep breath and focused again, seeing her magic stirring within her with flames dancing along its edges. Again nothing. Then she felt Daegan sneakily grab hold of her elbow. Where his skin touched hers, there was a crackling energy that she felt entwine with her own. Without thought, she looked to the arrows that were yet flying again and pictured them bursting into flame right as they hit their targets... instant fire.

"Nice," Metrí said in awe.

They watched as the flames not only pierced the Ónarach, but caused the chaos that they were looking for as they had desperately hoped not to have to fight these creatures without understanding their weak spots. The flames would not kill them, but they did begin to devour their cloaks and send them crashing into one another, trying to find a way to extinguish the flames.

It was at that moment that a large white bird soared overhead releasing a cry that was heard above the disturbance. Immediately following, Arileas turned to a brambling bush that was just on the other side of himself and began to spin his arm in a wide circle chanting something under his breath that most could not hear. But neither Daegan nor Kaeleigh were most. Even though it was undecipherable at the time, Kaeleigh could feel the energy put into it. She could see the colorful magic swirling so fast it was creating an opaque surface.

"It is time! Quickly, through the portal, every one of you. Go." Arileas spoke loudly enough to be overheard by those he called, but not distracting enough to lure the Ónarach into his domain. That would be catastrophic.

Finn and Ella grabbed Chel and Metrí by the arms and pulled them along as they ran full speed, not hesitating for a second, into the circle of swirling magic. Halister then followed with Daegan, who pulled Kaeleigh along behind him. The archers let loose one last round of arrows, holding the creatures back as they screamed and hissed and made sickly sounds while the flames licked at the hoods of their cloaks near their faces. The archers of the Ehsmia ran into the portal. The last in grabbed Arileas—who had to remain the last in order to hold the portal open—by the arm as he stepped in to ensure that the Elder made it through. Arileas. As soon as they entered the other side, Arileas released the magic of the portal and it collapsed immediately. The Ónarach and the trap set for them remained on the other side.

"Take a deep breath and welcome to Ehsmia," Arileas said. His ancient eyes twinkled and he spread his arms wide as he proudly introduced them to the land within a land—the land of the hidden people.

CHAPTER ELEVEN

ELNYE. THE CASTLE IN ELNYE, THE
CAPITAL OF FERAÁNMAR.

"Mother, why have you sent spies after my brother?" Rheina casually walked into the throne room where Maleina was standing off to the side, intently studying a large map of Alandria. The landscape on the page was alive with her dark magic as it rose into an active three-dimensional view of all that was going on.

Maleina raised an eyebrow at her daughter. They appeared to be the only two in the large marble room. The columns that lined walls on both sides were thick and tall, wrapped with vines and greenery. However, even that foliage was beginning to fade in color as much of the city's did as well. The cream color of the marble should have been more welcoming than it was, but the spidery veins that crept throughout the walls and wound around the pillars pulsed a bright red. Its color reminded Rheina of fresh blood and brought a creepiness over the whole palace. There was plenty of light filtering through the large floor to ceiling windows along one wall, but even that didn't sweep away the heavy feeling in the room.

"Rheina!" she declared, acting as if her daughter had said nothing. "Where have you been?" She studied Rheina from head to toe, taking in her aggressive posture. "Don't question me, daughter. You know nothing of what I do or why I do it," she tsked, waving her finger at Rheina.

"It is not necessary for me to question. I know the answer." Rheina stood tall and looked at her mother direct with unblinking eyes.

"Do you, child?" Maleina's eyes narrowed as she walked up to Rheina. She leaned into her daughter's face with a blaze of conflicted resentment in her eyes. Rheina was not intimidated and completely detached.

"Yes."

Suddenly, the air began to change in the throne room. The air was charged with electricity. A breeze swirled around Rheina as her head shot back with her eyes closed. When she brought her head forward again and opened her eyes, they had changed from green to granite gray. Her eyes, now colored with age and wisdom, gleamed when they pierced Maleina with their stare.

Maleina gasped, for a moment caught off guard, then became infuriated.

"How dare you use my daughter to spy on me! Who are you?" she demanded with fierce sparks of anger.

Rheina's voice took on a different, wispier tone. "It matters not who I am, but that I am here. There is but a little light left inside you, a small hope. If you do not find it, you will not survive what is to come."

Maleina eyes slightly widened revealing, a warmth that had been there once long ago, struggling to be seen as it was drowned by her overwhelming greed for power. Then her gaze grew narrow again as an evil laugh rose out of her.

"You have come to warn me? Me?" Her laugh became tainted with an edge of danger. "You are right about one thing, it matters not who you are, nor that you are using my daughter. She was proving to be unuseful to me anyway. Much like her brother. I will offer you this though; it's a promise from the bottom of my heart." She paused for effect. "*You* will not survive what is to come." Maleina laughed again as she returned back to her map.

Rheina simply stood there, quietly staring. The breeze calmed and the charge in the air fell flat. The skies reverted to the lifeless light that filtered in the windows. Her eyes changed back from gray to her natural green. As they changed, a single tear escaped Rheina's eye.

"I will always love the mother you were to me as a small child. Find yourself, Mother, or you will lose everything."

Maleina stopped laughing and for a brief moment something akin to regret flashed across her face. She quickly looked away and out the large windows, dismissing her daughter.

"Goodbye, Mother." Rheina turned and walked away from her mother and out of the throne room.

"You have failed me, daughter! And now you desert me?! Stay out of my way," Maleina shouted at Rheina as her daughter stormed down the hall.

Quietly, Wren stepped out from the shadows behind their thrones where the doors to their individual chambers were.

"You have managed to push away all our children. Will you rid yourself of me as well?" He let the silence linger for a moment. "You have a chance, my love. A chance to make all this right," he pleaded with his wife, the woman he had fallen in love with many years ago. "Make this right. I need you, Maleina. I want you to be the woman I have loved all this time. Free and full of passion and joy. Pouring your life into all living things around you! That is the woman this realm needs. That is the woman and friend I need."

Maleina could not look at Wren as she stared at her map. "I can't be that woman anymore," she replied with vehemence. Then her voice quieted. "I am no longer her."

"That is not true, my love. You are still her." His voice cracked with emotion.

"No!" Maleina turned toward him. She then grabbed her skirts and stormed passed him to her chamber. "She is gone."

She left Wren rooted to the floor where he stood, alone and broken.

✧✧✧

Rheina stood at the edge of Guardian Grove, the forest behind Elnye that skirted along the edge of the Gáraldrath Mountains. She knew this was the path she was to take. It was right, but there were still the flutters of nerves in her chest. Compounded on top of the sharp pain and hollow feeling left in her heart from the encounter with her mother, she was raw and on edge. The *other* voice in her head had been quiet since she came forward in the throne room. For the moments of solitude, Rheina was grateful. She hadn't had much time, but she packed a few necessities and some food and threw on her traveling cloak, as much for warmth as for shielding her from watchful eyes.

Twilight had fallen in Alandria. The two moons shone bright in the night sky and would guide her path without the assistance of additional light. She was able to sneak out of Elnye, her home, virtually undetected; either that, or no one cared. Rheina hoped it was due to her covert abilities. She took a deep breath, threw her shoulders back, and stepped into the forest and under the protective cover of the canopy of green.

She hadn't gone more than a few steps into the forest when she saw Valus leaning casually against the trunk of a tree, waiting for her. He was hard to spot in the shadows of the other trees unless you knew to look for him, which she did.

"It's about time, Rheina-lee." His voice was calm and casual like his posture, but Rheina knew underneath all that, he could be fierce. He wasn't a warrior like her brother or Daegan, but he did remind her a little of her Hal. He was comfortable and casual with people like Hal, but Valus used it to hide a sharp edge. He had a dark side and it made Rheina nervous. But what concerned her more was how much it didn't scare her.

"It's been awhile. I haven't seen you since your coming of age party," he said as he pushed off the tree. The man before her watched her closely. "Are you all right?" His face was pinched with concern.

Rheina nodded, but when her eyes met his she couldn't contain the sadness hers held. Without needing details, he gathered her protectively in his arms, stroking the back of her head, running his fingers through her hair. Rheina froze, uncomfortable with the sudden affection. She liked Valus, but she wasn't sure how much yet. This was the first time he had shown so much physical attention to her. He backed up a step and cleared his throat as if he was as surprised at his actions as she. Valus was tall and muscular, but lean. He had intelligent gray eyes with long dark lashes and a head full of wavy golden blond hair. Valus didn't belong to Alandria, but because of who—or *what*—he was, he had the ability to come and go as he pleased. Rheina had yet to fully understand him. Now they would have time.

"It appears that it is time for us to go," he observed, changing the topic.

"It is time. This is my path and I will see it through." Rheina stood tall and her green eyes met his gray ones with fierce determination.

"Then we need to move quickly, before anyone sees us." Valus started walking deeper into the grove toward the mountain.

"Valus, will your brother meet us?"

"Yeah, Rhys said he'd be there. So he better be. He knows the land better than I do. I try not to spend much time in those parts. It lacks a certain hospitable quality that I seem to look for in a home." Valus winked at her and they kept walking.

There was much Rheina wanted to ask Valus about Exhile. She had never been there and truthfully, hoped she never would. Extreme situations called for extreme action. This was what her visions showed her, and they had not been wrong thus far. So into Exhile she would go, but at least she would not be alone.

"Did you call me 'Rheina-lee'?" She scrunched up her face when she looked up at him.

Valus shrugged. "You needed a nickname. It just came out. I can keep trying."

Rheina looked at him thoughtfully. "It might grow on me." Then she gave him a small smile before refocusing on their journey ahead.

CHAPTER TWELVE

EHSMIA. THE HOME OF THE HIDDEN PEOPLE.

H al clapped Daegan on the back as he walked past him, looking up at the vast expanse of the amazing space. "It doesn't get old, does it?"

Kaeleigh looked around in awe. Suddenly, she halted, then bent down to admire the little flowers. Orchids. Her eyes filled with emotion. She breathed their fresh scent deeply then looked up to Hal then back at Daegan. "You have been here before?"

"Once. Recently," Daegan answered.

"Actually, you have been here a few times before that, young Daegan," Arileas interjected with mischief in his face.

"You mentioned that last time," Daegan spoke skeptically.

"You do not yet remember." Arileas spoke it as fact and not a question, but Daegan shook his head nonetheless. "But you will."

"We do not have time for riddles, sir," Finn spoke up from the back. "If you have something that could help us, we would be in your debt."

"I believe you already are, Master Finnlan." Arileas raised an eyebrow and gestured behind them at the portal they had just arrived in.

"Grandfather, perhaps we can show them around and offer them rest and refreshment. After all that just happened, I am sure they are weary and drained," Ella spoke sweetly as she looped her arm through the arm of the older Faerie. He was quite aged looking, but there was still a spark of youth and excitement in his eyes.

Even though the group had many questions, they were also entranced with the beauty of Ehsmia. It was, essentially, the inside of a mountain, its domed center so high you could not see the top through the canopy of tall trees. The colors were all so brilliantly bright that many times it looked white in one angle and then full of color at another. A stream that ran through the center sparkled and glistened as if filled with tiny diamonds reflecting the light. It was the bluest of blues and yet upon closer look it was crystal clear. Rocks and stones were smooth, looking soft at the bottom of the stream bed. Fish like they had never seen in the mortal realm swam and played around rocks. They even jumped up, kissing the air to see new visitors.

"Are those real diamonds?" Metrí whispered to Kaeleigh, who was walking next to her. Kaeleigh shook her head, but then looked closer.

"I don't think so, I think it's just the light reflecting."

There were trees of all kinds—a quaint forest within the land—but they did not clump and block the light; instead, they seemed to absorb and steep in it to then release and enhance the light around them. Every single tree flourished in its respective type, growing and blooming to the fullest. Up high in their branches, a multitude of butterflies, dragonflies, and other small flying creatures flitted about.

Gasping, Kaeleigh watched them as the small creatures frolicked. "They are beautiful."

"Everything is beautiful," Chel spoke in hushed awe as she too looked around, taking in everything she could.

"Watch your step and please follow us," Ella spoke, bringing them all back. They stepped onto a bridge that crossed the stream, leading them toward the back of the mountain.

"Are we in a volcano?" Chel asked, craning her neck up looking as high as she could.

"In a matter of speaking," Ella responded, speaking as if she had stepped into the role of tour guide. "It is not active if that is what you mean. It is more of a hollowed out mountain. However, it is also not as simple as that. If you come to the outside of the Kandrian Mountains—even if you found the correct tunnel entrance out of the hundreds that are there—you could not just enter. If you began to dig into the mountain you would also not reach us. Similar to the realm we were just in—we created that to be a pocket realm, much like a bubble within a body of water—it is a land separated by magic, but it is not in a different realm. We are in the same plane as Alandria and still considered a part of Alandria, though most do not believe us to truly exist."

"The hidden people," Finn spoke softly. "Even though I have known you for some time and known that Ehsmia exists, I have never had the honor of being here before. It's truly magical, Ella."

Ella stared at Finn, lost in a momentary memory, before she nodded and they continued to move back toward the large waterfall cascading from somewhere high above at the back of the mountain. "We have taken great precautions to remain hidden as we are, to not correct the tales, and even create some of the rumors ourselves."

"But why?" Kaeleigh asked.

"It was not always like that, dear Kaeleighnna, but when darkness had been allowed into Alandria from the previous realm, time and experience had proven that our kind, our race, was sought for our magic to be used for selfish gain. We tried to show good faith by sending our prince to lead Elnye for a time, but we were then dismantled and so we remain hidden until it was our time once again." Arileas spoke with wonder in his eyes as if he was seeing something far off. "But that is for another story. We have much to cover, young princess, but let us get you nourished." Arileas's eyes twinkled once again as Kaeleigh's footing got tripped up.

No one had really mentioned the "princess thing" since Hunter had passed on. It made her heart hurt a little bit, but it was also something that seemed so foreign and distant from who she knew herself to be.

"Princess?" Metrí asked with confusion and awe.

"We can talk about it later," Chel whispered conspiratorially.

Metrí watched Kaeleigh for a few minutes, studying her under new light and perspective. She seemed to decide something as she nodded to herself. "I can see it." She said it matter-of-factly even though no one had asked.

"Have you seen your little friend?" Hal asked Daegan with a wink. At the confused faces of the others with them, he explained. "Last time we were here, Daegan seemed to have an affinity with the smallest creatures."

Daegan gave Hal a stern look telling him to leave it, but of course he did not.

"One of the butterflies talked to him." Hal's words were full of light, but he was not making fun of the butterfly. Actually, he had pride in his eyes. Something about the interaction had endeared himself to the butterfly that she would choose Daegan to connect with.

"Wow," "That's cool," came from Kaeleigh and Chel, but Metrí had turned around her back to them. When she turned around, her eyes were large. "Like this butterfly?" she asked. Holding her arm out, she displayed a beautiful large butterfly that was crawling up her arm. She was an exquisite creature. Much like butterflies in the mortal realm, this one was much more ethereal. She was shimmery white and had large wings; the two in the back extended longer and trailed behind her. The butterfly had large obsidian eyes that focused with a knowing depth, but also a playful curiosity.

"She is extremely honored and special in all of Alandria." Ella spoke reverently, and then she glared at Hal. "She is also quite magical and not to be disrespected."

"No disrespect intended." Hal bowed his head.

Metrí giggled. "She tickles my arm hairs." Chel and Kaeleigh slowly crept closer to look at the amazing little creature.

"I think she likes you." Kaeleigh smiled.

"Mmmm." Chel closed her eyes, humming.

"Can you understand her?" Halister asked as he came up beside Chel.

"She's speaking about Metrí's magic." Chel smiled at Metrí. "She says you're special, important, and powerful. She likes you."

"Well done, Chel of the Shifters," Arileas observed quietly. "That is, in fact, exactly what she said. Metrí, we welcome you here and will do what we can to help you find your magic if that is what you seek."

Metrí nodded with a big smile and watery eyes that barely contained her emotion. Kaeleigh placed her hand gently upon the young girl's shoulder. After she did, the butterfly fluttered to Kaeleigh and slowly made her way up her arm. Kaeleigh watch in awed silence. When the butterfly had almost reached her shoulder, Kaeleigh inclined her head. "Hello, lovely lady." The butterfly looked at Kaeleigh for a long minute, then moved even closer, making her way up to her head. She fluttered in the air by Kaeleigh's ear for a moment then kissed her cheek. She then floated in front of each of those there and stopped briefly in front of Daegan. He inclined his head to her and said, "It is nice to see you again, thank you." Then she fluttered high into the trees after a brief circle around Arileas's head. He bowed to her as well.

"Wow," Chel breathed out. They all watched until they could not see the little butterfly any longer.

"What was that all about?" Finn asked quietly, looking between Chel and Ella.

"There was so much emotion in her little feelings. It was hard to decipher. Her passion was so great, but I couldn't put most of it to words," Chel replied, frustrated.

"There were words, my dear, and there was much in them. We will discuss this very soon." Arileas spoke as he turned and continued walking to the waterfall.

❖❖❖

After what seemed like a longer time than it should have taken to reach the waterfall, they stopped in front of it. Chel turned around to look behind them with a confused look. "How did it do that?" Chel looked to Kaeleigh to see she was trying to figure it out as well. "It shouldn't have taken us that long to get here. I see the beginning where we started like it's only a few minutes away."

"I know. It's strange. I can see threads of magical energy running along the path we took. So whatever it was must be some kind of magic." Kaeleigh shrugged and looked at Chel, who seemed satisfied with that answer.

"That is cool!" Chel grabbed Kaeleigh's arm and they scooted in closer to hear what the others were talking about.

"Why are we allowed to see you this time?" Hal asked, remembering the last time he and Daegan were there they had been asked to wear blindfolds so that they would not be able to be witness to the accounts that the Elder was informing them about.

"The time for secrecy has passed. The Sol-lumieth has been brought back to the mountain." He gestured toward Kaeleigh with his head. "The time for preparations of things to come is now upon us." As if that should be a sufficient answer to Hal's question, he turned and beckoned them to follow his lead back behind the waterfall.

Instead of walking into the den-type room that Daegan and Hal had been in before, they entered a short tunnel lit with small round torches of blue flames that opened up into a large rustic kitchen. It still looked like it was carved out of a mountain, but it had all the necessary conveniences for a modern eatery. There were several workers in the room that froze with shock as the entourage walked in, staring at everything in sight.

"Please excuse the intrusion, Grya and Lendi. These are our guests for the time being. Please see that they are fed properly." Arileas smiled at the Faeries in the kitchen. They looked pretty ordinary and could almost blend into the mortal realm if they wanted to, except for the slightly pointy ears and the *otherness* that was in their pale skin and lavender eyes.

Not sure who was who, one a man and the other a female, Kaeleigh went up to the woman and extended her hand. "Hello. I'm pleased to meet you." The woman looked at her hand then up at Kaeleigh then over to Arileas in obvious confusion.

"In Alandria, it is not custom to shake one's hand as you do in the mortal realm. Simply incline your head in a show of humility and respect," Hal instructed as he showed her how it was done.

"Please forgive me, I meant no disrespect." Kaeleigh bowed her head and lowered her eyes. The woman's face lit up.

"She is from the mortal realm?" She looked to Arileas, but did not wait for his response. "I am Grya. Welcome to Ehsmia." She extended her hand to Kaeleigh. She, too, could adapt to one's customs. Kaeleigh smiled at the woman. They all said their greetings and then Ella pushed them further into the room to a spattering of tables and benches to await their meal.

Not long after they had gotten cleaned up and seated, hot steaming bowls of some kind of soup along with trays piled high with breads and cheeses were placed upon the tables. A moment later, more trays were brought out filled with a variety of fruits—some of which the girls from the mortal realm had never seen—and another filled with meats and nuts followed shortly after that.

"Wow, this all looks so delicious," Chel said with her mouth practically watering.

Kaeleigh laughed at her friend, but she agreed. "We haven't eaten this well since...well, I was going to say since last Thanksgiving, but I guess we did eat pretty well in Elnye before Maleina threw us in the dungeon." Everyone stopped what food they had been about to put into mouths that were now gaping open at Kaeleigh. "Too soon?" She blushed and shrank into herself. "Sorry."

Chel brushed it off nonchalantly. "What do you do? It happened. We're free now so we should be able to talk about it. Shake it off, Kae, no worries here." Kaeleigh smiled at the absurdity of her friend and the bizarre look Hal was giving her—like she had grown a third eye or something crazy.

Hal eventually nodded. "I appreciate your candor and perspective. I am not sure how to respond as it was my family who placed you in such a situation. Which has placed me forever in your debt."

"Hal, it wasn't you, but your mother. However, if you need it, we totally forgive you." Chel gave him an awkward smile.

"Agreed." Kaeleigh nodded her head.

"It is remarkable how easily you are able to release forgiveness and move forward. Thank you." Halister looked down. A moment later, he looked to Kaeleigh. "I hope you know that I swear to protect you and your friends here"—he motioned to Chel then Finn and everyone at the table—"and stand with you even if it is against my own mother." Hal's eyes captured a normally hidden intensity that rose out of his sincerity. His life had been altered forever and he had chosen his path.

"Thank you, Hal. Your friendship and support are important to me, but I would never ask for that kind of an oath from you or anyone. However, if this is your heart's true path, I welcome you and I think we all do. I know Daegan trusts you. So I do too." Kaeleigh smiled at him and looked briefly at an uncomfortable Daegan.

"So long as we can keep him from the bar maids, I think we'll be all right," Daegan uncharacteristically joked, throwing a smirk across the table at his friend as he reached for some food.

"I resemble that remark! I mean, I resent that remark! I'm confused," Hal fired back playfully, giving Chel a dangerous glance to see her response.

"Okay, Hal's philandering aside," Finn interjected, clearly amused with where the conversation had gone, "I think it would benefit everyone if we began this feast, wouldn't you agree?"

Metrí's stomach next to him growled enough that the entire table heard it.

"Yes, please," Kaeleigh giggled at the small burst of humor from her usually all too serious warriors. "Let's eat!" She felt light for the first time since they had entered Alandria. This small group of beings, now her friends—old and new—were becoming more than that. They were becoming her family.

Chapter Thirteen

"There is no time to waste." The familiar sound of the Elder's words came as they echoed throughout the cavernous room they were all gathered in. "We begin immediately."

After they had eaten the night before, Ella gave them a brief tour of Ehsmia and introduced them to a few inquisitive people that ventured out of their cave-like dwellings; the rest stayed hidden from the newcomers' eyes, reserved but also uncertain. They were shown to a couple of different rooms which were cut out of the rocks; one for the girls to share, and one for the boys. The dark brown walls were an interesting texture. It appeared to be a mix of the actual wall dirt sealed with something that felt like paint. There were comfortable beds with soft, clean off-white linens, and there was a sweet aroma of vanilla and cinnamon that subtly permeated the air. It was cozy and offered an oasis of comfort. The floors were the same sealed brown as the walls flowing seamlessly from ground to ceiling, but they were covered in a spattering of thick, plush rugs. Oil lanterns were spread throughout the rooms for ample light. It was a nice soft glow that made you feel like cozying up with warm apple cider, a fire, and a good book on a cold winter's day.

"To begin, please draw near to me. I know you have many questions and there is much to share. We shall speak now and also continue while you train," the Elder began as he sat down on a chair thick and sturdy but made of branches that appeared out of thin air.

"Cool," Chel whispered in awe. When she didn't see any other chairs, she simply sat on the ground near the Elder, anticipating the revelations to come. Metrí sat next to her, followed by Hal. Kaeleigh noted that the other guys were not sitting down, each refusing to be the first to do so. She rolled her eyes and sat down herself, muttering something about stubborn warriors under her breath. Ella remained standing just behind her grandfather, but that seemed to be more for support than her desire to out-stand the guys.

"Kaeleighnna? Let us begin with you. What would you like to know?" the Elder asked, putting her on the spot.

Kaeleigh's eyes grew big. "I have so many questions, sir, and most I had thought I'd never see answers to but now that you are offering... I don't even know where to begin." Kaeleigh took a deep breath and briefly looked around at her group. When her eyes made it back to Arileas, she had decided on what she wanted to know most of all.

"Is my father alive?"

"Yes," came from not only Arileas, but also Aidón, at whom Kaeleigh shot a quick glare of unbelief.

"What? Why didn't you tell me? This whole time we were to-gether and you didn't tell me?"

"Forgive me, Kaeleigh, one thing happened after another and there did not seem to be the time to discuss it. I planned to talk to you about it once we got here." Aidón looked her straight on with no shame or unease. She appreciated that.

"You are right, there wasn't the opportunity." She looked back to Arileas and then again to Aidón. "Do you either of you know where he is?"

Arileas nodded to the other man. Aidón spoke up then. "Not exactly, but I do believe I can find him now that I am free of that glamour. It affected my mind so that it could not be infiltrated by anyone that should not be in there." Kaeleigh looked to him with emotion strong in her eyes. "We will find him, Kaeleighnna. I give you my word." She gave him a quick nod and a smile.

"Someone else go, I need to gather my thoughts," Kaeleigh blurted out, rubbing her hand over her forehead.

"Elder?" There was a pause as Hal searched the room to fix on something, avoiding all eyes. "Is my mother evil?" he finally asked, just above a whisper, bracing for a reply.

Arileas paused before he answered, his eyes finally catching Hal's. "Do you believe her to be?"

"No, sir, I do not. However, I know she is not good either." Hal looked off to the side. It was obvious that this was painful for him to talk about and spoke to his concern and love for his family that he brought up such things.

"We all make choices in the lives we are given—for good and for...not so good." Arileas looked at each of the members of the group. "There are many *gray areas* in life, not just black and white ones. Your mother's choices have not been good for quite some time." Arileas paused for a moment, his mind captured in a memory past. "She is not bad or evil, but her decisions are corrupting both her and the kingdom entrusted her. There is something else at work. I cannot see it clearly yet, but there is a greater, darker power that surrounds her. I would not be surprised if she is under the influence of another, more powerful than she." Suddenly Arileas was up from his chair, pacing over to the wall and leaning his hand against it, obviously deep in thought. "Yes, there is definitely a stronger dark power, and it is tangled within her, bound to her even."

"Does that mean she can be helped?" Daegan asked from the back of the group with his arms across his chest, his muscles tight and intimidating. Kaeleigh blushed, realizing that she had been staring at him instead of thinking of her next question.

"There is always redemption for those who realize they need it," Arileas said without hesitation. Halister nodded in acknowledgment of Arileas, but appeared to be distracted.

"Daegan's connection with Maleina... it's not broken, is it?" Kaeleigh asked next.

Arileas took a breath as he studied Daegan, taking in everything about him for the next few seconds. "No, not in its entirety. It is severely damaged thanks to whatever it was that you did. I can see the residue of your magic upon the frayed edges of the connection.

It is not an easy thing to see or to *do* for that matter. There is still the tiniest of connections that keeps you tethered to her, Daegan. We must find a way to sever it completely or it will regenerate, I am afraid."

Kaeleigh felt Daegan's anger rise at the truth of the matter, just before he consented to Arileas, schooling his features into a mask of stoic resignation.

"Wait, are you saying that Mother did something that connected her to you?" Halister's voice rose. Daegan looked his friend in the eye and nodded even though Hal knew the answer, having deep down considered such a possibility. Daegan rolled up the sleeve of his long-sleeved, loose-fitting shirt, revealing not only corded tan arms and defined biceps, but the mostly vanished marking of the snake he had had on his upper arm for most his life, since he had entered into the ranks of the Ferrishyn elite training program as a boy.

"When we had these done, she did something. Whether it was with a spell or an actual tracer poison I do not know, but it is how we have been connected, how she could see where I had been or who I had spoken with. How she would always know when we disobeyed her when we were younger." Daegan lowered his hand, allowing his sleeve to fall.

"I had no idea. I... I don't know what to say." Hal looked completely horrified and for a moment, even broken. Daegan clapped his hand upon Hal's shoulder and squeezed.

"It will be our priority, Master Daegan, to do what we can." Arileas inclined his head.

There was a moment of weighty silence.

"Let us begin at the beginning, shall we?" Arileas looked directly at Kaeleigh. Her shoulders relaxed as she took a deep breath and smiled at him.

"Yes, please. I have heard pieces of different things, but not enough of anything to make sense of most of it."

"You have heard of the prophecy?" he asked. Kaeleigh nodded. Just then, Ella approached him and whispered something in her grandfather's ear. He gave a small smile and nodded his head in agreement with whatever she said. He continued, "I will arrange a time with the scholars to present the original ancient document so you may fully understand."

"That would be helpful and much appreciated, thank you." Kaeleigh paused for a moment. "All right, so I understand how the land was created and where you came from, even that there was a prophecy. What I am not completely grasping is why you believe that this prophecy has something to do with me?" Kaeleigh asked, bringing them back on track.

"I believe we will need a demonstration." Arileas stood to his feet and handed Ella that cup of tea that she had brought him moments before. He walked off to the side of the group. His hand waved off to the side toward nothing, then suddenly it wasn't empty space. Instead, a beautiful ornately carved sword stood in the corner shining in all its glory. Arileas looked to the sword and then to the group.

Kaeleigh's eyes were wide with surprise seeing her sword, or what she thought of as 'her sword' appearing there. It had not been with her since she last had it in Elnye. She felt its absence, had longed for that connection again since it had disappeared, but she figured she must not have needed it at the time. Plus, she still had the one that Daegan had given her. Kaeleigh started to get up, but Arileas waved her back down. She thought it odd, but wanted to see what he would do.

"Ella, will you please try to wield that sword?" He directed her toward Kaeleigh's sword.

Kaeleigh frowned but let him proceed. Ella walked to the sword and respectfully bowed to it before she attempted to pick it up. It was heavy in her hands, in fact so heavy Ella wobbled with it and barely was able to lift it high enough to even attempt to swing it. She then carefully put it down.

That's odd, Kaeleigh thought.

"Finnlan, please can you do the same?" Arileas asked.

Finn walked skeptically up to the sword. He lifted it with little strain, but even with his great strength found it somewhat challenging to swing it. However, he was able to. The shocking thing no one expected was for Arileas to step into the swing with his own sword and block it. Finn recovered quickly and blocked the parry that the Elder sent his way. However, when he used the sword it became almost lifeless and lost its luster.

"Strange. It is very heavy, even for one trained with weapons. However, I could fight with it in a battle if absolutely necessary, but it would not be my first choice. I can feel it fighting against me. It pulls from me. I used it once before and do not recall it feeling like this," Finn said, confused.

"When you used it, was it to help Kaeleighnna?" Arileas asked, already knowing the answer.

"Yes, we were trying to save Chel from the Droch-Shúil and Kaeleigh had been knocked down. It still only worked magic with Kaeleigh, but it let me use it in that moment." Still confused, Finn looked to Kaeleigh, who shrugged as she considered what was being demonstrated.

"Chel, would you like to try?" Arileas gave a small smile, noticing the anticipation in Chel's face.

"Yes!" She bounced up and moved toward the sword still in Finn's hands. He handed it to her gently, yet she barely could stand as it fell to the ground. "Well, I guess it doesn't even want me to try," Chel laughed, but the disappointment was evident in her eyes.

"Do not worry, Chel, you'll have your own built-in weapon soon enough," Hal said with a wink in her direction, to which she smiled a big cheesy, flirtatious smile in return. It totally caught Hal off guard. Daegan even stifled a laugh at his reaction.

"Elder... Arileas, sir,... I've been told that the sword only reacts to me, but I don't seem to entirely get what you're saying. I'm obviously missing something."

"Kaeleighnna, would you please come hold *Nithylrith,* the Orchan sword? Yes, you are aware that this sword is special and has an energy all its own that reacts to you." Arileas beckoned her closer. "Please take the sword."

Kaeleigh walked up and took the sword. It felt comfortable and the weight felt perfect in her hands. It balanced well and felt once again like an extension of her arm. She felt at home as the energy of the sword welcomed her own. However... "This still does not explain to me what it has to do with me, specifically. Why me?"

"Why not you?" Arileas countered.

"I am nothing special. Up until recently I didn't even know I had magic."

"You have always been special. Think on it this way: perhaps it is more who your parents were... who their parents were. You see, you are not you in and of yourself." At her confused look he continued, "You are a result of each generation before you. You are a culmination of every choice they made, every seed they sowed, all of their magical energy invested into the atmosphere that has circled its way back to you. As are each of us." He gestured around the room. "In your case, there were certain investments and sacrifices made that culminated to this point in time and in your particular person. It is not because of anything you can do or anything you can be. It is because of what they have done for you, how they have enabled you for this purpose."

A lightbulb lit up in Kaeleigh's mind. This moment held significance. Her eyes glistened. She nodded. Then a moment later, she even went down on to one knee, following her instincts. "Then for whatever I can give, I accept the path that is before me for them... for my parents and my grandparents. I will be who I can be for Alandria."

"That is all we can ask of anyone: Be who lives inside of you." Arileas slid a glance to the warrior standing at the back of the room as Arileas helped Kaeleigh up and lifted her chin with his fingers. He moved closer and gave her a kiss upon her forehead like her grandfather had done. Arileas stepped back.

"There are many more questions, answers will follow. There will always be questions, but now it is time to train. Ella, let them in. I am bringing in some of my own warriors to train with you. They are trained as you train your warriors, Master Daegan and Master Halister, but I think you might find their unique style of fighting intriguing. Not only watch and train along their sides, but *feel* how they fight."

Finn and Hal stood, helping the other girls up and flanking them with uncertainty as Ella ushered in a group of about ten of their warriors. To all the girls' delight, there were women in the group of warriors. They had not seen many of these, if any, yet.

"Metrí, I think this is going to be awesome," Chel whispered conspiratorially to Metrí, who nodded in agreement.

CHAPTER FOURTEEN

The large room they had met in was also called the Hall of Warriors. It had a short tunnel extension, almost like a hallway, that opened into a much larger cavernous hall. It had the same high ceilings as the entrance into Ehsmia had and the same bright light—though not quite as brilliant. There were also trees scattered about, but the room's pièce de résistance was its height. There were no openings to other dwellings. This hall was simplistic and functional; it was a training space. An area near where they entered was filled with racks of swords and spears and other long weapons. There was a section for bows and quivers full of arrows. Various medieval-looking weaponry hung from the walls, all shined and begging to be handled. These weapons bore the echoes of ancient times etched upon blade and handle, but they were cared for with pristine guardianship. There were "oohs" and "ahhs" as the group followed the Ehsmian warriors into the room.

The difference in these fighters was immediately noticed by Kaeleigh, and Chel as well. They were also noticeably friendly and welcoming. They explained they would quickly go through basic fighting techniques to distinguish where each of them were at with their skills. Then they would apply various levels of magic. Kaeleigh had fought with Finn a little in this manner to see how she could handle it, but it did not last long. She couldn't seem to grasp how she could infuse her energy into her sword and still have some to fight with, not only her physical energy, but also her magical.

"Please choose a weapon that you are comfortable with if you do not have your own already," one of the Ehsmia instructed.

Even though most of them had their own weapons, they could not resist fawning over the ones at their disposal.

"I think I am the only one of us that doesn't have my own weapon," Chel stated as she picked up different lengths of swords then moved on to trying out the spears and sticklike weapons that resembled the katana sword.

"Remember, you *are* a weapon." Kaeleigh winked at her friend.

"Oh, believe me, I remember," Chel said with humor even though something flashed across her eyes.

Kaeleigh came up close to Chel so the others wouldn't hear her. "Chel? You don't seem okay. What's wrong?"

"Yeah. I just keep hearing that I'm my own weapon and the skills I *should* have... but I don't have them yet. I couldn't protect myself, or anyone else for that matter, if I tried right now. I mean, I know I have this extra senses thing going on and I can hear the animals, but I haven't shifted yet, and I don't know if I ever will, Kaeleigh. Maybe something is wrong with me." Chel was rarely that honest with her feelings and Kaeleigh was not about to let it pass by.

"Listen to me. You are Chel, my best friend. I know beyond any doubt that you would do whatever you could to protect me or anyone else that was in your vicinity. You are all that matters to me, in any shape or animal. If it is going to happen, then it will happen in the right time. It will be organic and seamless. Don't force it. You are everything you are meant to be, right here." Kaeleigh pointed to Chel's heart.

Chel took a deep breath and wiped a stray tear that escaped one of her eyes. She gave Kaeleigh a bone-crushing hug. "Thanks," she whispered in her ear before releasing her.

"Now, grab yourself one of those mighty sticks. I can totally see you being bad-A with one of those," Kaeleigh giggled, but was glad to see the light of hope in her friend's eyes again.

After they were ready, the warriors of Ehsmia took them to the center. There was some kind of mat area etched out in the ground.

There wasn't really a mat on the "mat area" like in mortal realm dojo, but it was lined out all the same. It encompassed a large circled area.

"When we have sanctioned fights among individuals, you stay within this circle," one of the women warriors instructed as she followed the circle area in the air with her fingers. "My name is Líyl. Welcome to our training hall." She was an average-looking female, Kaeleigh noted, with only a hint of "other." She stood out among so many of the other Faeries and their ethereal beauty, being the only reason Kaeleigh noticed. She was not ugly by any means, but just not as striking as some of the others. Kaeleigh wondered if it was because she was a warrior—if that meant anything. Líyl was about to demonstrate some of their fighting techniques with one of the other fighters, a man named Gyon that they had met earlier. *There is no way I'm going to remember all their names,* Kaeleigh thought to herself in frustration but determined she would try. As soon as they began their dance, clashing their swords together, their energies began to emanate outward from them, clashing in a dance all its own, and a glow that only Kaeleigh could see stirred Líyl's features and practically transformed her beauty. It was there all within her and it shined when she did what she was born to do. Kaeleigh envied the ease and fluidity Líyl moved with and wondered if she would ever have that grace and power within her steps and her movements. She realized for the first time she wanted that: to exude the power of a woman in full glory as she fought as Líyl did. It was enrapturing to watch. So much so she didn't notice that Daegan was in the back of the room with Arileas discussing something that seemed to be causing Daegan some discomfort. She could, however, practically *feel* it. The feeling of "connection" she had with that warrior was growing along with her care for him.

"I need to leave. I am putting you all in danger." Daegan was adamant.

Arileas stared at him as if seeing into the depths of his soul; perhaps he was. "No, it is not time yet. She needs you here," he said with the slightest nod in the direction of the center fighting arena.

Daegan stared directly at Kaeleigh sitting on the ground, watching the Ehsmia fight with rapt attention. However, she briefly broke her focus to turn and notice him out of the corner of her eye. She was always aware of where he was, as he was with her. It was unnerving and also comforting. "She will be safe here. There are others that will train her and get her ready."

"That is not what I mean. I think you know that."

"I have nothing to give her in this life or another."

Arileas stared at Daegan once again. "You still are not aware of who you are."

Daegan leveled the Elder with a look that would have had almost anyone in their right mind creeping low and away from danger, but not Arileas. He simply smiled.

"Then enlighten me. Who am I?" Daegan almost shocked himself at how disrespectful he was being toward an Elder, but he was nearly at the end of himself. He knew it was only a matter of time before he led Maleina right there not only to Kaeleigh, but to the whole race of a people that had been able to remain hidden and out of sight for centuries.

"Let us remove your hindrance before your memories surface. It is not yet Maleina's time to be aware of the enlightenment yet to occur."

"I do not understand your riddles. Can you really do what you say?" He placed his hand up high on his left arm where the marking had been slowly reappearing. "I would be forever in your debt."

"It is not for you to be in my debt. It has already been paid."

Daegan looked at Arileas with hope and deep questioning. Head cocked, he tried to read the energy and emotions coming off the Elder, but Arileas was locked tight in his mind.

Now go train with the others. I have preparations to make. The Elder surprised Daegan by speaking into his mind once again, obviously aware that Daegan had been trying to use his gifts on him. The Elder smiled.

Daegan nodded in defeated acquiescence and replied mind to mind, *Yes, sir.* When he turned to give the Elder a bow, Arileas was already gone.

"We should be protecting her! Not sending her out to fight. We are her warriors. As much as it pains me to say it, it is better there are two of us to keep her safe. This feels wrong," Finn adamantly growled at Daegan as he continued to throw magical offensive tactics at Kaeleigh.

Kaeleigh rolled her eyes for the millionth time at Finn. This was not a new discussion, but it was the first time all three of them had it together, not to mention while they were fighting and she was trying to focus. She knew Finn meant well, but she had to learn. "Finn, we have been over this. I need to learn. It is better I know how to defend myself in case I need to. I'm getting better and I have to keep learning. These new skills would have come in handy a few times already."

"But Kae, I can't protect you if you are out in the middle of the crossfire. We don't know what we will be coming up against. You need to be hidden somewhere safe until it is all over, then you can step into your role as the new leader of Alandria."

"That is why we are training her, Finnlan. We will do everything we can—and more—to keep her safe, but it is part of who she is. She is part warrior, it is in her blood—it is in her destiny." Daegan was exasperated with Finn. He was done with it. Daegan lunged toward Kaeleigh with his sword, which she in turn blocked and parried. He nodded at her quick thought and focus.

"Well, I care about her enough to want to keep her from that life. To keep her safe from battle and the stains of death that come with it." Finn knew he was challenging Daegan, but he had to do it. He had to know.

Seamlessly, Daegan spun Kaeleigh out away from him with a push of his sword and a little magic and engaged Finn with his sword. Without missing a beat, Finn pulled his knives to defend himself. The two warriors began battling each other with more intensity than each of them had with Kaeleigh. "That is not what I understand love to be. It is caring enough to prepare her to survive and to succeed without us there. To make her ready and to support her destiny no matter what it might be, beyond personal feelings. To believe she can do it beyond all shadow of doubt, so you can stand in confidence that she is ready."

Kaeleigh stood by watching her sword, now dropped at her side with her mouth practically hung open. The intensity radiating off the two warriors was thick and the discussion heavy. Daegan continued to drive Finn backwards as they clashed swords and knives, thrusting and blocking, spinning and deflecting. Finn's face had gone three shades whiter. Kaeleigh focused her magic, feeling she needed to do something to contain them and allow them to hash out their issues before there was a battle, before she needed them. She threw her fingers outward, visualizing containment. A little bit to her surprise, a thin barrier of energy surrounded Finn and Daegan as they continued to move within their circle. It was like they were in their own little bubble of war.

Feeling the containment, Finn pulled back, lowering his weapons, and scowled at her before his expression softened. He asked her seriously, "That's why it's him, isn't it?"

Uncomfortable as to where the conversation had turned, Kaeleigh looked away, biting her bottom lip. Daegan had also dropped his weapon and stepped back.

"He loves you enough to let you be who you are and who you need to be, not just who you were. I loved you too tightly, trying to keep you away from all this. Kae... I'm sorry. He's right." Finn looked down, still breathing heavily. Then he looked over at Daegan, whose face reflected intense resentment at Finn's blunt assessment. Finn then stepped away from Daegan and Kaeleigh, out of the circle, and pointed his finger back at him. "How does a Ferrishyn raised by that witch Maleina know such things of love, while I come across the fool? In truth, it appears that I am the one more like her. I am the fool," he said sadly.

"Hunter taught me, he showed me. She taught me nothing," Daegan said in hushed tones as he remembered his old friend, offering nothing more.

"It is my shame. I served under Hunter as well, for so many years, but I kept my fears in front of me when it came to matters of the heart." Finn's eyes exposed his complete brokenness for a brief moment. He took a deep breath and inclined his head toward Daegan. Finn then looked warmly at Kaeleigh and spoke with resignation. "Let me out, Kae."

Kaeleigh dropped the magical boundary. She wanted to stop him. Her eyes pleaded with him as she called out, "Finn?"

With big, vulnerable hazel green eyes, Finn opened his soul to her. "I need to go for now. Please understand." Without waiting for her to reply, he turned and started out of the hall.

Kaeleigh nodded with unshed tears in her eyes and a hitch in her chest. "Okay," she whispered. Her tears began to roll down her cheek as she watched him leave.

After a moment of awkward silence, Daegan spoke. "Kaeleigh... what he said, I—"

Kaeleigh cut him off flatly through her emotion. "I know, I know. He was in the heat of the moment. You don't need to explain it all away, Daegan. I know how you feel." Then she walked away.

After she was almost out of sight, he took a deep breath watching her walk away. "No, you do not."

"How long have we been training? Has it been days or years?" Chel said, exasperated.

Halister let out a huff of annoyance. "It has only been a few hours. Has your sense of time not adjusted since being here?" he asked seriously.

Chel squished up her face at him. "How would I know?" she replied sarcastically as she lowered the spear that she had been sparring with and breathed heavier than she would have liked.

In that moment of brief distraction, Hal moved with amazing speed. He grabbed her spear, twisting her arm around with it, bringing it up behind her back and effectively pinning her in front of him, his other arm in front of her neck preventing any upper body moves. She sagged defeated in his arms.

"Why do you always..." Her sentence broke off with her elbow ramming up and into his ribs, catching him off guard. His grip on her loosened. She spun around then hooked her leg behind one of his, yanking him to the ground. However, she did not fully adjust her movement and overshot, causing her to tumble to the ground with him landing partially on the hard dirt floor and partially draped across Hal. "Gotcha!"

Hal laughed. "Yes, you did."

"You let me do that, didn't you?" Chel sighed in irritation.

"Let you do what?" Hal winked at her. "No, you bested me fair and square. I was caught off guard by your intoxicating scent and your breasts heaving against my arm, which was, of course, my purpose from the very beginning."

"You are a... a... a very bad word. In Missoula, Montana, we have names for guys like you," Chel finally resolved, crossing her arms over her chest.

Kaeleigh laughed from the sidelines. "Is that the best you could come up with?"

"Yes. I vowed not to actually curse in this realm and I couldn't come up with—JACKELOPE! That's what you are," she accused him with her finger.

Hal just looked at her like she was crazy or he was intently trying to remember what that word meant in the mortal realm. Apparently it wasn't a creature they had in Alandria.

Kaeleigh laughed even harder. Finn came up beside her and she quickly summarized the story while still trying to actually breathe.

Finn laughed more at Kaeleigh trying to tell the story than at the actual story itself.

"Fine. Laugh it up, you two, I've got both your numbers too, you know." Chel pointed directly at Kaeleigh.

The other warriors had now all stopped what they were doing and gathered around with curiosity.

"Oh! I apologize, I did not mean to interrupt your sessions," Kaeleigh said, bowing her head reverently.

"Do not apologize, Kaeleighnna. Laughter is an important part of training," Líyl said with a small smile.

"How so?" Metrí asked, standing there with her sword still ready in her hand.

"It brings light to your soul and clears the darkness which brings heaviness, confusion, and fear," she stated as a matter of fact.

They nodded and all got to their feet. "Should we begin again?" Kaeleigh asked.

"It is time to break for the day. We will continue more tomorrow," Ella spoke as she set the weapon she used back on the racks. However, she kept her personal weapon strapped to her body.

The girls left the hall while Finn and Hal began gathering the weapons they had strewn about the floor as they tried out different ones. "I still don't understand what a 'Jackelope' is," he muttered as he shook his head.

"It's a type of rabbit with horns like an antelope. It is rumored to be a myth, I believe," Finn replied like he was reading from a dictionary. "I think it was meant to be an insult."

"I'm sure it was, but I am not sure how it applies and why it would be so bad. She must not know we have such an animal here, the Lielmär, an extraordinary animal. Either way I do enjoy that Shifter's insults," he mused quietly to himself with a smile.

CHAPTER FIFTEEN

EXHILE. THE LAND OF THE UNFORGIVEN DEAD.

"**H**ello, my pets." *She* sauntered in through a black tunnel doorway and into the cave. It had not been there before, but what had been a solid rock wall a moment before stretched tall revealing an opening then closed just as she stepped through. *She* trailed a hand along the rough reformed wall. Eyes of red glinting in the rising darkness—the Droch-Shúil—followed closely behind her, wrapping its smoky tendrils around her body as she moved. "You have been quite busy during your stay here with me. Contacting whoever you can reach out to, making new friends. Tell me, have you found the Sol-lumieth? And that Ferrishyn warrior, isn't he one of your kin?" *She* crooned then moved closer to the *Orchids* that stood together. "That was not wise. Or was it? Perhaps your cunning will be the end of me." Slowly, *She* walked in front of each of them as they approached in an informal line. *She* continued to trail her delicate and thin fingers along the shield of energy that contained them. "Perhaps it will all work out perfectly." *She* laughed with disdain. Her eyes were wide and knowing, the blacks of her pupils swallowing any color remaining in her irises. *She* could cross the barrier if she chose to, but there were other plans taking shape in her mind.

The *Orchids* remained still and quiet, watching her, awaiting her next move. Except for the two women with the most to lose—Eva and Cley-una. Each of them started forward, but caught themselves. *She* waved her finger in the air. "Tsk tsk, don't dare to hope, ladies," *She* sneered. As if hearing their unasked questions, *She* smirked in their direction. Closing her eyes, she breathed deep, absorbing their barely contained fear as it leaked out of them little by little. Her eyes flashed open as she reveled in what she was about to do.

"What do you want with us?" Cley's husband, Dy'lánd, once a fierce warrior, now captive in Exhile, stepped forward with his arms crossed over his chest.

She studied him. "You are a brave and delicious one, aren't you?" Moving in his direction, "Because you asked so nicely, I will tell you." Her smile grew feral and her eyes narrowed, removing the whites of her eyes and leaving only the black. Her voice turned grave and held an edge that evil balanced precariously upon. "My plan for you is simple: I had you killed and brought here to my domain. I contained your souls and gathered you so that you would not pass on to the In-between. That part was all really too easy. Now..." *She* looked them over hungrily, licking her bottom lip. "Now, the time is almost precise to glean your magical essence straight from your souls."

Many of the *Orchids* inhaled sharply. "It is not possible!" Tylna the elderly Faerie with the blue tinted hair hissed as she made her way to the front.

She laughed. "Oh, I assure you it is."

"Why? Why would you do this?" Cley-una cried out.

Eva gasped. "To enter Alandria," she strained out a whisper.

"Very good, Highness. You are more than just a pretty face," *She* mocked with a hint of jealousy.

"But you are dark. How can you sustain the light that make up our souls?" one of the Shifters asked from the side.

She glared in his direction. "I no longer want to share with you. Perhaps I will simply show you," she snarled.

Closing her eyes, *She* placed her palms flat against the energy barrier separating her from the *Orchids*. *She* took three deep breaths and began to chant. Her voice was guttural and deep. The words were foreign to the Alandrians and sounded ancient. Where she stood it was calm, but within the containment the air grew thick. Wind thrashed around the enclosed area, throwing their hair and clothing all about. It began with low moans and whines, but soon several of the *Orchids* were screaming. Dark energy swirled around each member. Red eyes pierced that darkness as the Droch-Shúil gave it direction. As it touched them, it leached out and stole remnants of their souls, the very essences of their current presence. If it continued, however long it would take, the *Orchids* would cease to exist—their souls disseminated.

To their surprised relief, *She* spoke a word and everything immediately ceased. The darkness stopped moving. The Droch-Shúil retreated, their souls still intact, the *Orchids* stunned with shock and fear.

She soaked up the bit of energy she had taken from them. Her body was aglow from ingesting the purity of its life for a brief moment, before the darkness within her digested and tainted it, giving her evil a deeper shine as if kissed by hell itself. *She* laughed loud and deep from her core, her head thrown back, power flooding her with a temporary burst of strength. "I must test the limits of this." *She* looked back to the *Orchids*. "You know what is coming. There is no escape. I will return and then I will finish this." Without another word, she turned back to the part of the cave wall she had entered through, now closed again. She placed her hand barely even upon it, flicked her wrist, and a doorway yawned effortlessly open for her. The Droch-Shúil trailed behind her, a train of creeping darkness with eyes burning red.

The *Orchids* stood stunned, their faces revealing their despair. However, there were two mothers whose eyes gave no quarter to despair. There was still hope.

CHAPTER SIXTEEN

EHSMIA. THE HOME OF THE HIDDEN PEOPLE.

E veryone was gathered in the Ehsmian Great Hall. As Kaeleigh walked in, she surveyed what appeared to be a full house. It looked like part of the mountain was carved out to fit a cathedral-style building smack in the middle of it. It was cavernous, similar to the other rooms that they had been in, but this one was spectacular. Yes, the walls were still sealed packed dirt the color of dirty rust, but there was something sparkling all the way up to where the pinnacle of the room met. When the firelight from the many wall sconces on each side of the room flickered, the diamonds in the walls would sing the chorus of their song and shine in magnificent unity. There was a heavy reverence, thick with sacred tradition and magic that rested, but it wasn't judgmental or pompous. Instead, it felt welcoming and peaceful. The way tradition full of history should feel—inviting, asking, welcoming you to be a part of it.

"Is this like a church?" Chel whispered to Kaeleigh, who only shrugged with her mouth open and eyes wide with wonder.

"This is the Great Hall," Ella began, "where most of our traditions and sacred gatherings that involve everyone in Ehsmia happen. It is also used for banquet meals when we are celebrating or having honored guests."

"Who are you welcoming, Cinderella?" Metrí asked, her face wearing a mask of pure enchantment.

Ella scrunched up her nose in confusion. "I am not sure who Cinderella is, but tonight we are welcoming you," she said with a smile as she gestured around to all them.

"Oh wow," Metrí and Chel spoke at the same time. Kaeleigh looked down with a slight blush creeping up her neck and squeezed her hands nervously, not wanting to be in the spotlight. She sensed him before she looked his way. His presence was soothing; she could almost feel his hand on her wrist sending waves of peace through their connection. In reality, he was at the other end of their small entourage, too far to touch. When she did turn to casually look his direction, she couldn't help but be snared in his deliciously warm eyes. Her breath hitched and she turned back to the room. She would rather face a crowd of strangers at that moment than face what she was seeing in Daegan's eyes. The crowd was staring at her with curiosity, but the other... he was staring with an intensity that only continued to add confusion and stir chaos within her soul—not too mention those pesky butterflies in her stomach.

"Follow me." Ella waved at them as she walked toward the other end of the room which had a window-type opening in the wall. It opened up to look out at the entry that they had walked in upon when they entered Ehsmia. It was a gorgeous view. She could sit and stare for hours and never get bored admiring it.

"Please take your seats here at this table." Ella gestured at the table now in front of them. "Our meal will be served shortly." She sat at a seat next to the head of the table. There were a few others already seated, scattered amidst the settings along the table. It was not a formal event, but it looked lovely and planned out just the same. Kaeleigh walked past the table right up to the hole in the cave wall to admire the view. When she looked out she realized that they were actually higher up than she had been before. She had noted on their way to the Great Hall that it seemed they were walking uphill, but she didn't think it had been that high. They were easily three stories off the ground. Looking out over the grounds below, it looked like the Garden of Eden.

"It's amazing," Kaeleigh said with awe as she turned back to Ella and everyone still standing behind their chairs, obviously waiting for her.

"Thank you," the Elder Arileas said as he came walking up behind the other tables, making his way to what must have been his place at their table. "It is what home should be... to me. I am glad you appreciate it." He nodded his head toward her. Kaeleigh smiled at him then returned her gaze out the window. She extended her hand up and through the window. *Through?* With confusion etched on her face, she reached her hand once more tentatively where she had assumed glass was.

"What?" she asked out loud as she continued to feel through—not through, but into. "I can put my hand through it, but it doesn't actually go *through* it. It's like there is still something there as a barrier, but it's not liquid. What is it?" She turned to Arileas.

"There is no name for it in the modern language of the mortal realm, but it is essentially an energy that is made viscous—not liquid nor solid—infused with magic, of course," he said with a wink.

"Of course," Kaeleigh said almost with a giggle. The things magic could do that she hadn't thought of made her feel light and full of possibilities. "Will I be able to learn to do things like that...with magic, I mean?"

"Of course. It is in your blood. Hunter was the one who instructed me on how to accomplish it. You just have to find it, within yourself." He gently led her back to the table by her elbow. "Come, let us eat."

They ate in silence for a short time, sating the ravenous appetites they had gained from training. Kaeleigh and her friends were spread out amongst the Ehsmia and it made her smile to see everyone getting along, and to find some peace even if for a short time. They were safe. They were taken care of, and they were finally getting some answers.

"Elder Arileas? Would you mind updating me as to what has transpired in Adettlyn?" Aidón asked.

After swallowing a bite of his food, Arileas nodded at Aidón. "Yes, and may I say it is a pleasure to see you again, Lord Aidón." Arileas inclined his head to the Elf, who had once been titled as king-in-fact for a short time of Adettlyn. "I am most happy to see that you are well again and once more fully yourself."

"As well as I, sir, thanks to my lovely grandniece, Kaeleighnna, and her friends." Aidón inclined his head to them all. Kaeleigh blushed slightly at the compliment but turned back to her food. "I remained in that place of darkness for too long." Sadness passed through his eyes, but he did not dwell there. Instead he looked to the Elder for news of the present and hopefully a glimpse of the future.

"Adettlyn has been under the rule of Syén—this, you knew. What he does not yet realize, or perhaps he does, is that he is also under the rule of Maleina of Elnye. She has plans that are vast and unknown." Arileas suddenly looked aged as he thought. The lines around his eyes deepened and the shadows behind his eyes darkened. "She has managed to gather not only her own fleet of Ferrishyn to bend to her will, but she has also created allegiance within each of the territories except Ehsmia, as she cannot find it to this day much to her diligent seekers' attempts. She is in league with the darkness to an unsettling depth: the Droch-Shúil, the Ónarach—as you saw—and I fear that she is somehow even working with forces within the realm of Exhile."

Gasps came from around the table. Halister's face paled. He looked as if he would fall over. Chel, next to him, reached over and squeezed his arm, which he did not even acknowledge. No wink, no witty response, nothing. It struck fear in Kaeleigh as she watched the revelations hit him in ways the rest of them had no way of understanding.

"It is a blind spot in my sight. That is one reason I am believing she could be in league with Exhile... that and the *Orchids* are not in the In-between awaiting their rebirth as they should be." He sighed deeply.

"How do you know that, sir?" Kaeleigh's voice was small.

"I have a gift to communicate with those in the In-between. It is not something that is widely known," he said, acknowledging the wide eyes from even some of his own people. "There is a great disruption in the natural order of things. If the *Orchids* do not make their rebirth or are unable, Alandria may cease to exist. It was created by their joint energy. If their energy is not returned to it, I fear for the stability of our world." Tears formed in the old man's eyes. He looked directly to Kaeleigh. "Do you know... if that is where they are?"

Kaeleigh took a deep breath. Panic started to bubble in her chest. *Do I know?* She looked around the table, then paused at Daegan's eyes intently searching hers. It was unsettling, but not in a bad way; in fact, she felt a certainty there. It gave her peace and she suddenly remembered the dreams and visions she had over the last many years, well most of her life. Another deep breath. She nodded.

"I have seen them. At least, I think I have." Pausing, she took another breath and continued at Arileas's encouraging nod. "I have had dreams and I sometimes get visions. I have seen my mother. I've seen others with her. They seem trapped, unable to leave where they are. It is always the same, desolate, dark, and empty. Not like this." She gestured toward the light and warm atmosphere within the expansive room they were presently in. "It's dark, dangerous, and lonely... and there is someone else. Someone that is keeping them there. I can't ever see who it is, but their presence is heavy, oppressive, and cold." Kaeleigh didn't even realize that she was shedding tears of gold as she spoke. She could feel the despair and the anguish that she had woken up feeling for so many years. Beginning to be able to vocalize what she had felt, and realizing that there was actually a reason for it, lifted a weight she had carried for most her life.

Arileas wore a slight look of shock upon his face. The news was not what he had expected. "Are you sure? They are all together?" He barely waited for her nod before he stood up from his seat and began to pace in front of the window. "How? How did she accomplish that? Why can I not see them? This is disturbing. The ramifications are..." He paused then shouted, "They are not to be there!" A flash of energy mixed with anger jolted everyone in the room.

"Sir? Where are they?" Kaeleigh interrupted his burst timidly.

He turned toward her and looked to them all with a grave expression. "Exhile. They are trapped in Exhile." A pin could drop and no one would hear it in the deafening silence of the room. The air was thick and all breathing ceased. Time stood still if for only but a moment. Then chaos ensued. Everyone began talking at once, theorizing hypotheses of "how" and "why," devising plans of what could be done. Daegan stood, causing everyone around him to suddenly still at the sight of him and the weight of the calming energy he was putting forth. He looked to Arileas. "I have heard them. They have spoken to me as you said before. I will go. Perhaps I can find a way to set them free. I am willing to do whatever is required."

Arileas stared in return for longer than what was comfortable, not in challenge but more in examination. "That is the next step, yes, but not yet." *You must be set free to travel undetected into that realm. I must find a way to sever your ties to Maleina completely or it will all be for not.* Arileas spoke into Daegan's mind. Daegan nodded his understanding.

"I want to go too!" Kaeleigh declared confidently, standing and looking at Arileas.

"No!" Daegan said flatly. Kaeleigh almost buckled under a sudden force of pressure upon her shoulders. She placed her hands on the table, possibly so she would not succumb to it. It was powerful. It wanted her to relent. She refused and pushed back with her own energy as she raised her eyes, filled with determination but also anger that he would use his magic against her. Glaring at Daegan, she threw her energy at him and found a slice of satisfaction that he flinched under the spark of her magic that hit him.

The air crackled with the intensity of their energy. Arileas watched them both with intense study. Everyone else seemed unsure what to do, but couldn't keep from watching.

Arileas interrupted the tension. "Yes, she will go. You will need her. You will need each other." He paused. "Now, release it." It was not a request. The air cleared remarkably fast and everyone took a deep breath. "Sorry," Kaeleigh mumbled as she looked around briefly and took her seat.

"No," Daegan said, looking at her but directing his words at the Elder. Then he turned and stormed out of the Great Hall.

Silence was present for several minutes.

"So he's kind of scary intense," Metrí muttered to no one in particular, but Chel responded, "Oh, girl, you have no idea."

CHAPTER SEVENTEEN

Kaeleigh couldn't believe how Daegan had stormed out of the Great Hall the night before. She had never felt his power used against her before. Well, she took that back, it wasn't *against* her. She knew he would never hurt her. It was more him trying to dominate and tell her what to do by using great power. That was almost worse. It infuriated her. She couldn't sleep. She had tossed and turned most of the night, agitated by the dictating ass he had been. But then, almost as quickly, worried about what the near future was about to hold. Worried for Daegan, worried for the rest of her friends—old and new—and worried about what Maleina or whoever was behind all of it was doing to the *Orchids*.

In the morning light that filtered through the canopy of trees overhead, she took a deep breath and inhaled the soothing currents of energy sifting off the little river that flowed through Ehsmia. Kaeleigh sat under one of the large trees by the bank of the river. She watched the vibrant schools of fish as the sparkles within the water glimmered in her eyes. She watched as the smallest beings of Alandria flew by her and flitted about. There was a beauty here in this place that could not be described. It was more than what the human eye could behold, and the brain could process. It was mostly a feeling and an energy that could be absorbed into the very fibers of one's soul. It merged with who you were and the magic you possessed. Kaeleigh found it refreshing, and all she wanted to do was bask in it for all eternity. But she couldn't, so she would take the few moments of peace that were offered her.

Raising her chin up to the warmth of the sunlight, she closed her eyes and simply *felt*. It wasn't long before she sensed a shadow creep over her face, her peace interrupted by a presence that was almost as familiar as her own. "Pull up a root. It's quite comfortable." She smiled, then finally squinted her eyes open as he sat next to her.

"I was looking for you," Finn said quietly. "Are you all right?"

Kaeleigh gave a small smile and a nod to her friend. She had missed simply hanging out with him the way they used to back in her apartment in the mortal realm, but that was another life ago.

"Yeah, I'm fine. Just thinking. I needed some time to myself, ya know?"

"I figured, but others were wondering where you were, so I thought I'd check on you." He took a look around the place they sat. "It really is something else here, isn't it?"

Kaeleigh nodded. "Had you really never been here before?"

Finn shook his head. "Nope, I spent most my days in Adettlyn, serving the king—your grandfather—or out on missions..." Finn looked sad for a moment.

Kaeleigh looked over at her friend. "I'm so sorry, Finn, I forgot that you worked closely with him, too."

Finn nodded. "I spent a lot of time on errands for him and trying to stay undercover." He continued speaking more honestly than he ever had with Kae about his past. "A lot was happening in Alandria at that time, much as it is now, but it was more underground and concealed than it is now. Things are now coming into the light." Finn picked some grass blades and began to split them one by one. He squinted up into the light and looked at the walls within Ehsmia. "Do you think that's where most of them live?" he said, nodding his head in the direction of the little openings in perfect lines that ran up the sides of the walls surrounding the entire entry of Ehsmia.

"Yeah, I think so." She also looked up in their direction. "I never see anyone in them though. Maybe there aren't actually that many of them. It's very mysterious," she said with a small smile. "Are you okay, Finn? Are we okay? I haven't really gotten a chance to talk to you since"—she paused—"since the other day."

He smirked, hiding emotion. He looked away and then back at Kaeleigh. "I'll be fine, Kae. I've done many things with my life. Some good and some I deeply regret. I'm sorry about what happened at the training hall. And I know I said it before, but I can't tell you how sorry I am about not being honest with you about who I was, who you were, that you had a grandfather... all of it." Finn's voice cracked and he looked down at the blades of grass in his hands.

Kaeleigh grabbed his hand and squeezed. "I know you are. We can't change that now, but I do forgive you. You are one of my best friends, Finn." Kaeleigh breathed in the soothing air around her. "I know things won't be the same as they were... probably ever again, but know that you will always have a piece of my heart and a place in my life." She started to pull her hand away, not wanting to give him more than a you-are-just-my-friend hand hold and confuse the situation again. She knew now, for certain, he was not the right path for her. She hoped he felt the same way, but when he refused to let her hand go, she wasn't sure.

Finn moved to where he was directly in front of her so she would have to look him in the eyes. "Kae, listen to me. It was unfair of me how I made you feel. I realize now, I feel for you what you felt for me all along. I was too close to remember why I was there and what I was supposed to be focusing on. I had just been sent from my home and I was angry." He looked out to the water below them, then back up at her with a twinkle in his eyes that she had seen there before. She wasn't sure where he was going with his next words, but she liked seeing the sparkle of hope in his eyes. There had been too much despair and pain for too long. Finn started once again. "Did you know before I left to be your guardian, one of my secret missions was to seek out and gather the Twined with Ella? It was a long time ago. I forgot how much I loved finding them and teaching them about who they could be."

"Oh, Finn..." Kaeleigh started in with a guilty voice before he stopped her.

"No, Kae, I am not telling you that to make you feel bad. I wouldn't be part of who I am today and you wouldn't be a part of me had I not gone to the mortal realm with you. I do not regret any of my time with you. I deserved to have been banished, but I did miss the Twined and..." He paused with a sheepish look on his face that Kaeleigh for sure had never seen.

"Ella." Realization had dawned on Kaeleigh as he was talking. "Do you love her?" No jealousy, no regret at letting him go, simply curious as his friend.

Finn looked out, then back to Kaeleigh with a small smile on his face. He nodded.

"Does she know?"

"She did once upon a time, but I think she is hesitant because she knows my position with you and I'm sure she could sense my guilt and misplaced affection." Finn picked at the grass once more.

"She needs to know, Finn! I can tell her we are only friends."

"No, I will tell her when the time is right. I need to prove myself to her, to the Twined cause once more." Finn paused with a brief look of sadness and purpose mixed together. "I don't know if I will ever feel at home or feel the pull to Alandria as I once did. It saddens me, but it also makes me feel alive when I think of working at the camp in Tylínyth again. Ella has really done an amazing job there in my absence. I missed her."

Kaeleigh squeezed his hand before he let go. "I'm glad you told me all that. Thank you."

"No, Kaeleigh, thank you. Thank you for everything. For loving me and letting me be a part of your life. I will always, always be there for you when you need me to be. I have a feeling the Twined will be needed and in your service in the near future."

"It sounds like you are saying goodbye, Finn," she said with a curious and concerned voice.

"Not yet. But I feel I will be going a separate way soon. There is much training to do, and you really don't need me for that part. Not anymore." There was a temporary silence as they both knew what he said was true.

"So, last night was fun," Finn said with a way too big of a smile.

"Ugh, don't remind me."

"Really though, Kae, your power has grown considerably since you found it. You are one powerful girl," he said with a wink.

A wink! "Did you just wink at me? Where is my gloomy, moody friend, Finn?" Kaeleigh laughed.

Finn ruffled her hair and laughed back. "I don't know what you are talking about."

"What *are* you talking about?" Out of nowhere, Chel came up behind them. "I have been looking all over for you guys." She put her hand on a hip, then stalked toward them with a frown on her face. "Here you are having a little heart-to-heart or whatever and I am wandering around by my lonesome to find you!" Slightly put out, she plopped down next to them and looked at each of them. "What's going on here? Finn smiled at me," she said to Kaeleigh as she looked back and forth between each of them. To which Kaeleigh and Finn simply laughed.

"What's up, grumpy pants?" Kaeleigh asked Chel.

"I'm worried about Halister," she said bluntly. "He went for a 'walk' and I haven't been able to find him either. He seemed to be in a real bad way though. He is pretty beat up with all the new intel on his mom's betrayal. I mean wouldn't you be?" She was practically defending him, but to whom?

Kaeleigh placed her hand on Chel's. "Yes, I would be too. Come on, let's see if we can find him. Maybe Daegan can do some of his 'connection voodoo' stuff and find him." Chel looked at Kaeleigh funny, but let it go and helped each other up. Finn walked with them for a bit, but Kaeleigh spotted Ella out of the corner of her eye watching them, and apparently so did Finn. He looked to Kaeleigh, who smiled.

"I'll catch up with you guys a bit later." Finn put his hands in his pockets and turned the other direction toward an opening in the wall. "Oh, and Chel?" He looked back at the girls. "You could find people faster if you learned to use your nose." He turned and jogged over to where the lovely white-haired Ehsmia Faerie stood.

Chel scrunched her face up, "We could've used his help, but whatever." She rolled her eyes. "Use my nose!" she grumbled sarcastically under her breath.

Kaeleigh grabbed her arm within her own. "Chel, he will be all right. We'll find him."

Almost to the other side of the entry into Ehsmia, where they first entered, Kaeleigh could tell Chel was not only worried, but starting to get pissed too. Laying her hand on Chel's arm, she tried to give her friend comfort.

"We'll find him, Chel. I'm not concerned about that, but I am a little confused at your reaction. What's up? Do you like him?"

Chel crossed her arms in defiance and turned up her nose. "I am simply a concerned citizen. Sure, I like him, who wouldn't—have you met him?"

Kaeleigh simply leveled a knowing look at her friend and crossed her own arms waiting for her friend to spill it. She would wait quite a while if she had to. This was the most time they'd had to themselves in a long time.

Chel rolled her eyes and sagged her shoulders, dropping her arms in defeat. "Fine. There might be something about him that is capturing my attention, but it's probably nothing more than my ability to admire fine art," she said with a twinkle in her eyes. "Plus I still have Samuel waiting for me at home—at least I think I still do," Chel added thoughtfully with a slight frown.

"Kaeleighnna, would you and your friend please come to the Great Hall? I have something to show you. Could you also retrieve Daegan from the training tent?" Arileas called from somewhere and nowhere all at once. The girls both looked around, unable to see where his great voice was booming from. Seeing some of the other Ehsmia not reacting at all to the voice, Kaeleigh looked at Chel with confusion.

"I guess we're being paged," Kaeleigh giggled.

"I guess I'm the 'friend' then, since I heard it too," Chel grumbled. "I always thought when it came down to it, I would be the superhero and you would be my loyal sidekick. Oh, how the mighty have fallen," Chel elbowed her friend in the ribs and took off before Kaeleigh could grab her playfully back.

Kaeleigh caught up to Chel quickly. "I bet Hal will be there when we get there. You know how he hates to miss out on anything."

"Go get your warrior, I'll meet you there." Chel winked and stuck her tongue out at Kaeleigh before she ducked off in the other direction.

My warrior? Of course, Kaeleigh had thought of both Finn and Daegan as *hers* along the journey. But it sounded different when it came from someone else, even Chel.

CHAPTER EIGHTEEN

Kaeleigh walked into the training arena where they had practiced earlier to find it almost empty. Almost... except the one Ferrishyn she happened to be looking for. His back was to her, but she knew he was aware of her presence.

"Why, Daegan?" Kaeleigh slowly approached him. His shoulders stiffened. She didn't need to explain her question; he knew exactly what she asked about.

Without turning toward her, he sighed and hung his head for just a moment before looking up at the point in the ceiling where all the sides of the large expanse came together. "That should never have happened. There is no excuse for my behavior. I... I am truly sorry, Kaeleighnna."

Kaeleigh was now right behind him. "But why, Daegan? Why were you trying to force me to back down?"

"I... I can't protect you if I am not fully focused on what I'm doing. If you're there, with me... in that place... I can't..." His head was bowed and his breathing labored.

She lightly placed a hand on his back. He flinched. Kaeleigh pulled back a fraction before he whispered, "Do not go... please."

Taking that as an invitation, she moved both hands to his shoulders, simply resting them there, while individually they took shallow breaths. Neither spoke. There was a slight tremble in Kaeleigh's hands when she ran them slowly from his shoulders down over his arms all the way to his hands. Neither breathed. Her own hands rested on his before she moved them underneath, lacing her fingers with his, holding them for a moment before gliding her hands back up his arms. Suddenly overwhelmed with emotion, Kaeleigh wrapped her arms around his stomach from behind and held tightly to him. An awkward moment passed before she felt his hands cover hers where they gripped his shirt at his stomach.

"I remember being held only as a small child. It is... nice," Daegan said almost at the level of a whisper. Kaeleigh's heart broke and gripped him tighter. Then he stiffened, pulling her hands and arms away from him slowly. He stepped out of her embrace, putting distance between them.

Kaeleigh straightened her shoulders and held her chin high. "Don't do this. Don't shut me out, Daegan."

"It is better this way." He turned partially back toward her. His eyes were guarded, his expression hard.

"Why?" Kaeleigh's voice rose.

"I cannot be the one for you. I need to protect you. That is my promise, that is my oath."

"Protect me from who?" she ground out of her teeth.

"From the Droch-Shúil... from Maleina... from *me*." It would have been easier if he had shouted at her. It would have justified her, but the stillness of his voice, flat and void of emotion, infuriated her.

"I'm not *asking* you to protect me, Daegan. But I am asking you to open up to me, to not push me away from you." Her voice lowered. It was almost pleading. "I don't want to be away from you. I want you!"

Daegan looked her in the eyes, searching as deep as he could see. He saw in her his equal match, a partner, but also something he could destroy. That was unacceptable. "I feel crazy in my head around you—I do not know if what I feel is from you or because of you. I cannot think. I am not free from the darkness inside me. It is a danger to you. I am a danger to you!" His voice raised, he paced with his hands on top of his head, fingers fisting through his hair. He stopped only to see her begin to walk out, anger mixed with pain etched in her face and tears threatening to spill from her eyes. He had hurt her. He meant to push her away. Make her angry enough to keep her distance, but never hurt her.

"Kaeleigh, wait. Kaeleighnna!"

She didn't stop. Just before she got to the exit, he grabbed her arm. She spun and he pulled her none too gently back to his chest, holding her tightly in place. Kaeleigh wouldn't look him in the eyes. She couldn't or she would lose it.

He reached out and tipped her chin up with his finger so he could look into her beautiful, otherworldly green eyes that brought him to his knees.

"Kaeleighnna, please understand. It is not that I do not want you. I do. I want you, more than anything I have ever wanted before. That is why I cannot." His eyes grew sad.

One of her hands made its way up to the neck of his shirt. She played with the string there for a second while searching his eyes. Her fingers moved up his neck and to his cheek. He gasped at her attentions. "You distract me. I am not just the warrior when I am with you, but a man. We are about to enter danger unlike any we have seen so far and I need to know you are safe at all times."

"It won't matter if I'm with you or not, I am not going to be safe. This is war, Daegan. It is dangerous. Even more reason to grab hold of the things that are important. The things that give us something to fight for. The people that give us hope."

"No. I will not see you risk your life because of my own selfish desires, my weakness." He gently pushed her away from him. His breaths came deeply.

"That is not a good enough reason, Daegan. I'm going to risk my life with you or without you," she resolved with a whisper.

"I cannot lose you," she heard him whisper. "I have lost those I have held closest to me. They get taken away from me. She always took them from me. She will do it again," His voice cracked, choked with emotion.

Kaeleigh moved back to him. Just then she realized how broken he was... how lonely he had been. The self-inflicted isolation simply to protect everyone else, but also himself. Reaching up, she pulled his face down toward hers. She looked him in the eyes. Strongly and confidently, she spoke to his soul. "Not this time. This time we do it together. This time we fight back." Then she kissed his lips brazenly with all the love she had within her, desperate to unleash it into his parched soul.

Daegan hesitated as the explosion of Kaeleigh's love blasted through him like a bomb. Kaeleigh sighed as his strong arms pulled her up into himself. He kissed her back and his returned passion washed over her, a passion he had been waiting to release his whole life. He held her tightly to him; she fit within his arms, against his body, like she was made for him. One of his hands found its way up her spine and held her at the base of her neck, the other secured against her lower back. Their mouths moved in sync as if they had been kissing forever. For the first time, he felt a hope that only love brought. They would fight, but they would fight together. She made him stronger. Her love and confidence made him feel invincible. With her, he realized, he could be the Ferrishyn he was always meant to be. He was home.

CHAPTER NINETEEN

"**Y**ou have now all heard the prophecy. I have *seen* some truths and I would like to look deeply into it to hopefully show it to you as well." Arileas stood at the head of a long rectangular table. He addressed them all as equals, open to their opinions and suggestions.

The Great Hall was much more ominous without all the carefree chatting they experienced during their meals. It was still beautiful and the sparkles in the ceiling shimmered, reflecting a brightness into the room and giving it a white look even though the walls were the brown of a typical Ehsmian cave. Of those present, some were in chairs made of spindly branches yet sturdy in their makeup, and some sat several to a bench. The natural elements were a lovely juxtaposition against the brightness and the white wood of the table. The gathering consisted of those in Kaeleigh's group and the few Ehsmia that participated in their training sessions along with a group of others that Kaeleigh had not seen before. They reminded her of pious church elders with their heads held high; the only way for them to see you was by looking down their noses. Their dress was similar to Arileas's with long robes of various natural linens, but theirs revealed the stains of judgment and gave off the stink of intimidation.

Arileas did not seem fazed by their presence. They either answered to him, or he simply didn't care. Kaeleigh only cared for what Arileas had to say and it was obvious that he was in charge. In light of this, she refused to let their roving eyes of dissent seer into her skin. Kaeleigh envisioned a curtain around her mind, but also around her body until she didn't feel their eyes any longer. She could feel the magic buzzing under her skin so she knew something had happened. When she opened her eyes, she looked up to find not only one, but three pairs of those judgmental eyes watching her with haughty looks of surprise. She felt Daegan's eyes also on her, reading her, but his were not of judgment but deep care and concern.

"Well done, Kaeleighnna. You sensed a threat against you and you took care of it in a manner you thought appropriate. I assure you, these among me"—he gestured to the pious three—"are here at my request and are merely curious, though they may not come across that way. You always have the right to protect yourself as you feel needed. I have asked them here because they are among my greatest scholars of the ancient texts and have found a possible discrepancy amidst the written document of the prophecy we have."

At that, all eyes went to Arileas in confusion. Suddenly Kaeleigh's insecurities faded away and she was trying to understand why the shift in the atmospheric intensity.

"Elder, what do you mean there is a discrepancy?" one of the Ehsmia Kaeleigh hadn't met yet asked.

"I am not certain myself, but it appears there is a newly added variance in the script. The writing is the same as the original, which was scribed by one of the fallen *Orchids*. We possess the only copy and it has not been moved from where it was secretly kept." His face turned red with a sudden fury. "It is a sacred text!" Arileas shouted, pounding his fist on the table in an uncharacteristic show of emotion. "I will not apologize for my rage. Foul deeds are at work here. I am most disturbed at this revelation. My blindness to this is shameful." Arileas yelled with one hand on the wall as he looked out the opening at Ehsmia. Then his tone softened. "I know what I saw when I first received this ancient text. It is recollected in my memory from the day it was delivered, but I am an old man. It is possible that what is in my mind is not as it was originally delivered. I rely on these original texts of the past to ensure that which is in my mind is accurate. I do not know fully if I am in error or if the scroll we have is the one potentially polluted."

"What do you believe to be true, Grandfather?" Ella asked from several seats down.

Arileas's stern expression turned to a smile as he looked on his granddaughter. "You have always had a way of reminding me of truth. We should always believe our hearts and our spirits that guide us. I believe what is in my memory to be true and untampered with, but the fact still remains that we have or have had in our midst one who has betrayed us." With heartache etched on his face, he looked out the window, taking a moment for himself.

Everyone was silent, weighing the gravity of what was just said. "Sir?" one of the pious three spoke out. "You asked us to bring the scroll to read it against the original version in your memory to see where and why it might have been tampered with. Would you like us to reveal it now?"

The fact that he alluded to the original version being what was in the Elder's memory gained him points with Kaeleigh. He would not speak against the Elder and believed him solely on his word—that showed trust and loyalty to her. Still, she didn't like how he carried himself, like he was above everyone else. Perhaps he was, for all she knew of this realm, but she didn't have to like it. She let it go for now. Shaking herself out of her current train of thought, she watched as the three scholars hefted a large dusty and tattered scroll onto the table. At Arileas's nod, they proceeded to place it lengthwise on the table and began to unroll it. It was longer than Kaeleigh thought it should be for the prophecy she had heard the Elder speak. Rapt with attention, everyone sat at the edge of their seats, waiting to get a look at the ancient passage.

"There! That was not there before." Arileas pointed to the end of the written text. "I cannot read it, for it is warded with magic!" Arileas's shock was evident. "I need to think on this. I have not *seen* it."

As it slowly continued to unroll, Kaeleigh leaned forward. Her breath caught at the magic she could feel reaching off the scroll.

The words were not in English, but the strange symbols embedded on the page and etched into Alandrian history slowly rose off the page and rearranged themselves into words she could understand. It still didn't seem to be English, but Kaeleigh could understand it anyway. All except the last stanza, which remained indecipherable. She gasped when she realized she was reading it.

Chel looked up at her from her seat next to Kaeleigh and pulled at her sleeve. "What is it? Can you read it?" Kaeleigh only nodded with a baffled look on her face.

"All but the last bit," she replied quietly.

Halister had been quietly in attendance sitting across from Chel at the table. He had only acknowledged her with a slight smile when he caught her eyes questioning his state of well-being. Hal now stared at the ancient language with confusion etched on his face. "I cannot read it," he simply said. Then he looked up at Daegan, who seemed to be lost in his own head by the vacant expression he wore. Daegan shook his head and pinched the bridge of his nose as the onset of another headache began.

Arileas looked on with rapt attention as he watched the expressions of those all around the table. Something about others being able to read it must have been fascinating. Aidón, who had also been scarce since they had arrived in Ehsmia, looked on then back up to Arileas. "I cannot read it either. I was never the student as my brother was when it came to the ancient languages."

"Young Master Daegan, what about you? Are you able to decipher the ancient language?" Arileas asked.

The question made Daegan squirm. There was a struggle in his eyes but he refused to look at the text. There was determination in his demeanor. "I will not try with the darkness still attached to me for the safety of this place." He sighed in frustration. "I will not hold back my knowledge from you though. I am able to pick up quite a bit of it, or at least the essence of it, through Kaeleigh's emotions. She tends to broadcast quite loudly though she has been instructed not to." He looked at her pointedly with a scowl. Kaeleigh's eyes flashed to his sharply and though she was angry, she could see the growing struggle in his features. She took a moment and closed off her emotions and magical release of energy. He nodded at her that she had done it.

Arileas contemplated something as he looked to each of them. "I have foreseen this. I do not yet know what it will mean, but I want you to look at the document only and purposely open yourself to her... to Maleina." Daegan threw a look of questioning frustration at what the Elder was asking of him. "Show her," was the only command Arileas gave, but Daegan stared long at the Elder, reading his resolve. He relented with a nod.

Daegan took a deep breath and shut his eyes, moving closer to the table. Then he opened them upon the ancient text, absorbing it all into his mind. To his surprise he too could read the language. In his mind, he willed the prophecy to Maleina. He could almost sense her shock at him taking control of the connection—that he had figured out how to turn the tables on her—but her greed to know the entirety of the prophecy that had been hidden for too long outweighed her curiosity at this new discovery and how she could use it or how she could keep it from backfiring at her. Daegan could feel her greed, could feel her plans taking shape. He could feel her hatred for him and her desire for his power. *His power?* That was something he did not fully grasp nor took the time to weigh it in front of her. When he finished reading the scroll he prepared to shut her out with a final message that he hoped was loud and clear: *I WILL NOT BE USED.* In return, he *felt* almost as strongly as if he had heard it with his ears, her laughter born from evil itself. It sent chills up his spine.

Halister move up beside him and turned Daegan's face so that it was right in front of his alone and opened his soul to show his hurt, his anger, and his brokenness to his mother. He knew she would see him. He wanted her to see him, see what her quest for power had done to him and to their family—turned him against his own mother. Hal closed his eyes. So did Daegan as the connection was lost. Daegan looked back to Hal—his friend, his brother—and placed his hand on his shoulder. Words were not needed. Their bond was strong.

"This ends now." Arileas moved up beside Daegan. "May I?" the Elder asked, seeking Daegan's eyes, letting him feel his intentions. At Daegan's nod, Arileas placed his hands on the warrior's shoulders. Daegan stood taller than the Elder, but somehow Arileas managed to look straight into his face. Without breaking contact, Arileas addressed the others. "Join your magic, join your energy. We break the connection that binds Master Daegan to the evil within the Paladin."

Everyone gathered in close. There was nervous anticipation swirling about, but also confidence and strength from the Elder's magic that was contagious as it jumped from one to the next. Halister stood next to Daegan on one side and Kaeleigh flanked him on the other. She joined her hand with his infusing her magic directly with his. His fingers squeezed hers in response. A breeze began to blow in the Great Hall. The sparkles on the cavern walls flared in bright erratic sparks. Magic consumed the air, thick with possibility and hope.

"Release your magic. Sever the tie that binds." Arileas muttered a few words in the language of the Ehsmia. The words held weight and the power for freedom: *Thantül Kothnyte lan du illeyll.* "Daegan, you have the power within you to push her out. We are assisting, but it is you that must remove the anchor darkness holds inside you. She has no right to have this hold over you. FORCE her out!" Arileas's voice boomed in the room, echoing throughout the Great Hall, reverberating on every surface. Intensity exploded in the room.

Daegan's face was pinched as if in pain. Kaeleigh sensed he was on the edge of something, and she squeezed his hand again, reminding him she was there with him. Daegan threw his head back and roared, shaking everything in the room. His roar surpassed the shout of the Elder before him. It rattled each of their souls. It was the sound of bondage, pain, regret, humiliation, possibility, hope, and freedom all wrapped into one. It was terrifying and liberating.

There was an audible "snap" and then Daegan sagged to his knees, breathing deep, his chest rising and falling. Kaeleigh sank down beside him, still gripping his hand.

"You are free," Arileas whispered into the charged atmosphere. "You, young prince, are free."

"Yes. I can feel it," Daegan whispered as he caught his breath. "Thank you." Daegan breathed deep, relishing the freedom he felt.

The room was quiet as they watched Daegan recover. The air was thick with a multitude of emotions and spent energy. Kaeleigh beamed up at Daegan, her grin reaching her teary eyes. Daegan started to move in close to her face, hesitated for Kaeleigh's sake, then gave in to his heart's desire and pulled her into him. He lightly brushed her lips, but then Daegan growled and crushed his lips against hers in exclamation and freedom.

CHAPTER TWENTY

M etrí, quiet up until then, still not wanting to interrupt Daegan's newfound freedom, snuck up beside Arileas. She beckoned him down closer to her level and whispered, "So I'm hoping someone will explain what just happened later, but I'm curious about this prophecy. Is it possible to hear it, Elder Arileas, sir?"

"I have an idea, if you will indulge an old man for a moment." Arileas smiled conspiratorially at those still gathered. "Kaeleighnna, I would like to stretch your magic to see how you have grown."

Kaeleigh nodded and stepped up to where Arileas was standing. "What would you like me to do?"

"Instead of me reciting an old text, I would like to see if you are able to show everyone. There is something to experiencing an event firsthand as opposed to hearing about it, do you not think?"

"I am not sure how you want me to do that, sir. I did something similar once, making light in darkness to see, but I was able to envision it. I don't know how to project something I have not experienced myself." Kaeleigh scrunched up her nose in thought.

"No, that would be most difficult," Arileas said. He then turned to her right. "If you are able to channel the experience from me and push it into Kaeleighnna's mind, I believe she will be able to externalize the vision for us all to see."

Kaeleigh didn't even have to turn around to know that the Elder was addressing Daegan behind her. Who else did she know that could draw from others' feelings, emotions, and apparently images?

"Oh sure, why not? Easy peasy," Chel muttered under her breath sarcastically.

"I want to try. That is, if Daegan is willing to help." Kaeleigh turned to him with questioning eyes. He looked curiously at her with eyes full of love, then nodded his head.

"I will admit, I have not done what you are asking much, and only then it was attempted in smaller amounts of magic," Daegan spoke humbly. "If you are projecting your memories loudly enough, then I should be able to draw them out. I am more uncertain of pushing them into Kaeleigh's mind." He turned to her. "It will not hurt, that I am aware, but I have never tried to send that big of a vision before."

"Then we will learn and try together," Kaeleigh said matter-of-factly.

"As Chel said, 'easy peasy.'" Arileas winked at her.

"Let us begin. I will call the ancient words from my mind, releasing the magic of the event so very long ago." Arileas took a step or two back from the table. Everyone at the table watched him with bated breath, awaiting what might transpire.

He closed his eyes and spread his hands wide. The Elder began to emit a low hum that was melodic and even haunting. A light breeze playfully swirled about the Great Hall, tickling the ears of each individual there before it rested around Arileas. This breeze was different from the previous, more deliberate wind. The air in the room chilled and silence weighed heavy like a blanket upon them. The brightness of the hall began to dim, allowing the glimmers of the cave walls to shimmer even more like millions of tiny diamonds embedded into the walls. And the lanterns that were lit slowly dimmed to barely a flicker. With just enough light to see, a thin mist rose into the air. It took a few minutes for Arileas to be ready, but when he was, the energy in the room shifted and built to an intensity that was strong, though not frightening.

"Come, it is time," he said with his eyes still closed. He reached out to grab Daegan's arm.

Daegan gripped the Elder's arm in return. Daegan did not close his eyes, but he stared intently at Arileas as if through his eyes alone he could draw out the memories. Perhaps that was how it worked. The air in the Great Hall shifted once more. A crackle of energy pulsed throughout it, chasing the tails of the finicky breeze. A moment later, Daegan reached back and grabbed Kaeleigh's hand, pulling her close to where he and Arileas stood.

"Now, Kaeleigh," Daegan said barely on a whisper.

She turned so she faced the table and everyone that was waiting. Kaeleigh nervously clenched and unclenched her free hand over and over. She caught Chel's eyes and when she winked at her, Kaeleigh took a deep breath, believing she could do this, she would do this... show them Arileas's vision of the past. She nodded and closed her eyes. Kaeleigh could feel it channeling into her mind from Daegan. It was like she could individually pick out the different strands of energy in her head. This had gotten easier for her the more she practiced, but it was always people around her, not all in her head. She saw glimpses of Arileas's energy as it wafted in her mind on the color purple and then she could of course feel Daegan, his strand the most familiar of them all. This time, though, she noticed it was different. Before, it was blue tangled with wisps of black and felt murky and inky. This time it was a clear, brilliant deep shade of blue. It felt solid and whole. The result of his new freedom.

She took a deep breath and began to make sense of the disjointed pictures she was receiving in her mind. Her energy was stirring within her, building in her chest. It almost hurt, but mostly it was just pressure. She envisioned pushing her magic up into her mind, slowly and methodically gathering all the images and sorting them out like a puzzle. With great control she saw her magic pull the pieces together like a film strip and push it out of her mind. Kaeleigh felt a release. She knew it had worked. The confirmations of gasps from those in front of her helped too. Afraid to open her eyes, afraid she might lose it, she decided to trust her magic, trust her energy to finish what it began. Slowly opening her eyes, she saw what everyone else did. Like a movie, there was a vision playing out before them on the opaque screen of mist and fog. The image of Hunter stood in the air above the table. He looked much younger, but it was definitely him. Green eyes that she had recognized upon her first meeting with him were the same eyes that were now focused on another group before him in a very different land.

Arileas's voice reverberated through the room as he set the stage. He spoke the words and the cadence of a different time. It could also have been simply that it was a prophecy and the words flowed from him ensconced with a deep and ancient magic. It felt different than even what Kaeleigh had experienced in Alandria thus far.

It was a different realm, the one before Alandria was even a conceived thought. It was home, the land from which we came. The beauty of it, even more otherworldly than this one. It was peace, it was serenity, it was Lenoria. Until the time when the darkness slowly crept in and then was unleashed. It was forceful and destructive and swept across our land with a vengeance that no one expected and has not been seen since. The only escape was to flee or be destroyed. The death toll was horrific. However, there were those who were able to flee to other realms, including the mortal realm. The Elders—the Orchids as they were called—gathered to bring their power together, to unite as they sought answers... a way to save their people and their land. They could not. In their time of desperation, a prophecy was brought forth...

A storm of red stains the skies of Alandria.
The darkness brings cleansing to a world run thick with confusion and conspiracy.
Behold, a union of strength rises.
Mystery comes with strength and compassion.
The shadow gives way as the Orchids bloom.
Seats of power are set to the right,
As things once held in sleep and night
Have now crossed over.
Awake, Alandria!

The sword is upon you.
There is hope in the hidden,
Destiny revealed in the unknown.
Awake.

There was an abrupt silence followed once more by Arileas's voice as it echoed through the hall.

The Elder that delivered it was extinguished with his last words. His soul, sent to the In-between for rebirth, which he was. Your grand-father, you knew him as Hunter. We always knew him as Ryek Sayaelith of Lithnai, the king of not only Adettlyn, but the head of the Orchids in our mother realm. He was given the inspiration and the magic to create—using all of our combined power and energy—a portal that would simultaneously create a new realm that had never before existed. Alandria. It would be what Lenoria failed to be in the end—an oasis.

In Lenoria, the source of the darkness had been contained, as far as we knew. That realm, sealed off and destroyed by its own fire and darkness. We began again. To his, and all of our disappointment, darkness found its way in, once again, into the hearts of our people slowly saturating and growing until it could no longer remain hidden.

The vision blinked out as Kaeleigh and her Ferrishyn conduit released their hold on the Elder. Arileas began to look tired and even older, if that was possible. Daegan helped Arileas back to his chair. Kaeleigh looked to him, worry etched on her face. She felt fatigued and drained, but surprisingly, nothing like she had experienced before when she used that much magic. Kaeleigh wondered if it had to do with the vision not being her own and she simply functioned as the funnel, or if it was the fierce warrior who fed her the vision. She let him help her back to her chair, noting that he seemed unfazed from his part of what had just happened.

"Are you well?" Daegan asked her.

"Much better than before. Thank you." Kaeleigh then looked once more at Arileas. "Elder? Are you all right?"

"Yes, child. I will be replenished and fine in moments. I simply need to go sit in my garden and absorb life from the lovely Alandria. She heals me and rejuvenates me."

"So you were there? At the destruction of your other realm and the beginning of this one?" Chel asked.

Arileas nodded with a twinkle in his eyes. "Yes, I am quite old, eh, Chelnáh?"

The shock on Chel's face was priceless. Kaeleigh watched her friend try to recover. No one ever used her given name. Kaeleigh almost forgot that she had one.

"You know my name?"

"Indeed. I know your parents as well. Did you know that you were actually born in Alandria?"

Chel shook her head back and forth so fast, Kaeleigh worried it might fly off. "No. I mean I knew my parents are from here and left after Kaeleigh did, but I believed I was born on the outside." Her expression was curious, as though she was counting the years. "How is that? Because I am only a little younger than Kaeleigh."

"Actually, Chel you are older than Kaeleigh by no more than a few days." It was Ella, this time, that spoke. "Time moves differently—slower—here than in the mortal realm remember? Your parents adjusted to whatever age you would have appeared when you arrived in the mortal realm."

"Okay, that makes sense," Chel said, nodding her head, but her expression still held confusion. "It is just hard to grasp. I guess it doesn't really change anything." She looked to Kaeleigh with a smirk. "Except now it makes sense why I am so much more mature and responsible than you."

The room filled with light laughter, breaking up the intensity of the moment to everyone's apparent relief. "Of course, that's it!" Kaeleigh smiled at her friend and grabbed her arm, giving it a squeeze. She noted that even Daegan grinned at the humor of the moment.

After a moment or two of silence following the laughter, the three scholars put their heads close together and spoke quietly amongst themselves. They looked back to the Elder. "We will need to look at the scroll again and think on what the new addition could mean and how it could have come to be. Perhaps, the Sol-lumieth would join us, if she has the strength." They all looked at Kaeleigh simultaneously, expecting her compliance.

She looked to Arileas then to Daegan quickly, but their faces did not say anything so she assumed it was her choice. "Yes, I will do what I can to help."

They nodded.

Arileas stood with the assistance of Ella under his arm. "Might I suggest we take a short rest and gather again for the evening meal. We shall discuss more. For now, I need rest."

"Finn, would you help me get Grandfather to the garden?" Ella asked.

Finn quickly moved toward the Elder. He stopped at Kaeleigh's chair briefly and touched her shoulder. "You sure you're good, Kae?"

"Yeah, thanks, Finn. Please help Ella." Kaeleigh squeezed his hand on her shoulder before he pulled away.

After they had escorted Arileas out of the Great Hall, the scholars all started talking at once. Others around the table joined in and Kaeleigh, along with her friends, simply listened. Confused by what they were saying, she tried to keep up with them. The main thing she took away from their words was they were confounded as to how anyone could have retrieved the scroll from where it was hidden and alter it to the state it was now in.

"Do you think it was purposely given to Alandria in a shorter version to understand? Or are you saying you believe the Elder wasn't truthful long ago?" Chel voiced the thoughts that were being expressed on many of the faces around that table. There was a heavy moment of silence.

"No child, we are not saying the Elder was dishonest. More that a future was foreseen long, long ago and only part of the prophecy was given and transcribed for all of Alandria when they passed from Lenoria into this realm. The *Orchids* and those that traveled with them were deemed trustworthy with the future of the new realm. But, perhaps, it was King Ryek who saw something that would suggest to keep such truths hidden until an appointed time... this appointed time." The scholar with the long face, the pointy ears, and ethereal beauty in a nerdish sort of way spoke for all three of them. The others nodded their agreement. Kaeleigh felt a weight lift off her that they weren't going to have to debate the trustworthiness of one specific Elder. "The baffling part is that we have read this specific text before and witnessed that the new segments were not there before now." They all frowned, deep in thought.

"That, what we just heard, was similar to what Elder Arileas spoke to Daegan and myself when we visited here not too long ago, before Daegan went to the mortal realm in search of you, Kaeleigh," Halister said, thinking out loud.

Kaeleigh cocked her eyebrow with a questioning expression as she looked to Daegan. "I thought Maleina sent you after me."

"She did. They both did."

"Care to elaborate on that?" Chel joined in as if showing she was on Kaeleigh's side—not that there were any sides.

Daegan sighed and gave Hal an annoyed look. Hal simply shrugged, not bothered by it one bit. "I'll elaborate for him," Hal began. "Mother dearest sent us looking for information on the Sol-lumieth which she had gotten wind of somehow. We found Ella, who brought us here saying her grandfather was waiting to speak with this handsome lad next to me." He gestured at Daegan. "Arileas explained what the Sol-lumieth was and how he might go about finding her and that he should bring you here." Hal looked all around with his arms spread wide as if it was obvious that was what they had done. But they hadn't.

"Wait. Are you telling me that we were supposed to come straight here all along? That had it not been for the way we went, we wouldn't have encountered the Droch-Shúil in those caves? That we would never have gone to Elnye and had to be trapped in that detestable dungeon? That we could have avoided all encounters with that insufferable woman?!" Chel's volume rose as she vented her anger and fears from the last many days spent in this land.

Hal's face blanched at her fury. He looked quickly to Daegan and then to Kaeleigh and then to anyone else's eyes he could catch, searching for something, anything that could get him out of the hole he apparently dug for himself. He gulped audibly. "Chel..." he started, then his face fell.

"Yes, that is what he is telling you," Daegan intervened. "I had loyalties. I was unsure they were truly on the wrong side. I had considered all options. I did not plan on encountering all the dangers and injustices that you faced. I would change them for you if I could. I am truly sorry for that." Daegan came before Chel and kneeled in front of her. Tears now streamed down her face. "I was wrong. Can you please release Halister from this anger you now harbor?" His head was bowed.

"You do not want forgiveness for yourself?" she asked.

"No, it is not deserved. But Halister acted under my direction."

Chel took a deep breath, looked over to Kaeleigh, and then considered something. "Yes. Hal is forgiven... and so are you." Chel stood tall and wiped her eyes dry.

Daegan cocked his head and looked at Chel with thoughtful amusement and admiration at the notion that she could so easily forgive them both. "You are generous with your heart. Thank you."

Kaeleigh stepped forward. "What has happened has happened. It is done. We cannot change it. It happened for a reason; whether that reason was solely on you or not, we will never know. But it has changed us and made us stronger and more aware of who we are to this land. It has given us a reason to fight and to dig into what is happening to Alandria." She took a breath. "I'm seeing some things in this prophecy and have questions for Arileas and all of you." She looked to the scholars and then to the other Ehsmia.

"We will discuss it with him when he returns for evening meal," Líyl, one of the Ehsmia warriors replied above the others.

CHAPTER TWENTY-ONE

EXHILE. THE LAND OF THE UNFORGIVEN DEAD.

S he was there. Waiting. She shouldn't have to wait. Pacing in the tight space once more. It seemed that was all she did lately. Paced and waited on Maleina. Her hair wild with madness and entangled with strips of darkness. *She* was normally so controlled, but Maleina put her on edge. Absent-mindedly, she ran her hands back and forth across her stomach and down her legs, her fingers caressing the fabric. She still wasn't use to it. It had been centuries since she had a form—a body.

"What is taking her so long? She knows I do not like to wait!" *She* spat out as she turned to the darkness in the corner of the cave she called home. *Home?* It seemed she had one once before. She had no recollection of where it was or *when* it was, for that matter. Did she know people? Did she have loved ones? HA! The very thought was absurd and she shook it off with arrogant flourish.

"Maleina!" *She* called to the darkness as she ran her finger through a reflecting pool of the blackest water possible. It rippled in response, but stilled quickly as glass once again. Nothing. No response. *She* had called to Maleina quite some time ago, definitely sufficient enough for her to find a secluded place to speak with her.

"Incompetent woman!" she spat. "She had such potential to come along my side too. Pity," she whined as the darkness from the corner had slunk closer to her as a pet seeking attention. *She* beckoned it closer still to her and as it visibly nuzzled under her hand she crooned to it as an owner, as a lover. "I think she is losing her edge. Perhaps she is giving in to the side of the light or... OR..." She whipped around, her hair following as the end of the whip with a lash. "She is turning against me! Using my plans in her own hands! Ungrateful, weak-minded little witch! She has no idea what she is doing; what will happen once she has crossed ME!!"

She stared at the black water with a murderous glare, willing it to respond to her desires, her wishes. She could not yet leave her forsaken, desolate kingdom but she would find a way to enact her plan and execute her revenge. It was her entire means of survival.

"Maleina will pay for this!" *She* began to storm away when she heard the rippling of the portal waters.

"What is Maleina going to pay for?" A snide voice came filtering through the glasslike water turned mirror.

Stopping at the entrance of her chamber, she contemplated simply walking away and letting Maleina guess as to what her plan was. Instead she opted for civility. *She* may still be in need of the wretched Faerie yet.

"I called you quite some time ago."

"I was trying to manage my kingdom in this realm. There was some unease that needed... smoothing," Maleina said silkily.

"And did you *smooth* everything?"

"Of course. I am aware of everything happening in my territory and even beyond." Her tone hinted at something.

"I would have chosen another if I had suspected anything less. Now on to the matters at hand..." *She* paused, thinking over her next words. Shrugging to herself, she flipped her hand in the air as if flippantly deciding on a different dress to wear to a ball. "This will be your only warning, Maleina. If you betray me and take this plan into your own hands... well, let's just say that there are worse things than death. I am proof of that. You will be reaching for anything that will extend the mercy of your last breath, but will be unable to obtain it."

There was silence then a cackling from opposite the scrolling mirror. The anger etched on the evil woman's face would have melted the skin right off of Maleina's if she could have seen her. Luckily for her, she couldn't, at least not yet. "You think I would betray you... *YOU*? After everything you have done for me and the power you have bestowed upon me. I am faithfully yours, my lady."

A sneer spread across the woman's face. "When those who claim loyalty to me, when those whom I love refuse to communicate with me, what else could I assume? You will soon rule at my side. Do not give me a reason to doubt you again." *She's* own words were slippery and seductive. "When I call for you, my love, you WILL answer." *She* was a viper, ready to strike at a moment's notice. Her fingers drummed methodically on the edge of the dark basin, until she stopped and her eyes grew wide.

"Maleina, daughter of my heart, those who have put the rumor out there will be punished, of course, but I will need some kind of further assurance to show all that you truly are mine. Have you anything you are willing to offer me? Something of value you could prove your loyalty? Beloved, you are my daughter but I do not trust anyone, sadly not even you." She relished putting this pawn in her place.

There was continued silence as she awaited her slave's reply.

"Of course, my lady. I have something to offer you. How shall you retrieve it as we are not in the mountain of Gáraldrath?" Maleina asked hesitantly.

"You have more than enough power now and combined with mine, you do not need the portal within the mountain. I will give you the words to open a temporary portal through the scrying bloom. Simply insert it there, assuming it is not too large for the opening. But I'm sure you are powerful enough to accommodate that even if it was. Repeat after me..." *She* spoke a few words in a language that was familiar to the Faeries and yet much older, tainted and dripping with evil.

There was a momentary stirring in the black waters not made by the woman with eager anticipation in her eyes staring at her own reflection before it. Suddenly the fastened end of a chain necklace came straight out of the water. Grabbing the chain, she gave it a slight pull but not too much as the process was slower than she would like. Finally, the end of the necklace emerged from the dark water. It was a crystal—a white crystal with a swipe of blue through the center of it. It really was beautiful and she could feel the energy within it, but she did not quite understand the significance of it. She examined it for a moment to see if it would speak to her. Trying to coax the blue out of the crystal, she frowned as she could do nothing more than stir it. Before she could ask, Maleina's sultry voice came through the water.

"It is the essence of a Ferrishyn that I have been tracking."

"Why would I want a lowly Ferrishyn? What good is this to me? What foolishness is this!? Have you—" *She* was cut off by Maleina.

"No, you misunderstand, my lady. It is a piece of his soul; a piece of his very essence. You may track him or use him," she said smugly, loving that she had something that *She* didn't even seem to understand.

"Whose, Maleina? I tire of this game," she spat.

"The Ferrishyn called Daegan."

Another moment of silence that seemed to stretch the moment far longer than it was. And then... a throaty, deep laugh that echoed throughout not only the cave in the mountain reaching far beyond it, but also through scrying well straight into Maleina's chamber. When Maleina added her own haughty laugh, it felt as though an eruption of evil shook the atmosphere. Each laughing for different reasons.

"Well done, my love. This will suffice. The time is approaching quickly for our next move. Be available next time I call. We will proceed with our plans right on time." She touched the blackest water with only the tip of her black fingernail, but it severed the connection instantaneously.

❖❖❖

"I have her!" Cley-una shouted ecstatically. "After so many tries, I finally have her. Okay, okay, focus," she said to herself as she calmed herself down and slowed her pacing back and forth, wringing her hands anxiously. "Breathe," she whispered as she did so. "In and out. In and out. Okay, I am good now," she spoke serenely to Eva, who was standing next to her now holding her hand.

"Send her the message, Cley. Our time is running out." Eva didn't whisper but she spoke low enough that only a few nearby could hear her.

Cley nodded, bobbing her head swiftly. She closed her eyes tight, tuning out everything around her: the constant hum of low chatter, the bickering of the elderly Faeries, the deep slow breaths of her friend of many years standing at her side, the never-ending drip of water down the side of the cave wall. Peace. She needed to find that place of peace and connection where she could slide into the channel of energy that was specific to whoever it was she was making contact with. In this case, specifically, it was Kaeleigh.

"Kaeleighnna. Can you hear me?" Cley-una whispered gently into Kaeleigh's mind.

Surprised, Kaeleigh answered with hesitation, *"I hear you. Are you one of the Orchids?"*

"I am Cley, of the Orchids and a friend of your mother, Eva. I am also Daegan's mother."

Kaeleigh gasped. *"Oh! Please tell her I am here. Should I find Daegan? He is near."*

"You have no idea how tempted I am, but there is no time. I will try again with him. Tell him to be open." It was quiet so Cley-una continued. *"The woman who holds us in Exhile is about to do some-thing, but we do not know on what scale. You must tell Arileas it is time for you to meet the hidden. Do you understand?"*

"Yes, but we are currently with the Ehsmia, where they are hid-den."

"No, child. Tell him: it is time for you to meet the hidden. He will know."

"Okay."

Cley-una could tell Kaeleigh was confused, but it would have to be enough. *"I have to go. Take care of him please."* Cley tried not to let Kaeleigh hear the emotion in her voice as she was about to lose contact with her only connection to her son.

"I will. Please tell my mother I love her. Cley?"

"Yes?"

Cley-una could barely hold the connection open to hear Kaeleigh's last words, but she managed to just before the presence of the woman of the mountain, the mistress of darkness, made her way closer to their prison they called home for the last many years. What Kaeleigh said gripped her heart with more hope than she thought could be contained. Tears streamed down her face, but hope beamed through her eyes as she pushed her thoughts into Eva's mind as she gripped her hand tightly.

"We are coming for you... for all of you. You will be free. Tell the others. Tell my mother: I'm coming for her. You will be free."

CHAPTER TWENTY-TWO

EHSMIA. THE HOME OF THE HIDDEN PEOPLE.

I t had been most of the day that Elder Arileas was in the gardens nearby the entrance in Ehsmia, soaking up the energy of the mountain. The garden was really just a condensed area of the large open atrium-style entrance that they all had walked through. It was lush and quite purposely overgrown. It was an oasis unto itself even amidst the serenity that was Ehsmia. Kaeleigh had stopped to let Arileas know what had happened when she had gone back to her room to rest for a bit. Arileas sat on a bench that practically blended in with all the greenery surrounding it. He did not seem surprised the *Orchids* were now confirmed to be in Exhile. What did surprise him, however, was that it was time to meet the "hidden." He frowned and grumbled to himself so low even Kaeleigh couldn't decipher what he was complaining about. She excused herself, not wanting to stick around. After all, she was just the messenger in this case and did not even know who she was supposed to meet, nor what their value was to the future of their cause.

After another day of training and learning to use both magic and weapons, Chel and Kaeleigh both had gone back to the Great Hall to help prepare the tables for the evening meal. Chel was in a mood, apparently. She set dish-wear down as if it bit her.

"What's up, Chel? You seem, um, a little agitated," Kaeleigh asked quietly to not draw too much attention to her friend as they were in the presence of the few others that also helped.

Chel snapped her head up. She looked at Kaeleigh then back down to the silver that was apparently causing her much grief. "It's nothing, Kae, don't worry about it." She continued to set plates down with such force Kaeleigh was surprised they didn't break or at the very least make a loud racket.

Okaaaayyyy. "Well, breaking the dishes isn't going to help, and something is obviously wrong. Why won't you tell me?" Kaeleigh pouted her lip, trying to get at least a laugh out of Chel if not more.

"Nice. Very mature, Kaeleigh." Chel rolled her eyes.

"Is it Hal? Didn't you guys talk?"

"No, I mean yes, we did talk. No, it's nothing to do with him, at least not directly." Chel sighed. "I haven't shifted yet."

Ahhh. Realization dawned on Kaeleigh. "It'll happen when it's the right time, Chel, please don't worry. I hate to see this eating away at you."

"It's upsetting. Apparently, it is something I *should* be able to do and yet I can't!" Her voice started to rise, and Kaeleigh moved closer. "I mean, look at you. Your powers are growing and you are getting more control. I'm learning to fight, but that's it! I have no idea how to access my 'inner animal' or whatever it's called and you know I hate feeling like I *can't* do something. UGH!!" Chel threw a spoon down on the ground with a clatter. Her shoulders slumped in defeat.

"I have to say, I'm impressed with how long it's taken you to freak out about this," Kaeleigh said with a sly smirk.

"What?" Chel shrieked.

"Well, I know you, Chel. This would be bothering me a LOT and I knew it bothered you. I was just waiting for you to realize it yourself or to finally lose it."

"I am not freaking out OR losing it!" she practically shouted.

Kaeleigh put her hands out to pacify Chel's wrath. "Listen, I'm only saying that I am impressed with your patience and level of self-control. You've grown a ton. There's no way you would have lasted this long before."

With her eyes closed, Chel took a deep cleansing breath and held it for a second before she let it go again. "Hal taught me breathing exercises. When I feel stressed it helps me get control," she said with her eyes still closed.

"It's working."

"Yeah, it definitely helps." She opened her eyes and gave Kaeleigh a small smile. "I'm sorry. I was being pushed so much in training and they kept talking about how when I can shift into an animal I will still use the techniques but I will have to alter them accordingly and... and..." Her breathing accelerated and her hands started to shake. She closed her eyes again and concentrated on her breathing and slowing it down. "And I guess I just snapped a bit. Poor Gyon, he was training with me today and I totally bit his head off." Chel laughed a little.

Kaeleigh put her hands on both of Chel's shoulders, "Look at me, Chel." Chel did even though her eyes shifted away momentarily then back. "It will happen. I have full confidence in you and what you can do now and will be able to do when you shift. You know why?" Chel shrugged. "Because I know *you*. I know your heart and what kind of person you are. Even if you end up being the only shifter who has never shifted, I will still love you and believe in you. Even if you are more of an 'unshifter' type shifter." Kaeleigh waited while that sunk in and watched Chel's eyes grow wide and infuriated.

"I will NOT be the only shifter who has never shifted!! I can't believe you even said that to me Kaeleigh-whatever-all-your-new-names-are-Johnson! An unshifter! Really?! Of course I will shift. It's in my blood. It's part of my heritage and I claim that fully. I thought you believed in me," Chel said, somewhat hurt.

Kaeleigh just smiled a big cheesy and satisfied grin.

"You totally set me up, didn't you?!" Chel put her hands on her hips and looked to the ceiling of the Great Hall and sighed. "And

I walked right into it. Okay, you're right. Yes, I will change when it is the 'appointed time,'" she said, using air quotes to reference what their fearless leader Arileas kept saying. Both girls erupted in giggles right in the middle of the Great Hall, startling the few others that were there helping to set up. Kaeleigh and Chel hugged each other then continued going about their duties for set-up. No one had asked them to help—after all, they were "guests"—but Kaeleigh wanted to be a part of the community and not above it.

Everyone had gathered in the Great Hall for the evening meal just as they had done the night before. Arileas seemed to have what might be referred to as an inner circle of followers that were loyal to him and whom he trusted implicitly. He had never said as much, but it was obvious to Kaeleigh, as they were the same group that sat at his table during meals and were the same ones called when he had special meetings.

Arileas appeared back to his "normal" aged self and not the actually "old" looking man he had become after the prophecy had come forth. Kaeleigh felt anxious about that. There was still so much to understand.

Arileas stood and raised his glass. A hush came over the group in anticipation. Everyone did as he did, raising their glass. "A toast. I know you have seen them around, but I wanted to fully introduce our honored guests that have been in your presence these last few days. Please stand when I call you so that we may all greet you."

Kaeleigh's hands started to sweat and her leg under the table started to bounce. Daegan, who sat next to her on one side, raised a subtly amused eyebrow in her direction. Then in an uncharacteristic move for him, he placed his hand on her knee under the table. She knew he must just be trying to stop her nervous bouncing, but the nerves were shooting up her leg where the heat of his hand seared through her pant leg, seeping into her very skin. Her heartbeat began to accelerate and her breathing became slightly erratic. She couldn't believe her traitorous body; after all the control she had learned with her magic, she still had no power over her teenage hormones. In the background, Arileas was saying something but it was just jumbled words in her foggy mind at the moment. Chel stood up across from her and gave a wave and a slight bow and then there was applause. *Oh dear gods please let him move his hand!* Taking a breath, she gently tried to push her energy to guiding his hand off of her knee. Daegan smirked in response and instead of removing his hand, he slowly slid it up just past her knee closer to mid-thigh. Kaeleigh was about to hyperventilate. *Has he lost his mind? Is he teasing me? MOVE YOUR HAND OFF!* She sent him with a blast of energy from her core. It was a bit more powerful than she had intended but he did indeed move his hand, only it flew off her knee under the table and hit the back of his hand on the underside of the table itself with a loud thud. Everyone immediately looked her direction to see what the commotion was. Daegan looked completely innocent in his smugness and Kaeleigh's face was turning a bright shade of turnip.

To save her more embarrassment Arileas distracted the others by then introducing Halister of Elnye to the group. There were gasps from some that knew who he was, or rather who his parents—his mother specifically—were, and were not sure how to react to him being in their midst.

"I understand my presence may cause you discomfort, but please know I am here to fight for the cause of Alandria—yes, against my own mother. I am here to serve your people and protect. I have made an oath to the princess, to this place, and to my brother Daegan." Halister bowed and sat back down.

Before Arileas moved on, he gestured toward Hal. "My friends, I want you to know he has my trust and I hope you will give him yours as well."

With that the people gave him applause. Arileas turned to Kaeleigh and nodded at her that she was next. She took a deep breath and straightened her shoulders and gave herself a little shake to shake off whatever nonsense—glorious, dream-worthy nonsense—Daegan had just tried.

"I would like to introduce this special young woman to you now. You have heard rumors, some of you have met her yourselves. She comes to us from the mortal realm but she is indeed one of us, from Alandria and from the Ehsmia." There were gasps of awe from the audience. "This is Kaeleighnna iliatheyll Sayaelílth, the daughter of Princess Eva Eytht of the line of iliatheyll from under the mountain. She is the rightful heir to the throne of Elnye and the territory of Feraánmar. However, she is also the daughter of Prince Brandt, son of Ryek Sayaelíth, king of Adettlyn, and also the rightful heir to Adettlyn and the territory of Lumari."

This was not only a surprise to the audience, but to Kaeleigh. If she had really thought about it, she could have possibly connected those dots, but it seemed so far out there and out of her reach and so unlikely that she never believed it was possible. Yet here, in "appointed time," Elder Arileas decided to share that information with the entire clan of the Ehsmia. Kaeleigh gasped for air. Her legs buckled like noodles as she fell to her seat. Arileas gazed down at her with a twinkle in his eye and bid her to rise and greet her people. It was overwhelming and daunting and Kaeleigh wanted nothing more than to run out of the Great Hall screaming and throw herself into the river to cool off and find some air. But it wasn't possible. Everyone was applauding and cheering and she didn't know what to do.

Daegan grabbed her arm and pulled her up to a standing position once again. "They are your people: the Twined, the Faeries, and the Elves. They need to meet you. Stand and be who you are—their leader. Embrace them, you are their hope," he whispered into her ear. His confidence and apparent lack of shock gave her strength. He sent waves of peace through his touch to her arm where he held on. She took every comfort he gave her and then she looked to Chel, who was beaming ear to ear and nodding at her. She stood a bit taller and looked out at the many faces seated at multiple tables and smiled at them. She wasn't really sure what to do next. She looked to

Arileas, who smiled sneakily at her then bowed on one knee in her direction. The crowd did the same; as if in a wave they all went to one knee with a fist over their hearts. It was silent in the room and Kaeleigh looked wide-eyed around it, in sheer panic at the thought of trying to lead a people. She had no idea what to do, or how to do it. Suddenly everyone at her table did the same, even Daegan, who was still supporting her arm. He looked up at her out from under the curtain of his thick, long eyelashes, pledging his allegiance to her. He would not have done it unless he really meant it, even if it meant he was the only one in the room left standing. Tears of gold sprung from her eyes with no hope of containing them. She looked out, taking in the moment, and nodded her acceptance as her eyes met the hopeful gazes of friends and strangers alike. Lightly, she placed her hand over her heart in silent acknowledgment.

After a short moment, Arileas stood and called everyone to their feet for their last introduction. He called on Daegan to stand and began his introduction, reintroducing this Ferrishyn warrior who was in Ehsmia not for the first time. However, what he was about to say would shock everyone, including Daegan.

"So as we celebrate our friend visiting us a second time, the moment has come to reveal something that is of great importance to us all." He paused for effect. "Daegan is the other half of the Sol-lumieth that is prophesied," Arileas said without any hint of deception. The room gasped and Daegan turned to him sharply, absolute confusion mixed with horror etched upon his face. "It is true, Master Daegan, I had my suspicions, but when the prophecy was relived and I communed with the Ancients, it was confirmed. It is clear now that we all did not understand completely. The Sol-lumieth is not one being alone, but it is two. It is the two of you together. It is why your power is greater when put together, why you are so connected, why this path has been obscured from yours and all our eyes."

Kaeleigh quickly grabbed Daegan's hand, in a show of support but also to hold him there. She sensed his panic, which scared her. He looked out to the hundreds of people before him and whispered,

"This cannot be. I do not deserve this title." But the people did not hear him as they all in unity bowed before him and Kaeleigh together. He looked to Kaeleigh in horror as if she was a stranger. He was not seeing her, though, he was somewhere else in his mind. She squeezed his hand and then pulled him down with her to kneel before the people that were blindly putting their faith into the apparent embodiment of a prophecy. It was surreal. Kaeleigh wanted nothing more than to flee the Great Hall and absorb all that had been said. Arileas sensed and understood their discomfort with a knowing smile, as he transitioned the now buzzing room for their evening meal. As everyone resettled for dinner, Daegan quietly let go of Kaeleigh's hand without saying a word and excused himself, quickly leaving the hall. Kae didn't know what to do as she looked at the Elder for a clue. He simply nodded. *He will be all right. Rest and eat,* he spoke calmly in her mind.

The rest of the meal was a complete blur to Kaeleigh. Her right side felt completely cold and empty waiting for Daegan to return to dinner, but he didn't. She worried for him and wanted nothing more than to find him. However, she knew for the moment he had to work through it on his own. She was overwhelmed with her own revelations as well. Chel kept trying to talk to her and get her to answer questions, but Kaeleigh had nothing more than one-word answers. It was all so much... it was too much. She knew her mother had been a princess, and she had hints at who her grandfather was, but the thought of being a princess from two separate lines was a huge brain cramp for her; exactly what did that mean anyway?

Chel escorted her back to their room as Kaeleigh simply followed her lead like a numb zombie following the scent of fresh meat, blinded by the thoughts and possibilities that were moving so fast and shouting so loud in her head she could barely keep from covering her ears and burying her head in the sand. She remotely remembered Chel tucking her into her bed and telling her to rest for a while, before the sweet oblivion of sleep swallowed her whole.

❖❖❖

Daegan left. He could not believe the cowardice and weakness that he felt exposed within himself. He did not know what to feel or if he was simply losing his mind. He saw and felt keenly Kaeleigh's panic after she was announced. But this... this had never even been a thought in Daegan's wildest imagination. His own intense anxiety brought back flashes of when he was a boy and out in the wilderness of Alandria on his own. There were times he was not even sure he would live to see the next day, the panic was so overwhelming, but he would think of his parents and the sacrifice they had made for him to be free. Thinking of them would calm him while simultaneously breaking his young heart all over again.

Where would he find peace now? He longed to be close to Kaeleigh. In her, he truly did find peace, but not this night. He needed to straighten out his mind, his emotions. He was desperate to simply sit in solitude and let these new revelations absorb into his unsettled mind. Again, recalling his days alone as a child, he remembered... the trees. He went to the biggest tree he could find in the middle of the hidden mountain. By the small river near the entrance of the land of the Ehsmia, the tree grew strong and sure. It was a tree unlike the others. There was an energy force stronger than the others coming from this tree. It was an ancient oak that had roots firmly planted deep into the soil and shot out into the stream to drink its fill. The glory of its canopy was unmatched and the strength of its branches unchallenged.

This tree called to him. As he approached it, he placed his hand on the large trunk and felt the gnarled and rough bark under his fingertips. He asked permission for the shelter this tree would provide and sanctuary he might find in it. Using his gifts, Daegan could see the green energy pulsing all around the outline of this tree. It welcomed him and even sent some of its energy to fill Daegan and offer him peace. Daegan lowered his eyes and bowed his head in thanks to one of nature's Ancients—the NaNai. While humbled and honored, he was also a bit surprised to find the tree so inviting of him. What surprised him even more was the tree used its energy to speak words that he would understand, more than simple feelings and emotion that Daegan could gleam, but actual words into his mind.

"You are troubled, young warrior. So much conflict within you. Your mind does not remember. You shall see soon enough."

"How do you know?" Daegan questioned.

"I am of the NaNai, I know all that has happened on the soil of Alandria."

"There are some things I would rather not remember," Daegan whispered with heavy sadness.

"Follow the thread of truth through the past, the light within the darkness. The rest will unfold itself as you are ready."

"What if I am not ever ready? What if the truth hurts too much?" Daegan choked out desperately.

"You are ready. It would not be revealed if you were not."

"But I feel so weak. I cannot see the greater outcome this time. I only know my love for Kaeleigh. It is the only thing that is clear in my mind. I have never counted myself as necessary, wanted, or needed by anyone. Not until I found her," Daegan admitted.

"You need her and she needs you. If you are not together, the magic of this land will wither. You will die and she will perish as well."

"I cannot lose her."

"Neither can we. And we cannot lose you either, young prince."

Daegan's heart constricted, the pain in his chest so deep it caught his breath. He knew the great tree was right. He went down to one knee, a hand on the ground and the other fisting on his forehead. He was ashamed at his selfishness in so abruptly leaving the dinner—and Kaeleigh. His love for her and for Alandria began to flood his senses and brought with it an excitement and even hope. "I will not lose her," he whispered to himself.

"Be at peace, son of Alandria. The time is coming nigh for each of you to live your role. Have courage, Ferrishyn, son of Elnye."

Daegan looked up, then lowered his eyes and turned so he was kneeling before the great tree—an Ancient of Alandria, the

NaNai—in gratitude. *"Thank you for coming to me, your presence was most gracious."*

"The NaNai are with you. It is time. To you, Daegan Tokníyth, we pledge fealty and will serve Alandria as she has served us. We are ready and will be waiting."

With that, the energy of the tree retracted almost jarringly, leaving Daegan grateful and questioning as to what the tree's words meant. The name the tree used was not one Daegan knew, yet there was a nudging at the back of his mind, a tickle of a memory that was buried under layers and layers of dust locked away in the recesses of his mind. His mind continued to stir. He sat still and quiet, allowing the memories to slowly rise inside him. It was not all at once, but one by one they came. And then... he remembered.

CHAPTER TWENTY-THREE

T he next morning Daegan walked back into the Great Hall only to find everyone he was looking for already there. Arileas was going over the scroll that the altered prophecy was written on. It sounded like an open discussion as different ones were offering their interpretations. Even Kaeleigh was explaining what she saw when she looked at it and could almost point out where magic had erased or changed parts. He remained in shadow by the entrance for a brief moment taking it all in. Instead of waiting for an opportune time, he decided interrupting was just as good. He did not even need to say anything. His mere presence was demanding attention before he had even made it more than a few steps into the light.

Everyone stopped what they were saying and looked sharply over at him, examining him. Kaeleigh stared with tears in her eyes when she took him in. There was something different about him, he could feel it, though he was not sure that the others would see it. It was quiet. Out of deference, Daegan looked at the Elder for what was to come next.

Arileas wore a crooked grin as he looked at Daegan. "I see something has happened." It was not a question. Daegan nodded. Arileas's smile grew as he spoke in a hushed tone. "You remembered."

"Mostly," Daegan confirmed. "There are still spots of obscurity in my mind."

Arileas nodded as if it was expected.

"What is happening?" Chel asked no one in particular. She looked at Kaeleigh, who, wide-eyed with love, was watching her warrior. Hal began to approach Daegan, but Arileas held his hand out to give Hal pause. He questioned the Elder with his expression, but did not counter him.

"What do you know, young Daegan?" Arileas asked with a profound tone.

"I know who my parents were. I know what has been done to my mind."

"What else?" Arileas coaxed with expectant eyes.

"I know who I am."

They stared at each other for more than what should have been comfortable. Daegan allowed the Elder to search his mind; for the first time an open book. Kaeleigh continued to stare in awe. Chel elbowed her and whispered, "I'm confused. Don't we all know who he is?"

Kaeleigh whispered back but didn't take her eyes off of Daegan. "I think this is something much more significant."

"Indeed it is, and it is just the right time." Arileas looked over to the girls with a slight rebuke for their whispering.

"Daegan, what is going on?" Hal finally voiced directly to Daegan. The look of confusion on his face mirrored almost everyone in the room. Ella had moved up by her grandfather and placed her hand on his shoulder, also with a knowing gleam in her eyes.

Daegan looked over at Hal and responded, "My parents kept my family in hiding for many nights, always keeping us from Elnye where they had once called home. My grandfather had fled Elnye in one of the last battles. My father was born as a nomad, but trained with my grandfather to be a Ferrishyn. When he was old enough, they let him return to Elnye under a different name and under a glamour that would disguise any distinguishing features."

"Do you remember your parents' names?" Hal asked.

Daegan nodded slowly. "And more than just that. I remember their legacy." He took a deep breath and suddenly looked uncomfortable, rubbing his hand through the hair at the back of his head.

"Go on, Daegan, please," Kaeleigh petitioned, still sitting at the table looking up at them.

"My grandmother's name was Et lyn Waeth and she married my grandfather, named Ryethni Tokníyth. They had a son—my father—Dy'land Waethni Tokníyth, but for their protection they dropped the last name. They became of the Waethni line even though there had never before been one." He looked to Halister to see if what he had said registered with him. Apparently, something had as Halister stared at him as if he were seeing a ghost. Others looked to Arileas to hear him counter what Daegan had said, but he did not. He simply held his head high as if he was a proud grandparent witnessing his grandchild's new discovery.

"I'm not quite caught up. What does that name mean?" Kaeleigh asked hesitantly, looking directly at Daegan.

"I am Daegan Waethni Tokníyth, the heir..."

"Prove it!" Finn practically shouted at him from across the room with his arms crossed.

"Finn!" Kaeleigh was shocked at Finn's rude outburst.

Finn glared at her then explained, "It is a grave accusation to make, Kaeleigh. I need proof."

"What accusation did he make? I'm really getting tired of people not giving me the answers I need—and why for the love of all things holy, Daegan, are you untying your pants??" Kaeleigh practically shouted then immediately a blush ran up her neck when she realized what she had shouted and that a very attractive warrior was indeed lowering a part of his pants. "No, really... what is he doing?"

"I am showing Finn what he is looking for." Daegan looked into Finn's eyes as he exposed a part of his right hip where there was nothing to see. "Remove the glamour, Kaeleigh."

Kaeleigh's eyes snapped back to his. "What?"

"Please remove the glamour. Or at least see *through* it and tell Finn what you see. Otherwise he will think I placed it there for him to see." Daegan looked at her a little softer, with eyes pleading for her to simply do as he asked.

She nodded and stepped forward. It made her blush to be that close to him and with his pants slightly hanging down even though there was nothing more to see than his very defined hip bone surrounded by tight muscle that led to other areas of him still covered. That blush was rushing on full throttle from her stomach all the way to the top of her head. It was all Kaeleigh could do to keep from reaching out with her fingertips to trace the lines of each muscle. Daegan cleared his throat, causing her to flinch back into her mission.

She took a step back to help her think a little more clearly. Kaeleigh concentrated on the smooth tanned skin where his hip was. Suddenly an image appeared in front of her eyes and she sucked in a breath. "I see a small black orchid marking," Kaeleigh said. "That's all I see."

"Can you show us, Kaeleigh? Remove the glamour?" Arileas asked calmly.

"Okay, I'll try." She focused her magic to dismantling the threads of a glamour she could see surrounding the image. It really wasn't that hard compared to what they'd had to do with the glamour surrounding Aidón. She heard several gasps from around the room, so she assumed what she did worked.

"There is your proof, Finnlan." Arileas nodded at the marking on Daegan's hip.

"I also have this," Daegan said to Arileas as he held out his hand. "My father's ring. He gave this to me when I saw him last, right before they were killed."

Kaeleigh knew the ring; Daegan never took it off. He said a few words she did not recognize but her mind quickly translated, and softly said, "*Reveal.*" His ring altered its appearance in both texture and design to something much more ancient looking. It had a small green stone that glimmered like new in the center. Kaeleigh was transfixed on the ring and how it had changed before her very eyes. Then suddenly she realized that everyone around her had gone down to the floor on one knee, bowing to Daegan. This time was different. She could feel it. Everything had just changed.

She quickly took her own knee, only to have Daegan raise her eyes to his with his fingertips lightly brushing her chin. "You do not bow to me, Kaeleighnna." He helped her to her feet. "Neither do you, my friends. I have done nothing yet to deserve the honor you are giving me." Daegan looked down, humbled, and showed slight emotion. "My parents never got the chance to serve you or be honored the way you honor me."

Arileas stood and walked closer to Daegan. "They knew who they were and who they were protecting. They would do it again to ensure that you were in this time and in this place. I know, they told me so. They will be honored properly when this is over." Arileas smiled at Daegan. "I know you will see to that."

"So, I'm assuming Daegan is some kind of royalty since we just pledged our lives to him or something," Metrí whispered to Chel, who was chewing the inside of her cheek but nodded her head in agreement.

"Yes, young one." Arileas spoke directly to Metrí with an almost giddy grin. "I present to you Daegan Tokníyth, the heir to the throne of Elnye and the territory of Feraánmar," he declared, arms open toward Daegan and jubilation in his eyes.

The room buzzed with excitement as Daegan's face slowly began to frown as a thought and question rose in his mind. He began pacing the room as everyone looked on. He looked to the Elder. "Did Maleina know? Is that why she sought after me and took me?"

"Yes, I believe she suspected, but did not actually know."

"That would explain so many of her actions toward me. She was threatened by me even as a boy. That must be why she orchestrated all that she did and put me in the position I held, to keep me under her thumb and watchful eye."

"Yes, that does seem to line up," Hal mused aloud, looking down and running his hands through his hair. He was deep in thought as his eyes raised sorrowfully toward his brother and now his king. "I never knew, Daegan. I was blind to it. I swear I would have told you if I did."

"I know." Daegan looked at Hal with a smile. "You are my brother and you will always remain so." He thought for a brief second and then nodded his head as he spoke more softly. "And Rheina is my sister. I'm not sure what she would say about that, but

I like to think she would feel the same, in her own way," he finished with a smile.

Hal chuckled. "I think little sister has had her own hand in things and her own part to play all along. She is a mystery to me." His expression grew serious and far off. "I hope she is all right."

Daegan reached over and gripped Hal's shoulder. "I hope the same," Daegan whispered.

Arileas gave them both a conspirator's eye, "Your sister has had her own part to play indeed. She is quite special. I do look forward to what comes next on her path."

"You know something, Elder?" Hal asked.

"Of course he does!" Daegan declared with a smile, showing brief affection and emotion for Arileas. "This man always seems to possess the right secrets at the right time. Are there any more secrets we should know right now, Elder? Perhaps involving our sister?"

"One more, but it is not quite time, I am sorry to say," Arileas said with a smile. "Shall we proceed with deciphering the prophecy?"

Everyone agreed and went back to the table where the scrolls were laid. Daegan grabbed Kaeleigh's hand quickly and pulled her to his chest. She gasped out of surprise. He would never have shown affection in front of others before. Her eyes grew big as he leaned down, his mouth so close to her ear she could feel the warmth of his breath as he whispered for her ears alone. "I am yours, Kaeleighnna, if you will have me." He did not even give her a chance to respond, but let her loose as he went to a seat beside Arileas that was left open for him.

Kaeleigh was left staring into a corner of the Great Hall. Her legs were shaking and her eyes felt pried open, unable to blink. She clutched her arm where he had just held it.

"Come on, so a boy whispered in your ear. That's nothing new, right? Shake it off. We got stuff to do." Chel laughed and winked at her friend as she conveniently helped her to a chair at the far end from Daegan. Chel had decided her friend needed some breathing space. Kaeleigh gave Chel a grin and then rolled her eyes and shook herself to clear her head.

"See, now you can just sit back and watch him from here," Chel said snarkily, but Kaeleigh just continued to grin.

It seemed like hours had gone by as they studied the ancient magical text. They could see where it had been added to, but understanding it was proving to be more complicated. There was quiet frustration in the room. Kaeleigh had a thought and stood up abruptly. "I keep feeling like I get close to something and I get 'rerouted,' for lack of a better term. Could there be a magic to confuse us on it?"

"Is that such a thing?" Chel asked.

Arileas cocked his head for a moment as he stared at the parchment, but he was seeing something other than what they were all looking at. He appeared to be searching it thoroughly. After a long time, one of his eyebrows rose. "I believe you may be on to something, Kaeleighnna. I have detected something that should not be a part of either the old version or what it should say."

"Okay, well, what do you suggest we do?" Kaeleigh asked slightly impatiently as if he was waiting for them to all figure out the riddle before they could move on.

"Metrí. She needs to begin training as well. This is something I want you to work on, Metrí. There is unknown magic here. I think if I point you in the right direction, your magic that is such a mystery may have something to offer." He spoke sagely to a young Metrí, whose eyes had grown quite large, but she quietly nodded as she began focusing on the parchment.

"I think it best if I can have some time with Ella and Metrí as we finish, to help her focus her magic. A lot has transpired today. So much has been revealed and there is more to come. I am so grateful for you all in this time. Rest well." The Elder's eyes twinkled at them as he shooed them out of the Great Hall.

"Wow. I am exhausted," Chel yawned out as they left the hall into the perfect night air. The trees practically glowed in the shimmering light of the blue moons as it streaked through the tree canopy above.

"I know! I feel like I don't even know you people anymore," Hal joked as he gave Daegan a light slug as he passed. "We've got kings and queens among us just like that!"

Daegan let out a laugh as he pushed Hal before he got too far out of his reach. Hal was accustomed to the more playful side of Daegan, but none of the rest of them had seen it before. To Kaeleigh especially, it was breathtaking.

After Finn and Ella had walked past as well, Kaeleigh steeled her resolve and turned toward Daegan. "I have news for you, your Highness." Her eyes danced as they looked into his. "You were mine long before you acknowledged me. Just for the record." She spun to keep walking and perhaps play a little hard to get, only to have him catch her arm and twirl her back to him.

"Is that so?"

"Mmhmm," Kaeleigh hummed through her lips. Lips that he was staring intently at before he looked back to her green eyes.

"We are even then," he said.

"Not quite," Kaeleigh smirked then reached up to grab his hair in her hand and pressed her lips to his. This was not their first kiss, but it felt different. It was mutual and acknowledged. It was more than a kiss of desperate emotion bubbling forth, it was purposeful with focused passion. Kaeleigh could feel him—the real him, the him that was deep inside of his rough exterior—it was his soul. The kiss they shared was one soul reaching out to the other's soul. It was magical and full of energy that surrounded them both. Kaeleigh could feel when her energy entwined with his own. It was electrifying, similar to what they each experienced when they would touch skin to skin in the past, but so much more. Daegan's lips began to intensify on hers, their kiss deepening. His tongue reached out to the seam of her lips, coaxing them to open to him. She let him in, opening her mouth and tangling her tongue with his. It was a dance that they had not dared get near before, but now... but now, they belonged to one another.

The energy within Kaeleigh sparked, starting at her wrist where Daegan was holding her, and then from her wrist up into her hand as he kissed her senseless. It was a shock that neither could ignore, however, and they stepped apart with enough room to look down at her wrist. The marking on her wrist that had been only partial before was now fully apparent.

"Whoa!" Kaeleigh managed to get out as she was trying to refill her lungs with air. She was afraid the magic of a dream come true might snap and shatter before her. "Look at that!"

"I see," Daegan said, smiling as he examined her wrist. Where his fingers traced the marking, he left a wake of fire burning along the nerve endings of Kaeleigh's wrist. "It seems to be complete. Though I still have never seen a marking like this."

"I wonder what it means," she said, no longer disappointed by how different her markings were, but now knowing clearly for the first time who she was and who she belonged to.

He tipped her chin to look her squarely in the eyes. "It's beautiful, I know that much. I have a feeling that our resident Elder will know or at least know something about it." His eyes went distant as he thought.

"What is it?"

"It happened after I kissed you."

"Right..." She looked at him to continue.

"After I remembered who I am to be. After I declared myself to you. After I gave you my heart. Arileas said we were two halves of the Sol-lumieth together. Maybe it has something to do with that." Daegan shrugged one shoulder.

"Maybe you are right." She thought for a second. "Wait! Did you say you gave me your heart?" Kaeleigh's eyes filled with emotion and she tried to swallow it down, but her throat was so tight she almost ended up choking.

"Yes, my choosing you is my way of giving you my heart. I have given it to no one before you and I would give it to none other than you." She gasped and took in a staccatoed breath. "There is no other for me, Kaeleigh. I want you. Always." Then he kissed her. Because it was the perfect time to do so, because he wanted to, because he could.

In between kisses wet with salty tears and Kaeleigh gasping for breath she responded, "I... want... you too. You have my heart." She pulled back enough to see his eyes. Kaeleigh whispered, "Forever." Then she lay her head against his chest as they held each other close for another moment. Nestled within his strong, muscled arms, Kaeleigh felt everything was suddenly right in her world. She was safe. She was loved. She took a deep cleansing breath, feeling lighter than she had in a long time.

They both turned to walk in the direction of their friends, who had now long disappeared on the path ahead. Daegan grabbed Kaeleigh's hand and slid his fingers in between hers as they walked together under the star-studded Ehsmian night sky.

CHAPTER TWENTY-FOUR

For the first time since they had all found each other and embarked on the journey from the mortal realm into Alandria, there was peace blanketing their small group. There was an unspoken unity amongst them—they would fight together for Alandria and all her people. In the training room that next morning, they took turns sparring with each other using various weapons. This time Kaeleigh faced off with Finn. She almost hated sparring with Finn, because he was so good at fighting simultaneously with his swords and his magic. They had also learned he was a skilled archer. Kaeleigh had tried to learn to use his bow, but she wasn't connecting with it like she did with her sword. She thought she might be able to shoot an arrow to save her life or that of another, but it would take more time and effort than she was prepared to offer learning to master it.

Facing Finn in the designated ring—a circle of dirt dug out of the ground that was a lighter color than the rest of the ground—Kaeleigh centered herself and became one with her magic as he had taught her.

"When you're ready, Kae," he taunted her. She looked to him with a smirk and waved him forward, mimicking Neo in the old *Matrix* movies they used to watch back in the mortal realm. He let out a laugh, shaking his head. He did his best Morpheus expression and nodded her way. She stepped forward to make the first move. Then everything was practically a blur as they danced with swords flying in perfect rhythm. They were faster than humans, and their senses were all enhanced to varying degrees—Kaeleigh's especially—and with magic as that little bit of "extra," it was hard to keep up with them.

Kaeleigh was finally able to hold her own against most of her opponents. This time was different though. She could feel her body anticipating Finn's moves almost before he even made them. She was there to stop him and counter his moves. She pushed her magic at him, to trip him up when she could. He had to respond in kind. Sword for sword and magic for magic. It was like four people fighting within two bodies. When magic was involved, wind reacted, flying back and forth between fighters, electricity soaring from the one bidding it to the other. She had the benefit of the elements more so than Finn as she was part Faerie. Kaeleigh concentrated her magic, asking the wind to help her as she sent it toward Finn. The wind swirled together in a swift yet fierce twister in front of her before it flung itself at Finn. He barely had time to jump out of the way, landing on the ground looking up at Kaeleigh with eyes of shock and awe.

"Kae! I didn't know you could do that!" Finn shouted.

"I couldn't before. I guess now I can." Kaeleigh laughed as she did a little dance at having bested Finn in such a manner.

"What else can you do?" Daegan asked from the sidelines.

"I... I don't know. There were a few things I wanted to do before but was never able. Let me try. Finn, you game? Or is someone else volunteering?" She looked out to the crowd now gathered.

"No way, I'm out, Kae." Finn got up with a smile on his face, teasing her.

"I will let you have fun with me, Kaeleighnna." Líyl of the Ehsmia stepped up. Kaeleigh had fought with her before but had never won. She was hesitant, but excited about giving her magic another try. When Líyl stepped into the ring, they faced each other and bowed respectfully to each other. Then it began.

The women went at each other with everything they had while still protecting each other from harm. It was a very even match with weapons and endurance, but then Kaeleigh pulled the magic from her core, which was coming much easier and faster than ever before.

She tried beckoning wind and energy within the air at the same time and pushed it at Líyl, with the intent only to throw her off balance. Her magic responded beautifully, knocking Líyl onto her back before she even knew Kaeleigh had summoned magic. It was smooth and graceful and Kaeleigh felt strong and beautiful—more than she ever had before. She felt like her true self, what she was made to do, who she was created to be. She felt almost fully in control of her magic and her skills.

Líyl looked up to Kaeleigh, nodded her defeat, and then bowed her head to Kaeleigh.

"You are ready. You and your magic are one now." Arileas spoke from the back of the crowd where he had been watching silently. As he moved forward, the people parted a path for him to easily reach the front. "May I see your wrist?"

Kaeleigh held out her wrist with the complete marking now free for everyone to see.

"Oh wow, Kaeleigh, when did that happen?" Chel asked.

"Just before last night, when Daegan..." A blush flushed her cheeks. Chel's expression said she understood just what she and Daegan had been doing last night.

"Yes, it seems that was what we were waiting for," Arileas said unabashedly.

"What is that?" Finn asked hesitantly.

"For the Sol-lumieth to come together in unity," he said matter-of-factly.

"What?!" Finn growled at the same time Hal said, "It's about time," and Metrí said, "When did you have time for that?" There was a lot of commotion. Daegan simply smiled while Kaeleigh was mortified.

"No, wait! Oh my gosh, you guys, we just kissed. There was no 'unifying'!" Her air quotes didn't help the laughter that was swirling throughout the room, and Kaeleigh thought she had never been so embarrassed.

Daegan came up to stand with her in the center of the training ring and held her hand tightly. "She is mine and I am hers. We fight together, we serve together, we love together." Kaeleigh knew he meant well, but seeing Chel trying to contain her laughter with Metrí huddled next to her only made her all the more uncomfortable.

"All right, you guys," Kaeleigh followed up, growing tired of the joke. "Let's just be clear for future reference, any 'unifying' that does or does not happen is nobody's business." Everyone nodded with contained laughter and smirks of joy. She finally let out a laugh as she took Daegan's hand and walked over to Arileas. She held out her wrist for him to see more clearly. "Do you know what this particular marking means?"

He examined it then looked at her. "No."

Kaeleigh's frustration burned across her face. "You don't have any kind of guess or gut feeling?"

"You did not ask me that," Arileas said with a twinkle in his eyes. He laughed. "I do believe it is a marking that is special to you alone. You are the only one with your Twined bloodlines—if I may use that term. You see, you have blood of your father's line, the Elves." He pointed to a piece of her marking that resembled a bit of the Elf marking. "You have the blood of your mother's line containing Ferrishyn and Faerie as well." He pointed to a different piece of her marking. "And you have the blood of your great-grandfather, who is of the Ehsmia race of Faeries," he finished, tracing yet another part of her marking. "The only blood of Alandria you do not have is Shifter and Dryad, but they accept you nonetheless."

Kaeleigh thought on it for a minute as a smile grew on her face. She stared at her marking. "So it is not saying that I am different. This mark shows that I belong." Her eyes beamed and she held her wrist as if cherishing it. "I love that."

Arileas smiled in return. "So do we."

"Group hug!" Chel called before smothering her best friend, bringing Metrí with her. There was laughter and joy and freedom in simply being together. It strengthened them and brought them together.

"Clean up, then meet me in the Great Hall. I have someone I would like you all to meet." Arileas turned and walked out, Ella trailing behind him.

CHAPTER TWENTY-FIVE

O n their way back to the Great Hall, Ella stood waiting just outside the doors.

"Grandfather decided to make this meeting a more intimate meeting. Kaeleigh, you and yours please head into Grandfather's private chamber through this tunnel." She directed them with a hand off to the side from where she stood. It did not stand out as a tunnel that was widely used. In fact, it was dark and hard to see unless it was directed to you or you already knew of its existence. Kaeleigh nodded, but Chel cocked an eyebrow, questioning Ella.

"There's something I can't put my finger on about her, Kae," Chel whispered.

Kaeleigh thought about it for a moment, then shrugged. "I like her. I'm not sure what you are picking up on, but I'm not discounting it either. Feel it out, see if you can decipher it."

"Maybe it's just 'cause she's gorgeous and confident," Chel complained.

"So are you, what are you talking about? Don't tell me you are feeling insecure all of a sudden." Kaeleigh knew that would push her friend.

"Of course not, I was just saying," Chel grumbled as they continued to walk into the entrance to the tunnel with the warriors following behind them.

Chel stopped abruptly at the opening to the dark carved out hole in the wall of a mountain. "This seems like a tunnel from a horror movie," she said, eyeing the entrance. "We ladies should definitely not be going first to our doom inside the dark creepy tunnel." She sighed with feigned helplessness like a true southern belle as she fanned her face with her hand.

Hal chuckled quietly from behind her and Finn rolled his eyes at Chel's sarcasm and let out a sigh of exasperation.

"Step aside, dear lady. I and my warrior brethren will take the lead and slay the beasts of the dark," Hal spoke valiantly, and he puffed out his chest as he moved to the front.

Chel batted her lashes and swooned. "I knew chivalry wasn't dead."

There were several muted laughs as they walked into the tunnel, which ended up being not as dark as it looked to be from the outside. It turned out to be the back entrance into Arileas' study.

They gathered together in the Elder's modest study with the others. There was Kaeleigh and her entourage of five companions. Ella and Arileas stood waiting, along with Líyl and Gyon and a couple other Ehsmian warriors. Showing up last were the scholars as they slowly entered the room, filling it to capacity. It was a cozy fit, but the room seemed to expand on its own to make the additional space. The warriors were all gentlemen and allowed for the women of the group to sit in the seats that were available while they stood at the edges of the room. Arileas stood by the door that they had just entered through.

"I have some very special people that I want you to meet. By agreeing to be here, you are under the strictest vow to not reveal who you have met—although most would not believe you. I fear it has been too long." Arileas scanned the room, reading the eyes of all and confirming their agreement. After each had given their assent, he took a deep breath and went to a covered entrance that was not there moments before right next to the one they had entered through. He opened the curtain.

"We are all gathered. You may enter if you wish."

There was a heavy silence in the room as they all looked intently at the opening, with great expectation. Stepping through the curtained entrance was not one but three elderly beings. One woman was obviously Faerie, with her silky smooth skin and pointed ears and chin, and bits of leaves randomly placed through her short dark hair. The other woman had a more ancient, ethereal look to her. She stood tall and had piercing green eyes and pale skin, with dark purplish hair that fell in long rings. Her eyes were much more aged looking than the other woman's, but still her appearance and body had only aged maybe comparable to a seventy-year-old mortal. Her skin was porcelain and smooth, her features sharp, but there was kindness held within her eyes. The other was a man. And the way he held and escorted the second woman, they appeared to be a couple. He was strong still, as one in command, with wisdom in his eyes. His hair was held at his shoulders, stick straight and chestnut brown. His eyes were warm grayish brown and they too seemed kind with the wisdom beyond all ages.

Kaeleigh looked with surprise as Daegan walked slowly past her with eyes fixated on the first woman who had just entered the room. He walked right up before her and reached for her small fragile feminine hand and held it gently within his larger, stronger one. His eyes were soft and full of love as he searched her face.

"Grandmother?" he asked with the hope of a small boy lost long ago.

"Yes. Yes." She smiled with joy. "My Daegan. How strong you have grown." Her eyes shone at him with pride. "You are a warrior just like your father before you. You are more handsome than I could have imagined. I am so proud of you." Her voice quivered with emotion as she paused and looked at her grandson, slowly sliding her hand down his cheek. "I see your parents in you. They would be so proud." A sparkle of love glimmered in her eyes.

A single tear escaped Daegan's eye and slid down his cheek. "You are alive!"

"I am so sorry. There was no way for me to come find you. Forgive me, please." Her look was hesitant, afraid he might turn away from her.

Daegan reached for her and hugged her as tightly as he could without fear of breaking her. Then releasing her, Daegan spoke eagerly. "It was as it should be. She would have killed you if she knew you were alive. Have you been hiding here all this time?"

His grandmother nodded. Daegan turned to Arileas and bowed before him. "Arileas," Daegan stated with intense emotion, "you have my eternal gratitude."

Arileas nodded his acknowledgment and then turned and addressed everyone else softly.

"It is my pleasure to introduce you to Et lyn Waeth Tokníyth, wife of Ryethni, Prince of Elnye and Daegan's grandmother." Arileas bowed to her along with everyone in the room.

"Rise, all of you. You need not bow to me, it is I who bow to Arileas for his shelter and protection all this time," Et lyn said humbly as she inclined her head.

Standing just behind her was the couple that had followed her in and they were staring at Kaeleigh. Arileas stepped forward and gestured toward them. "Also, with us—" But before he finished, the scholars had quietly fallen to their knees once again. Kaeleigh and Chel turned to look at them inquisitively then back to the Elder.

"This is Wyéln and Kaeylnísa iliatheyll... thebelieved 'fallen' king and queen of Ehsmia and the hidden people," Arileas announced, again with a bow.

Instantly everyone else in the room fell once more to their knees, even to their faces to get as low as they could. Something tickled the side of Kaeleigh's arm. Irritated, she slid her eyes to her friend without moving her head; she really didn't want to get in trouble for being disrespectful in such a serious situation. *What?* She mouthed to Chel.

"Doesn't that name sound familiar?" she whispered back as quietly as she could, knowing Kaeleigh could hear her especially being so close.

"Yes, it should sound very familiar, Kaeleighnna iliatheyll Sayaelíth, great-great granddaughter of the Ehsmia," Arileas voiced out above their heads. Kaeleigh snapped her head up, looking at the Elder, then she moved her gaze at the king and queen that stood before her... looking intently at her.

"Ohhh!" was all Kaeleigh could get out of her befuddled mind. She had been told that she was a descendant of them, of course, but she never thought that they would be alive... that she would get to meet them! "Forgive me, I think I am in shock." Chel nudged her to get up off the floor.

"Rise, child," the man... the king... spoke as he beckoned her toward them.

Kaeleigh walked slowly and unsure of herself toward the only living grandparents she had left—that she knew of—and was insecure of how they would accept her. The honor and power they projected into the room was amazing and intimidating to Kaeleigh as she moved quickly to them. She curtsied in front of them.

"It is an honor to meet you," Kaeleigh said with her eyes lowered to the ground.

The woman reached out with her long, frail fingers and raised Kaeleigh's chin. "Kaeleighnna, the honor is ours." They nodded their approval and love as they took in the beauty of their granddaughter.

Kaeleigh was beyond words. She didn't know what to do. She looked at Arileas for support and he simply nodded with a smile and took a step back into the shadow. The king reached out for her hand and Kaeleigh placed her small feminine hand inside his much larger one. She instantly felt a familial connection, warm and loving.

"I don't even know what to say. I have been searching for family... for you, all my life. And now I have found you." Kaeleigh smiled, a single golden tear rolling down her cheek. Her grandfather reached out and wiped the tear from her face. He gave her a small smile.

"Golden tears... just like me." He proudly showed his finger to the queen. She gave him a knowing smile.

"Just like you?" Kaeleigh's eyes lit up. He nodded at her and squeezed her hand.

"We have been in hiding for a long time, but we see your mother and her ancestors—including our son—in you. We are so grateful to have this chance to meet you and hopefully be a bigger part of your life," her grandmother said as she lovingly ran her hands down Kaeleigh's hair.

"I cannot express how excited I am to have more family in my life now, when I have had none for so long." Kaeleigh paused and grabbed Chel as she walked close by, looping her arm through Chel's, inviting her join their conversation. "This is my best friend, Chel. Her parents helped take care of me in the mortal realm."

Chel smiled and bowed. "It is an honor to meet you, Majesty. Ehsmia is beautiful. It really is an amazing place. We have felt right at home here."

"Thank you for your loyalty and love to our Kaeleighnna." The queen inclined her head to Chel with a sparkle in her eye.

After a few minutes of visiting and introducing the rest of those in the room to her new family, Kaeleigh took a deep breath, sad to interrupt the love for the true nature of them coming out of hiding.

"You have been in hiding. It seems quite a few of the Elders and royalty in Alandria went into hiding. The *Orchids* asked for you to be brought out of hiding at this time for a reason." Kaeleigh fidgeted with her necklace that she always wore—the orchid locket inscribed with her name that she had with her since she was a small child.

"Yes, but as everyone believes us to have died long ago, we have remained in hiding to help protect our people and assist when Arileas needed our council. He is the true leader of this people and has kept them safe for all this time," the queen, Kaeylnísa said.

"Kaeleigh, did the *Orchids* contact you recently?" Daegan asked, confused.

She reached out to grab his arm as he was standing close by. "Time slipped by and I did not tell you yet. She came to me." Kaeleigh glanced up at his grandmother who was also listening intently. "Your mother, Cley, she spoke with me and told me to tell Arileas that it was time to meet those in hiding. I did not really understand what she meant until now." Kaeleigh looked sad for a moment as she saw the lost little boy in Daegan's eyes. "She also told me to take care of you." At the glimmer of hope in his eyes, she sounded stronger, with greater resolve than she had a moment before. "I told her to tell my mother and the others that we were coming for them—to free them." Kaeleigh stared deeply into Daegan's eyes, infusing her purpose into his own. A fire burned in his chest as he acknowledged it.

From near the back of the room, Kaeleigh heard Chel whisper, mostly to Hal, "Have you noticed the longer she is around your brother, the more she starts talking like him? You know, without any contractions." There was a low chuckle, but Kaeleigh tuned it out. For some reason it made her smile inside.

Kaeleigh looked to the leaders, who stared at her with anticipation and pride. Arileas stepped forward. "If I may, it sounds like you may have your next part to this journey laid before you."

Kaeleigh took a deep breath. A flitter of panic seared through her body, but she realized it was nothing compared to the resolve she felt inside. Her power was strong and gave her confidence unlike any she had known before. There was a rightness to what Arileas had said. She knew it deep down in her soul that this was what she needed to do. She had promised the *Orchids* she was coming and she would. She just needed to be sure she was ready for whatever they would encounter in Exhile. The only problem was, she had no idea what that might be.

"So, I am assuming that you are not able to freely leave Ehsmia, or possibly even your protective hiding place. What will you do now?" Kaeleigh asked the newly found royalty.

"No, we will not risk all that has been planned until the appointed time," Et lyn, Daegan's grandmother, said softly.

"Now it is time to plan." Her great-great grandfather stepped up and put his hands on either side of Kaeleigh's shoulders. "We will prepare you for all you need to know and instruct how we can. You will be our connection." He winked at her. He was much more formal than Hunter had been, but he was still warm and kind. She hoped the future would provide more time with them. She saw quite clearly that Daegan wished the same as he looked at his grandmother. Kaeleigh could feel his love pouring out of him in waves toward his grandmother. He had not let go of her arm since they had reunited.

Chapter Twenty-Six

Exhile. The Land of the Unforgiven Dead.

Holding the necklace Maleina had given her into the light of the fire blazing at the top of the mountain, *She* seethed with fury. After several failed attempts to track Daegan by his entrapped soul, she knew that Maleina had just declared war against her. The blue wisp of his soul that had life when she first received it had lost any energy it had. On top of that, somehow Maleina had blocked all communication with her. *She* could not figure out how she had done it. Maleina would either have had to grown more powerful or had assistance from someone with the capacity for stronger magic.

I have the Orchids. They hate her as much as me. Who would do this? How did they do this? Who would rise up against me?!

She threw her head back and shook the cave walls with a scream of fury like none other before it... like a trapped fire-breathing dragon. "Maleina will die by my hand. She will not keep me here. She will not stop me." She laughed from a depth beyond the body she inhabited.

With conspiring and shifting eyes, she stood looking out from a high mountain vista surrounded with jagged and sharp edges at all of Exhile before her. Scattered around her were the sacrifices of various animals that survived in the desolate lands of her entrapment. This was a major setback. It was not part of her plan, but something went wrong when the spell that gave her this body was executed. *She* blamed the body that she inhabited. It was a useful tool, especially being a witch of elements—that combined with her own essence of darkness made her the strongest she had been in any realm and in any lifetime previous. *She* had been around a very long time even if the body hadn't. *She* would find a way out. *She* was so close, she had come close to creating a safe portal she could physically traverse. However, the enslaved soul she sent first through the portal, as a test, was incinerated after just stepping into it.

A pleasant surprise had, however, come out of Maleina's betrayal. There was a different woman who was, in fact, linked to the necklace. *She* had tried to use it to trace back to Maleina, but apparently Maleina was not the one who had commissioned the item. After slaughtering her sacrifice to the elements, the ritual for this particular dark magic was enacted. *She* would leave the slashed carcasses to be consumed by the large creatures that flew the gray skies and the others that lived in the rocky peaks. The crystal on the necklace was tied to a young woman; the connection was strong. In the smoke screen of the fire, she could see her face and even into her location. *Perhaps this was a useful gift after all, She* mused with interest. The woman she saw—a soul stealer—was very rare indeed and if the magic around her location was any indication, Maleina had reinforced it recently and knew it as well. *She* would find her.

She wiped away the blood that was left on her chest, arms, and legs with a piece of cloth she had carried up with her. Turning toward the fire, she threw the cloth into the flames. It ignited with a burst of sparks, nothing to be heard but the hiss and pop of an angry blaze. The scent of blood in the smoke called all the flesh-eating creatures to come and devour what was left for them. *She* turned and departed through the opening into the mountain, her silky black dress trailing on the ground behind her practically floating over the rocks and stones. Glowing with a new vibrance from her ritual, *she* was ready for her next move.

CHAPTER TWENTY-SEVEN

EHSMIA. THE HOME OF THE HIDDEN PEOPLE.

H is voice was sincere and concerned. "It will be dangerous. Most that go to Exhile who are not supposed to be there do not come back." As the king of the Ehsmia, and Kaeleigh's grandfather, spoke, he looked into the eyes of his granddaughter. She had decided that it was too much to say "great-great-grandfather" and so settled on simply calling him "Grandfather."

"I understand, but I feel in my soul that I must follow through on this. I promised them," Kaeleigh said with resolute confidence. Daegan stood by her side and nodded his agreement. Her grandfather's eyes lit with hope at her declaration.

He nodded in return. "So be it. And may all the magic of the Ehsmia go with you." Wyéln looked to the Elder Arileas, who nodded his approval, and then to his own wife, Kaeylnísa. She stepped forward next to her husband as he began to speak with an instructional tone.

"There is a way, a hidden portal into Exhile far from the pathways of the Ferriers as they escort the souls beyond, either into the In-Between or into Exhile. However, this portal has never been found in the age of Alandria. Most have disregarded its existence entirely. Its origins date back to the founding of the previous age. I believe our greatest hope to finally find this portal is found in the pages of the Book of Lenoria. It is an ancient tome containing the founding documents of that age. It is a living entity unto itself, enriched with the magic and life force of the 'originators' long ago."

Kaeleigh's grandmother spoke up as he finished, with her gentle voice. "It has been in our guarded care for as long as the Ehsmia have existed. As important as it may prove to be in finding Exhile, it may prove even more important for getting yourselves out."

"Where is this book?" Daegan asked cautiously.

Her grandparents looked at Kaeleigh, then back at Daegan, and then to everyone in the room.

"We do not know for certain, child. The magic of Alandria helps keep it hidden; the land protects what is her own. You would do well to remember that as well. We do know it is guarded by the Ehsmia, but not here."

"How, then, do we get it?" Finn asked from where he sat rigidly, arms crossed and scowl firmly in place. Ella sat next to him completely relaxed, quite the opposite of him in almost every way with her white hair and her otherworldliness, as contrasted to Finn, dark and brooding, with more of the mortal realm rubbed off on him.

"You do not," the king replied without malice. "Kaeleighnna does."

"Not alone," Daegan corrected him with no apology.

"Correct, she will not go alone, but she is the key," Grandfather amended. "She has always been the key. Yes, she is part of the Sol-lu-mieth, but in the prophecy of her birth she is the key with regard to 'the book.'"

"I could do with less of these prophecies," Chel whispered to Hal, who sat next to her on the edge of his seat. He nodded his head with a smile and a wink.

Kaeleigh blew out a sigh, her hand shaking with slight tremors. She closed her eyes and took a deep calming breath. It was usually then that she could feel Daegan's energy sending her waves of peace. Instead, she felt his large masculine hand slide into her own delicate feminine one. Their hands locked like lost puzzle pieces finally fitting together. Instantly, she felt calm. Kaeleigh opened her eyes and looked straight up into his warm gaze watching her protectively.

Her heart stuttered a little at the sudden openness she saw within his soul. A slight blush crept up her neck and she turned back to the king and queen, who were unfazed by their quick public display of affection. Chel, however, was beaming from ear to ear as she watched them unabashedly. There was a throat clearing at the front as Arileas stepped up next to the king and queen.

"In the mortal realm, there was a company of Ferrishyn who guard the book. They are more heavily bound by glamour than even you were, Kaeleighnna—of their own choosing—to appear mortal to anyone other than is deemed worthy by Alandria to find them. I believe this realm has chosen you to find the book, and will allow you to do so." Arileas spoke with a confidence that Kaeleigh suddenly didn't feel.

"So there's a chance that she won't be able to find the map and thereby the book?" Chel asked.

"There is a chance, but I do not believe that is the outcome. I cannot see it clearly, but my heart says it is time for the book to come out of hiding," Arileas replied.

While he was talking, Kaeleigh had wandered over to one of the walls. Maps of Alandria and each territory, along with drawings of creatures and weapons, were hung strategically on the cavernous walls. There were even maps of the forests as some of them were quite vast. On the opposite wall hung a collection of actual weapons that looked ancient. They had obviously been used at one time, but had been cleaned, leaving only the scars of scratches and knicks in the metal along with wear to the leather of the handles. Kaeleigh reached out her hand to touch the edge of one of the spears that had beautifully engraved symbols and words in an ancient tongue. Before she remembered what had happened in the dungeons at Elnye when she touched the walls, she was in the memory of the weapon.

Flashes of many battles long past flooded her mind. She was aware of what was happening this time where before she couldn't differentiate what was her mind and the memory of others. This time was different. It wasn't the memory of different beings, but of the actual weapon itself as it fought in various battles. She could feel the honor and duty it felt at its ability to serve and be what it was created to be. The spear was strong and confident. It was at its best when it felt at one with its wielder—when the wielder was confident and directed its path with precision and decisive execution.

Kaeleigh found it strange to be in the memory of the weapon itself, but there was also something very enlightening in feeling the connection it had. She suddenly heard Daegan saying her name both out loud and in her mind, trying to break her connection to the weapon. She heard him say something about blood and she felt herself let go of the wood with a parting infusion of gratefulness at what she learned.

Falling back into Daegan when she released her hand, she heard him asking her, "Are you all right? Where are you hurt? I felt your pain, but I cannot find the source of the blood."

"Blood?" Kaeleigh asked as she sat up quickly and looked at her hands covered in blood. Shocked, she wiped her hands on her pants only to realize the blood was slowly disappearing as if never there. No stains. She and Daegan both looked at her hands, turning them back and forth, front and back. Nothing.

"Fascinating," her grandfather breathed over her head as he too watched along with everyone else in the room.

"I felt pain, are you in any pain?" Daegan asked her again, more direct.

"No, I didn't feel any pain. Except... well, I could feel what the weapon felt. When it pierced flesh, it didn't exactly feel pain but it absorbed the pain of whoever it had punctured and took in some of the blood. Maybe somehow I absorbed some of its blood when I touched it? Is that possible?" Kaeleigh looked at Arileas and then at her grandparents. Daegan's grandmother was also in the room. She was quiet, but considering what Kaeleigh had said.

"I think that is exactly what happened, Kaeleighnna," Arileas said. "I have never seen it to that degree, but your mother could project images like you can with her magic. Perhaps you can also take in physical experiences. That is something you will have to be very careful to understand. It did not appear to inflict you with the actual pain and injury, but the mental anguish that you might face could be tragic." Arileas frowned. "In fact, that information does not leave this room. It could be used against you."

Great. One more thing to "protect Kaeleigh" from, Kaeleigh grumbled in her own mind. Someday she would be the one to guard those she loved. She vowed it to herself then.

"It could also be quite a useful skill, child." Daegan's grandmother came up beside her and placed her hand on Kaeleigh's arm. "Guard it, but do not discount it. It is a part of who you are." She smiled and patted her hand before walking back across the room in thought.

"So, now what?" Kaeleigh asked, trying to divert the attention from her. "We go to the mortal realm again?" Her eyes lit up with the prospect of possibly getting to see her home and Chel's parents. She realized that she missed them; she couldn't imagine how Chel felt having been so far from them.

Everyone turned to look at the Elder Arileas. He sat rigid with his eyes glossed over. "He is having a vision," Ella spoke as she came up next to him and stood protectively beside him. "We will wait until he has returned to us." Suddenly Ella remembered the king and queen were there and she took a step back with her head bowed. "Unless you have other instructions. My apologies," she uttered.

"No apologies necessary, Ella. Your grandfather has been governing for a long time and you now at his side. Your advice here is worth much," the queen replied with softness.

"Thank you, your majesty." Ella gave a small smile and stepped back beside Arileas.

Not but a few minutes later Arileas's eyes cleared and his rigid body relaxed. He took a deep breath and looked around the room. "Time grows short. The darkness is growing. It will not remain contained as it is. I am afraid that we need to not only free the *Orchids*, but also strengthen our numbers with incredible haste. War is upon us. The *Orchids* are calling for allies—Alandria needs to know who fights for her." His deep soulful eyes bored into each of them in the room. "We need to know who is with us."

"I have allies that will be loyal to me in Adettlyn." Aidón stepped forward. "I will go to them and prepare the territory of Lumari." Head bowed and arm raised to his heart, he waited a breath of a second before he looked to the king and queen. "It has been too long. It will be my honor to fight alongside you and yours once again. Not only are you beloved royalty, but I count you as beloved family as well."

The king had a knowing grin on his face as he nodded his approval. The queen gave a loving glance at Kaeleigh and then back to Aidón. "We are family indeed." Then her eyes intensified with a smile. "Our people will come together once more." Kaeylnísa threw off customary protocol and embraced him, uniting the house of the Elves with the Ehsmia. "Make haste, Aidón, surprise will be your ally and stealth your guardian. As much as you will be drawn to your home, to your son, you must find our allies or there will be nothing for you, or any of us, to go back to. The state of Adettlyn will break your heart if you see through its glamour—of this I am sure you will—but stay the path. Your journey will be well received."

Aidón nodded. "I will leave at first light. Perhaps our scattered departures will bring confusion to those that might be tracking our movements out of this hidden place."

The Elder along with the royalty nodded and murmured their agreement.

There was more discussion of loyalties, allies, and where they could assemble them once they came. Finn had been talking with Ella off to the side in what was clearly a private conversation, but Ella did not look too happy with the outcome. She sighed then stormed away from him. "So be it."

Ella spoke out when there was a brief moment of silence between the planning. Arileas and the king had been poring over a map that they had taken down from the wall. "Finn and I will go to the Twined camp and gather the warriors that have been training. It's time to follow through on our promise. It's time to give them their chance to be a part of Alandria."

"Yes," Kaeleigh interjected confidently. "I could not agree more. They have won my heart. I believe they have won all our hearts. Let them join us and let them call Alandria home, if they so desire." Suddenly aware that they were all staring at her, Kaeleigh stepped back with a moment of hesitance and insecurity. But then she felt Daegan at her back, strong and solid. She could feel the heat coming off his body. Confidence began rebuilding itself within her.

"Do not back down from any decision you have made. Stand firm in your belief. They respect you," he whispered right next to her ear, sending shivers all the way down to her toes. His warm breath on her neck made her want to curl up in a ball and snuggle into him. She caught herself leaning back into him and stood tall. She could feel a chuckle silently shake his chest just before he moved back to give her decision space.

Kaeleigh shook her shoulders and regained her stature. She looked at her grandfather and was humbled to see pride in his eyes.

"It is a well-deserved proposal," Hal spoke up. He had remained quietly observing up to that point. "They have been either ostracized or ignored along with the Shifters of Alandria for far too long. It is a wrong that my family has condoned and I want to make it right." He paused and took a breath. For some reason, he seemed nervous about what he was to say next. "I would also like to suggest that I go to Mandü tré Lan with Chel to find allies among the clans of her race." Hal's eyes shifted to where he could see Chel out of their corner, gauging her reaction. It seemed she was surprised by his suggestion, but then perhaps excited about seeing her ancestral home.

"I would like to see where I am from," Chel said, biting her lip as she thought through the plan. "But what about going with Daegan and Kaeleigh?" She directed her gaze at Hal, knowing he would want to go with Daegan.

"It will be easiest if our journey is quick and focused," Daegan said.

"Translation: without distraction, quiet, and so you don't have to watch out for everyone." Chel winked at him.

"Not exactly, but we will be in situations where fewer people involved will be to our benefit. Stealth in the mortal realm, with beings both good and evil hiding in plain sight, is essential. There are those with dark hearts seeking the same thing we are, and they have been seeking it for centuries. They will not hesitate to murder us without thought if we are discovered. Stealth in Exhile is even more imperative." He did not intend his words to be a harsh dose of reality, but that was exactly how they came across.

It was quiet for a moment as the weight of what they were all doing settled upon the room. They were fighting for a realm and the future of so many. It was daunting. The air was thick with a united faith in their cause mixed with anxiety and fear of what was to come.

CHAPTER TWENTY-EIGHT

S tanding at the entryway into and out of Ehsmia was Aidón. He was surrounded by Kaeleigh and the entire group as they came to wish him well. He checked his weapons to ensure they were securely in place for his journey. One of the Faeries that worked in the kitchen handed Ella a satchel, which she in turn handed to Aidón.

"Food for the journey. It is not much but it is enough and it will be light for you to carry swiftly." Ella bowed her head to him before stepping back.

"My thanks to you and gratitude to the hands that prepared it," Aidón said humbly.

Everyone said their farewells and wished him safe travels back to Adettlyn. Kaeleigh was last to approach him. Hesitant, she stood in front of him, willing herself not to cry. She would see him again. She had to. He was family.

Aidón placed his hands upon her shoulders and looked into her eyes. As if reading her mind, he spoke confidently. "We shall meet again, Kaeleighnna. I would not be here if it were not for you and your friends. We have so little time, but it is our honor to be destined for such a moment of great importance. However, with it comes sacrifice and duty." Kaeleigh couldn't speak for fear of losing the emotional net she was barely containing. She nodded, understanding. Aidón looked to Daegan who stood not far from her, then to all of Kaeleigh's friends. "Take care of one another. You will be tested of your strengths and loyalty to this cause, of this I am sure. Stay true to each other and the light of Alandria. She will guide you and we will meet again." He placed his fist to his heart honoring them all, then he turned to walk out the portal into his unknown adventure. He would unite those willing to fight for Alandria. He would do all that was necessary to bring peace back to his home of Adettlyn. Even if it meant the death of its dark ruler, his own son.

"Wait!" Kaeleigh shouted. She ran to him without shame and threw her arms around his neck and hugged him, truly not knowing if she would see him again. There were no more words needed; they were above all, family. She released him after looking into his tear-filled eyes. He smiled and turned quickly away, vanishing within seconds.

"This is fascinating," Kaeleigh commented as they watched Arileas work with Metrí in the training room. Seated with legs crossed on the ground facing each other, Metrí and the Elder closed their eyes. They were supposed to be meditating and focusing on their inner energy and releasing their magic for different tests.

"Yeah, except Metrí seems distracted. That's like the tenth time she has dropped her item," Chel whispered.

"Well, it's good they switched to wooden and natural items, I think she broke an entire place setting of dishes," Hal interjected from behind Chel. They were sitting on the ground off to the side, watching the training. They were supposed to be doing their own meditation to learn to join their magic as one, but so far they hadn't been able to accomplish that. Their thoughts were scattered as they pondered the future. They needed to take a break, and so they did.

"Maybe if you would stop talking and do what you're supposed to do, I wouldn't be so distracted!" Metrí snapped, her eyes still closed and her hands still relaxed on her thighs.

"Oops," Chel snickered. They were all quiet for a change as they continued to watch for a few more minutes.

Scattered around the two in the center ring were various items they scrounged from around Ehsmia: wooden bowls, a few things that looked like wooden children's play toys, some shattered pieces of glass from the dishes, a spear—they all opposed Arileas when he laid out one of his small swords—and a few boxes of various sizes. Most were inconsequential items, except for a smoky gray orb of glass that the Elder kept at his side. They had not yet worked with that item, but Kaeleigh watched as Metrí kept sneaking a peek at it as if it had done something different, which it hadn't.

Thud. Another box made of wood, similar to a crate, fell to the ground, luckily not cracking into several splintered pieces. Metrí sighed and her shoulders fell. "What am I doing wrong? And don't say I am not concentrating hard enough, because that was the hardest and longest I have ever focused on anything."

Arileas opened his eyes and looked at the young girl with the bouncing blond hair. She had innocence written in her features, but there was also a relentless curiosity to her. Metrí was sweet and snappy, strong and yet a slip of a girl, curious but also guarded. She seemed to have formed an attachment to Daegan that the others didn't really understand. He looked at her like she was a painful memory come back to life. Even now, he focused intently on her training with the Elder—not in a creepy way, but like he was studying her, understanding her. With his empathic abilities, perhaps he was able to read her better than even Arileas.

"It is not something you are doing wrong, child. I believe it is more what we are not doing right," the Elder said.

"I'm confused. Isn't that the same thing?" Metrí groaned.

"Think of it more like a puzzle to which we need to fit the correct pieces together."

Metrí just looked despairingly at the Elder. Anyone looking at her could tell she was on the verge of either a colossal fit or a breakdown. Suddenly the gray orb next to the Elder began to levitate off the ground just above Arileas's head. It lit up with a soft white-gray light. Surprise lit not only Arileas's eyes but also those of Metrí, who obviously did not intend for that to happen. It fell from where it hovered, snapped out of the air by the quick hand of the Elder before it could crash to the ground.

Daegan cleared his throat. They both turned to look at him, one curious with relief and the other with snapping agitation.

"Her magic feels different than yours or Kaeleigh's or anyone here actually. I believe it will react and be trained differently as well. Do not glare at me like that, little one," Daegan admonished her. As soon as she softened her expression—eye roll and all—he continued. "What I feel from her is a mess of emotion and chaos. She needs to loosen herself from the inside out, to find unity with her energy. It is the how of it that I am uncertain of," Daegan said with a frustrated frown.

"I see something when I *look* at her. I do not know if it would help, but may I share?" Kaeleigh asked as she stood up.

"I do not know," Chel mimicked in a whisper to Finn. "There she goes dropping her contractions again." Chel smirked and shook her head, muttering, "More and more like him, I swear."

"It's not just him, though, most speak that way here if they have had no interaction with mortals," Finn stated quietly as they had a side conversation.

Chel frowned, the wheels in her head turning as she nodded. "Hal doesn't."

"If there is occasion to be formal, notice that he does. But I think he's more humored by it and chooses it because it is different."

"Why don't you do it more since you're back then?"

Finn frowned, suddenly closed off. "Because I choose to retain the mortality I have adopted." End of discussion.

Chel looked up to see Kaeleigh staring at them with her eyebrow cocked. "Do you mind? I'm trying to offer my profound insight here." Chel gestured her hand in a sweeping motion for Kaeleigh to continue.

"Webs. That's what I see. Tangled and broken webs in and around her. They aren't scary or malicious, but layered protection." Kaeleigh looked at Metrí with soft understanding. "I think she is the only one who can unweave them enough to control her magic. I can tell she contains quite a bit of raw energy and I've felt her magic when she's used it before, but it's stifled."

Tears filled the young girl's eyes. The warmth in Kaeleigh's voice and her perceptiveness made her feel vulnerable. The instant she let it hit her, though, she stiffened and held back the rush.

"Well perceived, Kaeleighnna," Arileas said as he watched Metrí. "The question for you, Metrí, is if you will choose to untangle the webs of your past and see what your potential is to create your future."

Metrí looked away from everyone. With a sigh she released her greatest fear. "My future couldn't be that great if whoever abandoned me didn't want me in theirs." Tears began to fall from her eyes, slowly chipping away at the dam constructed around the young girl's heart. "I have nothing," she whispered as Kaeleigh came up behind her and simply held her. It was uncomfortable and slightly awkward for everyone in the room, but something in Metrí broke as she began to sob, turning into Kaeleigh and gripping her tightly.

After several long moments, Metrí hiccuped and took in deep lungfuls of air trying to settle her breakdown. She wiped the tears from her eyes and her face and, embarrassed by the outburst, she let out a strangled laugh. "Oh, look at your shirt, Kaeleigh, I'm sorry."

"Don't be. I chose to hug you. You must have needed the release. I always feel better after a good cry." She smiled at the girl, looking over her now blotchy red cheeks.

Metrí looked up to see Arileas in a state of meditation on his own or perhaps another vision. But to her relief and continued embarrassment, she had driven everyone else out of the training area. Except for the shadow of a bulky Ferrishyn off to the side leaning casually by the weapons near the entrance, giving them the semblance of privacy without going too far. He was probably more there for Kaeleigh than for her, but it still warmed her heart that he was there. She always had wanted a big brother.

Arileas opened his eyes to see straight into Metrí's soul. She was caught off guard and even a little startled, but that only made her mad so she stared back, challenging him to look at what he would with her arched eyebrow and attitude. Unfortunately, it only made the Elder laugh out loud with a deep belly laugh.

Metrí glowered. "That's not usually the reaction I get to my attitude." She looked over at Kaeleigh, who only smiled.

"I am sure it is not," Arileas answered in a semi-grandfatherly manner, "and while many would not tolerate it, I am amused by it. Your spirit and fire are important to who you are, but do take care with whom you use it and use it sparingly with purpose." He stood up and reached for her to take his hand, pulling her up, and then he offered the same to Kaeleigh. "Now, I do believe I have what could be an understanding to your magic. I believe what Kaeleigh has said is right and true. This is a battle within yourself. It will be a day-to-day unraveling until you have found the center and source of your magic. I do not know why I did not consider it before now, but I had a brief vision of you in the mortal realm and your magic's reaction to the land. I believe your magic to be elemental. That is not a magic derived from the source of Alandria's magic." Both Kaeleigh and Metrí looked on with intense interest. "Some might call it a human magic or even witchcraft or wizardry. It is very much the same as magic here, but it is different in that the sources are different. Kaeleighnna, your magic comes from the energy within you that makes you who you are, born of the energy of Alandria. Metrí, your magic comes from the elements themselves. They combine with your natural energy that has an affinity—in this case a very strong affinity—to accept and use them. Our earth Faeries use the elements, but they are elements strongly rooted in Alandria. Their magic would suffer greatly in the mortal realm without stronger blood or gifts—which some have been given, but not as a whole."

"I think I understand." Kaeleigh practically bounced.

"I don't," Metrí replied with a wanting expression.

Arileas explained further. "Your magic will still work here because we have elements that are basically the same as in the mortal realm. However, you will have to learn to navigate their properties in different areas. This is actually very exciting! I have not met an elemental before and have only heard of them as being extremely rare in the mortal realm."

"So this is something I can learn? Can you teach me then?" She looked expectantly at the Elder.

"In a manner. Some of it will be experimental, I am afraid, but I will help you. Your patience and understanding will be required, of course," he said.

"So... basically, are you saying that I'm a witch?"

"An elemental, but in simple mortal terms... basically, yes. But you do not need spells and things for a casting—as far I understand," Arileas considered with a slight frown.

Kaeleigh watched cautiously, waiting for Metrí's reaction. She was thinking so deeply the crease in her forehead was taking the form of a canyon. Suddenly the girl's eyes lit up.

"So instead of being a freak in this realm, I'm actually a freak in my own realm." Metrí looked back and forth between Kaeleigh and the Elder, then also noticed Daegan had come out of the shadows and stood waiting and watching.

"Sweetie, you're not a freak—" Kaeleigh began.

"But don't you get it? I am, but that's okay with me. I always knew I was some kind of freak, I just hated not knowing how I fit. And while I'm still slightly different than all of you, this tells me who I am. Now I can finally figure out how I work." Her genuine excitement was infectious as Kaeleigh's face lit with reserved amusement and then a gleeful grin.

"This will change things for you, warrioress," Daegan informed her.

She nodded with exuberance. "I'm ready to realize who I am and see what I can do." She was excited, yet also aware of the possible challenges that were now before her. But, at least she had an idea of what she would face.

The unknown was a dark and lonely place, Kaeleigh knew. Even on the edge of it, it was enough to change people and challenge who they believed themselves to be with who they thought they were not. The confusion and insecurity of the unknown could tear a person apart from the inside out if they do not have something to anchor their beliefs to: a revelation, a dream, a drive, a soul mate... anything that would face them with the truth of who they were and to remind them of why they were there.

Kaeleigh turned to Daegan's face and searched his eyes. He was her anchor. He stepped close to her, so close they were front to front but not quite touching. He laced his hands with hers and whispered, "You are mine as well." Then he moved away and placed a hand on Metrí's shoulder, giving it a brotherly squeeze. "How long until you think she might have a little more control of her power, Master Elder?"

Arileas cocked his head, scrutinizing the young girl before him. "Not long. She is ambitious, perhaps a couple days for her to re-arrange the webs in her attic, so to speak, and then she will feel what her magic is truly responsive to." He winked in Metrí's direction. A blush crept up into her cheeks, creating a nice rosy glow.

"I think it is important for her to stay here in Ehsmia and continue her training."

"What?" Metrí turned on Daegan, her eyes smoldering with the injustice of his words.

"You would be safer here and can train more focused with your magic. I know you are significant in the freedom of Alandria, but I need you to be safe and learn all you can," Kaeleigh pleaded with the girl.

Metrí's eyes softened and covered her disappointment with her bravado. "Safer? I can still outmaneuver you on the field, Lumieth girl."

Kaeleigh gave her a funny look. "You need to work on your smack talk too." She giggled, but then turned serious eyes to Daegan, who spoke.

"It is a feeling I have. I understand it is disappointing and it is not that we do not want you with us, but I know this to be the right path for now," he said with conviction.

Metrí stared at him intently for longer than comfortable to others in the room. Conceding to his "gut," she nodded. "Okay. I trust you."

"Thank you." Daegan smiled at her and then ruffled the hair on the top of her head.

CHAPTER TWENTY-NINE

ELNYE. THE CASTLE IN ELNYE, THE CAPITAL OF FERAÁNMAR.

M aleina's steps were loud as she walked into the old wing of the castle. The slap of her heels on cold stone reverberated off the walls, the sound empty and lonely. She walked slowly, her movements svelte and purposeful. Her emerald dress trailed slightly behind her. She walked down one side of the hall and held out her hand, her fingers absently trailing the stones in the wall. Her fingers itched for the powerful energy she could feel buried behind the stone. The walls in the rebuilt part of the castle were smooth ivory marble decorated with spidering veins of red, whereas this was an older section of the mansion. It was what was left of the original castle before it had been mostly destroyed in the last great battle along with the slow decay of time. The library was sheltered in this part, but other than that there wasn't much left in the old wing. At the end of the hall, there was a discreetly sheltered stone stairway that was originally used for servants. Also sheltered at the end of the hall was a hidden doorway. A doorway that led to the floor below.

The closer Maleina walked to the end of the hall, the stronger she could feel the pulse of magic that drew her there once again. No one followed her, she made sure of that. With single focus and intent, she stopped before the stone wall. She walked around the false wall encasing the old servants' stairway leading to the upper levels and into the darkness that lay below it. A flick of her index finger lit the first torch, guiding her foot down the stone steps that led below. With every few steps she took, the torches lit, continuing to light her path down the spiral. The temperature began to drop, as the air became moist. She couldn't see the bottom—all that lay below was darkness—but she did not fear the dark or what lay beneath the library.

At the bottom, she took a deep, heady breath. The scents of mildew and moss were strong, but the scent that drew her above the dankness was bitter and metallic. She could see her breath as she exhaled. As she continued to step further into the room, the torches sprung up all around the room that was not much bigger than the library above it. It looked like a cellar encased by ragged stone rock walls. There was a hum of energy that drew her to a wall off to the side. She could hear the faint rhythmic beat. *Thump thump... thump thump.* She smiled.

To anyone besides Maleina, it appeared as the rest of the stone walls in the lower level: stone standing the test of time, the foundation of a castle's former glory. As she rested her hands upon the stone, infusing her magic into the rock, it slowly shifted. The wall groaned as it slid apart at the middle like two doors opening. Opening several feet, it revealed another wall behind it. This wall, however, was different. It was made of different colored stones, yet similar in the smooth texture of the other walls. These stones appeared to be porous and even had mosses of light-deprived green growing on them. It was humid. It had the same musty smell, the same overriding scent of metal that she encountered upon first entering the room, but stronger... much stronger.

There was what looked like a spindly tree growing against, and attached to, the stones of the wall. Rooted into the ground through a crack in the floor, it then grew up from there and continued through multiple cracks in the ceiling. The branches were not brown or green like vine, but a deep red. This was no plant at all but it was alive. It was life itself. It was a vein and in it, blood flowed. Darkness radiated from this monstrosity that grew under her home.

Maleina could feel her magic responding to the beat of the sound she had heard. It was usually enough to siphon the essence of it from the very veins spidering throughout the castle trapped within the marble walls. It should've been enough for her to simply stand before the veined tree to absorb the energy it provided. However, this time was different. She needed more. Maleina had done what *She*, her now former mistress, had told her wasn't possible. Maleina had broken her tie with the witch in the mountains of Exhile. Maleina was free and could now reign in Alandria on her own, or so she believed.

Reaching her long, slender fingers toward the source of the veins at eye level, she punctured the thin skin surrounding the blood with one of her sharp red fingernails. Leaving her finger in the tiny hole she made, she turned her hand palm up and let the blood drip down her finger onto her palm, pooling there until the trickle became a steady stream. Taking her other hand, she sliced open a thin line of her skin just below her wrist parallel to her arm. She tilted her arm, and the blood flowed from her palm down a path straight into the open wound as her energy directed it. Maleina's eyes fluttered as she absorbed not only the blood—the life essence of those she deemed unworthy of existence in her kingdom—but the energy and power that dwelt within it. The first hit of energy was intoxicating. She swayed with the weight of it as it entwined with her own.

As she finished, she sent a surge of her energy into her fingertip to cauterize the hole she punctured into her morbid "tree of life." She felt strong and sated. The power circulating in her body was tangible and she could feel its current paving its way from her head to her toes.

At the top of the stairway, she sealed the doorway, placing her hands upon it. Her magic was instantaneous and fluid. As she sauntered back down the hall of the west wing, her image was one to behold. She was striking. Her eyes shone with the newly consumed power.

Passing the library entrance, she felt a presence and turned sharply. There was no one there, not even a shadow. She cocked her head, listening. Nothing. Continuing down the hall, she again felt a presence following her. There was a faint hint of laughter, dark and mysterious, that seemed to surround her. Maleina was not afraid, but she was irritated and curious. She kept walking, the sound of her shoes clipping along as she picked up her pace, daring the presence to follow her.

Her steps had reached the end of the hallway when upon passing a mirror, she almost tripped on her polished high heels. Maleina did not stop to linger, but what she saw in the mirror sent shivers down her spine. She felt the blood begin to pull from her head.

"It's not possible. *She* cannot be here. I have wards. *She* is in Exhile!" Maleina defiantly declared under her breath. Again the eerie cackle lightly swirled around her as she turned from the old wing, heading toward her personal chamber.

In the safety of her chamber, Maleina paced in a tight space in front of her dainty, yet ornately carved wood desk. Filled with new power, she let it wash over her. She inhaled slowly and deeply, letting her anxiety leave with her exhale. She leaned forward, placing both her hands palm down on her desk. After a moment, she stood up straight, running her hands down her green dress.

"They are mere echoes of the past, Maleina," she whispered to herself with relief. Deciding to dress more appropriately for her journey to Adettlyn to meet with King Syén, she chose a traveling dress and cloak. After changing clothes, she stood regally before the full-length distressed silver framed mirror. Just as she was turning to retrieve her cloak, her image floated in the mirror once again. *She* leered at Maleina and threw her head back with a haughty laugh. The laugh was dark and occupied the small chamber as it squeezed the air right out of Maleina's lungs. Maleina fell back against a nearby chair, overwhelmed with shock as she looked back at the mirror in horror. Them Maleina felt a surge of anger rise in her chest as she pushed up from the fallen chair, bringing it with her. She swung the wooden chair with all her strength directly at the mirror, shattering the glass all over the ground, effectively banishing the unwanted intruder from it. Maleina breathed heavily. She straightened her dress, grabbed her cloak, and fled her own chamber.

On her way out the entrance of her home followed by a handful of her guards, she passed not a mirror, but a maid on her knees on the marble floor, scrubbing it, sloshing water about the floor. Maleina's intake of breath startled the maid, causing her to cringe and quickly scoot to a doorway beyond her. The sound of evil laughter followed her out the open doorway.

"I will find you, my pet." The voice belonging to the mistress of darkness surrounded Maleina, wrapping seductively around her. Maleina looked around, but no one else seemed able to hear her. *She* was in her head. *She* was surrounding her.

"I am coming!" *She* shouted so loudly, Maleina physically covered her ears. The laughter grew louder and louder, following Maleina out to the stables where her horse and guards traveling with her awaited. Maleina's anger burned along with a growing uncertainty and fear. She was determined to see her plan fulfilled. This path had cost her everything, and she was so close. Flames rose in her eyes as her indignation surged within her veins, dancing with her new power. She could feel the energy slither under her skin, ready to strike. Syén awaited her at Adettlyn with the reinforcements she had asked for. They would be there or else. Syén's usefulness was beginning to wear thin. Maleina and her entourage headed out, riding fast and hard toward the territory of the Elves.

Maleina would see her victory. No one, not even *She*, would stop her.

Chapter Thirty

Ehsmia. The Home of the Hidden People.

"We're leaving today, Kae." Chel choked on a sob. "I don't want to do it. Not without you. I have this terrible feeling. I'm not sure if it's regarding you or me or just a generic sense of doom for all living things, but I don't like it! And now I have to be alone with a very pretty Faerie boy!"

Kaeleigh bounced on her friend's bed that was in the cavernous room the girls all shared and squeezed her tight. She held onto Chel for dear life, as if that could keep them together. "I don't like it either. I have a feeling too, but I don't know what it means," she said with a frown.

"Have you had any visionary"—Chel waved her hand, searching for the right word—"revelationy things in a while?"

Kaeleigh's eyes sparked with amusement. "No, I haven't in a while. Arileas said that was a gift I shared with him and my mother as well. He's really the only one I can learn from to try and understand how it works." They were quiet for a few seconds just being with each other. "Hey, have you had any other feelings like you might shift?"

Chel scrunched her nose up, "Not really. I talked to Hal about it, though, he said not to worry about it—like you did—that it would happen when it was the right time. Maybe being around others like me will set something off." She shrugged.

"I will be pissed if I'm not there when it happens." Kaeleigh pouted and folded her arms like a petulant child.

"Why?" Chel pushed her friend over on the bed.

"Are you kidding me? Because it's a huge part of you and I don't want to miss it or not be there for you," she said, trying to hold back her own tears.

"I'll try to hold off, you know, wait until after you come back for me," Chel teased. Kaeleigh retaliated and pushed her back.

"That 'pretty Faerie boy' better take care of you, or I'll find a nice home for him in Exhile," Kaeleigh said, now serious.

Chel blushed uncharacteristically. "He said he would. Well, his exact words were: 'My sword is yours on this journey and I will serve you with my life and protect you with my death.' That's a little intense for me, but I appreciate the sentiment."

Kaeleigh's jaw opened and Chel reached over to snap it shut with a flick of her finger. "Whoa, Chel, that's pretty big. He could have just said, 'Hey baby, I'll keep you safe and warm.'" The girls giggled. "What about Samuel? Have you given him any more thought? I mean you supposedly live with him back home."

Chel frowned. "I know. I'm not sure what to think. Honestly, I haven't really thought much of him since being here. That's bad, isn't it?"

"Not bad. I think it means something though." Kaeleigh shrugged, trying not to lay on her opinion of Samuel too thick. She had thought from the beginning something was off about him and that they rushed things really fast. "Give it some thought, though, when you're on this journey with Hal."

Chel nodded with consideration. "I wonder if he misses me. Sometimes it seemed like he didn't even really like me that much, but just wanted me to be with him, if that makes sense." She shrugged. "I mean he's probably moved on thinking I wasn't coming back or something. Plus what he doesn't know won't hurt him, right? Maybe I'll give Hal a shot. After all, we are going to be all alone on our little adventure." Chel winked at Kaeleigh, trying to move on, uncomfortable with where the conversation had gone. Kaeleigh rolled her eyes. "Speaking of alone... what is going on with you and Daegan? Spill it!" Chel was practically bouncing on her bed, jostling Kaeleigh all over it.

Kaeleigh's cheeks flushed crimson and she looked around the room, avoiding Chel's penetrating stare. "Come on, Kae! You can't ask those questions and then not answer mine!" Chel, no longer bouncing, protested with hands on her hips and a glare in her gaze. Kaeleigh sighed.

"He basically opened up to me. Said he wants me and apparently is not leaving my side except for when I'm in here with you." She closed her eyes tight as if anticipating the look on Chel's face which would not disappoint. If Chel's eyes grew any wider they would probably explode and the Grand Canyon would lose the competition with her mouth for openness. Then the mother of all squeals pierced the momentary pause for shock. Kaeleigh had to cover her ears. In fact, she toppled over onto her side in the fetal position, covering her ears and closing her eyes as Chel jumped and rocked the mattress. Suddenly a large weight crashed on top of Kaeleigh practically suffocating her.

"I knew it!" Chel whispered next to Kaeleigh's ears.

"I knew it, I knew it, I knew it!" she repeated louder and at light speed.

"Fine. You knew it. Can you get off me now?" Kaeleigh struggled to get the words out with her friend crushing her lungs. Chel rolled off the top of her and they both lay side by side on the bed, quietly contemplating. Then they both started giggling.

"We sound like teenagers with girly crushes," Kaeleigh laughed out disgustedly.

"We *are* teenagers with girly crushes. Get over it. It's awesome!" Chel stated proudly.

"Yeah, it is." Kaeleigh smiled, her thoughts going to a very muscular, dark, stoic Ferrishyn warrior who had stolen her heart. A warmth flooded her soul and relaxed her body. *He's mine,* she thought with confidence.

And you are mine, Daegan replied in her mind, sending his own feelings of warmth and happiness to her through their connection.

You can hear me?

I can, he replied. *You are getting stronger and our connection to each other is stronger. You are projecting to me specifically, that is how I heard you.*

Kaeleigh sat straight up from the bed. She looked to Chel, who was totally unaware of her private connection with Daegan. She smiled and wanted to try it again. *I'm saying goodbye to Chel. Are you with Hal?*

I am. Meet us out by the entrance when you are ready.

Kaeleigh nodded, forgetting he couldn't see her. *We will be there shortly.* She closed her mind to him and focused on Chel, who was now looking at her curiously.

"What are you doing? You seemed to be concentrating extremely hard," Chel observed.

"Nothing. You ready to head out?"

Chel took a deep breath and looked around the room to see if there was anything else she needed to take with her. They didn't have much with them, but some of the Ehsmia had given them clothing and few necessary items. Chel picked up her bag and looked at the food items placed inside it for their journey. "I don't think I will ever be a vegetarian again. It's too hard to survive out there without hunting and eating whatever you can find. It's so conflicting to eat a little furry animal when I know I could possibly one day shift into one myself." A pained look crossed her face.

"Maybe Hal can help you learn which leaves and berries or whatever else that might not have legs you can eat on the way. I bet the shifters might have tricks for it as well. You'll see." Kaeleigh smiled.

"Way to find the silver lining, Kae." Chel smiled in return. "Okay, let's get this show on the road... or dirt path... or whatever it is." They walked out of their room, arm in arm off to meet the wizard—or the warriors as the case may be.

After several more minutes of hugs and tears, Hal and Chel were ready to head toward the Shifter territory of Mandü tré Lan, where they would try to find new allies. Chel, of course, hoped to learn more about her heritage and perhaps even her family, if there were any distant relatives to be found.

"Please take care of her. I know you will, but... she's my family," Kaeleigh pleaded with Hal as she grabbed him before he put his pack on his back.

He smiled and nodded at Kaeleigh. Putting reassuring hands on her shoulders, he looked directly into her eyes. "I will protect her as my own... family, I mean." Halister backed away with a slight flush in his cheeks that took Kaeleigh aback for a brief second. Then she glared at him. "If you break her heart, I will come after you and find some magic that will hurt you in some"—she stumbled on her words realizing she really didn't want to be mean to Hal—"in some bad way on your body or something painful. Oh heck with it, just please don't hurt her." She glared at him, half smiling at her bungled insult, until he nodded in complete understanding.

Hal backed away from her and turned to Daegan, who surprisingly couldn't hide the quirk of his lip. Halister questioned Daegan with a look, but only received a shoulder shrug in turn. "She is a mean one, brother." Hal winked playfully at them all then reached his hand out to Daegan. Daegan reached his hand out, grasping Halister's forearm as they had done many times before, and then they brought each other in for a brotherly hug, slapping each other on their backs. "Take care of each other. We cannot lose either one of you and especially not both. She will come after you and I have no idea what she is capable of." Hal's mind filled with anguish at the thought of his mother hurting anyone, let alone Daegan. "I hate that I will not be there to have your back." He looked to Kaeleigh as well. "Either of your backs."

"Bring it in," Chel commanded as she pushed all of them together for a group hug.

After a few more minutes together, they said their final goodbyes. Kaeleigh didn't go far as she watched Hal and Chel fade from view as they entered the tunnel. She stood on the edge of where the soft emerald green grass met the compacted dirt that opened into the tunnel that would take them to the portal out of Ehsmia and into whatever was waiting for them. She really hoped there was nothing waiting for them. Kaeleigh could never live with herself if something happened to them.

"No!" was all she could say out loud and then taking a deep breath, she ran to the tunnel and out of sight after them.

"Kaeleigh!" Daegan turned around just as she disappeared into the tunnel and tore after her. He reached her as she stood directly in front of where the portal should be, but instead she found solid rock and dirt. Not taking the time to create light, he followed his ears to find her in the dark. Like a blind man, he felt for her and found her braced with hands against the tunnel wall, her back heaving, wracked with sobs. His heart broke for her in that moment.

"I can't find the opening! What if I just sent them to their deaths?" Kaeleigh could barely get the words out and breathe.

Daegan wrapped his arms around her from behind, bringing her back away from the wall. His wide chest solid at her back, he held her. Sending peaceful energy to her, he tried to calm her down. He rubbed his hands up and down her arms as he whispered soothing words of another language next to her ear, his head resting against hers. She turned her head into his, cheek to cheek. Then mouth to mouth. Hungrily, their mouths danced, seeking comfort and reassurance. Kaeleigh turned into him, pressing her body against his, desperate for his warmth and the feel of him against her. Grabbing his shirt in her hands, she pulled him into her, chest to chest not close enough. Too many barriers between them. She felt her way up his chest, entwining her fingers into his silky hair at the base of his neck. Their kisses escalated into something far more raw and needy. His hands felt their way up and down her spine, one holding her neck at the top of her spine. Their passionate energy sent sparks into the darkness; it could have lit a torch when Daegan grabbed her leg and hoisted her up closer to him. She wrapped her legs around him as he pushed her back into the tunnel wall, knocking loose some of the dirt which then rained down upon her head. Some of it fell into her eyes, causing her to blink agitatedly and pulled back from his full and very kissable lips.

"What..." Kaeleigh tried to wipe the dirt away and then giggled slightly from the realization and possible embarrassment of what they had been doing, but also from the intoxicating energy he was pouring into her that made her giddy. Chest to chest, they were both breathing erratically, their energy still swirling about them in a soft glow allowing them to see each other in the darkness. Forehead to forehead, they tried to catch their breaths also bringing with it a sense of awareness. He released her legs but she did not release her arms around his neck. His hands were steady at her hips, fingers imprinting their design upon her. She played with the hair her fingers were tangled with. They simply held each other. After a few minutes, they both had calmed but her body was shaking. He scooped her up in his arms and walked her back through the tunnel into the light of Ehsmia.

"They will be all right," he said confidently.

"How do you know?" she asked weakly as she laid her head on his shoulder.

"Because they have to be."

CHAPTER THIRTY-ONE

"**A**ll these goodbyes are killing me," Kaeleigh groaned as she walked with Metrí. It was already the next day and they were headed to where Ella and Finn were saying farewell to the Elder Arileas and the king and queen of Ehsmia. Daegan had respectfully said his goodbyes then headed off to gather a few extra things for their own journey. Kaeleigh watched him for a moment as he went his way. Her stomach fluttered and she smiled briefly, reliving their make-out session in the dark tunnel the night before.

"You okay?" Metrí asked, eyeing Kaeleigh suspiciously then shifting her gaze to Daegan.

A blush flooded Kaeleigh's cheeks and she quickly turned her head back toward the destination ahead of them.

"Uh-huh, sure." Metrí started giggling.

"What?" Kaeleigh asked innocently enough.

"You totally got it on with him, didn't you?"

"What? No!" If possible, Kaeleigh's face turned even more red than before. "It wasn't that at all. We just... kissed." At Metrí's girlish gasp, Kaeleigh rolled her eyes. "Kissed. Just kissed... a lot." This time Kaeleigh giggled.

"I knew it!"

"No you didn't. You thought we 'did it,'" Kaeleigh reminded her complete with air quotes.

"Nah, I didn't really, I just wanted you to tell me what you really did do." Metrí, apparently satisfied with her accomplishment, skipped—actually skipped—up to Ella with a big cheesy grin on her face.

Kaeleigh sighed and walked up to Finn with her arms wide open. Finn returned her embrace. "You all right?" he asked into her hair.

"Yeah, I just hate saying goodbye." Kaeleigh's eyes filled with tears. "Both of you are going to be gone. I've never been without even one of you for very long." Tears started to flow down her face. "I mean I know this is what we need to do, I feel it is right in the very depths of me, but I still don't want us to all be separated."

Finn sighed and looked at Kaeleigh with soft eyes. "I know. I don't like it either, but we *need* to do it. This is what we were meant to do and now we're actually doing it." Finn held her arms' length away from himself so he could look into her eyes. "We are all going to be fine. You are going to do amazing things. I wish I could be there to see it, but Daegan will be with you.

"The point is... if it is right for us to be doing this, then Alandria will supply what we need. It doesn't mean it will be easy or safe, but the greatest results never are."

"I always know you're right when you sound like Gandalf the Grey." Kaeleigh wiped a tear and smiled.

"Excuse me, my friend, I am Gandalf the White," Finn corrected her with mock seriousness.

"Gather the Twined, then find us again. We need them and we need you." Kaeleigh couldn't handle more than that and went to give Ella a quick goodbye. When she stood before Ella about to reach out to hug her, Ella did something Kaeleigh wasn't expecting. She got down on one knee and bowed her head to Kaeleigh. Kaeleigh was shocked, but something in her was also humbled and accepting of the loyalty and honor that Ella had just bestowed on her. Kaeleigh reached down and placed her hand on Ella's shoulder.

"Rise, Ella of Ehsmia." Kaeleigh didn't know where the words came from but she felt them so she went with it. Ella stood up and looked to Kaeleigh. "You honor me and you honor Ehsmia. Accomplish your mission and do not tarry in your return to your home." Satisfied that Ella didn't laugh at her, she then threw herself into Ella, wrapping her arms around her in a tight hug. Then she whispered into Ella's ear, "Please take care of him. He needs you—I think he's always been in love with you."

When Kaeleigh pulled back, she saw shock and even a slight glimmer of hope in Ella's eyes. Smiling, Kaeleigh stepped away and ran into the Great Hall. With every goodbye, she felt her heart tearing into even smaller pieces. Shivering with the cold reality of loneliness, she wrapped her arms around herself and sat at the table that faced the back wall of the large room. Oddly, there was no one else in the Great Hall at this time.

A few moments later, she felt him. Kaeleigh turned to find Daegan standing just inside the entrance. He was leaning with a casual grace against the wall next to the doorway. His arms were loosely crossed, accentuating the definition of his chest underneath a black loose-fitting linen shirt with a mostly open collar barely held together by two ties meeting in the middle. Daegan's eyes lit with a fire only caused from a ravenous hunger.

"When you look at me like that, I feel I might lose control, Kaeleighnna," he said, his voice rough and his eyes lit with desire. But he remained where he was against the wall and did not move closer to her.

"Would that be a bad thing, Daegan?"

"Not bad, but there are other matters we have to engage ourselves in. As much as I want you to myself, Alandria needs you and I will not take you until we have been pronounced properly." His stare told her how serious he was, but the fire in his eyes expressed how much he desired her.

Feeling emboldened by his words, she slowly rose from where she sat and moved toward him with purpose, with intention. He simply watched her, his gaze taking in all of her. For the first time, she *felt* him looking at her, really looking at her not only as someone to watch over and someone to train, but as a woman. A woman he wanted as his own. The butterflies were swarming in her stomach, but she continued to move toward him. She was right in front of him, taunting him as she looked longingly into the deep set of his eyes.

"You are quite the vixen, aren't you? I have not seen this side of you before." He quirked an eyebrow at her.

"You make me feel bold. You make me feel strong and secure." She reached up with both of her hands and entangled a finger of each hand in the ties of his shirt. She gently tugged him down toward her. Looking into her eyes, he could not refuse her. She lifted up on her tiptoes then lightly kissed his full lips. They were soft and pliable. He placed his hands gently on her hips, letting her take the lead. After a moment of her feathered attentions, a growl rumbled from his chest. She took the bottom of his full lips and tugged lightly on it with her teeth before she giggled and turned her back to him as she walked back toward the table at the front of the Great Hall. She could hear his deep breaths behind her and gave herself a satisfied smile. She had not really ever been the "temptress" in a relationship before. Usually that was more Chel's style, but something about Daegan's rightness and honor made her want to break the rules with him and push him to his limits.

"Elder," Daegan quickly acknowledged as Arileas entered the Great Hall.

"Daegan. Kaeleighnna. I am glad you are both here. I hope I am not intruding on anything, but I wanted to see you and say goodbye. Is there anything you wish to discuss before you journey to Exhile?"

Kaeleigh was grateful her back was to both men. She was embarrassed that the Elder almost walked in on her taking advantage of her warrior—*her warrior!*—and didn't want him to see her face flushed. It was still very surreal that Daegan wanted to be with her.

"Kaeleighnna? What do you see in that image?" the Elder asked sincerely as he came to stand beside her with Daegan following on his other side.

She cocked her head as she looked at the mural that had been imposed onto the back wall. It was an extremely large painting that covered almost the entire wall. She had looked at it before during meals and meetings when they had been in the Great Hall, but today it shone like it was standing out for her—calling to her. "I'm not sure yet, but it is drawing me in, asking me to see it. I just am not quite sure what I'm suppose to—"

Kaeleigh gasped then ran up as close as she could get and still see the entire image. To other eyes that looked upon the image, they would see layer upon layer of the evolution of Alandria. All the territories and races were accounted for. It was like a collage of all your friends and family and favorite pictures all arranged in some kind of way that either made sense to the artist or was simply haphazardly placed to fit like puzzle pieces forced together. But when Kaeleigh looked at it with even the slightest release of her magic to see beyond the paint, she saw each layer three dimensionally, like looking into a funnel of time and history. After layer upon layer of beauty then destruction, peace then turmoil, incredible color then shades of darkness, and at the epicenter was an image of desolation and barrenness. And there in the midst of it all, she stood, a blazing light around her and the shadows of who she recognized as the *Orchids*. It was what she imagined Exhile to look like.

The pictures then swirled, pulling her to follow its lead. Pulled in without leaving her place in the Great Hall, she moved through still images of beings either in various acts of battle and devastation or through the fields and valleys of color and abundant life and beauty. She took a deep breath and leaned forward, touching the wall. Kaeleigh became one with the art and suddenly everything sprung to a life of its own. Battles commenced as if she were really there. This one in the past. The valley she had been in, she recognized as the one they had traveled through after leaving Hunter's house. Then she saw him; Hunter was outside his house right before he died at the hand of Maleina then transformed into the rare white bird. It looked directly at her as if he knew where she was before he took to the sky. Her image swirled around and pulled her into the realm of Exhile she had seen herself in before. She could feel the magic needed there, could feel the desperation of the *Orchids*, could feel how she needed to set them free.

Then she had to grip her stomach for fear of losing its contents as she was ripped from that image into another battle. This battle she had not seen before, but somehow knew it was one they had yet to fight. Then she recognized face after face, people—beings—she either knew or had seen before... her friends... Chel, Hal, Finn, Daegan... and many others. Her heart was gripped with the horror and turmoil of what battle could look like up close and personal.

Her stomach rolled again. Then she followed the pull of the image to where she was face to face with herself. *She watched herself fight with not only her sword, but also magic she hadn't yet realized she possessed. The scene was horrific. Beings filled with darkness, beings believing they were fighting for what was right, beings filled with light and goodness all scattered about the field. War did not discriminate—casualties littered the ground for both the dark and the light. Kaeleigh took a moment to be grateful that the scene she saw, she now realized, was in black and white and shades of gray. Her stomach couldn't take seeing it in living color. It was bad enough. The face she fought belonged to Maleina. It did not surprise her, but the other images flickering in and out did. There was also the face of another woman—a dark and vile woman with jet black hair and eyes of fire. Then it was Maleina out of control and encased by serpents and a fog of darkness. Kaeleigh saw her sword glow as the image seemed to be trying to show her something important.* The field lit with a light so blinding, it threw Kaeleigh out of the picture and she flew back into the table in the Great Hall she had started at.

CHAPTER THIRTY-TWO

Panting and trying to regain her breath, Kaeleigh gripped her head with both hands. She could feel Daegan's hands on her.

"Kaeleigh!" Metrí shouted as she ran through the Great Hall, having just entered.

"Are you all right?" Daegan asked as he stroked his hand down the back of her head offering a touch of peace.

"I think so. My head just hurts," Kaeleigh said, still clutching her head with one hand. Metrí rushed up next to her, not sure what to do, but there just the same. She tried to get up on her own, but both Metrí and Daegan grabbed an arm on either side and helped steady her. Arileas was surprisingly quiet. They all looked up to him, but he was lost in a vision, his eyes glazed over almost to the point of whiteness. His body was rigid and tense.

Kaeleigh turned to Daegan. "Can you tell what he is seeing?"

"No, for some reason when he goes into a vision it is like he is untouchable. I can only get vague senses." Daegan stared at the Elder, making another attempt at reading his emotions. Suddenly Daegan's head snapped toward the doorway and his eyes narrowed. "Something is wrong..."

"Danger," both Daegan and Arileas uttered at the same ominous time just as Arileas came out of his vision.

"Freaky," muttered Metrí under her breath.

Kaeleigh agreed. "What?!" she asked, trying not to panic. "What is it?"

"It seems you are going to have to leave sooner than you planned. Maleina. She is in the forest." Arileas took off, still in a slight daze. They all followed him as he shouted commands and orders to various Faeries they passed.

"Metrí, run and get my pack from the room, please," Kaeleigh requested and the young girl nodded and took off without question.

"Meet me by the entrance. Do not go through that tunnel without me," Daegan issued as a command and a plea at the same time. He took off toward the training area. Kaeleigh could only guess he went for more weapons, even though he was never without all of his.

Kaeleigh continued to follow closely behind Arileas. She didn't realize that the old man could still move so fast. He was driven and completely in charge and everyone obeyed his command. Then she realized that he had extreme motivation as well: Ella. She and Finn had left not that long before. Kaeleigh's steps picked up and she came up beside the Elder. "What can I do?"

"Ella sent me the vision. Prepare yourself. For now is a time to fight. I do not know what she has intended, but she has brought the fight to our door and invoked the wrath of the Dryads by involving the trees of this forest," he ground out.

"The trees?"

"She is burning the forest, flushing us out, I am sure. We are purposely walking out into a trap." His voice was weighty, but filled with confidence. He knew what he was doing and they were prepared for whatever came to their doorstep. It was why the Ehsmia had been able to stay the "hidden people" for so long.

Daegan had come up behind them and began issuing his orders, instructing the warriors around them what he knew of Maleina's capabilities, which he realized he did not know near as much as he would like when facing an enemy, even an enemy he had grown up with. Her duplicity kept him from understanding her twisted ways.

Kaeleigh slid her hand into Daegan's strong masculine hand, taking comfort in being close to him. "What did you go back for?"

"A weapon," he said with a glint in his eyes and a smirk on his mouth.

Kaeleigh questioned him with her face, but he didn't give her any more than that. He squeezed her hand and tugged her along by his side. She had to move fast to keep up with his longer strides. Metrí ran up beside Kaeleigh and handed her the satchel she had prepacked. One of the cooks in the kitchen had packed all of their bags with provisions that very morning, not realizing it was only supposed to be Ella and Finn departing—or perhaps she had known they would all be leaving. Kaeleigh was always surprised at the different types of magic each had and their gifting that went along with it. She was learning not to question too many things anymore.

"We go out in small groups. Blend into the shadows. Assess the situation and surround the enemy. Two of our own might be out there. Keep eyes out for them." With that last instruction from Arileas, they did exactly that. He held Daegan, Kaeleigh, and Metrí back by him. "Let them get in position. We do not know what we face," he instructed.

"I do not stay in the back, Elder. I fight at the front of my men," Daegan said with clenched teeth. It was heavy upon him that he was not out there.

"I understand, but you are in a slightly different position this time," Arileas said, nodding not only to Kaeleigh but also Metrí. Daegan nodded. "It is imperative that your mission not be compromised. This time you must stay to the outside, prepared to get to the portal that will take you to the mortal realm."

"I was not aware there was a portal to the mortal realm in this region of Alandria," Daegan said.

"And for good reason. We prefer to keep it that way. You will still have to journey to find it. It is in the valley beyond the Kandrian Mountain, past the village of Klavaí and beyond the reaches of the known parts of Alandria. It will be a challenge. Follow your instincts, Daegan, they will show you the way. The path has been imprinted on your soul by your grandmother should you ever need it."

Daegan looked to the roof of the tunnel lit only by a few torches. He quickly remembered standing in that very spot with Kaeleigh not that long ago... in the dark. Then he quashed those thoughts quickly, replacing them with thoughts of his grandmother who earlier that day had already said her goodbye. She knew something would take him away sooner than she had planned. When she had hugged him she whispered words that he remembered her whispering when he was young, but this time instead of taking away pieces of his memory, they revealed more than he was prepared for.

"Then that is where we will go," Daegan resolved.

Arileas put his hand to the dirt-covered tunnel wall, whispering ancient words to conceal and guide as they went. Each of them placed their hands against the wall as they took a step forward and stepped into the dirt wall that shimmered, becoming a transparent veil to walk through.

CHAPTER THIRTY-THREE

As Kaeleigh stepped through the veil and outside of the mountain, she noticed the sky was gray and ominous. It was the first time she had been back out in days and when she took a deep first breath, she almost choked on the bitter air. They could see the smoke. It was right along the path that Finn and Ella were to take back to the portal into Tylínyth. They had been ambushed right near the portal.

Those exiting the veil were still a ways away from what seemed to be the center of destruction, but it stung her eyes and they instantly watered. Her teeth were gritty and her tongue dry. It was what she imagined it would be like to eat charcoal. Her stomach roiled at the stench of it. It wouldn't be so bad if it had smelled like a giant campfire. Most people like the smell of campfires, but this... this was so much worse. It smelled like death. A screech rent the sky. Kaeleigh threw her hands over her ears and almost crumpled to the ground as her knees buckled.

Daegan reached for her, hauling her to his side, his strength supporting her as they moved swiftly to the side to allow for the others to come through the veil. They all coughed and pulled their clothes or hands or whatever was available up over their mouths to not breathe the thick air. The sounds coming from the forest surrounding the mountain were unbearable. The pain, the terror, the destruction... Kaeleigh couldn't take it. She pulled against Daegan. He looked down at her with question, but instantly his face changed to one of resolve.

"We can't leave them! We have to help them, Daegan," Kaeleigh pleaded.

"Agreed." It was all he said, but his support and need to do the right thing warmed her heart, but also made those pesky butterflies of nerves soar at the prospect of fighting.

"You have to get to the portal, Kaeleighnna. That is your objective. That is what will stop all this." Arileas fiercely gestured back to the forest. His eyes were ablaze with determination as to what he believed was truly the best course of action.

"No. We have to help them! Ella is in there. Finn is in there." Kaeleigh's voice cracked. She did not have time to fall apart now. No, she would follow her heart. She would fight. Kaeleigh felt a weight at her back that had not been there for the last couple days. She smirked as she reached behind her and confidently pulled from the holster at her back the sword that had chosen her, then she quickly replaced it. The path that Ella and Finn had taken was in the opposite direction they were headed, but she took the sword as a sign.

Arileas's eyes went wide at the sword's timing to reveal itself and what it meant. He took a deep breath and nodded his head sharply. "So be it."

"You do not leave my side unless it is absolutely necessary. We fight as one," Daegan commanded sternly as he looked deep into Kaeleigh's eyes.

She nodded and agreed. "One."

Something deep in Kaeleigh began to stir and rise up out of her. She was made for this. It was part of her heritage. She had the blood of a Ferrishyn, but not only that, the blood of the Ehsmia and the blood of the Elves. She felt the strengths and gifts of each race rising up within her and coming together, uniting for a purpose higher than any she could have created for herself. It was ancient and powerful. This was her land and these were her people.

They snuck through the forest to get as close as they could without revealing their presence. If they crouched low, the air was thinner and cleaner. It was not such a struggle to breathe. Holding Kaeleigh's hand, Daegan led the way, deftly avoiding downed

branches and sidestepping fallen trees. Little blue fires were spring-
ing up in random places, magic their guide, as they wrought destruction with every lick they took. Once the fires latched onto something
they could burn, they were unstoppable. A sharp inhale came from
Kaeleigh as they were maneuvering around a tree that was on fire
and still fighting it with its green energy. Kaeleigh could *see* it. All
over the tree, its life energy—the very magic that made these trees
what they were—was flowing and pulsing, pushing its magic in
concentrated bursts where the fires were attempting to combat it.
It was not working.

Kaeleigh pulled her hand from Daegan but he only held on
tighter. He did, however, allow her to pull him with her toward the
tree. She glared at his hand where he refused to let her go, but he only
nodded his head toward the tree, telling her to focus and do what she
came to do. Kaeleigh went right up to the tree and placed her hand
on its trunk where fire had scorched a path straight up into the "Y"
of the tree where it began to branch off—its weakness. The bark was
rough and brittle under her hand, but the pain she felt coming from
inside the tree, from the very heart of it, broke her own. Daegan did
as she did and placed his hand on top of hers. His energy flowed into
hers, entangling with her own as they poured into the tree. Arileas
snuck up behind them and placed his hand on Kaeleigh's shoulder.
He sent a surge of his own power into her as well.

Their united power burst into the tree. Kaeleigh could feel the
tree welcoming their energy with gratefulness and relief. The little
fires that were eating their way through the thick foliage and strong
branches were suddenly doused, leaving trickles of smoke in their
wakes. There was an audible sigh from the tree. Kaeleigh wrapped
her arms around the tree and sent another blast of her energy its
way. The tree began its regenerating healing faster than it would have
under normal circumstances.

"Kaeleigh, we have to go," Arileas prodded. She looked back at
him and nodded.

"There are too many trees, we cannot save them one by one this
way," Daegan offered, full of thought.

"I know but we have to try!" Kaeleigh whispered as loud as she could without actually using her voice. She didn't want to give away their presence.

"Kaeleigh…" Daegan took a deep breath, his frustration clear. They had to move. They had to act. They had to help. They had to fight, but he didn't know where to start.

"There!" Arileas whispered as he pointed. Off to the side a ways into the foray, Ella and Finn were crouched behind a large bush, but would stand and send out blasts of energy in the form of fireballs toward something they couldn't see through the smoke. A moment later, a returning fireball would soar straight overhead, but thankfully missing them. They began to see others of the Ehsmia strategically placed at a wide circle focusing on that very area that Ella and Finn were facing.

Daegan searched out all the possible angles. Kaeleigh could see the strategic wheels in his head moving as she tried to think of a way to help.

"Elder, will you cover Ella and Finn while Kaeleigh and I circle around to the opposite side. We will attack whatever is in the center of the smoke-induced circle at once. Do not overshoot though. We need to contain and then dismantle whatever is behind this attack. I am certain Maleina will be found here, but I am not sure what or who else is with her," Daegan growled out.

Another screech of epic proportions pierced the forest. Kaeleigh's head snapped toward the smoke-filled center. "Holly," she whispered, her voice strangled with terror. "I know that tree. Hurry, we have to finish this!" Kaeleigh grabbed Daegan's hand and began to pull him.

He quickly took the lead and directed her around the circle, once again ducking and leaping over branches and rocks that littered the forest floor. There was a heaviness mixed with vibrating fear that was taking over the trees that they passed. They were mourning their fallen. Daegan would reach out his hand and touch as many as he could as they passed. Sending bursts of healing energy and courage into them, he whispered in his foreign tongue. Kaeleigh saw what he was doing and could actually *feel* a change in the spirits of the trees. She began reaching out to the trees on her side that he was missing. As a team they strengthened and poured new life into the forest. Every once in a while Daegan would say, "Call to her. Bring her." Kaeleigh wasn't sure who he was referring to, but she joined him.

"Who are we calling?" she asked after a minute of doing it.

"Andreinna."

Ah. Kaeleigh had met the Dryad priestess of the forest. "Wouldn't she know what was happening in her forests?"

"The trees are hiding her. They will die before letting her come to harm. She needs to be called."

Daegan and Kaeleigh found cover behind some rocks on a slight rise in the forest terrain. They could see what was happening in front of them much clearer from their position.

"Maleina." Daegan gritted his teeth. Kaeleigh reached out and placed her hand on his forearm. He took a breath and surveyed the area. "What can you see?"

Kaeleigh looked around, squinting and moving her head at various angles. "Nothing. I can't see anything beyond that smoke."

"It is a diversion. Think of it as a smokescreen. What can you *see*?" he asked again.

Understanding dawned on Kaeleigh and she focused her magic to filter through her eyes to see beyond what was in front of her. "I see her!" Kaeleigh excitedly exclaimed with a whisper. Then carefully and more studied, she added, "There are dark vines or threads of magic surrounding her. They twist and wrap around her with a life of their own, but they are definitely tied to her. And eyes... " Kaeleigh gasped. "Those aren't vines, Daegan, they're snakes! They are entwined in her hair, but have free range over her body." She looked to him with panic in her eyes.

He looked into her eyes, and his lack of surprise told her he had seen this before. "What else?"

"Those zombie-looking guys from the other day are there too."

"The Ónarach."

"Yes, them. They're the ones throwing the fireballs, but Maleina seems to be concentrating on something. Her eyes are wide open but unseeing, like she's in a trance." Kaeleigh glanced at Daegan, who was nodding like he expected what she said. Kaeleigh felt a chill run up her spine. "What's our plan?"

"I am going to distract her. You will stay here and focus on creating a shield around me with your magic, in case."

"What?" she looked at him like he had suddenly grown two heads. "No way. In case of what? How do we take her down?"

"I do not know if we do. The most we can do is distract her and wait until the priestess arrives. This is her domain. We need her additional power, Kaeleigh." Daegan ran a hand down his face. "Maleina has grown strong. I am not aware how strong yet and I am not willing to put you in the middle of it if we do not have to."

Kaeleigh suddenly felt a concrete resolve settle within her mixed with rage. "That is not good enough! We have to fight," she demanded.

"Yes, we do." Daegan did not argue. "However, there is a time for it and my soul tells me this is not it. Now, we save the trees. We save Finn and Ella so they can get to the Twined. We save ourselves so we can free the *Orchids*."

Something in his eyes jumped out at her. She could see the pain and the conflict there. He would end it now if he thought they could. Her rage softened as she felt Daegan's inner compulsion to do what was necessary and get to the *Orchids* as fast as possible. She complied. "All right. After I *try* to put a shield around you, then what happens? Do I try to take them out?"

"No, then it will be my turn to step in," a strong and angry feminine voice whispered all around them. Kaeleigh couldn't tell if it was in her mind or said out loud. There was no one nearby, then suddenly through the smoke just beyond them stepped Andreinna, the Dryad priestess. There was a very ethereal air about her; she was visible but she didn't quite seem solid. She floated through the smoke like a ghost stepping out of one tree, wildly sauntering into the next, advancing on them. Kaeleigh watched in awe. She was pretty sure her mouth was gaping open. The Dryad's beauty, wild and untamed, was striking as she got closer. Her eyes were glowing white hot anger.

Daegan shifted onto a knee, bowing his head in respect. Kaeleigh glanced over at him and quickly did the same. She didn't think the priestess would hurt them, but her power was pushing upon them, seeking out enemies and allies. Andreinna stopped right before them. She was still not completely solid in her state. Hair the color of sunset, complete with branches and twigs, flowed with a life all its own as if she had a fan blowing in front of her.

"So the time has come. This is the beginning. Maleina is pulling on a power that does not belong to her or to this realm. She must be stopped." Her voice was an ominous monotone until her eyes shifted directly to Kaeleigh. "Your power is strong, but this is not your time. However, for the moment, I gladly welcome your power into my fight."

"My power is your power," Kaeleigh offered.

"Given freely?" Andreinna was suspicious.

"Yes." Kaeleigh kept her head down, but her eyes looked up into the Dryad's. There was hope in them.

"You will make a great leader, Kaeleighnna." The priestess' eyes rose to peer through the smoke that was billowing before them. "Follow your plan. I will do the rest."

As Andreinna slowly turned back toward the fighting, she whispered into both of their minds, *From this day forth, the Dryads now fight with the Sol-lumieth... no matter the end.* She glanced back at them with blazing eyes and a confident smile.

CHAPTER THIRTY-FOUR

"**I** know you are there! Come out and face me, *nephew*," Maleina taunted. "I can *feel* your presence along with that little witch and her deception."

Behind the bush, Kaeleigh looked up to Daegan's fierce eyes with question. "Me?" she mouthed as she pointed to herself. Daegan frowned, but there was a slight twitch of his mouth as if he was amused.

"I can burn down this entire forest, Daegan. COME OUT!" she shouted. Her voice carried through the smoke and seemed to seek his presence out.

Daegan began to rise, to go out and meet her face to face. Kaeleigh reached out and gripped his arm. He looked down at her with his eyebrows pinched. There was a war in his eyes. He did not want to leave her, but he knew he had to go out there to protect her, to protect what was his. For the first time, he felt it—this land, this people, were his to protect. And he would.

Kaeleigh let him go. She would expect him to do the same, when her time arose. "Go. But you better come back to me." She pulled him down into her face and pressed her mouth against his. The kiss was short, but it was not sweet. It was passionate and aggressive, a promise of a future together for him to fight for. He responded in kind then drew away abruptly, his chest heaving for breath. Without pulling his face too far away, his gaze searched her eyes and reached into her soul. He opened himself up to her, allowing his soul to connect with hers. She inhaled sharply at the welcome intrusion. It was not painful but warm and gentle like a cozy hug, but on the inside. Their souls longed to be together and so they were.

"Shields up," he whispered. Before either of them could say or do anything else, he jumped up and boldly walked into the smoke.

Andreinna was still standing there, ready to advance as Daegan walked toward Maleina. Her presence was powerful and eerie at the same time. "You do not need to fear, Kaeleighnna. This is not the end."

"Thank you," Kaeleigh said, not sure what else to say. She took a deep breath and turned back to look through the smoke. The way the smoke danced and billowed, there were often breaks of air that allowed for a visible opening without Kaeleigh needing to use magic to see. It was becoming second nature to her. Sometimes her magic reacted before she even intended it to. Her eyes followed Daegan's back, strong and solid with muscle and pride. She took a deep breath and focused her energy to surround him as best she could, satisfied that it would help at least for now. If he took too long, she was concerned she wouldn't be able to hold it. However, lately, her magic felt far more effortless. She had learned how to pull energy from the land and the resources everywhere around her. With the blood of her Elf side, she could draw energy from the sun and the moons. From her Faerie/Ferrishyn blood, she could pull from the grass, the foliage, any living plant containing energy. From her Ehsmian heritage and the ancient bloodlines of royalty, she could pull from the old magic that was still foreign to her, but it seemed to respond to her nonetheless. Kaeleigh's magic was strong and adapted to her needs and compensated accordingly as if it were a living entity on its own.

Through the distant areas of smoke clearing, she could keep an eye on where Finn and Ella and Arileas were. She tried to locate others of the Ehsmia that she knew were out there, but she had a hard time with all the smoke and the encroaching Ónarach that were not only surrounding Maleina, but also advancing in small groups to try and engage those fighting against her. They were grotesque in appearance and even looked worse for wear than the first time they confronted Kaeleigh and her friends. They moved in groups of three to five, marching in unison as puppets responding to their master. Perhaps that was what Maleina was controlling with her moments of entrancement. Through a clearing in the smoke Kaeleigh looked back to her, but Maleina's eyes seemed lucid as she looked hungrily at Daegan as if she was about to devour a savory piece of meat. She was practically salivating at the raw power she felt coming from Daegan. Some of what she felt most likely belonged to the shield of energy Kaeleigh had surrounding him, but it would also be attributed to Daegan's fresh remembrance of who he was and the power he contained along with his freedom from her wicked clutches.

Maleina sauntered closer to Daegan, her hand stretched out, caressing the air around him as if she could feel the energy radiating out from him. Daegan held perfectly still, but in the way of confidence. He was an intimidating sight to behold. He was also creating quite the distraction simply by being himself. Several of the Ónarach loosely surrounded him, enclosing him with Maleina.

"Where is my disloyal son? I thought he was always with you, following like the puppy he is," Maleina questioned with a sing-song voice that skirted the edge of sanity as she continued to move around him, distracted by his energy.

Kaeleigh was a little surprised to realize he was doing it on purpose to keep her close. Kaeleigh wanted to try something. She sent out a flare of her energy that was tied with his. Kaeleigh watched as Maleina's eyes widened at the visible surge of power, her tongue even licking her lips hungrily. Kaeleigh reined it in, pulling it back into herself as she watched Maleina grow agitated and try to grasp at something not there.

"What was that?" Maleina growled out.

Daegan frowned at her. "What is this all about, Maleina? Why the Ancients, the trees...the Dryads? What have they done to make you lash out at them this way?"

"Absolutely nothing, pet," she crooned, then hardened her features. "They have never done anything for me either!" She practically spat as her hold on sanity appeared to be slipping even more.

"That is why... they will not join me and so they shall perish. Plus it got you to come home to me, now did it not?"

"You are mistaken. I am not with you, Maleina." He paused, looking into her eyes with irreverent confidence. "I know who I am now..." He waited for that to sink in. Her face contorted into a rage that he did not think possible. Her features seemed to morph as darkness surged from within her. "I suspect that you knew who I was all along. Why did you not just kill me when you had the chance?"

"I had suspected, but I could not be certain. You showed many signs, but your bond with Halister..." Her voice faded as if she caught herself finding compassion for a young boy and could not admit to it. "I suppose you think I was foolish. But you were so useful. You could kill when I needed you to. In fact you did, you were my enforcer. So loyal," she sneered with silk-like manipulation.

"Those days are finished," Daegan flatly replied, giving her no quarter in his mind.

Her face took on a dark rage that seemed to bubble up from within her. "The throne is mine! It no longer matters who you are!" Maleina shouted, eyes fixated on Daegan.

"I do not want it. That is the difference between you and I. I will not fight for your power or the throne you have stolen, but I will fight for Alandria. Every living thing in this realm will be free and you will surrender or die," Daegan growled in return.

Maleina took several steps back from Daegan with a sneer on her face that could rival an evil from any legend ever told. She began to cackle, her laugh taking on different sounds as if she were possessed by something with a voice of its own. Suddenly, the snakes that were still swarming her body stopped. Simultaneously, they slithered off of Maleina and out from her, disappearing into the forest beyond where she stood. Maleina shuddered at their absence and her eyes glossed over momentarily. There was one snake that remained comfortably wrapped around Maleina's neck. The rest of the snakes slithered up various trees that were either still standing or still struggling to put out fires.

Kaeleigh's eyes widened and her body leaned forward as if she would lunge into the action. She had a very bad feeling about what just happened. She feared for Daegan. Watching him intently, she did not miss the slight shake of his head telling her to stay put. Her eyes shifted quickly between Daegan and Maleina. She was ready. Quietly, the priestess of the forest came up next to her. Kaeleigh turned to watch her as she crouched down. The Dryad was graceful and beautiful, especially for someone with appendages that changed between flesh and branches as Andreinna's energy shifted erratically.

"It is time," she whispered, her voice turbulent as the wind in a rising storm. "She will pay for what she has done. It will not be today. There are darker things at work here. Today we send a message, but her time will come." Andreinna's eyes caught Kaeleigh's own. The vengeance she saw there made her breath hitch. "Wait for the signal, then shift your power to Maleina, to the snake you see around her neck."

"What about Daegan? I'll be leaving him without a shield."

Andreinna cocked her head at Kaeleigh with an odd smirk. "He can take care of himself. Or do you not trust his power?"

"No. I do...completely." Kaeleigh nodded her head with finality. "I'm ready."

"Take care of the remaining snake, Kaeleighnna. I will take care of the trees. Daegan and the others will take care of the Ónarach." Andreinna stood up and began to back into the closest tree. "Remember, wait for the signal. You will know it when you see it." Then she stepped into the tree as she became completely transparent again.

Kaeleigh gazed back at the center where the smoke had begun dissipating. The fires were no longer as prominent; she could see a lot more clearly without using her energy. She could feel Daegan's strength as he faced off with Maleina.

Just then Maleina's eyes, filled with fire, snapped up toward Daegan. "The Priestess is here. Why is she here?!" Maleina practically hissed.

"You are threatening and destroying her kind. Did you really think she would not come?" Daegan taunted her.

"No matter, my snakes will take care of the remaining trees. You could still join me, Daegan. Just think what our magic combined could do!" The hunger blended with a fresh desperation in her eyes. It was disturbing.

"No. You will lose everything, Maleina. Does that not mean anything to you? You have already lost the loyalty of your son. I imagine that of Rheina as well. Where does Wren stand? Does he continue to stand with you? Only out of love, but that will be lost over time. There is still time for you to stop, time for you to fix what you have done."

"I lose nothing if they do not support me, they will only pull me down. They would try to take my power for themselves."

Daegan was trying to distract her as he saw Andreinna making her way from tree to tree from his peripheral vision. She was healing fallen trees as quickly as she could, then sending a surge of her power into all the others. She was uniting the trees for something specific.

"They take nothing for themselves. All they have ever wanted from you was your love."

Kaeleigh's heart pinched. She couldn't help but wonder if he was including himself in that statement.

"Lies. All of it. I see them watching me, waiting for a moment of weakness. They mock me as do you. They have never loved me! They would not stand with me then and they do not stand with me now. So they have become my enemy," she spat out with rage.

"They are your family!" Daegan shouted, maintaining his diversion. "You are not fit to be a mother, Maleina. Your end is coming. Your choices will be your demise!" Daegan tried to hold still, but the anger and the power was building so strong within him. He could only think of Halister and Rheina and even Wren and what she had put them all through. He saw Andreinna give an imperceptible nod out of the corner of his eye. "This will end!" he shouted, almost exploding as he held back his rage.

She jerked back, her eyes aflame. "You know not what you provoke, young prince. If I go down, you are going down with me! *She* will find you. If I do not destroy you, *She* most assuredly will."

Maleina cackled. At Daegan's confused look, she twirled slowly with her arms outstretched. "Watch the snakes, Daegan. Watch what I can do!" The snake that was around her neck unwound itself behind her head as it stretched and moved to slowly slither down one of her arms, encircling it as it went. When it reached her wrist its head reared back, exposing its massive set of fangs, and then it lunged into her flesh, biting her deep. Instead of screaming, Maleina's eyes rolled back in ecstasy as a sigh of pleasure shivered through her body.

Daegan took a step back; clearly this was not what he was expecting to happen. His eyes shot to where Kaeleigh waited anxiously on the balls of her feet, ready to leap into action when the signal came. She was confused why they had not acted yet. What was the purpose of Maleina allowing the snake to bite her?

Maleina began to laugh once again as a wisp of darkness seeped out of the puncture wounds the snake had left. "Poison, Daegan."

Suddenly, everything around them stopped. The fires, the fighting, it all came to a standstill of dark expectation. It was eerie. Kaeleigh felt it within her before it began. There was a surge of darkness and then there were screams. The screeching, screaming sound was coming from the trees. It was a cross between a human scream and the souls of the trees escaping their wounds for all to hear. The snakes had all bitten into the trees, unleashing their poison into the very veins of life underlying their protective bark.

"Now, Kaeleighnna." Andreinna's tumultuous voice carried on the wind straight to where Kaeleigh waited. Without hesitation, Kaeleigh let her energy build up in her core, pulling back from what she had sent to Daegan and gathering what was available at her core simultaneously. She felt the pressure build until she didn't think she could contain it any longer, then she let it build a little more. Finally, she directed her magic straight at the snake wrapped greedily around Maleina. She had never directed power at something so small and attached to a person, but her magic flew sure and pierced the snake with a blinding flash of light. It fell lifeless at Maleina's feet with an audible thud. What was left of it was charred and unrecognizable. It smoked and smelled like sulfur and burnt flesh.

A moment later, the Dryad priestess bent down and put her hands to the ground and released her magic. It soared through the network of roots that united all the trees in the forest like an electrical current. Visibly, it could be seen traveling up into each of the trees through their trunks and into their branches. Andreinna's energy joined with Kaeleigh's as each collided from opposite sides in the forest, one through the trees and the other through the snake connection.

Suddenly, all around them they heard hisses mixed with small screeches. The leaves of the trees shook as snakes fell from trees all throughout the forest. Singed and burnt, lifeless and charred, they littered the forest floor. Simultaneously, the Dryad priestess rose above the ground her magic lifting her in all her ethereal beauty, the light of her magic piercing the darkness of the forest. She then moved fast from tree to tree, stirring their life and their magic. Then calling upon their energy, the priestess released her magic to join with the power that the Dryads were pushing out from their glowing limbs. Visible streams of green energy flowed through the forest as it pulsed with the power of their priestess. Suddenly, an explosion of brilliant green energy shot up into the sky. Then just as quickly, it came back down and burst out into the forest as far as the eye could see. Kaeleigh watched in awe as it began healing and restoring the trees back to their original strength and stature. It was magnificent.

Daegan had pulled out his sword from his back and was fighting Ónarach two and three at a time. He moved fast and sure, not entertaining but dispatching them one by one with ease. The other Ehsmian warriors joined the fray. Finn jumped into the chaos as well and fought alongside Daegan. They fought together back to back, destroying their enemies from all sides. With focused strikes, they took down one Ónarach after another. It was easy once they realized that each of the abominations had no master to guide them.

Kaeleigh stayed where she was as Arileas and Ella came running up to her. "Her retribution will be harsh and swift. We need to go now," Ella panted out. Her clothes were singed and she had black marks on part of her exposed skin, but overall she appeared unharmed. Arileas looked completely unaffected as if he just had joined them even though Kaeleigh saw him fighting with weapon and magic. He confounded her in so many ways.

Arileas says it's time to retreat, Kaeleigh whispered to Daegan's mind.

No. We finish this. We finish it now. I have a Quarian Sun. Close your eyes, he whispered in return.

"Close your eyes!" Kaeleigh yelled to anyone who would hear her. Like a bomb, there was an explosion of light that was so bright it blinded everyone in the forest, causing them to drop their weapons and cover their eyes.

"NOOOOOO!" Maleina screamed with rage that gave way to defeat, her body expressive with arms flown out from her sides, suspended in air. Her face contorted with horror, she screamed again. It tore throughout the forest, the tremors of her voice shaking everyone and everything in proximity.

When the light from the Quarian Sun subsided, it revealed the efficiency of the warriors of Ehsmia. They had Maleina completely surrounded with spears, swords, and bows drawn and aimed at her. The Sun had fulfilled its purpose for distraction and incapacitation. Maleina remained still with a haughty air about her, refusing to look any of them in the eye, especially Daegan.

Andreinna stood behind the line of warriors. Green energy still visibly crackled all around her as she moved through the fighters with not only grace and beauty, but a fierce indignation in her eyes. She raised her palms skyward as if she pulled something invisible from the ground with them. Suddenly, large roots and vines of various sizes shot through the ground, raining dirt down all around them. They were crawling and wrapping around Maleina's legs, ensnaring her and pulling her down to the ground. On her knees, she glared at the priestess as she was encased in a prison created by the trees. Still she said nothing.

CHAPTER THIRTY-FIVE

A NEW ENCOUNTER.

D aegan looked around at the still slightly hazy battlefield, the green energy having chased away the smoke. The clearing was littered with fallen Ónarach. Suddenly, the ground shook with slight tremors, cracking open just enough to pull the bodies down into the very land itself to be absorbed. He had seen this once before, long ago. What he was surprised to see was Maleina, on her knees, her face clenched in pain and a gash dripping blood down the side of her otherwise flawless face. There was a part of him that wanted to release her, but his heart knew better. He reached out for Kaeleigh's soft, warm hand—a hand that knew no violence or hatred or evil—and he gripped it inside his own. His hands were not innocent, but he would choose redemption over revenge.

Daegan stepped through the line of Ehsmia as the priestess had, Kaeleigh gripping his hand as she moved with him. She watched as Daegan looked on Maleina. There was conflict in his eyes. Through their bond, she could feel him torn with the evil that she had become and the mother figure he had known. Kaeleigh gave his hand a reassuring squeeze and felt an answering resolve from his energy. Maleina had made her choices and now he had made his.

Ella came up beside Kaeleigh and whispered in her ear. "The portal back into the Twined realm is through that cavern, straight ahead." She pointed to it. "Finn and I must leave you now! There is no time. Stay safe." She then went to Arileas and grabbed his hand, whispering something into his ear before she and Finn turned to go. While it was a victory, everyone knew in truth, this was just the beginning of the war for Alandria.

Daegan took another step forward to address Maleina. Right as he was about to speak, Maleina's body shook all over as she moaned and then instantly, she went rigid then sagged uncharacteristically. They all stopped dead in their tracks. Finn and Ella turned, curious to see what was happening, and returned to their place at Arileas' side.

Maleina looked up without lifting her head, her gaze finding Daegan instantly. Her black eyes—*black eyes? The other woman*—bore into his own from under her lashes. Daegan stiffened as did everyone around him.

"Who are you?" Daegan demanded.

She glared at them with hatred and unfounded victory. Her lips were thin and tight as she surveyed the group in front of her. "Those in the mountain of Exhile call me *She* or the Mistress of Darkness, but I have also been known by other names."

"You are not welcome in Alandria." Kaeleigh stepped forward boldly.

"You?" *She* eyed Kaeleigh then laughed darkly. "So you are the Sol-lumieth?" She laughed again as she looked pointedly at Kaeleigh. "I expected more." It was eerie hearing emotion in the words, but not seeing it expressed on her face. Maleina's face was flat, every emotion shut down completely except the black in her eyes that conveyed pure evil. "I will deal with you severely, young princess... when the time is right." She paused with a thought. "Or perhaps you will find me?" the woman said snidely, her eyes boring into Kaeleigh for a brief moment before shifting her gaze to Daegan. Her voice purred, "You truly resemble your father."

Maleina's eyes closed and her head dropped. Everyone stood quiet, watching and waiting for only a short moment. Then quietly, she began to sing, her eyes still closed. Her voice was a high-pitched and eerie whisper as she began, "I have found my little poppet. I told her I always would. She thought she could undermine me. She was wrong!" The last of the song growled out of her with the grinding rasp of unfiltered hate.

Maleina's body held limp as *She* used her like a marionette. Her lip lifted in a sneer just as her blackened eyes shifted in the direction Ella and Finn had been heading. She raised her finger in their direction, her mouth forming indecipherable words. They carried on the wind, before anyone realized what she had done. Daegan heard the words of an ancient tongue, words laced with darkness and destruction first.

"Down!" he yelled, throwing himself on top of Kaeleigh from behind, knocking her to the ground with a thud and a squeal.

The cursed energy slammed into the rock face of the mountain in front of them, traveling through the entrance straight into the portal. The shimmering edge of the veil leading into Tylínyth was just barely visible, until hit with the force of magic. There was a burst of light. The magic didn't explode right away; it attached itself to the portal barrier, weaving its curse into the fiber of the veil until it finally shattered. The magical detonation shook the ground of Alandria, bringing down a small avalanche of rock and effectively sealing off the entrance into the cavern. Raising their heads up from the ground, Kaeleigh, Daegan, Finn, and Ella along with everyone else watched as the only portal into the Twined realm from Alandria was destroyed.

Numb. No one moved. There was a deafening silence. Ella turned her head back with vacant eyes, seeing Daegan and Kaeleigh but not seeing them at the same time. Either she was in complete shock or she was attempting to communicate with someone other than Arileas. Everything seemed to move in slow motion and then speed up all in one movement. Daegan hauled Kaeleigh up to her feet as they ducked and ran up to Finn.

"Get her up!" Daegan yelled to Finn, pointing at Ella. They all were to their feet with Daegan and Finn pulling the girls closely behind them. Ella turned her glare, full of hatred and unspeakable things she would like to do to Maleina or whoever was using her. They all stared at the center of the clearing where Maleina still remained. She was awkwardly struggling against the vines and roots that held her down. It looked forced and full of tension; her body held at strange angles and a mask of pain and rage seemed a permanent etching upon her face. The black eyes of the other woman shone like polished obsidian stones as they sought out Kaeleigh within the group.

There was an ominous, dark chuckle in the air as the wind picked up. Black wind swirled around them, teasing Kaeleigh's hair, taunting them with its approach. Kaeleigh almost screeched as she saw red eyes fade in and out of the darkness, as if the Droch-Shúil were not truly there, but figments of their essence.

"Kaeleigh, you have the light in you. They cannot approach it. It will drive them back from us." Daegan looked over to her with full confidence in his eyes. "I will help you, but I need you to visualize your light surrounding us and shielding us."

Kaeleigh nodded. She could feel the darkness within the wind. Shivers wracked her body, but she focused on her energy within—her light to shut out the darkness.

Their energy, the magical light within them, shot out and instantly joined together, striking down like a bolt of lightning. It created a strong wall of light in front of them then continued to form all around them. Kaeleigh watched as the darkness reacted to their light. There were hisses and shrieks of frustration from all around them. The darkness slithered in on itself like a den of angry vipers with jerky movements of chaos and confusion. The red eyes blinked out, the light blinding them. One more burst of their light dispelled the darkness. The wind surrounding them calmed. But those obsidian orbs now residing in Maleina's eyes glinted with the blue light of the moons above, now clear of the smoke.

In the center of the clearing, the black winds suddenly swirled to life around Maleina's body. There were mysterious words uttered in a low, guttural voice—words that had not been spoken in Alandria before. Then Maleina was gone. Vanished with the wind.

No one moved, they simply breathed. It was astonishment mixed with relief. Then simultaneously, as if on cue, the creatures of the forest began to stir. They could hear singing and chattering in the forest again. An audible sigh was exhaled from the trees themselves. There was still some mending to do with the trees that had been the worst off, but they were alive and they were together.

Arileas approached Ella and Finn. "No longer does the portal into Tylínyth exist. We cannot simply reconstruct what was built from such ancient magic in one day. Ella, you and Finn will need to accompany Daegan and Kaeleigh as they go into the mortal realm. This changes things considerably, but there is a portal there from which you can enter the Twined realm." The Elder turned to Finn. "Finnlan, Ella knows where the entrance is on the mortal side, but she will need your assistance and knowledge of the mortal realm to help her navigate the journey." Finn nodded and went to stand close to Ella.

"Daegan and Kaeleigh, your path has not changed. Make haste and be safe." Arileas smiled and held his hand out to Daegan in the manner the Ferrishyn were used to. "It is now in your hands. The war has begun. Metrí and I will remain in Ehsmia and prepare for battle. There is much to do."

Arileas bowed to Daegan and then turned to Kaeleigh, lowering his head to her also in a show of respect. Kaeleigh stretched up on her toes and surprised him by kissing his forehead and whispering, "Be safe, my friend. Thank you."

Andreinna stepped up beside them, inclining her eyes toward Kaeleigh and Daegan. "I will guide you to the end of my forest as you journey to Kandri. Beyond my borders, I cannot protect you. However," she paused, "it does appear that your path is already in place."

Daegan bowed his head with some emotion. "My priestess, since I was a child, you have been gracious to me." He looked up at her with the sincerity of a child and then spoke in another tongue. "I thank you, great lady of the forest. You have honored me in battle and now again as you help us on our way. The future seems dark, Priestess."

Her eyes looked with compassion at Daegan. Then she smiled and spoke in a manner all could hear. "It is always dark before the light bursts forth."

Everyone smiled as her words, laced with peace, washed over them.

Arileas waved them off with his hands as he spoke, "Off with you then and may the heart of Alandria go with you all." Then he turned back toward the entrance to Ehsmia.

And so their new journey began as they followed the priestess of the forests leading them on their way.

The forest was alive and cool, vibrating with the magic that had been unleashed throughout it by its priestess. Kaeleigh was mesmerized as she watched Andreinna move. Finally, walking peacefully and not under threat, she could observe so much more. Kaeleigh admired the priestess as her legs didn't seem to touch the ground, but instead she glided between trees, all the while barely touching the earth beneath her. They were initially tired, but the energy that came from all the life and light around them rejuvenated their bodies.

Refreshed, they reached the edge of the forest. It was an abruptly defined demarcation. The trees simply all stopped in a line, creating a border between shelter and a great, wide open plain. It was filled with nothing but field grasses—dying and brown—and brush dotted with a spattering of large boulders.

"Be well, my friends. You will know the way from here." She looked to Kaeleigh and Daegan, pride and honor gleaming in her eyes. "The power of the Dryads will always be your ally. However, I can take you no further than here. But remember, even the rocks choose their friends. You will find many supporters along your path." She stepped back into the closest tree, becoming one with it. Then she vanished completely. Andreinna was gone.

A new journey was beginning. The four of them looked with contemplation out at the open space before them and the mountains that walked along next to it.

Chapter Thirty-Six

Outside the Territory of Lumari. Journey to Kandri.

"**I** don't understand." Finn's face was lost as he took in the desolation before him. "What happened here?" he asked, looking at Daegan and then to Ella.

"I did not realize it was this bad," Ella said with as much confusion, taking in everything in front of her. There was even a boundary line in the sky. Everything this side of the tree line was browns and grays, sickness and death.

Daegan was kneeling on the ground with his hand flat on the land and his fingers digging into the dirt. His eyes were stormy and tormented. "Maleina has been sucking the land dry, feeding her own magic. I have no idea how she is doing this. This is not a magic from Alandria," Daegan spat out in disgust. "It is tainted and poisoned, slowly killing the land. I have seen areas in Elnye that are glamoured with life and greenery, but underneath feel like this. I do not know how the illusion feeds the people though. There must be enough life energy being recycled to not allow them to feel it."

He bowed his head and spoke to the ground. "*Kothnyte. Thantül. Gallten. Brachtah.* You will be set free. I will find a way," he uttered as he withdrew his knife out of the sheath at his side. In a swift, fluid motion, he sliced his palm and gripped a handful of dirt, mixing it with his blood now pooling in his hand. Squeezing tight, he then sprinkled the dirt, returning it to the ground. Kaeleigh knelt down beside him and held her hand out for his knife. He frowned but she only continued to hold forth her hand, palm to the sky. He handed her his knife, blackened at the edge with deep inscriptions of symbols and words ancient to her. She took it and without thought, cut her own hand. Taking some of the dirt she mimicked him, mixing her blood and making a silent vow of her own. As she placed her hand down into the ground, he placed his hand over hers and squeezed it, united in the dirt, their blood mixing, strengthening their vows together.

Kaeleigh jerked her hand back suddenly, as the ground heated in response beneath their hands. Her eyes wide, she looked to Daegan. "Alandria accepts our vow, and is showing her thanks." Kaeleigh smiled, then awkwardly patted the ground. Daegan's lip lifted tightly in silent amusement. Daegan rose then extended his hand to lift her to her feet.

"Thank you," Kaeleigh said.

"The pleasure is mine," Daegan whispered close to her head, sending shivers down to her toes.

When they looked up both Finn and Ella were staring at them with a mix of respect and simple curiosity before they began surveying the land.

"What did you say?" Kaeleigh asked quietly.

"The words do not translate the same, but I vowed to give the land release and then offered the land my blood, binding my words," Daegan replied softly.

"Wow, that is powerful and beautiful."

"I might add you did as well." Daegan smiled proudly at her. Kaeleigh nodded her head in agreement.

After a moment, they looked around at the land before them.

"There is not much for shelter," Finn stated the obvious.

"We cannot stay here," Daegan replied with his own obvious statement.

"Well, I think that much is given," Kaeleigh said, practically rolling her eyes, but then she thought better of it. "Is this the only path to get to the portal Arileas told us about?"

"Yes," Ella answered definitively. "We can skirt the edge of the mountain range there." She pointed off to their side. It was an extension of the range that the Kandrian Mountain was a part of. The range was tall, barren, and rocky. It was a contrast to what the other side of the mountain looked like, lush with greenery and life and even snow-capped. "It will provide at least some shelter and obscurity."

Daegan and Finn both eyed the way that would lead them beside the mountain, nodding at the prospect of it. "I think she's right," Finn added. "At least we wouldn't have to watch our backs from all sides."

"It will also lead us into Kandri," Daegan said flatly. There was a hard edge in his face as he gritted his teeth. Kaeleigh wanted to ask, but thought there might be a better time. As it was, they would be walking for a long distance if the edge of the mountain range had anything to say about it.

"I don't know what's there, but I don't think we have a choice but to follow the mountains. We can't go back," Kaeleigh said.

Daegan looked into her eyes. He had shut down for a moment, but she returned his gaze, enforcing that she was there with him. His gaze softened and he reached for her hand. She quickly gave it to him and he led the way.

Kaeleigh turned back to give a small smile to Finn and Ella following behind them. Everyone was quiet, the mood heavy and somber, their thoughts weighted with concern for the Twined camp and for those they left behind. Not for the first time, Kaeleigh's mind wandered to Chel and Halister on their own journey. She didn't know if there was a god, but if there was she prayed for their safety. Kaeleigh beseeched Alandria to guard over them as she sent her intent within a wave of energy into the land. She wished the group could have gone with them. But they didn't have a choice, they couldn't go back. They could only continue forward, their journey taking them to the mortal realm in search of a map to an ancient book with the key to freeing the *Orchids* from Exhile and the evil that has trapped their souls. The journey felt never-ending at the moment, but then the light from Kaeleigh's energy tickled her in her chest as it swirled about with its own intent. It cocooned her heart, spreading warmth throughout her body. Something bubbled within her—hope. They were getting answers and they were making progress or the darkness would not be so threatened. That thought alone gave her determination and hope for the future. They were stronger than they had been—she was stronger. She had Daegan and together, along with their friends, they would not let the darkness destroy Alandria. They would not fail. They could not.

Sensing her new resolve and feeling the overwhelming sense of hope radiating from Kaeleigh, Daegan stopped and looked back at her with a glimmer of purpose and hope in his own eyes. Then he looked to Ella, who couldn't help but feel the blanket of hope and love for Alandria that was emanating from Kaeleigh, and watched a lone tear fall from her eye. She raised her eyes to his and then to Kaeleigh's and nodded. Finn came up behind her and placed his hand at her lower back. He too embraced the hope and a fierce determination shone in his face.

"We do this together. We carry on for those we love, for this land that gives us life." Daegan spoke with pride and an authority he was embracing as his own. "We will find redemption." Then his gaze matched the look of fierce determination on Finn's face. "And we will drive out the darkness from our land." His jaw tight and his teeth gritted, he held his hand out to Kaeleigh and turned to follow the mountain into the valley of Kandri.

EPILOGUE

The Journey to Mandü tré Lan.

Halister's hand clapped over Chel's mouth as he dragged her back to his chest, maneuvering them both into a crevice behind a large boulder barely big enough for the two of them. "Shhh..." Hal whispered close to her ear as he held her tightly against him. Chel squirmed in his arms, but they were locked down. "They are tracking us," he uttered quietly.

Chel froze. All the blood drained from her head down to her toes, leaving her dizzy and slightly numb. He removed his hand from her mouth and she tilted her head back on his shoulder so she could see his face. His face was tight, his eyes roaming, seeking out the danger hunting them. As he looked down at her face, she questioned him. He seemed to understand and nodded.

The only thing that brought her terror like that was the Droch-Shúil. Chel gulped and tried to move back even further into Hal. If she could have climbed inside of him, she would have. He gripped her shoulder tightly with one arm wrapped above her chest. The other was around her waist, effectively pinning her arms down as well. One of her hands found his thigh and dug her nails in as deep as she could while the other hand had come up to grab his forearm encircling her stomach. She could feel his body tense against hers.

"If you claw me any harder, I might scream like a little girl. Then we'd really draw their attention to us," Hal whispered sarcastically through his gritted teeth. Her death grip loosened just enough that there was no danger of causing him real damage. He relaxed a little behind her. "That is better, thank you."

Chel rolled her eyes to keep from making a snarky comment in return. Self-preservation was more important right now than a good comeback.

"Was there something you wanted to say?" he whispered once again into her ear as his head came forward. Chel looked back up at him with a scowl on her face. *Be quiet,* she mouthed to him. He went back to scanning the area beyond their little hiding spot.

Instantly, Hal's relaxed posture went rigid and the lines on his face grew tight. Chel's head whipped around to face what lay outside the craggy rock opening they were in. She sucked in a silent gasp and held her breath. Unable to take it, she wiggled just enough that she could turn around and bury her head in Halister's chest. He pulled her in tight and held her still. Neither one moved. Even with her head buried in his warm chest made of solid muscle defined and chiseled over time as a Ferrishyn warrior, she closed her eyes. She took a deep breath, inhaling his scent of pine and clove, and found comfort there.

Suddenly Halister leaned down into her hair. Barely audible, he whispered, "Not a sound."

He pulled them into the rocky crevice as far as they could go. His back, up against the abrasive wall, bore the brunt of their temporary shelter. It was rough and dark, but he was grateful. The terrain in this part of Alandria was harsh and chapped, but all the hills of rock and stone provided many small shelters from weather or predators. He just hoped they didn't find their way into the shelter of someone or something they should be avoiding.

Outside the rocky crevice, the wind picked up. There was an eerie feeling carried with it. It grew dark just over the area where they were. It looked like shadows dancing across the desert, but these were no ordinary shadows. It was the Droch-Shúil and they had found them. Red eyes turned toward where they hid, seeking their prey. Suddenly the shadows all moved in another direction led by a larger set of red eyes. Diverted. Hal took a deep breath. Still holding Chel so tight that he was afraid he possibly suffocated her, he whispered, "Like I was saying, you could do without the relentless eye rolling."

Afraid and perturbed that he would risk their safety by correcting a habit induced by adolescent rebellion, she leaned back and scowled up into his face. He looked down at her, standing a head taller than she. "What? It is not becoming on a young female." Hal shrugged his shoulders then winked at her.

So many words went through her mind, but all she could come out with was, "Female? Female? Really, Hal?" She tried to pull back from him but he wouldn't let her. "I'm assuming it's safe to chat now, since you would have already given our position away to our friendly neighbor out there." She jerked her thumb out the entrance behind them. Realizing she still had his shirt in the death grip of her other hand, she let go and tried to smooth out his now wrinkled shirt.

Quietly, he watched her. She looked up into his eyes. Caught off guard by the intensity she saw there, all she could do was stare back. The moment changed into something charged and electric. Chel leaned in a fraction. Hal matched her movements inch for inch. She looked at his very full and enticing lips, and licked her own. Rising on her tiptoes, she was about to close the deal when a handful of pebbles and stones slid in front of their hiding place from above. Chel snapped back away from Hal and then spun around and froze, thinking their evil followers had found them.

"Chel?" came a scratchy male voice from above them.

Chel turned to Hal with complete confusion written on her face. Hal pushed Chel behind himself, but inched his way to peer outside their shelter. Someone jumped down right next to him. Hal didn't flinch. "Who are you?"

"Who are you?" came the same male voice that was now much more familiar to Chel.

Chel peered out from behind Hal's back, surprise and shock fighting for dominance in her expression. "Samuel? What are you doing here?"

"I'm here to take you home where you belong, Chel."

✽✽✽✽✽

Thank you for reading *Fractured Darkness*! I hope you enjoyed the third installment of Kaeleigh and Daegan's adventure! Things are getting intense!! Don't miss their continued journey as this unlikely group goes in search of allies for the coming war. Discover who they will find in book four: ***Fading Light***!

FADING LIGHT:

Kaeleigh, Daegan, Finn, and Ella have just escaped the Forest of Lumei, surviving with the help of the Dryad Priestess, Andreinna. Now, focused on getting to one of the few portals leading to the mortal realm, they continue their journey together through the desolate lands of Alandria. They witness the truth of the land's fading magic before making it to the portal, and their help is needed in the small town of Kandri where the darkness has infiltrated in mysterious ways.

Pairing up, they set out on three missions: Finn with Ella, seek allies amongst the Twined residents of Tylínyth. Kaeleigh and Daegan search for a map to lead them to the Book of Lenoria in order to reach The Orchids. Meanwhile, Chel and Hal seek allies among the Shifters of Mandü tré Lan with a few surprises of their own.

She—the mistress of darkness who resides in the mountains of Exhile—has tried time and again to free herself from captivity. The Orchids unknowingly provide her a source of energy to accelerate her plan for freedom, but how much more will be required? Her power is growing and She is amassing forces of her own.

The allies are gathering, but will they come together in time?

Will Maleina's plans for ultimate power in Alandria be her own undoing?

The light of Alandria is fading. But the fight is far from over, in fact, it is just the beginning.

One-click FADING LIGHT today!
Or read on for an excerpt from Fading Light (Book 4)...

EXCERPT 1 OF FADING LIGHT...

BOOK FOUR IN THE AGE OF ALANDRIA SERIES: CHAPTER ONE

The Realm of Alandria. Kandri. *The plains next to the Kandrian Mountain outside Adettlyn.*

It hadn't taken long for Daegan, Kaeleigh, Finn, and Ella to flee the Forest of Lumei. Maleina Endíl, the paladin and leader of Feraánmar the territory of the Ferrishyn warriors and Earth Faeries, had thrown what amounted to a large tantrum in protest at Daegan's defiance: joining ranks with Kaeleigh and her Alandria supporters. Against the very principals of an Earth Faerie, Maleina had poisoned the trees with lethal bites from her poisonous snakes. Thanks to help from Andreinna, the Dryad priestess and guardian of the forest, Maleina failed to destroy the trees and their life-giving energy. A darkness not from Alandria inhabited Maleina right before the group's eyes. The dark and ancient entity—an unknown female presence—possessed and proved her power by destroying the only portal within Alandria to the Twined realm of Tylínyth through Maleina. Her actions rerouted Finn and Ella from their previous direct route to the pocket realm—a realm within a realm—causing them to join Daegan and Kaeleigh on their journey to find the mysterious portal to the mortal realm. Each pair with a separate mission now joined together to battle what intended to stop them.

For the first time since exiting the forest under the guidance and protection of Andreinna, the four-some were utterly alone. At first they traveled swiftly through the land just beyond the forest; land seemingly barren and bereft of Alandria's magical energy, leaving it simple to traverse. Though they were moving through quickly, it felt unnaturally depressing. Maybe it was their isolation, or the barren expanse they continued to walk. In fact, even the atmosphere weighed in on the group, silencing any conversations they attempted. The group, trapped in a void that sucked not only the life from the ground but tempted them at their core with despair, but they pressed on for the sake of the mission.

"What is this?" Finn finally stammered out. Even for someone usually brooding, Finn appeared worn and withdrawn even more so. The warmth of his hazel eyes muted, and the usual luster of his sandy brown hair dulled.

Ella turned her head toward him. Her short blonde spiky hair fell unnaturally limp. Bleak shadows passed across her usually sharp grey eyes, altering her overall flawlessly bright expression as a Faerie but also what simply made Ella... Ella. As the granddaughter of Arileas, the governing leader of the Ehsmia people, her confidence exuded every aspect, but in this moment her shoulders slumped.

The group hung their heads, each one feeling oppressed, yet unable to explain exactly why or how. Despite not being able to express themselves on the matter, clearly Alandria was dying.

"It has to be Maleina," Kaeleigh muttered, her hand at her heart and moisture within her eyes as she surveyed the land.

Daegan eyed Kaeleigh, speaking the silent *Why don't you elaborate?* Naturally, Kaeleigh shrugged, but then went ahead and put words to her thoughts. "I mean, she is growing in power exponentially from what you," eyes narrowing at Daegan, "have told me about the past. How else could one do that? It stands to reason that somehow Maleina has been syphoning power from the very earth, right?" Her words grew quicker. "I don't know *how* she could be doing it, but I know she is connected."

"I believe you are correct, Kaeleigh, though I am still figuring how she accomplished it." Daegan pinched the bridge of his nose and sighed. "I feel like it is in the forefront of my mind, but just far enough away to keep eluding me," he growled in frustration.

His comment plunged them all back into silence, each one lost in his and her thoughts, the crunch of the dry brittle ground mixed with dead grasses under their boot-clad feet the only sound among them.

Daegan stopped and surveyed the grounds to the north, toward Elnye. The horizon stretched out in the bleakest way possible until you simply could see the land no more. Squatting down to the ground, he picked up some dirt, sprinkled it into the air, and watched it scatter with the wind. Frowning, he placed his hand flat on the earth, and dug his fingers deeper into the dirt. He whispered a few words under his breath—similar to how he had done when they first set out from the forest and made a vow to discover the source of Alandria's ailment. After not even a second, he made an inhumanly frustrated sound as he shot up from the ground.

"Daegan, what is it?" Kaeleigh had asked, rushing to his side, concern all over her face.

"It flows that way." He pointed toward Elnye. "There is a distinct current of motion under the earth, pulling in that direction." Wide eyes, saddened with despair and the reality of what he finally was grasping, he looked to Kaeleigh's for reassurance. "You are right, what energy is left in this place is flowing toward Elnye... to Maleina. I am sure of it. I must find out how!" His fists clenched at either side of him, unsure how best to express himself without having something to strike down with his sword.

Kaeleigh, more subtle than Daegan, reached for his hand and pulled herself over to him, resting her head directly on his chest only inches from his rhythmic heartbeat. Her calmness spread to him, and Daegan allowed it to, placing his hand around the back of her head holding her still. Absorbing her assurances of love gave him the confidence and serenity he knew he lacked.

"We will discover the source and the way of it," she had reassured Daegan. Squeezing his hand, she pulled out from his embrace, yet kept her hand within his.

Ella and Finn not unaware of the tryst between Daegan and Kaeleigh had begun their own conversation while waiting for Daegan's unorthodox ways of understanding the land to end.

Ella stepped forward and interjected herself into the conversation between Kaeleigh and Daegan. "I feel we have tarried here too long. We must keep moving, though I am loathe to interrupt your sacred moments, Daegan."

Daegan nodded. "Of course."

Traveling by foot during the day, building a fire and camping at night in the shelter of the base of the mountain, they were companionable at best but the lengthy silences were beginning to stretch Kaeleigh thin.

"These plains just don't end! They are much more vast than I originally could see," Kaeleigh suddenly announced after two days of walking in the shadow of the Kandrian Mountain. She paused, placing her hands one on her hip and the other shielding her eyes as she gazed up for the millionth time staring at the top of the sleeping giant they had skirted for what felt like forever. Reaching for her water bottle, she then gazed at her companions each beginning to look a little worse for wear.

"It is so quiet here," Kaeleigh huffed, not for the first time since they left the shelter of the forest. Rubbing her hands up her arms, she fought off an unwelcome chill that had begun to surround her. Daegan reached over and placed his hand beneath one of her elbows, sending waves of calming energy into her.

"How much further?" she desperately tried not to ask more than once a day but couldn't stop herself. "Still a day's journey," Ella had snapped at her the last time she asked.

"Sorry, I've asked that a lot haven't I?" she said sheepishly, looking past Ella out at the desolation all around her. As daylight grew scarce and night approached, Kaeleigh felt she might be swallowed whole by the bleakness around them. Even with Daegan sleeping by her side, keeping any boogeymen of Alandria away, the chill of the night still seeped in both physically and mentally. Kaeleigh wondered how they would make it much further in their current condition: weak and haggled from the draining journey.

Ella nodded but smiled sweetly, suddenly filled with grace once more. "I think all this..." she gestured around them, "death and despair is getting to me too," she admitted.

"It's getting to all of us, Kae," Finn answered, his hands busy building a fire for their camp and getting their sleeping packs set out.

Kaeleigh smiled at Finn, grateful for his reassurance even if he didn't show it the same way as she did. Her lack of understanding of Alandria still separated her from the rest of them, but what she did know she loved and wanted to continue learning. She couldn't imagine that desire ever changing or waning. In moments like these, she felt Alandria alive in her heart and that very life warmed her from the inside out, giving her comfort through the dark nights and focus during the days.

Unwilling to discuss some of the more unsavory parts of their journey in the dark such as Maleina or any evil, Kaeleigh smiled at Daegan her heart full of love blooming more each day. Climbing out of her sleeping bag she snuggled close to him, leaning against his legs where he sat on a fallen tree. She found more warmth from him than the sleeping bag itself. Kaeleigh looked up to him, her gaze adoring.

Before they knew it, the group drifted off to sleep, Kaeleigh finding her way back into her sleeping bag.

"Daegan?" Kaeleigh whispered.

"Yes, Kaeleighnna." Her name, a loving caress meant only for her to hear.

"Mmm, I like that." Kaeleigh's eyes closed for a moment, indulging the brief respite as she savored the sound of his voice. "I was wondering how we will find the Book of Lenoria once we are out of Alandria?"

"Yes, I too have been thinking on that," his voice rugged and sleepy from the late hour. "Arileas had told me to trust my instincts and to listen for the voices of the Orchids. They once instructed me on how to find you, you know," he admitted.

"No," she said with a gasp, suddenly feeling more awake than sleepy, "I had no idea!"

Daegan chuckled then continued. "When I entered Montana, a Wisp showed me the way to you. The Orchids also spoke to me, revealing more. So, I believe that is how it will happen again. Although I am not sure if the Wisps will reside where we will exit Alandria as they had in the mountains of Glacier National Park. That park is truly a magical place for creatures of such mortal magic to reside," he explained.

"Wisps are real in the mortal realm?" Kaeleigh's voice grew even louder.

"Kae go to sleep. We can talk about it in the morning," Finn shushed her.

"How can I? I just found out Wisps are real where I grew up, and you expect me to just push it to the back of my mind?" She was shocked.

"Yes, they are in the mortal realm, though there are not many of their kind left, especially in your United States. They originated from the isles of Scotland and Ireland, steeped in Celtic magic. And they only reveal themselves when directed strongly from outside magic such as my Alandrian desire for my destination, that and the influence from the Orchids overseeing the journey." He explained it all quickly and quietly, well aware that each answer would stir another question. "We can discuss that further along with the Orchids part in our journey in the morning."

"You know me well by now, oh wise one," Kaeleigh teased. "All right, for now we can sleep on that bit of information and the rest will wait until tomorrow," she relented, snuggling back down in her sleeping bag. Head to head, she looked back at him one last time before closing her eyes, but he surprised her by leaning forward to capture her mouth for a quick, silent kiss. Until she fell asleep, she would ruminate on his kiss, now mixed with the new magical information.

EXCERPT 2 OF FADING LIGHT...

BOOK FOUR IN THE AGE OF ALANDRIA SERIES: CHAPTER TWO

The Realm of Alandria. Kandri. *The plains next to the Kandrian Mountain outside Adettlyn. Continued.*

The next day brought Kaeleigh many forms of surprise, starting with the excitement of not only getting to further discuss Wisps, but also the discovery other non-Alandria, magical creatures were hiding *and* living among humans in the mortal realm. Kaeleigh learned that some of them were good and some of them not so good. Kaeleigh was baffled to learn other creatures—other magic—had existed right under her nose in the world she had called home for most her life.

"So you are telling me that there are multiple kinds of magic in the world... and not just that, but multiple worlds... err... realms?" Kaeleigh frowned, trying to digest the discordant information. Now too, that they were closing in on the end of the mountain ridge, she felt lighter than she had in days and felt the freedom to get lost in her thoughts.

Finn laughed. "Don't hurt yourself, Kae. He's right. Think of it like *Star Trek* and how they discover new life and ways of living throughout the galaxy from planet to planet. It's the same: Earth—just as with other planets in our own galaxy—houses many different beings and is surrounded by other realms interacting with it." Her pursed lips and scrunched brows prompted him to continue. "Is it that farfetched to believe each realm or planet has their own magic?"

"No, I guess not," Kaeleigh considered.

"That Earth has its own magic and some beings within it such as witches and other fae outside of Alandria have even found access to said magic? Is it that hard to imagine?"

"Okay, after everything I've seen I can imagine that."

"Magic is a type of language that different beings learn depending on where they come from. Some are able to learn from another, but the easiest is the kind you are born into." Finn watched her as understanding dawned on her. "Does that help?"

"Yes, Finn, thank you!" Kaeleigh's smile reached her eyes as she processed the overload of magical information. She was already seeing things in a new perspective and couldn't wait to apply it all back in the mortal realm. Would she be able to see the magic Finn spoke of when she did? Lost in her thoughts, she didn't pay attention to Daegan stopping in front of her and ran smack into his back.

"Oh sorry!" Kaeleigh mumbled scrunching her face and rubbing her nose. "Why did you stop?" When no one answered her, she peered around Daegan's muscled back and gasped. Coming fully around him to stand next to him, she couldn't take her eyes off the land before her.

"Wow!" she exclaimed. "How is it possible?"

Stopped at what appeared to be an invisible line drawn in the ground, separating death from life, each stood in awe. The mountain ridge cascaded majestically down, meeting the ground; a natural landmark signifying the division of land. The land they stood on remained desolate and barren—land void of magical energy or any energy for that matter. But the land one foot in front of them transitioned into a complete juxtaposition—plains alive with grasses of tans and light greens, rolling into hills of greener grasses dotted with a variety of greenery and boulders. The beginnings of tree copses accented with colored floral lined the skyline with height variations all moving and flowing with the natural order of the land.

"I've never seen this area before. It's horrific and beautiful all at the same time," Finn's voice ended on a high note. The group all stood transfixed.

"Nor have I," Ella added finally. "I did not realize such a tragedy was happening to the land here. I have not traveled out this far in a very long time," she added.

Kaeleigh fidgeted in the background, near bursting with curiosity at what they meant.

Daegan simply shook his head, astonished at the extremeness of what he saw. A footfall away lay a glorious Alandria, just the way history had described it, just the way it should be now.

"This is how Alandria used to be... everywhere. At least from how the stories are told," Daegan explained.

"Yes, it is," Finn and Ella both said wistfully, their eyes wide with amazement.

"This is how she should be once more then," Kaeleigh said decidedly. She took the first step. Life-invoking energy soaked through her feet. She sighed blissfully. "Step across! The magic is tangible, it's like life being breathed back into my bones." Kaeleigh practically cried with relief to be out of the desolation. Closing her eyes, she inhaled slowly and deeply. Daegan's hand slid around hers, warm and comforting; his touch hummed like home. That zing of electricity grew stronger when his touch accompanied the natural energy of the area. Where they had been, however, it had been dulled by comparison. "Alandrian magic is literally filling me, refreshing me, can you feel it?" she asked no one and all of them.

Gasps of delight and bliss were muttered in agreement. Standing transfixed each with either eyes to the sky or mouths open wide drinking in the air, absorbing the life energy into their very souls, it was exactly what they needed to continue the journey.

Moments later, rejuvenated and ready to move on, they rounded the mountain's edge with a new bounce in their step and hope in their souls.

Alandria in this part, was much more open with a large expanse of sky above them, plains surrounding them except for the sleeping giant next to them serving as their guide and constant companion all the way to Kandri. Fortunately, the pleasant weather held only a slight chill in the shadow of the mountain throughout the day. The lavender skies broke through the clouds, revealing a sun so much larger than what they'd been able to see in the mortal realm. Not only that but vast amounts of unknown grass and wild flowers gracefully swayed back and forth alive with the forces of the wind. Everywhere the group looked, they encountered a scene not seen in the mortal world.

"I miss Chel," Kaeleigh said again, thinking of her best friend away on her own mission to the Shifter territory of Mandü tré Lan with Hal also looking for allies. "Do you think there are creatures out here with us? Chel would know right away." As a Shifter, Chel's gift of being able to hear and communicate with the more animalistic types had developed more the longer they had been in Alandria and had become important—not too mention her optimistic outlook and shining personality had lightened many moments along their journey. "It makes me uneasy not knowing." Kaeleigh frowned.

"Yes," Daegan and Ella said in unison. Ella moved her head forward so as to begin speaking.

"If you listen carefully, not just to the silence but beyond it, Kaeleigh, there are sounds of creatures scampering through the grasses." Ella was teaching Kaeleigh a skill those raised in Alandria would have grown up learning. "Though I cannot tell what they are saying, they sound playful and chipper." Ella inclined her ear and closed her eyes briefly demonstrating to Kaeleigh.

Kaeleigh did the same and some moments later, smiled. "I do hear them! I also hear the whispering of the grasses, leaves moving on the trees, and the sounds of whistling as the breeze whips through nearby trees." She turned, wide eyed to Ella and threw herself at the woman, reaching out to hug her. Ella, unused to dramatic shows of excitement, stiffened. "Oh, sorry, Ella," Kaeleigh stammered, backing away from Ella embarrassed.

"It is all right, Kaeleigh. I'm just not used to others embracing me." Ella often saw Kaeleigh and Chel hugging—a demonstration of their closeness. "I'm not comfortable showing how I feel with casual touch," Ella explained, "but I know you must miss Chel and her affection for you." Both women looked away for a moment, searching for a way to get pasts the awkward moment.

"So now that we are in such a wonderful place, I've been wondering about something," Kaeleigh found her voice.

"What is that?" Daegan asked.

"Well, back in the forest when we faced Maleina this last time, well, someone else took over her body, right? Like Invasion of the Body Snatchers or something!"

Daegan and Ella both gave her strange looks. "Never mind, Chel would have laughed. Finn you got it right?"

"It's an old movie reference from the mortal realm," Finn explained and nodded at Kaeleigh.

"Thank you," Kaeleigh said with mock relief.

"I think that is exactly what happened, and it's not something commonly seen—even in Alandria," Finn replied.

"Yes, I observed the same," Ella said, her interest fully on Kaeleigh's words. "Such a strange sight to see Maleina used like a puppet under the control of another. The other said those in the realm of Exhile called her *She*. I am not familiar with one called that within Exhile."

Daegan stroked his chin thoughtfully, his fingers rubbed against the stubble having grown since arriving in Alandria. Kaeleigh just knew he was about to say something important and could scarcely wait to hear it. "I believe she is the one we seek in Exhile—the one holding the Orchids imprisoned—and perhaps still remains there. Her presence possessing Maleina back in the forest seemed for that moment; it did not appear she could hold her takeover the entire time but maybe in increments, at least for now."

"Makes sense with what we saw," Finn added, his face stretched into that familiar serious line.

"Does that mean Maleina is not at fault? Or that someone is controlling her? Or perhaps that the other woman is just not strong enough yet to control her?" Kaeleigh rapid fired her questions.

"I think it means all of those things but I don't believe she is being controlled completely. That is to say, I am fairly certain she did many things of her own volition." He paused with a frown. "I wish to understand the purpose of the other entity and what her end goal is... does she mean to possess a being of Alandria completely, is that even possible? Is she able to gain enough power to enter Alandria in her own form? And what kind of danger does she present to us or does she just intend to rule?" Daegan seemed to be asking his questions more to himself out loud for the benefit of the others.

"Oh! I saw her before."

"What do you mean, Kaeleigh?" Daegan asked.

"In the Great Hall, in Ehsmia. Remember when I got pulled mentally and magically into the mural on the back wall? I saw her, well, I saw Maleina but as I fought her the image wavered and another woman's face replaced hers—a woman with jet black hair and eyes darkened with evil yet lit with a flame of vengeance." Kaeleigh shook herself out of the memory.

"If you fought her in the vision, then I fear we will encounter her again in the near future," Daegan said, his tone full of morose.

Ella inhaled audibly and looked up at the sky thoughtfully, her short white-blonde hair barely ruffling in the breeze. "I agree. For now, we need to keep moving and find shelter."

"What is it? What do you see, Ella?" Finn asked suddenly at her side. As an Elf he had increased speed over a mortal as well as others from Alandria. Until recently, he had kept his speed and other traits hidden from Kaeleigh, but now she knew the truth of who he was—at least the parts he was willing to share.

"I feel something stirring on the wind," Ella replied, quickly on guard. She picked up her pace, encouraging the others to do the same.

"Daegan, what do you sense?" Kaeleigh asked quietly as she tugged on his shirt sleeve. Her face grew concerned, and her gaze darted to and fro though their surroundings offered nowhere for an enemy to hide.

Daegan strained his eyes searching for anything out of the ordinary. At first, he looked with his natural eyes and then also through the eyes of his magic. He shook his head slowly. "I also feel something stirring on the wind, but it is still too far for me to gauge what it is. I agree with Ella. It is time to find shelter and get out of these plains. We are not far from the villages outside Kandri. Let us stop there."

Finn, agitated with so much conversation and the slow pace, he couldn't help but let it slip into his tone. "Let's go then, already! Can't we keep going and discuss while we walk? Otherwise we will never get there."

Well let's go, Daegan's eyes said. He gestured gentlemanly to Kaeleigh to go ahead of him. Ella followed behind Finn. "Thank you," Kaeleigh almost whispered. Then sliding her hand along his forearm, she moved ahead.

The group moved on, chastened by Finn's urgency as well as by the idea of the unseen enemy waiting for them. Kaeleigh, not so keen on long periods of silence broke the quick though quiet pace. "So what's the territory we are headed into like?" Oddly, the already silent group fell into an even heavier silence. Kaeleigh couldn't figure out what might be wrong with the question she asked and just as she was about to ask, Finn spoke up. Surprised, thinking it would be Daegan, she felt for his presence at her back; he was there but their connection, normally strong and clear, had gone dark. In its place, the connection was thick and full of emotion, specifically anger.

Finn continued. "It's not a big area... well, it actually is large... but not too many live there... if I remember correctly. It's similar to Anise outside Adettlyn. It houses a combination of races." Finn recalled more. "Being further out as it is makes it easier for the inhabitants to not fall into the same pressures and outlandish perceptions as other territories have struggled with for so long. They are outside the judgement zone, so to speak." Finn stopped a moment, catching his breath. "It has been many years since I was last there, but even then..." Finn's face shut down all emotion, and his gaze went to the ground. "I did not tarry long," his voice drifted off thick and forced. Silence fell again as Finn said no more, knowledge or memories plaguing his mind.

"As for me," Daegan reluctantly began after searching Finn's face. Finn's strange reaction to Kandri stirred his own, "I have not been there since I was a young boy, and my memories of it are frail, barely holding together even with the ones recently restored." Not long before they had left Ehsmia, Daegan's memories of who he truly was—the rightful heir to the throne of Feraánmar—were restored after a visit with not only the ancient *NaNai* tree but his long-believed-to-be-deceased grandmother who had been hidden with the Ehsmia people. "I lived there for a time, but I do not remember much. My parents were protective and kept me sheltered. I now understand." He paused. "My parents and grandmother were in hiding, moving from place to place. The moment we would settle, or the whispers of pursuers surfacing we would move once more. It was not a life with roots and connections, but from what my grandmother helped me to remember, it was necessary to preserve our line."

"So so sorry, Daegan." Kaeleigh turned and gave him her hand, tightening her hold when he placed his large, tough hand around hers.

"It was long ago, Kaeleigh," he recalled.

"Yes, but it shaped your existence and left you without parents. It still hurts, and that I understand," she said more quietly, reflective of her own life.

"Where did your family go from there?" she changed the subject to a lighter one.

"Nowhere. This is where they were killed."

One-click FADING LIGHT today!

GLOSSARY OF TERMS~

PLACES

Alandria: A realm parallel to our mortal realm inhabited by several races of magical beings and creatures. Created by the Originators also known as The Orchids.

Exhile: Another realm—a pocket realm—where the condemned souls of the non-human go to spend eternity in unrest or until they are devoured and absorbed into the land, whichever comes first.

Lenoria: The original realm from which the creators of Alandria came. The darkness destroyed it. "Old magic" comes from this realm, but not much is remembered.

Feraánmar: The territory mainly inhabited by Faeries and the Ferrishyn.

Elnye: The capital city of Feraánmar.

Lumari: The territory mainly inhabited by the Elves.

Adettlyn: The capital city of Lumari.

Ehsmia: Home to the Ehsmian people (see below). A magical location hidden within the Kandrian Mountains, near Adettlyn, partially within the territory of Lumari.

Tylínyth: A pocket realm magically created via an overlay between the realms of Alandria and Earth (the mortal realm). It is home, sanctuary, and training ground to many of the Twined (see below).

PEOPLE/BEINGS/CREATURES:

Ferrishyn: (fair-i-shin) They are the warrior race of Faeries, mostly male, in the territory of Feraánmar. Physically more muscular and bigger builds than other faeries. Created to fight and protect. They serve as hunters, guides, and guardians. Elite members become a part of the royal guard or for the presiding Paladin.

Earth Faeries: The most common race of Faeries. They are cultivators and growers for the lands of Alandria, their magic strengthened from the earth itself even as they give back to it. A more peaceful people.

Ehsmia: (a.k.a. The Hidden People), An ancient race of faeries that have been in hiding to protect their race from extinction—though they are already believed to be of legend, if remembered at all. Their magic is stronger as they retain a fraction of the 'old magic' from their realm of origin—Lenoria—as opposed to the magic of Earth Faeries. Though they are blessed with long life, they are cursed with slow reproduction so there are not many remaining.

Elves: At one point were the majority race in Alandria. They have a base magic as most do in Alandria, but some are gifted with more abilities than others. Their magic is strengthened from the light of the sun, moon, and stars.

Shifters: A race of beings that have the ability to shift into an animal. Those of greater strength and magic, may have the ability to shift into more than one animal form rather than just one.

The Orchids: An illusive collective of heads from various races united together, originally to create Alandria, after they fled the darkness destroying their original realm of Lenoria. Considered the "Originators" and make up the group considered the Elders—though not all Elders are Orchids. Their goal: to unite Alandria against the darkness that stirs upheaval against the kingdoms.

The Droch-Shúil: Is an evil entity. It is an ancient host collecting souls that went bad—the unforgiven dead. It grows with the strength and magic of the souls it consumes. Also considered a kind of demon. It is subservient to whichever master controls it at the time, and ultimately will forgo its purpose to fulfill its master's wishes. Can be in physical form of a hooded dark creature or most often as a intelligent mass of darkness.

Ferriers: Not quite Faeries or Elves for that matter, an ancient creature nonetheless existing in Alandria but not of it. They are neither alive nor dead, but simply exist. They are not anchored to any particular realm as they are the ferriers. They escort souls to their beyond whether it be where they are transitioned into rest, reborn, or to Exhile. They are non-partial or so it is believed. They are not to be involved other than departures.

Ónarach: A faction of Elves—mostly—that chose to go against their nature and against their race by taking the lives of Elders in order to consume their magic for their own gain transforming them into something dark, creating the Ónarach. They are an unnatural abomination who take orders from a master. Usually, they function as multiples—clones—resembling something like the walking undead or a zombie.

Paladin: The governing rulers of a territory, specifically Feraánmar territory of the Faeries, that took reign when the King and Queen died.

Sol-lumieth: A new power, a new magic, that was foretold in an ancient prophecy to return the light and life—the hope—of Alandria.

NaNai: The ancient Oak trees that were originally used to contain and protect some of the ancient magic that was transported at the inception of Alandria. They were brought into Alandria and even scattered and deposited into the mortal realm by the original Elf lords of the forest, partners with the Dryads. As the ancient magic fails, so do the great oaks.

Dryads: Many came from the origin realm of Lenoria. Previously they had been a neutral party, refusing to get involved with the politics of magical beings. In Lenoria, they were threatened to be destroyed if they didn't side with darkness, but they did not. They are an ancient race driven close to extinction. Many escaped with the Originators and refuged in Alandria—some were taken into the mortal realm for safe keeping. They are majestic beings who protect and care for the forests of Alandria, guided and cared for by Andreinna, the priestess of the forests. Some can evolve into a human form, but others choose to become "grounded" and then are unable to move.

Twined: Half mortal and half Alandrian beings who were unaware of their magical heritage, and also mixed races within Alandria who fled recent persecutions.

* Several races that are present, or created, in The Age of Alandria series are inspired from various mythologies throughout history.

An Excerpt from DESCENT by Kallie Ross

A Young Adult Urban Fantasy Adventure

Chapter 1

"Ollie! Alexis just drove up!" My mom's voice cuts through the haunting lyrics bleeding from my speakers.

"I heard the horn! Can you stick your head out and tell her I'm not ready yet?" I bet it takes Alexis less than thirty seconds to get past my mom. I'm letting her use her epic fashionista gift to manipulate my wardrobe. It's been over nine months since my last style Smack-Down. I haven't had anything to do with trends or trusted friends since New Years Eve. I left everything for the exchange program in South America including a petite, feisty blonde with an addiction to accessories.

"Did you trade clothes with the natives before you came home?" Regardless of my appearance, Alexis wraps me in her arms. Her strength is a surprise, and her grip threatens to squeeze a tear out of me.

"I don't think I can go to a party with you if you're going to insult me, at least your brother would bring me flowers." There's nothing like a good dose of my sarcasm to cure a case of the misty eyes. I missed her, not so much her two-timing big brother. He was my first, and last, boyfriend.

"Good grief, woman! This girl's night out is for celebrating your return home, and teaching you the ways of an American teenager, young Jedi. Speak of the cheating scum, we will not."

"Now that you mention old, wise beings, I forgot to tell you that my mom is flying out on a business trip tonight. Are your parents going to be cool with you staying over if she's not around?"

"They won't care. What I care about is this whining music you're listening to. It's too depressing." Her eyes take in everything, starting with my iPod, moving to my disheveled suitcase on the floor, and ending with the window open to my neighbor's backyard. It's always hot in Texas, and my mom would kill me if she knew I had the window open with the air conditioner on. "Have you talked to Mateo since you got back?"

"I tried." The truth is my best friend, Mateo, won't talk to me, but I may have started the silent treatment. I've strained to listen to him playing his guitar over the rattling cicadas each night, since returning.

Alexis waves at the MP3 player and orders, "Give me that. A little Youngblood Hawke will make everything better."

I hand it to her, and force myself not to look over at Mateo's yard. I go through my limited options in the closet. As I shuffle through the tops, Alexis shuffles through my playlist. I pull out a purple tank top that has a peacock feather painted across the front and a plain olive-green t-shirt. "I missed your bossy face. Which one?" I ask, bracing for a bold opinion. I've been wearing a school uniform, made up of cargo shorts and polos for months.

"My face, hmm?" An eclectic beat begins to blare from my speakers. "That's better." Alexis looks up and points at the purple tank top, and I'm not sure if she's talking about the shirt or the music.

Walking over to the connecting bathroom, I change, then brush out the tangles in my hair. Alexis picks at her neon manicured nails. Next, I sit on my bed, and reach for the black sandals tucked underneath the dust ruffle.

"Ollie, please tell me you have shorts or a skirt."

"I do, but I'd feel more comfortable in jeans," I reply.

"Comfortable? We live in Texas, and it's June. Plus we're going to a party with boys, and boys like legs. One plus one equals two, so put on the shorts." Her stubborn streak is longer and stronger than mine. So, I grab the shorts from my suitcase and go back to the bathroom to change without arguing.

"You know you might have more guys looking at your legs if I'm in jeans." My shorts fall just a few inches above my knee, but they'll have to do. Alexis has a black skirt on, with a turquoise top that compliments her eyes, tan skin, and tousled bob.

"I'm not worried about guy-zzz, Ollie. I just want Graham's attention tonight." Alexis gestures toward my bare legs. "Now you have no excuse to sit in a corner by yourself if I'm hanging out with him."

"Is that what you're planning? I won't be hooking up with some guy I've never met before. You know, just because your brother dumped me, it doesn't mean you're responsible for finding me a replacement. The idea of being a third wheel at a party where I don't know anyone sounds pitiful." Hearing myself whine reminds me of the music I was listening to.

"Hey! I'm not leaving you high and dry at this party. I'm definitely not expecting you to hook up with anyone. Give me some credit, here. I just want to make sure you get your own attention. I'm sure the guys will be lining up to meet you! Maybe you'll see someone you know." Alexis has a huge grin on her face when I walk out of the bathroom, and she starts fiddling with my hair, tucking it behind my ear.

"I can just stay here, and you can swing by after you see Graham." Who am I kidding? I'll just lay in my room and pout, or stare out the window and watch for Mateo. "I'm just not good at boy-people."

"Fix that, I will. Love you, boy-people will after tonight." Alexis walks out of my room, and wonder how long it will be before she starts yodeling like Chewbacca. Grabbing my purse and shoes, I dart down the stairs to catch up with her.

~

After grabbing a quick bite, Alexis and I drive up to a neighborhood that looks like our own. Cars line the street, and she parallel parks her huge SUV with care. "I'm so full, no dancing for me for at least forty-five minutes. Isn't that the rule?" Alexis asks.

"Yep, that's the one." Anything to keep myself off the dance floor. "Those cheese fries were delicious, but dangerous. I haven't eaten anything that greasy in months." As I open the car door, I feel the bass bounce from two houses over. Alexis grabs my hand, pulling me with her to my first college party. In a few more weeks, I'll be a college student.

I hesitate when we get to the front porch. As Alexis opens the door, the music pushes every logical thought out of my mind. The beat is so strong and pressing that I'm afraid it will move me. I can even feel my bones vibrating. Alexis yanks me out of the thumping haze and through a throng of bodies dancing in the front room.

We squeeze through a suffocating hallway that leads to the back of the house, and I'm reminded of why I avoid shopping on Black Friday. Finally, we reach the kitchen, and Alexis turns to face me with a smile spread across her face. She gets close, and I notice beads of sweat have formed on her upper lip.

"He's here." She backs away, letting go of my hand. Then I look up and see a cute guy, a.k.a. Graham, hugging her. They start talking into each other's ears, and I know my wing-woman skills are not needed. I wish that super powers came with the title wing-woman, because I'd like to fly home or become invisible.

I'm quickly reminded of the fact that I don't know anyone here, because I feel invisible. No friends rushing to welcome me or guys throwing their arms around me. I spent my senior year learning about South American cultures and environments, and now I feel foreign in the place I grew up.

Within seconds my next goal becomes finding a place to think and breathe without inhaling some pungent apple-berry-vanil-la-perfume. Once I make my way back to the narrow hallway, I feel like a playing card being shuffled to the back of the deck. Moving with the crowd, the pace stutters, and I get jostled in the hot and muggy mix. A passing body thrusts me into the wall.

"Ouch! Watch it!" To avoid being the center of an Ollie sand-wich, I push the person's large, male back. "Is there a fire some-where?" I've always had issues with claustrophobia. Not to mention the stress of being at a party where personal space doesn't exist. Add the hashtag-fit-in-or-die American culture, and you could say I'm on edge.

The guy freezes, and from behind I can see he's wearing a blue t-shirt, khaki shorts and a baseball cap. Dark brown hair escapes the bottom of the cap in the form of curls, and I become aware that the cap is turning. Suddenly, I'm facing a familiar tan and flexed, square jaw. His eyes are so dark you could get lost in them, but they're squinting in frustration.

"Ollie? What the... What are you doing here?" As he waits for an answer, the bodies around us struggle to work their way past him.

"I'm peachy, thanks for asking." Mateo looks around us. "I'm here with Alexis." With no Alexis in sight, he starts to walk away.

"Hey! Where do you think you're you going?" I reach to fasten my hand around his wide arm and tug.

"Let go of me." He demands, but I'm determined. I grasp the edge of his sleeve, and drag him through the hallway. Colliding into every person we pass, I take a sharp left. He moves to stand in front of me, and we're face to face. I know I can't waste this opportunity to make things right.

"What are you really doing here? You've never been the partying type." Mateo's mouth twitches, and I can tell he's as tense as I am. I explore the small alcove we've ended up in and begin to back away from him to create some breathing room.

"So, how have you been?" My attempt at social decorum hits a solid wall of angst.

"I'm not going there with you. I already told you, I'm done being your substitute friend."

"At least tell me how Amber is? I didn't see..."

"I wouldn't know." That's one way to allude to a breakup.

"Oh. I'm sorry."

"Why do you suddenly care?"

It's obvious he doesn't want consoling. I've tried to apologize for not keeping in touch while I was on a different continent. Despite that, he's made it clear he doesn't want to be my friend anymore. The silent treatment, blatant avoidance, and sorry excuse for a conversation when he told me "We aren't friends," are proof.

I swallow the truth in silence. I've been a horrible friend to Mateo. The first month I was gone, we messaged and called each other, but then I found out my boyfriend, his best bro, was cheating on me. I know Mateo was as clueless as I was, but I couldn't deal with anyone from back home. I found out about the whole thing via a tweet-fest. After that, I committed social media suicide and vanished off the face of the computer screen.

"I'm here looking for Jesse." Mateo admits. "Have you seen him?"

"Nope, but I can help you look in some of these back rooms." I offer.

"Do you even know what people are doing back here?"

"Of course I do." But in all honesty, I don't have a clue. It's got to be a bunch of face-sucking happening, but I would hate to walk in on anyone doing more, especially being with Mateo. The only guy I've ever kissed is his best friend. "I'm on the lookout for a college guy that studies Political Science, and hopes to become a lawyer someday." I go in a sing-song way. "Once I find him, I'll schmooze my way through my MRS degree, and we'll get married. I'm planning on taking his last name, but I insist on hyphenating."

Mateo just stares at me, unmoved.

"What?" I ask.

"You shouldn't be back here." Mateo might as well be pointing a brotherly finger at me. He speaks at me like I'm his little sister, Perla.

"You need to stop being so condescending; you're not my mom. You don't even want to be my friend. Plus, I'm here for Alexis, who is my friend, and I thought I would hide out back here until she's ready to go. I don't even know why I'm trying so hard to explain this. It's not like you'll start caring. Go. Enjoy the party."

"I'm not here to enjoy the party. Getting Jesse out of trouble is still the highlight of most of my weekends." Mateo seems to find the hallway we just came out of more fascinating than me.

"Some things never change." The opportunity provides a way for me to make my exit, but Mateo moves in unison with me and grabs my shoulders. Maybe he does still care. His presence makes me feel small, and the sound of my own heart beating in my ears replaces the heavy beat around us.

"Everything changes, Ollie."

"I'm not that different. I'm still Ollie, the girl that's been your friend for the past seven years!"

"Maybe you aren't that different. You're definitely still stubborn.... What I mean is that I'm different. I've made other friends, and I'm growing up."

An awkward laugh escapes me. "Well, you have grown. You've got at least four inches on me now."

Mateo breaks eye contact, and releases his grip. My instinct to ease the tension with humor has had the same result as a rubber band being stretched too far.

"Okay, I promise to stop trying to joke my way back into your good graces. Why don't we agree to give each other a second chance instead of cutting each other out completely?" I plead.

"Ollie, you cut me out of your life months ago." His arms fold across his chest, shutting me out.

"I'm sorry." Head hanging, I watch his feet as they walk away. I'm not sure if I'll ever be able to make things right.

Mateo has always kept me grounded, but since I came home the weight of our friendship has been so heavy that I've felt buried by it. He's right, it won't ever be like it was before.

I maneuver my way back to the front room to escape my conflicting feelings. Hoping to find Alexis, I search the sea of people. I decide to get out, but see Jesse in the middle of the dance floor. I swim through the swaying bodies to reach Mateo's younger brother, and when he sees me his face lights up. Jesse pulls me closer to him and starts to dance around me.

The music is so loud that there's no way we can hear each other. Instead Jesse teases me by pretending to cast a fishing line in my direction and reels me in.

With a wink and a twirl, Jesse has me laughing harder than I have in months. After a few minutes of methodical movement, I'm lost in the chaos. His hand moves his around my waist from behind, and I enjoy the attention for a moment, but it feels wrong. He's my ex-best friend's goofy not-so-little brother!

My whole body stiffens and I realize that I'm not being me.

"Jesse!" He laughs, and cups a hand around his ear, obviously unable and unwilling to listen. It's no use trying to explain, so I move around him and begin heading to the front door. At the side of the room, Alexis, Graham, and Mateo stare in my direction.

"What?" I holler over the mob, and realize they're following me out the front door.

Once we're on the front lawn Alexis pulls at my shirt to stop me. "*What?* You have the nerve to ask us, what? You were just bumping and grinding with Jesse."

I look back at the two guys standing behind Alexis, and she turns to follow my gaze. "I found Jesse," I say to Mateo, and return my gaze to Alexis. "And, I was just doing what you told me to do."

"I didn't tell you to get jello-shot-jiggy with Mateo's little brother." Alexis says, but can't help but grin. "But he can dance, can't he?" She says under her breath with an eyebrow waggle. When I was gone Alexis and Jesse had a thing and she sent me some descriptive emails, but it ended before it really began.

"There was no jello, and I wasn't dancing with Jesse. I mean I was dancing, but we were just having fun. I couldn't think about Jesse that way. Honest." I hold up my hand like I'm making an oath.

Mateo takes a few steps closer, and looks lost. Maybe he's trying to find the right words, like I have been since I got home.

"I needed to release some of this physical tension." I gesturing between us with my hands, and Alexis snickers while turning and walking toward Graham. "Gah! This isn't coming out right."

The only thing that could make this situation worse is me sticking around, so I walk away. I feel Mateo hot on my heels, and when I stop and turn to confront him, *again*, he collides into me. My hands meet his chest, and the earth begins to move.

The ground shakes beneath us, and car alarms go off all around us.

"What was that?" I hear Graham ask Alexis after the tremor stops. I look over Mateo's shoulder and see them holding on to each other, and notice Jesse bracing himself in the doorway of the house. Strong arms tighten around my waist, and I can't believe Mateo is holding me.

"Are you okay?" Mateo's question interrupts the trembling I still feel in my core. Since when did he stir those kind of feelings in me?

"I'm f-fine." My response is generic, but I'm so far from fine. Like, five thousand miles away from fine. Maybe I've changed more than I'd like to admit.

DESCENT is available NOW!
Find Kallie at KallieRoss.com

About the Author

The Age of Alandria Series

Morgan Wylie is an award-winning and *USA Today* Bestselling author with several genres published from YA fantasy to adult paranormal romance and others in between. Morgan published her first novel, Silent Orchids, one year after moving across the country with her family on a journey of new discovery. After an amazing three years in Nashville, TN, and the release of two more books, Morgan and her family found their way back to the Northwest where they now reside. Still working everyday with great optimism, Morgan continues to embrace all things: "Mama", wife, teacher, host of The Lotus Bloom podcast for creatives, and mediator to the many voices and muses constantly chattering in her head... where it gets pretty loud!

You can find her and news on her books at the following:

MorganWylie.org

Morgan Wylie Books on Facebook

@MWylieBooks on IG and Twitter

The Lotus Bloom Podcast on most podcasting sites

Don't miss out! Join the Journey with Morgan today!

Newsletter of Enchanted Journeys

Or sign up at morganwylie.org

To show some love for this book, please consider leaving a review at the place of purchase or any of the locations it is sold. This means the world to an author!
THANK YOU!!

Also by Morgan Wylie

YA FANTASY:
The Age of Alandria Series:
Silent Orchids (Book 1)
Veiled Shadows (Book 2)
Daegan (Novella 2.5)
Fractured Darkness (Book 3)
Fading Light (Book 4)
Night Magic (Novella 4.5)
The Sol-Lumieth (Book 5)
The Rise of the Paladin (An Alandria Short Story Prequel)

YA PARANORMAL/SUPERNATURAL:
HAILEY: The Necromancer (A Shadow Realm Novella 1)
JAX: The Doppelgänger (A Shadow Realm Novella 2)
(A Shadow Realm Novella 3 forthcoming)
(A Shadow Realm Novella 4 forthcoming)

MISCELLANEOUS COLLECTIONS:
Dawn of The Witch Hunters (A Havenwood Falls Legends Novella)
Rise of The Witch Hunters (A Havenwood Falls Legends Novella)
Reawakened (A Havenwood Falls High Novella)
Rekindled (A Havenwood Falls Holiday Short Story Anthology 2019)
Redefined (A Havenwood Falls Novella)
Rediscovered (A Havenwood Falls High Novella)
Reunited (A Havenwood Falls Holiday Short Story Anthology 2020)
Reborn (A Havenwood Falls Holiday Short Story Anthology 2021)
Magic by Moonlight with Kallie Ross (A Havenwood Falls Spring Short Story Anthology 2022)
Remembrance (A Havenwood Falls Sunset Short Story Anthology 2022)